# THI ADVENTURE Yarns 2021

*Edited By* ROBERT GREENBERGER

CRAZY 8 PRESS

# THRILLING ADVENTURE Yarns 2021

**Contents for Winter 2020–2021**

# Thrilling Romance Yarns

# Thrilling Cautionary Yarn

# Thrilling Occult Yarns

*Cover Art by Gary Carbon*
*Logo by Jim Campbell*

| *Illustrations by* | *Peter Krause* |
| --- | --- |
| *June Brigman* | *Luke McDonnell* |
| *Kerry Callen* | *Ron Randall* |
| *Gary Carbon* | *Dan Schkade* |
| *Mike Collins* | *Bart Sears* |
| *Daerick Gross* | *Daniele Sera* |
| *Matt Haley* | *Jeff Weigel* |
| *Karl Kesel* | *Mark Wheatley* |

*To Ariel Brew, who always makes life a thrilling adventure*

# The Day It Came from Beyond Outer Space

By SCOTT PEARSON

**D**AN and Bobby came to a sudden stop as they walked around the corner of the old Swenson barn and saw the frightening invader. Wayne, close behind on his bicycle, baseball cards thrumming in its spokes, slammed on the brakes.

"What gives?" Wayne said.

Dan pointed at the unexpected visitor: a teenage girl in a white t-shirt, bib overalls, and Chuck Taylors, her long black hair in a sloppy braid. She stood in the shade behind the barn, a cigarette in her left hand, a surprised look on her face. They had to look up at her, because she was taller than all of them, especially Bobby, the youngest.

Dan blurted, "Who're you?" There'd never been a girl back here before. Bobby stepped behind him and didn't say anything.

Wayne jumped off his bike, letting it fall into the weeds by their well-worn path. "Yeah, this is our spot."

She took a puff on her cigarette. "Your spot?" She looked around at the barn, its overgrown pasture,

the nearby hayfield. "Which of you owns all this?" She pointed at them in turn. "Larry? Curly? Moe?"

Dan frowned. The Swenson place didn't belong to any of them, but Bobby's family harvested the hay since no one else did. "We always come here. We were here first."

"Not today you weren't."

Wayne said, "Are you living here like a hobo?"

She laughed. "No, I'm staying with my aunt for the rest of the summer." She waved in the direction of Old Lady Lehto's place, beyond some trees and across the road. It was by a pond, and the croaking of frogs wafted all the way to the barn.

"Well, that tears it," said Wayne. He already had three sisters to try to avoid. "Summer's ruined."

She smiled and stubbed out her cigarette on the foundation of the barn. "What do you do back here?"

"Play on the rock or in the barn, mostly," said Bobby, peeking out from behind Dan. He straightened his beanie over his fresh buzz cut, hiding the spots where his dad had nicked his scalp.

Wayne punched Bobby in the arm. "Don't tell her!"

She glanced toward the mostly buried boulder in the overgrown pasture. Dan figured she only saw a big slab of rock, but for them it was Marshal Dillon's office, or a flying saucer, or a castle, or a raft drifting down the Mississippi. Sometimes it was just for lying in the sun. It was a ways from the barn, which was half collapsed, its siding dark gray with age, only a hint of red paint left. They weren't supposed to play in there because their moms thought it was dangerous. If they got caught they'd get the worst chore in their own barns: cleaning out the gutter behind the cows.

"I'm Jo by the way."

Bobby stayed quiet, rubbing his arm. Dan scratched his nose. Wayne jammed his hands in his pockets. Jo watched them, raising her eyebrows. Birds sang in the background. Dan gave in before she started calling them Stooges again and said, "Dan, Wayne, Bobby." He nudged the other boys as he said their names.

Jo nodded. When none of the boys said anything more, she said, "What else do you do out here in the country? Do you watch *Alfred Hitchcock*?"

"We don't have a TV, and that's past my bedtime," Bobby said.

Wayne punched Bobby in the arm again. "Don't tell her!"

Dan opened his mouth as if to answer—then ran for the boulder. It was theirs, and he would be the king of the hill. But he heard Jo running after him. She was laughing and still catching up, which didn't seem fair. Soon they were neck and neck, stumbling over the uneven ground.

"Go, Dan, go!" yelled Wayne.

Jo was slowly pulling ahead. *Her dang long legs,* he thought. *I'm going to lose to a girl!* She gave him a sly sidelong glance and with three big bounds was at the boulder. Dan tried to stop, slipped in the grass, and went to his knees. At the same time, Jo staggered backward with a cry and fell off the boulder.

She rolled around on the ground, clutching her forehead, swearing like the boys' dads when their tractors broke down. Dan got to his feet, hitched up his short pants, and retied his rope belt. Wayne stepped up beside him. Bobby stayed behind Wayne. They exchanged confused shrugs and looked down at Jo.

"What happened?" Bobby said.

"Tripped and hit her head on the rock?" said Wayne.

"I don't think so." Dan stepped closer to Jo. "Uh...you okay?"

Jo took her hands off her head, revealing a growing bruise above her left eyebrow. "No, dammit."

"What happened?" Bobby said again, peeking out from behind Wayne.

"I hit my head!" Jo yelled, and Bobby jumped back.

"On what?" said Wayne.

"I don't know." Sitting up, squinting her left eye, Jo pointed into the air above the boulder. "Something up there." She pulled a pack of Luckies and a matchbook out of the big center pocket of her overalls and lit a cigarette.

"Something...invisible?" Wayne said. "You've flipped your lid."

Jo scowled at him and blew smoke in his face. She stood up, pointing at the bump on her forehead. "Did I imagine this?"

Wayne coughed and waved the smoke away. "I'll show you." He stomped up onto the boulder. "See?"

Bobby said, "But she's taller than you."

Wayne frowned down at him. "Not that much taller. And so what? Are you on her side?"

"No. But she hit her *forehead*, and she's taller—"

"Okay, okay. I'll show you too." He jumped straight up. There was a *thunk*, his head scrunched down between his shoulders, and he stumbled off the boulder.

Jo took a drag on her cigarette. "Told you."

Wayne said, "Something's really there." Bobby moved back behind him.

Dan pulled his slingshot out of his back left pocket and dug in his front right pocket. He picked up little rounded rocks wherever he saw one, often in his long gravel driveway. He loaded one up, pushed his left hand forward, drew his right arm back, and fired. There was a metallic *ping* followed by a high-pitched whine as the

rock ricocheted. All four of them ducked, but didn't see which way the rock went. Dan tucked his slingshot back into his pocket.

"What is it?" Bobby whispered as they straightened up.

Wayne frowned. "Commie spy stuff. An invisible Sputnik."

"Spying on an old barn?" Jo said.

"Nah, it just crashed here."

Jo shook her head. "Seems more like it's hovering."

"Like a flying saucer," said Dan. "Maybe it's from Mars." He loved books about Martians. *The War of the Worlds* was one of his favorites. He hadn't seen the movie; it came out when he was only seven. But he, Wayne, and Bobby had listened to the radio play last Halloween. It had given Bobby nightmares.

Bobby said, "We gotta tell someone if it's Martians."

Dan wondered how long the saucer had been there. They could have walked under it for days and not even noticed. "I'm gonna figure out what it is." He walked onto the boulder, stopping where Wayne had been. Reaching up with his right hand, his fingertips hit something he couldn't see. He pressed his palm flat against the invisible surface.

"What's it feel like?" Jo said.

"Cold, like metal." Between his fingers, he saw crows fly by overhead. Dan slid his hand backward. The surface curved upward for a foot or so then his fingers curled around an edge. Taking a step back, he put his left hand up to the edge as well. The rim of the saucer—he sure hoped that's what it was—was only a few inches from top to bottom. Dan gripped the rim with both hands and did a pull-up. As his feet left the boulder, he heard gasps from behind. When he hooked his chin over the top, he could peek down and see his feet swinging back and forth in the air. He dropped back down to the boulder and turned around.

Jo stood there wide-eyed, cigarette dangling from her lips. Bobby had edged away toward the barn, ready to take cover. Wayne was rubbing the top of his head.

"Come on," Jo said, punching Wayne in the arm as she walked toward Dan. Wayne hesitated, looking between Bobby and Jo. Bobby shook his head, but Wayne followed her. She reached up and stubbed out her cigarette on the invisible rim, leaving a dark smudge of ash in the air.

The three of them looked at that for a little while. Then Dan did another pull-up and tried swinging his leg onto the top of the saucer, but his foot slipped. "Boost me!"

Two pairs of hands grabbed his feet and lifted him—fast. Tumbling up and forward, he rolled onto his back, and slid across a flat surface until he hit something. The surface curved upward at that point. Dan lay there, staring up into the sky, until Jo suddenly scrambled up by herself and stood over him, hands on hips.

Dan also stood and said, "Guys, you should come up here."

Wayne hesitated again, and Bobby said, "I think you should come down."

"Never!" yelled Jo. She was a few feet higher in the air than Dan; she'd climbed up the rising that he'd bumped into. She squatted down and stuck out her hands like she was holding something in front of her. "I'm Wonder Woman flying my invisible jet!"

Dan almost pouted. He and Wayne and Bobby hardly ever got comic books. The Dime Store in Cloquet had some, but you had to go all the way into Duluth to find more.

Wayne said, "Quick, give me a hand." Dan turned away from Jo and reached down.

As soon as Wayne climbed up, he got on his belly, stretched his arms out, one hand open, the other a fist, and said, "I'm Superman! I don't need a jet to fly!"

Dan laughed and looked back at Jo. She smirked and rolled her eyes.

Acting like he was flying toward Bobby, Wayne said, "It's okay, Jimmy, I'll carry you."

Bobby shook his head.

Dan nudged Wayne with his foot. "Get up, let's see how big this thing is."

"Look out," Jo said, jumping down between Dan and Wayne. "Come on, kid," she called to Bobby, "this is more fun than an old barn."

"Fun as that goose egg on your forehead?"

"Worth it to discover an invisible flying saucer." Jo turned her back on Bobby and held her arms out wide, pushing the boys on either side of her. "Okay, spread out."

Dan edged out clockwise from Jo, sliding his feet to feel for the edge. A few yards away from her, he spread his arms to indicate the curve of the rim. Wayne was on the opposite side, arms out, a mirror image of Dan, and Jo was between them. The invisible surface was about twenty feet across, and seemed to be more or less round. With that higher spot in the middle. A perfect flying saucer. *So, is it hovering here or...?*

He stared down through the saucer. A few feet from the boulder, he saw a round indentation about a foot wide where the weeds were pressed flat to the ground. He circled along the edge, clockwise toward Wayne. Beneath the far end of the saucer he saw another indentation. He spotted a third closer to Wayne. "It's got three landing legs...like a Martian tripod."

"Seems small for a spaceship," said Wayne.

"It's bigger than our old Studebaker," Dan said.

"Where are the Martians?" said Jo. "Still inside?"

Wayne looked across the hayfield. "Maybe out exploring?"

Bobby must have heard that, because he glanced around and sank deeper into the weeds. *I bet he wishes he had Colonel with him,* Dan

thought. Bobby's family had had to put their old German Shephard down that spring. Out loud he said, "I think they'd only go out in the dark." He lay down and put his ear to the saucer. Even under the bright sun, the surface was still cold. *Of course, since the sun's shining right through it.* He closed his eyes to focus on listening. He hoped he'd hear weird Martian whispering, or maybe the beeping and whirring of computers.

"Anything?" said Jo.

"Nothing."

Wayne shifted from one foot to the other. "Knock to see if anybody's home?"

Dan rapped on the surface with his knuckles. Waited. Knocked again. "Nope."

"Let me," Jo said. She bounced up and down like a kangaroo: *thump, thump, thump.*

Wayne flinched. "Cripes, knock, not stomp!"

"Knocking didn't work."

"Doesn't mean you break down the door!"

"Shhh!" said Dan. He thought, just maybe, he'd heard a skittering sound, like his cats chasing each other across the kitchen linoleum. He pressed his ear tighter against the invisible surface...

*THUMP.*

Dan jumped to his feet, bumping into Wayne, who grabbed Jo's arm to keep from falling over the side.

"Did you do that?" said Wayne. Jo shook her head.

The three shared a look. They didn't need to talk to make a decision, and they all hurried over the rim of the saucer, dropping to the boulder beneath. They rushed to Bobby and hunkered down in the weeds next to him, staring back toward the invisible saucer.

A quicksilver shimmer, like air over hot blacktop, rippled above the boulder. Bobby was facedown, not even watching. Wayne gripped Dan's shoulder. The background chorus of birds and frogs was scared into silence by a hiss of static. Random splashes of color blossomed, hinting at outlines of a saucer, then vanished.

The static faded away as the flying saucer flashed into visibility, gunmetal gray with spokes of silver glinting in the sunlight. A rectangular section on the belly of the hull hinged downward with a soft hum. In the shade beneath the saucer, a deep-purple glow shown from within. As the hatch came to a stop, an arm—or was it a leg?—appeared, slowly stretching outward, soon followed by a second limb. The skin was lumpy and scaly, a mixture of toad and reptile, a mottled blend of dull blacks, browns, and tans, with a light speckling of yellows and greens. The limbs ended in three short fingers—or were they long toes?

A third limb appeared. Dan couldn't tell how many Martians were coming out. After limb number four settled onto the hatch, a head lowered into view on a longish neck. The Martian had a long, pointy snout, and three large, golden eyes in a horizontal line across its face. Swaying back and forth, it opened and closed its sharp, beak-like mouth. As it climbed out of the hatch, limbs five and six appeared, but it had no tail.

*There's six-legged Martians on Barsoom*, Dan thought.

It scuttled on all its legs out from under the saucer then raised the front part of its body up, standing on the four hind limbs, front limbs dangling. There was a harness across its chest. It looked over its shoulder, apparently trying to see what had made the noise on the saucer.

Dan felt a sharp pain in his left hand and realized Jo was squeezing it hard. Without thinking, he'd risen up for a better look. She tried to yank him down as the Martian turned back toward them. It opened its mouth, there was an exaggerated motion in its throat without sound, and Dan was punched in the chest by some sort of shock wave. He staggered backward and fell to the ground. There was a strange flurry of footfalls, because of the Martian's six legs, and suddenly it was straddling him, staring down with three unblinking gold eyes. Dan had lost hold of Jo's hand when he fell, and he didn't know where Wayne or Bobby were. It was like he and the Martian were the only living things in the pasture.

Close up, its face reminded Dan

of a turtle. The Martian clicked its beak open and shut and open again. Dan braced for another shock wave, but instead it made a screech that cut through his brain between his ears. He clenched his eyes shut, expecting his head to be eaten. Dan heard a crunching sound, but it wasn't his skull. He opened one eye. Bobby stood close by, holding a doggie biscuit in the palm of an outstretched hand. He always had treats for any dog he saw.

"Good boy," Bobby said. "You want another one?"

A long tongue like a tentacle shot out of the Martian's mouth, grabbed the biscuit, and yanked it back to be crunched up. Slimy crumbs fell onto Dan's face as Bobby dug in his pocket for more biscuits. Dan scrambled backward, pushing with palms and feet, to get out from underneath the Martian. He stopped when he bumped into someone behind him.

"You okay?" Jo said as she leaned over him. There were pieces of grass stuck in her hair.

"I guess." His chest was little sore, but that was all. He sat up and wiped the gooey biscuit bits from his face. Looking around, he saw Wayne peeking out from inside the barn.

Jo tilted her head to one side. "You sure?"

He realized how close he was to her, and scooted away.

"Jeez," Bobby said, glancing past Dan and Jo toward Wayne as he fed the Martian another biscuit,

"what a bunch of scaredy-cats."

Dan opened his mouth but couldn't think of anything to say. Jo giggled. The sound drew the attention of the Martian, who stopped chewing his biscuit and took a few steps toward Jo. When she went quiet, the Martian started chewing again but kept looking at her.

"Thanks," Dan said to Bobby. "I thought it was going to eat me."

"No, he's a good boy."

"Or good girl." Jo waved her hand back and forth, and the Martian's head swung from side to side following the motion. "How did you think of feeding it?"

"It seemed more like an animal than a person. Like that dog the Russians shot into space. All dogs like treats."

"Makes sense," Dan said. *You launch a dog or a monkey on a test flight to make sure everything works.*

Wayne stepped out of the barn. "Now what? Do we call the police?"

"No!" Bobby said. "They'll take him away!"

"You said we'd call someone if it was Martians."

"I was afraid of soldiers with ray guns!"

Wayne just folded his arms across his chest and scowled. Dan slowly got to his feet, keeping an eye on the Martian as it turned toward him. It was the size of a very large dog, even longer because of the extra legs. "What do you think?" he asked Jo.

She looked from the Martian to the spaceship. "Bobby's right. If we tell anyone, they'll take my flying saucer and Luna too."

"Luna?" Bobby said.

"A good *girl* like her needs a name."

"*Your* flying saucer?" said Dan.

"I found it!"

"Your stupid forehead found it," Wayne muttered.

Jo scoffed at him. "You're the stupid one, hitting your head on it *after* we knew it was there."

Luna's head jerked around as she watched whoever was talking. When they stopped and glared at each other, Luna ambled toward Bobby.

"I'm almost out of biscuits," he said. He dug in his pockets, handing Dan all he had left. "Keep feeding him"—he glanced at Jo—"or her. I'll get more."

"Hurry," said Dan. Luna was clicking her beak at him.

"Give me a buck?" Bobby said to Wayne.

"Sure." It was easy to give Bobby a ride because he was small. Wayne grabbed his bike and they disappeared around the corner of the barn, heading for the road. Luna started to follow.

"Whoa, girl," Dan said, waving a biscuit in front of her beak. Luna stopped and gobbled the biscuit. Rising up on her hind four legs, she stood eye to eye with Dan. There was a small, flashing purple light on the front of her harness. Luna clicked her beak and sidestepped in the direction Bobby and Wayne had gone.

"We need to distract her," Jo said.

"She's gonna take off after them and someone will see her."

"Let's get her in the barn." Dan tossed a biscuit in that direction to see if Luna would go after it. She just stared at him. "You wanna feed her?"

"Yeah." Jo held out her hand.

Dan gave her a couple of biscuits. Walking toward the barn, Jo waved them in front of Luna. She followed, swiveling her pointy head, flicking her tongue to pick up the one Dan had thrown.

There wasn't a door at the back of the barn, just a hole of missing siding. Once they stepped inside, the barn swallows that nested in the rafters started chirping and flying around, swooping just above their heads. Watching the birds, Luna appeared to forget about the biscuits.

Jo looked around the barn, wrinkling her nose. "What's that smell?"

"Old hay and bird poop."

"No wonder you love it in here."

"You get used to it." The hay was heaped against the wall in a mound about twelve feet high at the back, sloping down to spill across the concrete floor. Dan scrambled up the slippery hay until he reached the ladder, which was just boards between the studs. He climbed until he was a few yards above the hay and turned around, facing into the barn.

Jo, head tipped back, squinted up at him. "What're you doing?"

"This!" He jumped, somersaulted through the air, landed on

his back in the hay, and slid down the mound to floor.

Luna rushed over to him, clicking her beak. Grinning, Dan got up and gave her his last biscuit.

"That looked fun," said Jo. "But how much bird poop is in that hay?"

"Don't think about that."

"Okay." Jo struggled up the mound to the ladder. She climbed to where Dan had been then went up another two rungs.

"Careful!" Dan said, but Jo was already airborne.

She somersaulted onto her back in the hay, did another somersault as she slid down the mound. and landed on her feet on the floor. "Beat that!"

Luna rose up on her hind legs and looked at Dan, clicking her beak, as if also daring him. Jo tossed her a biscuit, which Luna snagged out of the air with her tongue.

"All right, I'll show *both* of you." Dan clambered back up, passing his usual rung and the rung Jo had used. As he stepped onto the third rung above Jo's, there was a scratching noise beneath him, and he twisted around to look.

Luna was climbing up behind him, clicking her beak. One of the rungs broke, but she kept coming, the wall shaking with her weight.

Jo yelled, "Luna! Luna, come get a treat!"

Dan clung to the ladder. More rungs broke, so Luna grabbed at the studs and siding, some of which gave way. Dan thought, *Maybe I should just jump now.*

Before he could, Luna opened her mouth without emitting a sound, and everything seemed to collapse.

When Dan sat up, he was on the concrete floor surrounded by broken rafters and scraps of shingles. The swallows were chirping angrily all around, flying through the dust-filled air. He coughed, then saw Jo sitting a few feet away staring back at him. He looked over his shoulder. There was a large hole in the back of the barn, and part of the roof had collapsed onto the hay. Luna was nowhere to be seen.

He crawled to Jo and sat down next to her. "You okay?"

She stared back at him. "Just scared." There were tear tracks in the dust on her cheeks. "How do you feel?"

He stretched his back. "I'm okay." Dan looked around the more-ruined barn. "Maybe we should get out of here."

"Yeah."

They got up, leaning on each other, and walked outside. Wayne and Bobby came careening around the corner on Wayne's bike, Bobby perched on the handlebars, and toppled to the ground as they saw the destruction. Swallows flew in and out of the hole in the roof.

"We heard the crash all the way to Bobby's," Wayne said as they got up. "You all right? Were you in there?"

"We're okay," said Dan.

Bobby didn't take his eyes off the barn as he took a biscuit out of his pocket. "Where's Luna?"

"She's gone." Jo turned away from the boys.

"Gone?" Bobby looked at the flying saucer. "Back in there?"

"Musta got scared by the collapse," Wayne said.

"She caused it!" said Dan.

Bobby walked toward the saucer. "Luna?"

Wayne said, "We promised Bobby's mom we weren't going in there, so I don't think anyone's coming." To Jo he said, "What about your aunt?"

Jo didn't answer.

"Hey," Dan said. "Will your aunt come looking for you?"

Jo shook her head, but didn't look at him. "She's kinda deaf. Probably didn't hear it."

Bobby came back. "The hatch is closed."

"She's not in there, she's gone," Jo said.

"She ran away?" said Wayne.

Bobby said, "We've gotta find her before anyone else."

Jo turned around. "You don't understand, she's *gone*. You can't find her."

"What do you mean?" said Bobby.

"I wasn't sure if I should say." She stared at Dan. "But... she's you."

*A rafter must have knocked her on the noggin,* Dan thought. He looked at Wayne and Bobby. They both shrugged. He turned back to Jo. "What?"

"You fell! All the way to the concrete, missed the hay." She stopped to light a cigarette. When her hands were free, she clapped them together. "Smack."

Dan made a face. "What're you talking about?"

"You weren't moving. Luna sniffed at you. Then her tongue shot out. Into your neck, like a needle. She laid down next to you. Turned into you. I didn't know what else to do."

"What do you mean?" Dan said. "What *did* you do?"

She took a deep drag. "I took your clothes off you and put them on you."

"She really has flipped her lid," said Wayne.

Jo sat down on the ground. "Go look for yourself."

Bobby said, "I'm just gonna see if Luna's in there."

"Good idea." Dan looked down at Jo. "Maybe I should stay with her."

With a nod, Wayne followed after Bobby, and they disappeared into the barn.

"Are you sure you're okay?" Dan said.

Jo looked up at him with a half smile. "You're like a... a carbon copy, aren't you?"

"I don't understand."

"Dan!" Wayne poked his head outside the barn. "Bobby found something."

Dan sighed and jogged over to his friend. Wayne looked pale, like he'd seen a ghost. Dan felt the hairs on the back of his neck stand up. "What's wrong?"

Wayne led Dan inside. Bobby stood past where Jo had been sitting after the collapse. As they joined him, he held up Luna's harness. The purple light was dark.

Dan's mouth went dry. "Where is she?"

Bobby shook his head and ran from the barn. Wayne pointed at the floor and went after Bobby. Dan took a step forward and looked down. Though it was pale, almost see-through, and flattened like a discarded mask, he recognized his face. His naked body was an empty husk, like a deflated balloon.

He turned to leave. On his way out, he noticed a large puddle of goo near the hay mound. Outside, Jo, Wayne, and Bobby stared at him. He took a deep breath and let it out. "I'm some sort of... pod person?"

Jo must have seen that movie too—he'd seen it with Wayne—because she said, "I guess so."

"But you seem scared," Wayne said. "Like a normal person. Not like in the movie."

"Yeah," said Dan. "I wonder how Luna could do that? And why?"

"Maybe that's what they're for," Bobby said. "Like those dogs that save people in the mountains. Except even after... you know."

"Yeah," said Jo. "Do you remember anything?"

"My whole life. I mean, me, Dan. Breaking my arm when I was five. All our pets. Taking a trip to the Badlands and Yellowstone, camping in one big tent. Wayne came with us. I don't remember... being Luna."

There was a long, nervous silence. Then Bobby said, "Wanna biscuit?"

"No!"

"Just testing."

Jo giggled first. It didn't take long until they were all laughing so hard they fell to the ground. After they were laughed out, they sat on the boulder under the flying saucer.

Wayne said, "Now what? Do we tell anyone?"

"No!" said Bobby. "They'll take him away!"

At the same time, they all remembered that was what he'd said about Luna, so they laughed some more.

Jo said, "I think it's gotta be our secret. Otherwise...well, otherwise it'll be like he's really—"

"Dead," Dan finished for her. She nodded.

"Pinky swear?" said Wayne.

"Pinky swear," they all repeated, managing to entwine all four pinkies at once.

They sat without talking. Jo lit another cigarette. Dan reached over Bobby and picked up Luna's harness. It was too big for his body, but he tried it on anyway. As soon as he did, the little purple light on the front flashed on. And behind them, they heard the hatch hum open.

They all turned around slowly and looked at the purple glow coming from inside the flying saucer.

"Well," Dan said. "Maybe we can figure out how to fly this thing."

# The Hardwicke Files: The Case of the Blue Helix

### BY RUSS COLCHAMIRO

FOUR hours. That's how long I've been ducking behind this rancid dumpster. My back and knees ache and I have to pee so badly urine is practically leaking from my tear ducts. I've also got a migraine, this persistent *wum... wum...wum...* above my left temple that nearly brings me to my knees.

But I can't leave until Michael Koop shows. He's trying to fence a cache of jewelry stolen from my client's store, including the second in a set of matching diamond bracelets that could pay for my retirement ten times over. I recovered the first one earlier tonight.

I debate running across the street to the Clay Street Diner—at least the bathroom is clean—when my phone buzzes. Normally I'd ignore the intrusion—Koop just turned the corner—but the caller ID says it's Frankie the Brush. He would never call at this hour unless it was important.

I tap my earbud as an arrowhead-shaped cloud drifts in front of the crescent moon. Shot through the heart.

"Bad timing," I whisper with clenched teeth. "Mama's grabbing some ice."

"Sorry, Angela. But I'm looking at something you really need to see."

Frankie the Brush is a general contractor and painter who works both sides of the street—commercial and residential. He also does galaxy renovation and polishing. So he's got every reason to know people in all walks of life.

"Can it wait? Between the part-time nanny and ahh"—I reach up to my throbbing head—"private school for Owen, I need this payday."

When you have a five-year-old like mine and the job I do, regular childcare doesn't really cut it. Been there done that.

"No, not really," Frankie says, the uncertainty in his voice clear to me even through the subspace communication channel. "I'm out in the Wilco sector."

"Wilco? Isn't that...?" Michael Koop drunk-fumbles with his keys. Which, despite my own blurred vision thanks to this headache,

*Illustration by Ron Randall*

gives me an edge, and explains why he's four hours late. I extend my taser. "Give me five minutes. I gotta go."

"No, Angela!"

"I'm gonna lose him, Frank."

I was going to have Whistler, my assistant, back me up, but he's got appendicitis.

"I'm tellin ya, Angela. The Universe. This whole thing. It's an imperfect place!"

"I hear ya," I say, ready to pounce on Koop. "It's a mess."

"No… I know you know. But you got no *idea* what I deal with all day. The Cosmos—and I'm talking all the dimensions and across timelines and parallel Universes, too—it's got cracks, leaks, bends, and breaks. It's littered with breaches, chinks, chips, and fissures of every kind."

Frankie's usually as cool as the dark side of the moon, but every now and then he gets all worked up.

It's annoying, but I kinda like it when he's like this. With a small business to run and a wife and five girls—including a newborn—it's nice to see him blow off steam once in a while. And Frankie doesn't blow small.

"But let's not forget the fractures, gaps, and gashes. And don't even get me *started* on the voids, gulfs, pops, and perforations."

"It's those very imperfections that keep you in business, Frank. Same with me."

"I know. But this one"—Frankie

sighs—"I've never seen this before. I'm scared, Angela. And I don't feel so good. My head, it's… I don't know what's going on, but I think it's bad."

In my soft-healed black sneakers and olive green utility jacket I sidle up to Koop who, despite bloodshot eyes and shaky hands, maneuvers his key into the lock. I get a whiff, but he's not drunk. It's something else. And then he reaches up to his temple. He's got pain. Same as me.

"Angela!" Frankie says in his commanding dad voice. "I need you. Now."

Koop turns to me. He's so disoriented I don't need my taser. I can take him easily. But that migraine, that *wum… wum… wum…* has got me light-headed, like I'm about to pass out.

"Hey," Koop mumbles, right before I taser him after all. "Who's Frank?"

CONTRACTORS signed to do any kind of repair work on the Universe are given job-specific access to intergalactic travel gates. Frankie keeps me on his employment roster for cases like this. I fight off the dizziness and cab it to the west side along the Rubiyat Highway, which snakes along the Chabaqua River.

Not my favorite part of town, especially at night, but a few winos, streetwalkers, and dealers aside, it's quiet.

Quiet for E-Town—the central

city in Eternity, the realm that supports and supplies the labor and services for the design, construction, and maintenance of the Cosmos.

Any other night I'd choke down some aspirin and two fingers of Whiskey, but something in Frankie's voice has me worried. He has the same headache as me. Michael Koop, too. The pain, the *wum... wum... wum...* is like a sonar of some kind, a persistent, repeating wave of dense energy that's disrupting my equilibrium. I'm nauseous.

All energy has a source. I need to find it.

Moonlight refracts off the chainlink fence fortified with an electric current and topped with barbedwire coils, security booth on the end. I show my access code to Latesha, the guard, who knows me well enough to let me pass without a hassle, but not so well to just nod me in. She makes me show my ID and put my eye to the infrared retinal scanner. It does its thing.

"Hey," I say. "You have an aspirin. Bitch of a headache."

"Nah, sorry. You, too? My head's been *throbbing*, you know what I mean?" She paws at her left temple. "Like I've been clubbing all night and the subwoofer's right against my dome, that baseline just humming and wumming. My ears are ringing. And I don't know why."

"Bad night," I say with a grimace.

"Real bad," she says.

Latesha buzzes open the fence, then walks me out back to the travel gate station along the river when the ground rumbles.

Streetquake. Hasn't been one in years.

The vibrations toss us aside, setting off alarms. Street lamps burst. Dogs howl.

Latesha and I are down on our knees, hands to our heads, praying for it to stop.

And then it does.

We look around, to see if it's really over. Some car windows are blown out, the river's dark waters riled up into waves, but otherwise, E-town seems to have settled down.

Back on our feet, Latesha nods to the shuttle. "You really wanna get in that thing?"

"Not really, no. But what's life without adventure?"

She squints. "Life," she says and walks painfully back to her post.

I HUNCH inside the shuttlecraft.

The Wilco Sector is a hundred and seventeen galaxies away, but programmed with the destination coordinates, the shuttle gets me to the job site in five minutes.

Gotta love gate travel. Although it takes all I have to keep from losing my lunch.

I dock near Frankie's shuttle van, a beat-up rig with more scars, dings, and dents than my soul.

He's set up outside an accordion-style lattice-work frame with interconnected platforms, spotlights, and junction boxes. Various tools are lying around, or floating in space, attached to tubes, wires, and hoses.

I forget sometimes all the equipment Frankie deals with, the guts of the jobs he takes.

He's encased in a clear, comet-coated bodysuit with the integrity to withstand the force and pressure of up to six black holes. The protective layer is a viscous fluid as thin as tissue paper, yet wonderfully malleable, permitting full tactility, sensitivity, and dexterity.

Inside my shuttle I step beneath a sprinkler head, then activate the device. It sprays me with the fluid, which slurps onto me. Whatever's in this fluid, it helps with my headache. It's not gone, but it's muted. I can deal with it.

The shuttle bay door opens. I walk down the platform, the nearest star system beyond our sightline.

"Okay, Frank. You got me here. What I am looking at?"

"Over here."

He leads us to what looks like nothing but empty space.

"What, Frank? You lost me."

He produces a wand with an LED light and magnifying lens on the end, leans forward on the platform railing, then waves the wand in tight circular motions against the black surface of space.

The LED light glows. "You see this here? How it's dented, this imperfection?"

I look closer. "Yeah, actually. I do. So?"

"Each quadrant of the Universe has its own containment grid. Invisible to the naked eye. But this one's damaged. They hired Sammy Krieger to fix the outer casing, repair the dent, and smooth it out. He used to do good work. But ever since he went corporate, he's spends more time wooing clients than overseeing the job site. He even left some gear behind. I was able to fix most of what he missed, but I'm not done."

"Frank. The dent is barely noticeable, even magnified to a factor of a million."

"It may seem small, but we both know it means the integrity of the space/time fabric has been compromised. A dent this small today could become a whole lot bigger tomorrow. And if that happens, the entire quadrant could collapse on itself."

"Fair enough. But why do you need *me*?"

He leads us to the end of the platform—which extends as far as he needs in any direction by way of hydraulic hinges—then punches a code into his phone. Before us is a rectangular carve-out in space, three feet wide, glowing green. Frankie puts his fingers against the surface, activating a hand-grip. He slides the panel to the side, revealing, through that rectangular window, what's behind it.

My breath catches. My heart pounds.

"Is that what I think it is?" I feel massive energy radiating from the other side of the gap. Even with the bodysuit, I've got goosebumps all over.

Trim for a middle-aged dad, Frankie looks at me and rubs his sausage link fingers over his bald head. "It's the DNA helix of the Universe. One of 'em, anyway."

The helix's twisted ladder formation is two miles long easy, the fluorescent blue strands of tubing at least fifty feet in circumference. Golden energy bands circulate through the entirety of the helix with that same persistent *wum... wum... wum...*

Huh.

"I've never seen one of these," I say. "I only heard rumors. I didn't know they were real."

"They're real, Angela. And classified. Which is why I never talk about it."

He punches in another access code into his phone. A red essence globe appears, the size of a basketball. Hovering in front of Frankie, the globe opens, gleaming a white cone of light. It lifts Frankie off the platform and scans his essence—analyzing his past, present, future, and the authenticity of his character—confirming he is who he claims to be. It sets Frankie down.

After scanning me, I'm surprised the essence globe doesn't spew clouds of black smoke then pour itself a martini. Instead it rolls its single eye at me. I hate judgmental essence globes. Like they're so perfect.

Cleared for work, Frankie punches in another code. A wall of space—revealing the entire DNA helix—slides back. Compared with this gargantuan interchange of pure energy, we are but eyes of flies against the galactic windshield.

Frank extends the platform—a seemingly endless apparatus—allowing us to walk beneath one of the helix twists.

"Look here. On this strand." He puts his hand on it, rubbing it gently, like the underside of a whale. Even though we're minuscule in its presence, the DNA helix responds with a surge of golden energy and guttural hum.

I reach out my hand, then retract it, as if pulling away from fire.

"It's okay," he says. "It trusts you."

"The Universe's DNA trusts *me*?"

"You wouldn't have gotten this close otherwise."

Still hesitant, I make contact. The casing is firm yet elastic, almost rubbery, with just enough give that the contours of my hand synch with the helix.

And then energy courses through my body. I tense up.

"Let it in, Angela. It's bonding with you. It's listening. You have to listen back."

"I don't—" My chest constricts,

my internal guardrails kicking in. But as that hum, the all-consuming energy, crackles along my skin, penetrating the very marrow of my essence, I relent. As if a valve within me I never even knew existed turns one rotation, then another, energy releases into my own essence tubes until, finally, I'm breathing easier. I feel the flow. I relax.

"Now listen to it," Frankie says. "Close your eyes. Listen."

I do.

"I've been out here for two days," Frankie says. "I've had these incredible headaches. They got worse as I got closer to the helix, but the suit helps."

"Same here. You've never felt this before? These headaches?"

"No, not like these. I thought maybe a wiring issue in the security matrix triggered a hypersonic frequency, but I did a full diagnostic. It checks out, as far as I can tell. I think..."

My mind immediately goes to Owen, when he had a tummy ache, and all he wanted was for mommy to rub his belly until he fell asleep. And then I realize.

"It's the helix itself. It's in pain. And it's asking for help."

UTILIZING the hydraulic-controlled platform, Frankie takes us about a half mile between the blue helix twists until we come to a section that is slightly... just slightly... pink.

It's less than a foot long and only a few inches wide.

"The outer casing has been compromised," I say. "It looks... wounded. I didn't know that was possible."

"Me neither," Frankie confesses. "I'm not sure I have the tools or skills to repair it. But even if I can patch it up, there's no guarantee it'll hold."

"So what now?"

"That's why I need you, Angela. You're the PI. If anybody can figure this out, it's you."

"I'm a private investigator, Frank, not an intergalactic forensics expert. I don't even know if there *is* an expert for this."

"I don't either. But I feel... sad. Dread. I think it's the helix. It's telling me... something. But I can't do this alone. Please. I need your help."

Easier said than done when the Universe's helix is like a wounded animal. So I ignore the scope of the case. Keep it simple.

"I'm assuming there would've been surface degradation or striations in the membrane if the helix had worn down or if some foreign object—a virus or particle—found its way into the helix and then ripped it open from the inside. Sound right, Frank?"

"Yeah. But this wound. It's clean, almost..."

"Surgical," I finish.

Frankie nods. "Maybe something brushed up against it. An asteroid or a comet? Satellite? Maybe a parasite gnawed on it. If it has teeth or tentacles, maybe it found a way to puncture the surface. Or maybe even a ship came out here, a raider. But I can't see how anything could get this close."

"Maybe it's sabotage."

"Sabotage? Why would anyone do that? And even if they wanted to, how could they pull it off?"

"Good question. Hey, look at this. Can you magnify the surface?"

Frankie illuminates the wound down to the tiniest threads of granulated tissue. There are new striations and microvessels, as if the helix is trying to heal itself.

"Gimme that, will ya?" I hold the wand close. "It's an incision. No way it was random. Too clean. We'd see rips and frayed edges if it had been torn. And look here."

"Is that circuitry?" Frankie says.

"Not circuitry. Magnify by a factor of ten. Nanobots."

"Nanobots? But the helix is organic tissue. *Cosmic* tissue. The Universe's DNA. How can there be nanobots... for this?"

"I have no idea," I say and study the mammoth blue helix strands engulfing this corner of space. "But what is DNA, Frank? What's *your* DNA, or mine for that matter? It's a string of complex molecules. It contains the genetic information of life and acts as an instruction manual for how to build and maintain... you. Each chromosome within you contains genes, very specific DNA strands, with detailed instructions about how to form every little piece of your physical self. Your fingers, your eyelashes,"—I take his hand—"your wrist." I let his hand go. "Package some of those genes, you get a chromosome. Package *all* those chromosomes, and in total, you have your genome. The Frankie the Brush genome. An instruction manual for *you*. And this massive helix here is a genome. A cosmic genome. An instruction manual for how to build and maintain the entire Universe. Or, at least, a section of it."

"I... I know, Angela, I just... I just never think of it like that. I never repair the helix. Just the grid that surrounds it. But why nanobots?"

"Think of the helix as a computer, with complex circuitry, code, instructions, pathways, and internal commands—mapping a blueprint for the Cosmos."

"And you think, what? Nanobots are trying to... hijack the helix? Take control of it? Technology imposing itself on organic matter?" Frank shudders, considering the abominations we've seen when tissue and tech co-exist against their will. "I hate when that happens."

We look at each other, our heads both pounding again, as the helix itself surges with that infected energy, that *wum... wum... wum...* drilling a hole in our temples.

"Unfortunately," I say, pressing my hand to my head. "I think it's worse."

"Worse? What could be worse than nanobots of unknown origin trying to take control of the Universe's DNA?"

I rub my temple, the queasiness roaring back with a vengeance. "I don't think they're just trying to take control, Frank. I think the helix has been sending out an S.O.S. because it's under attack. It's protecting the essence of its internal infrastructure, its identity. I think the nanobots are trying to rewrite the helix's entire genetic code. The helix is fighting for its survival. And by extension, the Universe."

Frankie stares at me, withdrawn so far into existential fear he can barely move. "Rewrite the Universe's genetic code? Why would the nanobots do that?"

I stare back, the surging blue DNA helix reflected in his eyes. My fear matches his, but I can't give in. I survey the work zone, a puzzle without a sequence.

"I have no idea," I say, and rummage through my pockets—weapons, phone, fingerprint and lockpick kit—reminding me that my own genetic code is still very much intact. For now. "So crack out your tool belt. We've got work to do."

FIGHTING off our throbbing headaches we rifle through Frankie's van for every diagnostic tool we can find.

"Hey, Frank. When you run diagnostics on the grid surrounding the helix, is it just one way? Does the grid to talk to your device, or can your device to talk the grid?"

"Both ways, why?"

"Can you ask the helix what's wrong?"

"I did."

"How?"

"There's a series of diagnostic codes. I ran a systems check."

"But did you actually ask it what's wrong?"

"You mean...?"

"I mean, key in the words, 'Hi, Helix. You seem wounded. What's wrong?'"

"No, but..."

I nod to him to do just that. He obliges, talking as he goes.

"*Hi... Helix. Are... you... o... kay? What... is...... wrong*?" He taps ENTER.

No response. The cursor on his device blinks. And blinks. And blinks.

"I don't think it works like that, Angela. This is a diagnostic process that—"

Blistering pain. Everything around us vibrates. His van, the lattice work, his tools. Even space itself rumbles.

The helix surges... *wum... wum... wum...* over and over, accelerating, as if it's building towards a systems overload. We squint in agony and press our palms to our heads, the migraines like diamond-tipped lasers burning holes in our temples.

"Do something, Angela! Unplug! Unplug!"

"No! Just give it a minute. Just give it—"

The shaking stops. We drop to our knees

"What...?" I start, gasping for breath. "What's it say?"

"Nothing," Frankie says. "It doesn't say..."

We both look at the device. A word appears on screen.

"*Brother.*"

Frankie's as puzzled as I am. "Brother? Brother what?"

I take the device from him, and key in my response. "*Can you explain 'brother'?*"

We wait. The cursor blinks. "*Brother,*" appears again.

"I don't have a brother," I say. "A sister. A few years older than me."

"You do?" Frankie says. "You never said."

I don't want to get into it. "We don't talk much. What about you, Frank?"

"I..." Frankie turns away.

"What is it?"

Frankie looks back to me, but his eyes reveal a depth of sadness I've seen far too often in my line of work. "Doug," he says. "He's been... gone a long time."

"I'm sorry, Frank. I didn't know. When did he die?"

"He didn't. At least I hope not. But either way, he's... missing."

"Missing? Frank! Why didn't you *tell* me? I could look for him. Find him."

"I tried, Angela. For years. It's one of the reasons I take so many jobs and travel as far as I do. But the trail went cold, and after a while I kinda... gave up. I keep an ear out, ask quietly here and there. But like you always say, some people, when they're gone... just don't wanna be found."

He's right. I say it a lot. Because it's true. "But sometimes they do, Frank. And it's your brother."

"Not just my brother," Frank confesses. He sighs, and nods at the helix. "My twin."

The helix surges. Words appear on the device. "*Brother. Twin.*"

Frank and I gaze at the helix, then at each other. I type again.

"*You have a twin brother?*"

"*Twin brother.*"

Frankie looks to me. I look to Frankie. "Twins," we say in unison.

A double helix. Of course.

"*Two brothers,*" I type.

The helix surges, that *wum... wum... wum.*

"*Brothers?*" I type again, fighting the pain.

Another surge. Only as Frankie falls to his knees, I notice something.

"You're grabbing your right temple. Is that where it hurts, Frank? Just the right?"

"Yeah," he grimaces. "Why?"

"Each time? Always the right?"

"Yes."

My pain is on the left. So was Latesha's. But Michael Koop, in the alley—I search my mind, study his face—his was on the right.

I key in another message: *"Your twin is your brother. But you are his... sister?"*

The cursor blinks. Then: *"Brother. Sister. Twins."*

*"And your brother is missing?"*

Another painful surge.

"He's not missing," I say aloud.

Frank squints. "Then what?"

I've seen this play out before. *"You know where he is,"* I type. *"But you just can't reach him?"*

*"No access,"* the readout says.

I think a minute. *"Can he access you?"*

*"Blocked,"* the readout says.

I respond. *"Blocked by what?"*

*"Grid."*

The pieces are falling into place. *"The containment grid? It's locked you in?"*

*"Twin,"* the helix responds.

"We know it's your twin," Frankie says. "What's she saying?"

"Twin," I mumble as my mind searches for the answer. "Twin-twin twin-twin-twin." My eyes go wide. "Twin! Frank! It's a twin. A twin grid!"

We look around us. Nothing but empty space.

"Frank. How did you find the grid?"

"I was given the coordinates."

"By whom?"

Frank retreats within himself, hesitant to answer.

I put my hand on his shoulder. "Look where we are, Frank. Looks what's happening. You need to tell me."

He takes a deep breath, holds it, stares at the injured helix, then exhales. "The CGMD."

"The CG what now?"

"Cosmic Genome Monitoring Division."

"The Cosmic Genome Monitoring Division. Right. And you never said because...?"

"Like I said," he says.

"Classified?"

"Classified."

The CGMD is one of the most ruthless organizations in the oversight of the Universe. No wonder Frankie kept his mouth shut. I would have, too. And yet he called me to help, not them. I get why. Which gets me thinking.

"Hey, Frank. How do you get clearance to be on site?"

He points. "We just did it. You have to... oh," he says. "I get it."

"Good," I say, and nod at the wounded helix. "Set it up."

ESSENCE globes do not appear on command, but Frankie knows his way around a construction site. By way of a coiled scraper, he collects a lump of spores trapped in the grille of his shuttle van, wipes them into a tiny pod, then ejects them into the work site.

On cue, sensing the life-form, the essence globe appears, hovering over the pod of spores. While performing its due diligence—the globe opens, and shines its cone of light—Frankie slips a conduction pole behind it, short-circuiting the globe.

"They're responsive," he says, "but surprising gullible."

Frankie jerry-rigs the essence globe with a custom star drive, then inserts the globe within a larger, magnetized gyroscope.

"Okay," he says. "Let's see what we see."

Frankie sends the gyroscope into the quadrant by remote, all three axes spinning as the central rotor maintains its spin axis direction.

When the gyroscope is out far enough, Frankie instructs the essence globe to open its dome, and scan in all directions. Searching for the missing life form. The second helix.

The missing twin.

"Anything, Frank?"

"No, not yet. But give it time." As small as stardust against the infinite cosmic landscape, it's difficult to miss the obvious. "There's a lot of real estate to cover."

NEARLY an hour goes by with no results. But as a private investigator, I know first-hand the value of patience and persistence on a stakeout. Even if I don't have the time.

True to his moniker, Frankie the Brush essentially paints the quadrant with essence globe light, up and down, down and up, one section at a time. It's a tedious process, but it's logical and consistent, one of the reasons I trust and rely

on Frankie as much as I do.

Which is why it's so satisfying when that patience pays off.

"You see that," he says finally. "It's a… tiny pink cloud. Over there." He magnifies on his view screen what the essence globe picks up almost a mile away.

"Yeah. It looks like radiation."

"A leak," he says.

"Frank. Magnify again. As close as possible." He does, and within that tiny pink cloud we see even tinier particles. But no. Not particles. "Nanobots."

Frankie throws up his hands. "*That's* where they came from. Sammy's gear. The tools he left behind. I tossed out the casing, because it was broken, but he must've used a Wylie-29 nanobot comet smoother on the dent. They don't *work* on space/time fabric. Nanobots are too coarse. And then they leak. I've told him that a hundred times."

And then it occurs to me. Sammy's not the only one who made a mistake.

"The nanobots aren't trying to reprogram the helix. The brother is trying to establish a link with his sister. I think the repeated vibrations—their extraordinary expressions—caused the initial dent. And then the helix repurposed those rejected nanobots for something they can actually do."

"Eat through the grid," Frankie says. "Creating a pathway from one helix to the other."

I ask the first helix. The sister.

"*Cut off,*" she confirms through the device. "*Communicate.*"

"*But why are you in pain?*"

The cursor blinks for what seems like an awfully long time. "*Infection.*"

"Ohh," I say sympathetically. "It's *infected,*" I type again. "*How did that happen?*"

The cursor blinks again. And then: "*Bots. Don't belong.*"

"*What was your brother trying to tell you?*"

"*Sad. Love. Caged. For so long.*"

"*So in trying to reach you,*" I type, "*your brother hurt you by mistake.*"

"*Help,*" the helix responds. "*No. More. Cage.*"

When I first met the helix it was like petting a giant whale. But I hadn't realized then it was such a gorgeous, soulful creature, forced into captivity, isolated from its family.

"Frank. Can you open the other grid? Can we reach her brother?"

"I can try."

His fingers clack feverishly at the terminal until finally he gives up. "I just don't have the programming skills. The second grid operates on an entirely different frequency. I don't have the codes."

Once again I survey Frankie's van full of tools. "Then let's go old school."

Frankie smiles. "Are you thinking what I'm thinking?" He sees that I am. "I like it."

I'VE seen the jaws of life in action more times than I care to admit. There's usually a mangled body to pry loose from the wreckage. But this is one time I'm happy to see that hydraulic spreader in action.

Only we make one adjustment first. The jaws of life won't fit into the tiny crevice in the containment grid created by the nanobots.

Frankie produces what looks like a massive leaf blower, but is actually a Shumpko L-760 portable miniaturizing and enlargement unit. He grabs the curved handle, points the outer tube at the jaws of life, and flips on the Shumpko.

From the tube shoots a fine yellow mist, which miniaturizes the jaws of life to microscopic size. Then with surgical precision, through his device and magnified on screen, Frankie remotely guides the miniaturized jaws of life through the crevice.

"Want to do the honors?" he says, and hands me the control.

I press the button, enlarging the jaws of life from miniature, to full size, and then beyond. The crevice in the second helix's powerful containment grid tears and wronks as it also enlarges—the jaws of life expanding like the mechanical beast that it is—until, finally, the crevice has been pried open wide enough, allowing the helix to communicate more freely.

From within we see a massive red glow. We feel it's *wum... wum... wum.* Only instead of resulting in our intense pain, Frankie and I both are overcome with relief.

The two helixes, brother and sister—twins—whir with energy until the containment grids around them both shatter, then disintegrate into cosmic dust.

After an imprisonment we can't begin to measure, the helix twins are, at last, free.

Like the giant whales they emulate, the siblings swim to one another, those two coiled DNA helixes hugging, I suppose, reveling in their reunion.

The cursor on Frankie's device blinks. And then: "*Gratitude.*"

A second message comes through. "*Remember.*"

Frankie and I smile at each other, then at the helix siblings.

"*You're welcome,*" I type. "*We won't forget you either.*"

Another message appears on screen, meant for me.

"*Glad to be of service,*" I respond. "*Call me any time.*"

One last message appears.

I steel myself, nod. "*I know. I will.*"

The helixes disappear then, off into the Cosmos.

"What was that about?" Frankie asks as he packs up his shuttle van. "Blowback from the CGMD? I'll need to watch my back with them. Sammy's on my shitlist for sure."

I slip my hand into my pocket, the two pieces of jewelry I'd repo'd between my fingers. I'd forgotten all about them. Twins, reunited.

"We'll discuss it over breakfast," I say. "And you're buying."

# The Shadow Lady of Docktown

## By Kelli Fitzpatrick

I NEED a shower, a good sleep, and a holo-show. In that order. Instead, I'm shined and crouched atop a bridge bolt, watching uniformed men on the dark dock below. I detach Tish from my jacket sleeve and send him to investigate. The little rag-bot flutters away like a bat wing in the night.

This job was supposed to wrap at last daybreak, but the targets didn't show, and if I don't find out what contraband they're hauling in those cargo cubes, I don't get paid. So I waited it out, twiddling my thumbs on a girder overlooking the loading zone. By harbor rules, those containers can only be docked for twenty-four hours at a stint, so I figured somebody had to show sometime.

Somebody did, just not the smugglers I expected. When I was almost ready to call it quits, an armored hover-skiff rolled up into the golden halo of a dock lamp. Out hopped two men in unmarked riot gear too high-end to be crime ring. They lifted two people by the arms from the back of the skiff and walked them stumbling into the container. I had to squint, but I could make out the bald head of Chief Forso exiting the passenger side. Police then? Or agents working for them? Most cuffs in this city don't actually serve and protect, unless you count serving their own interests and protecting each other from justice. Nobody does that better than Chief Forso. If his skeevy cocksure mug is involved, then this operation reeks worse than stagnant seawater. He turns and the lenses of his shine goggles catch lamplight. So...he's expecting interference from a puller. I smirk.

Tish flits back, fluttering silently in agitation. I check the scan data he's forwarding to my wristlet and see why: eight people are huddled on the floor inside that cube, including the two that were just dragged in. The passenger cars for Bridge transport are hanging high above us at the transit station. These containers are meant for Cendra company cargo only. What the hell is going on?

The Cobalt Reef hired me to get in, gather intel, and get out without being spotted. That's what shadow pullers are good at, and I'm the best puller in Docktown. I have the data they want—I'm free to skedaddle and let the Reef

*Illustration by Daerick Gross*

address whatever rotten scheme is brewing here. But abandoning people in boxes surrounded by shady cops doesn't sit right with me, so I decide to inspect the situation up-close. I'm already shined, making me invisible to all but the trained eye, so when Tish docks on my sleeve, he disappears too.

Luckily, sight is pretty simple to hack. Any half-decent photon-painter knows you mix light with shadow and you get a hazy glare. They cancel each other out, like a bright light shined in your eyes in a dark room. You see everything, and nothing. Too much, and therefore not at all. When I pull shadow from my surroundings and weave it into my body, I become the spark in the corner of your eye, the movement that's not really there. But it's a heck of a lot easier to do when I'm fresh. Forso's shine goggles will only reveal my form if he looks straight at me, so I'll have to be quick.

I slide down the tall pier to dock level and sneak around the end of the container toward the open door, timing my steps to the waves hitting the seawall so the cops won't hear me. I keep my eyes on Forso who is busy chatting with a dock worker, and slip inside the cube.

The close walls of the container act like a reverb chamber and it takes all my concentration to hold cover, but most of the people here have their head on their knees, or are staring blankly at the ceiling. They look, bizarrely, unperturbed. I crouch behind the one who seems most awake, a man in a tattered sweater. "Don't react," I whisper. He jerks his head, searching for the source of my voice but not finding it. "I'm not with them," I say.

The guy's breath hisses to the stuffy air. "Who are you? Do you know if we're traveling the whole way like this?"

"I'm spying for a group that thinks these cops are dealing dirty. Where are they taking you?"

He glances out the door where the cuffs watch some clip on a holo-pane and snicker. "I was arrested for vagrancy after I visited the cathedral. I'm not religious, but they advertised free confessions and I thought—"

"Hey!" one of the officers snaps. "Hush up in there. Silence was part of the deal, remember?"

The man clamps his mouth shut. I lean closer to his ear, still invisible. "You were arrested at the church?"

His voice is barely audible. "Not exactly. The priest—pastor?—whoever he is, led me into the confession booth, gave me this stone pendant to wear and said to pray for an hour in the chapel and my prayers would be answered. But I think he took something from me."

My gaze flattens. Only one priest-pastor-whoever I know who would steal from a desperate person. Galen Muldany. "What'd he swipe? Your money?"

"I think...I think he took my anger. I want to be upset at what's happening to me right now, but I'm not. At all."

My blood chills. Shadow pulling is not the only clandestine art afoot in Docktown, but I've never heard of *emotion* pulling. Muldany's enough of a nightmare on his own, but with powers? Shit.

"After I prayed, I left the cathedral and the cops sailed through a few minutes later."

What a coincidence. "That explains how you got picked up, but not why you're in a cube meant for rebar."

"Right. The police said if I agree to volunteer on a Bridge maintenance crew with Cendra Steel for a year, the charges will be dropped."

"Volunteer?" Since when do cops recruit for a corp? "That's a crazy dangerous job. Even convicts are supposed to get hazard pay."

"What else am I going to do?" he says, leaning his head back against the metal sheeting. "I won't survive prison."

He might not survive the Bridge work either—the list of risks is a league long, everything from ionwelding burns to falling into the radioactive depths. There's a reason the shipping industry died out. Or rather, all the sailors did.

Forso says something to his officers outside and makes a lifting motion, then walks off on a holocall. I don't have long.

"Listen, I'll sabotage the cube's hitch. If you decide you want out of this raw deal, you'll only have one shot when they transfer you to a different one. Tell the others." I pull a folded jackknife from my boot and slide it into his palm. To him, it probably looks like it's materializing from thin air. "The sooner you can duck underground, the better. Find the Reef. They will want your story."

I step onto the drawbridge-style door of the cube and smile at the extra effort the officers exert lifting with me aboard. I grip the top edge, ride it skyward, and leap onto the slippery roof as the door bangs shut. I can't see Forso from here, but this will only take a second.

Tish overheard the plan—he flies to the hitch of the container, spreads his flat body over the contact plate, electrifies, and sizzles till it looks like pitted tin foil. When the crane tries to lock on, it will find no purchase. I check my wristlet: Tish is low on charge and I'm beyond spent. Time to split before—

Something sharp rakes my left temple, narrowly missing my eye and throwing me off balance. I curse and my cover melts as I fall over the edge into a pile of boxboard and roll onto wet pavement. A throwing star tinks to the ground beside me.

"The Shadow Lady lives," Forso says, stepping forward. "I thought for sure you drowned in our last encounter."

I groan. "Those fancy new goggles say otherwise. Afraid to look me in the eye?" The left side of my body will be one giant bruise. Where is Tish? My wristlet shows him five meters away. Close enough.

Forso frowns and pulls his goggles up. "I don't know who you are playing mercenary for tonight, Delk, but maiming one cube is a futile move. In case you hadn't noticed," he gestures around, "I have plenty of resources at my disposal."

"You always do." I push myself up to an unsteady crouch.

One of the henchmen starts toward me but Forso waves him off. "I can handle her. I need you to reopen the cube. We have another Cendra volunteer." He smiles at me.

As soon as the officer rounds the corner and I hear the door unlatch, I draw a breath, lock eyes with Forso, and yell, "Tish, *mirror!*"

Tish zips between us and pulls his fibers into a tight metallic disk, rotating to a precise angle. I thrust my right hand to the greasy concrete and my left toward the Chief.

The bastard guesses what I'm about to do—this is not the first time we've tangoed—and he tries to shield his eyes, but I'm faster, using my right hand to yank all the shadow out of me through my feet with the force of a whip crack. Shadow always seeks balance, but the trip through the ground slows it down, leaving my torso briefly absent of anything but accelerating light. When amplified off Tish's surface, this photonic burst is temporarily blinding, even with eyelids closed.

Forso cries out, dropping to his knees. I hold up my forearm and Tish latches on, then I use what feels like the last of my strength to resume cover and sprint away, dodging into the shadows of the cargo labyrinth. I can faintly hear Forso cursing and yelling at his men. His sight will eventually return, but I've just poured saltwater in his open dislike for me.

I slide into a corner and listen for the drum-like thud of pursuit. Nothing. I lean forward and let my cover evaporate. Red dots drip from my temple onto my boots. The data! I punch in the clearance codes on my wristlet and forward the recorded data to the Cobalt Reef operative. The upload clears and I heave a sigh that eddies the yellow mist. Time to disappear underground till this blows over.

My wristlet vibrates and blue block letters zip over the display, but it's not the Reef. *Muldany in meeting, need your stealth,* it reads. Tharen. This web just keeps spinning tighter. I run a hand through my dark hair and a deep I-want-to-collapse-into-a-coma ache rolls through me. Not many souls in this world I would drop recoup time for, but Tharen is one of them, and she might have clues to whatever scheme is unfolding.

My holo-show will have to wait.

DUCKING through the milling night crowd in Docktown, I notice there's still blood dripping from my temple. That slice Forso blessed me with must be deeper than I thought.

"Tish," I say, and point to my head. "Sear."

The ragbot puffs off my sleeve where he was charging and wafts upward like a tiny ghost, folding over the wound and electrifying to cauterize. I grit my teeth—it hurts, for truth, but not as much as an infection.

Tish finishes and floats along beside me, pulsing like a jellyfish. He's been my buddy for three years, since I found him crumpled in an alley and finagled a repair. I've never seen a ragbot like him. Instead of typical programmed cloth for cleaning or whatnot, Tish is a square of weightless metal mesh. He looks like a puff of smoke, an appropriate sidekick for a shadow puller.

I sidestep a street vendor hawking the fur of some unfortunate gutter creature, and button the front of my grey trench—there's a damp chill that seeps out of the bones of the city. As usual, dirty fog drapes the whole oceanside district, a jagged spray of steel and glass reaching out over the water like an explosion on pause. Most buildings down here are low-rent hostels catering to travelers and transient dockworkers, rooms with windows and real beds—heck of a lot nicer than the sub-ground sleep boxes I usually spring for. Then, in the midst of the modern sprawl, like some ancient text slipped off the shelf of the past, there's my destination: Cherishdom, the church of the budget-conscious tourist.

Built on the perma-docks below the girders of the Great Bridge-Over-the-Sea, the Cherish Cathedral sports a grey exterior carved into sculpture of richly-dressed saints and peasant-looking people who are probably characters in some psalm I haven't read. The figures tower over the slummy streets, a caricature of our ridiculous economy that places leisure and poverty a half-step apart and names it normal. Maybe in its heyday, Cherishdom was a functioning place of worship for whatever faith originally bankrupted itself building it.

Now it's mostly an eyesore and a tourist trap, a play-acting farce in the grunge pocket of overpopulation that is Docktown. It is still a church, though, and churches are hotspots for a couple of things: sin, pride, and shadow. The church building is lit from above by a garish white spotlight that's supposed to simulate heavenly favor or something. It outshines even the neon flashery of the cuff station across the street. Bright lights and dark depths: my playground.

I climb the concrete steps of the

cathedral to Franklin Rex's cart. Same place as always, right by the entrance.

"Joriandis Delk!" His eyes light up. I swear Rex hasn't aged in over ten years. He still looks twenty-five and grossly full of verve, black shock of hair fuzzing over his eyes. "How's the Shadow Lady this evening?"

"Still not fond of that name." I nod down and Rex starts serving up whatever fried crap he's peddling today. His little tent's still pitched beside the cart, reflecting the polluted-light glow of the city sky.

"What's your target tonight?"

"Which one?" I snort, then nod up at the church.

"Not a good place for you right now." Rex hands me the hot paper packet and bats my hand away as I try to touch my wristlet to his collector. "On me. Just promise to stay shined and out of Muldany's path. He's publicly condemned all pullers as heretics."

"Jerk must think he's a real bishop." The fried crap burns my tongue but at least it's keeping me awake.

"You two have a history?"

"Let's just say he doesn't appreciate non-divine intervention." High above us, near the hat of a wizened saint, a tiny light flits around, then disappears. My spine stiffens. Light leeches—sky rats with fangs. That's really all I need tonight. Luckily it was just one.

"Last tour's ending, Delk." Rex points to the bubbly crowd pouring out of the building, holo-panes slung around their necks like medals. I lean against the cart edge as they file by, wondering what it is they will go home to. How different can two patches of the same planet be?

I swallow the last bite of food and chuck the wrapper into the nearest of Tharen's trashbots. The machine chews up the material and will later use it to 3D-print sleeping mats for the homeless around the neighborhood. Fricking band-aid on a missing limb, for truth, but sometimes a band-aid is all you've got.

STEALTH is not a matter of disappearing completely. It's about blending your presence into an eyeblink. Just a slight flash.

And then gone.

Sneaking along the aisle of the church, hiding from nun-actors and straggling rubberneckers, I test the shadow pool around me and find it rich as sin. The spotlight shines harsh through stained glass, casting all kinds of shades I can tap. Shadow pulling is not exactly viewed as a holy art, so me getting spotted by anyone who's not Tharen could jeopardize her job and my freedom.

Behind a stone pillar, I exhale slow, then bleed up some shadow from the floor and wink out in a glare, weaving the dimness into the light of my body. I'm there but not, the mirage inside your eyelid after looking at the sun. Assuming visual cover this way feels like sinking into cold water, smooth and clean and even. Sound, on the other hand, is a dawdling tease, and likes to dance with bits of pulled shadow—when I'm incognito, a tiny tap becomes a rustle, a click becomes an echo. I've spent years learning to snuff the sounds of my motion. Even the hem of my coat billows noiselessly—it must know I'm tired as hell and not in the mood for games.

Under the high arched ceilings painted holographic gold, I slip past the pulpit into a small chapel. Rays of light from skylights slant sharply through the dark. A dozen people sit in pews, staring with that same vacant gaze.

Several are wearing stone pendants.

I send Tish crawling over the wall like a spider to scope and record, then duck into an alcove and let the shadow slide back onto the floor. Holding cover this many hours in one day is daunting.

"Resting on the job?"

I start, then relax. "Priestess Tharen. It only counts as a job if you're paying me."

She smiles, grey hair coiled above a face too deep for her age, and stands with her back shielding the corner. "Not your usual discreet self tonight."

"You caught me coming off a beast of a job. I'm not exactly at my best."

"Who is, these days?" Her white robe shifts, streaked with purple triangles of shadow. "I messaged you because someone is interfering in my outreach. The people who wander in seeking help are disappearing. I can't explain it. I typically connect them with whatever resources I can and tell them to check in with me regularly. They quit doing that a few weeks ago. Galen says he knows nothing about it, but I don't believe him. I think they're in trouble."

"They're in *boxes*, Tharen." I sigh. "Muldany is grooming your down-and-out visitors for smooth arrest, some kind of emotion pulling I haven't seen before, and then passing them off to Forso who is selling them to Cendra as free labor. At least, that's what I gathered from my surveil at the docks."

"*God.*" Not sure if she's petitioning him or cursing. She pulls a cig from her bust and massages the bridge of her nose. "I'm tired, Delk. How am I supposed to sustain a shred of humanity in a sea of—" she gestures toward the sanctuary, "—men like him."

I lean my weight into the wall. Can I sleep standing up? "Darkness takes effort to pull out, priestess. From stone or society, doesn't matter, it won't stay on its own. Something has to hold it back."

"I guess that's us. We hold." The priestess flicks the end of the cig and it smolders angry red. "What can you see in here that will help me expose him?"

I check my wristlet for Tish's scans. "There is definitely an object, orb-shaped, exerting a pulling force from behind the altar, but I'd need a closer look." There's also two flickers of...something not orbish. "You notice a vermin problem lately, Priestess?"

"No. Unless you count the bishop."

The flickers disappear. I frown. Just in case, I grip the tall candelabra next to me and drain it of shadow, brightening the flames. That should occupy any hungry pests. "Look, I'll dig around back there and see what I find, but I can't promise conclusive evidence."

"Whatever you can do, Delk, is enough." She takes a long pull on her cigarette and huffs out smoke to swirl like incense in the grey light. "You should know, my authority on this is minimal. The Bishop could wrap his council meeting and drag the cuffs in here to arrest you and I'd have little grounds to stop him."

"Good thing I'm quicker than his fake sermons." With a smirk, I snag her cigarette and take a puff, surveying the room. Too risky to ask these people to leave—it might fast-track them into Forso's racket. None of them have seen me yet. Incognito it is. "I'll be honest with you, Priestess, I'm beat. I don't know if I can hold the cover."

"A little shimmer of holy presence never hurt anyone."

"And if it's more than a little shimmer?"

She shrugs. I hand her back the cig and she smashes it on the floor in a smear of ash. "I'd say we're overdue for a miracle."

I chuckle under my breath. "For truth."

PULLING abilities typically emanate from human bodies, but that thing behind the altar is definitely not human, it's tech. Which is terrifying—if anyone, with any agenda, can manipulate not just shadow, but emotion, the city just got a lot more vulnerable.

Standing shined before the chapel altar, I reach my left hand through an ornate carving in the stone to investigate the object wedged inside. I can sense the orb's presence like I can sense shadow. I reach further in and feel its jagged metallic surface that's warm to the touch. Now how does it communicate with the pendants—

And then something bites me. *Hard.*

Light leeches, a whole nest of them, each a rat-sized winged wad of glowing feathers and teeth, start gnawing on my left hand. Apparently the super-lit candelabra wasn't appetizing enough. I've been bitten before but not by this many. They can't chomp into the orb itself, so they're sucking light off the device *through* my body. Running light through a shined body is like touching ice to hot glass—something is going to crack. My glare flickers violently. The sudden energy transfer also seizes my grip—I can't let go of the orb. Frick.

"Joriandis. What an unwelcome visitation."

Bishop Muldany. *Great.* My insides cringe. He's directly behind me, sauntering up the aisle.

"We need to talk, Galen," Tharen says, in a voice that could cut steel. "I started the chapel outreach—"

"Out of my way, sister."

She moves her short body to block him. "Galen, we're actors, and this is not how a bishop should act."

"I said move!" Cloth scuffles.

I need to buy time. "Tish," I whisper, nodding toward the bishop. "Sear."

The ragbot sails through the air and clocks Muldany over the eyes like a rogue handkerchief.

With these few seconds of distraction, I try releasing a quick burst of shadow, hoping it will scare the leeches off, but it's not enough. If I release all the shadow I'm holding with the leeches jacking my cover like this, the sudden discharge could blow out my nervous system. Or, hell, maybe that of anyone wearing those pendants.

The bishop pries Tish off his face like Velcro, leaving a diamond of reddened burned skin. I smile spitefully, but my triumph evaporates when Muldany pins Tish to a pew with a stack of hymnals.

"Your demon-bot cannot deter heaven's wrath." He picks up a heavy iron candelabra like it's a broomstick and stalks forward again.

I'm no match for him in brute force, and at this rate, I won't get free in time to escape. There are too many variables in this room I can't control. "Tharen, get these people out of here," I shout, "and get those pendants off them!" Since I'm still shined, my words echo from twinkling air. People scurry away from my disembodied voice toward Tharen, who ushers them out to the sanctuary. There's no such thing as safety in the city, but at least those people won't be caught in this particular crossfire. Unfortunately, Muldany can tell a puller from an apparition.

He ascends the altar steps. "Caught red-handed defiling holy ground." He clicks his tongue at me though I'm still just a sparkly outline. "That's what happens when you interfere with God's plan."

He reaches for me, but I use the leverage of my apparently unbreakable grip to swing myself onto the altar in a crouch, one hand still stuck fast. Light coming off my form casts a long shadow behind him. "Is your little scheme with Forso part of God's plan too?" I say. "I'm guessing you're both getting kickbacks from Cendra for funneling them free labor."

Muldany's sneer unhooks itself and his dark eyes ignite in fury.

"You're using this orb tech to

somehow pull the fight from the desperate folks who mistake you for trustworthy. To make them more compliant, so they can be exploited."

"I'm making them useful to society. Something you wouldn't understand." He brandishes his forked weapon. With the scarlet face, he looks so much like the devil toys in the gift shop that I laugh out loud. The hell-branded bishop and the glittering heretic—what a darkly ironic transfiguration.

He swings the candelabra and I narrowly duck. At least it's not lit. But on the backswing he wedges the end between my body and the altar and wrenches. The leverage breaks my frozen grip on the orb with a painful zap. The leeches scatter. I arc through the air and slide on my already-battered side, colliding with a pew. I lean my head back on the cold tile and blink as the gilded ceiling spins.

"You're an abomination dabbling in darkness," the bishop growls, walking over and stepping on my bitten-up hand. I groan. My fingers feel like they've been dipped in fire. "The police have more than one warrant out for your antics. But I'm a merciful man. I might be able to convince them to put you in Bridge crew service instead of lockup, in exchange for changing your ways. A public recantation of your pulling, nothing less."

Screw that. I'd rather rot in a cellbox a mile underground than fuel his agenda. I try to rip my arm loose but he's too heavy. I can hear Tish buzzing, trying to get free, but he's stuck just as fast. Where's that damn miracle?

"Have you seen the light, Delk? Ready to work with me, or shall I summon Forso?" As he raises his wristlet to call the cops, I squint and notice Muldany's head appears ringed in a glow, a bizarre halo that throbs and squirms. Well, then. With my free hand I grab his meaty ankle and rip the darkness out of him in a brilliant photonic burst, briefly lighting up his bald head. The circling leeches lunge.

Pretty sure his scream wakes the nuns on the other side of the cathedral. I've done some miry deeds in my time, for truth, but I make it a point never to revel in somebody else's pain, even if they had it coming. Except this somebody. If justice exists at all, I swear to you on God's own shade, it's in the tenor of a corrupt bishop's howling.

Muldany writhes and bats futilely at the creatures sucking on the flesh of his head, his hands—heh, they're all over him. I take my time standing and brush the dust off my coat. Tharen pokes her head in, glances at me, then stares at Muldany in horror. Or is that relish? I hop the pew and shove the hymnals off Tish who flits up between me and the bishop and crackles with electricity, ready to burn someone's face off, but I send him to check the status of the orb. I cross my arms, blood from my bitten-up hand dripping down my sleeve, and watch Muldany flail.

"I might be able to scare them off," I yell over his racket. "In exchange for changing your ways."

OUTSIDE under a drizzly gold-grey sky, I lean back against the foot of a statue and watch the shadows fade in the wet dawn. One arm out of my jacket, I wind a strip of Tharen's robe around the bite wounds. With any luck, they'll heal before the next job. Tish hums over the bloody sleeve, attempting to remove the stain. He somehow never gets tired of handling my messes.

Muldany valued his own skin enough to agree to surrender the orb tech to me and bow out of Forso's racket. I also insisted he grant Tharen full autonomy over her outreach. Tish's audio recording of our conversation was helpful leverage to ensure he follows through—I am definitely *not* above public shaming. He will unquestionably find another way to profit off people, but for today, his pride is as chewed up as his scalp.

Rex slips out of his tent, yawning, hair askew, and rattles the solar starter on his cart. He glances at me like I'm part of the cityscape, a breath of fog, a pillar of stone. "Slept with the saints, ah?"

"Something like that."

He eyes my bandaged hand, then dumps dark powder into a pot while checking his holo. "Hey, look at this. A newsdrone recorded people escaping from a cargo cube on the Lower Docks last night." He squints sideways. "You wouldn't know anything about that?"

"Perish the thought." I smile. They actually made it. Now it's up to the Reef to make sure no more souls end up caged. And up to me to find a way to circumvent these new emotion pulling devices. If Muldany has them, so do others.

High above me, tiny lights appear, dozens of them, flitting about the heads of the saints. They bound off in a line through the air...toward the brilliant lights of the cuff station tower. The morning shift is out on the platform boarding their patrol skiffs.

I grin, cool rain slipping inside my lips. I might get that show after all.

# Hacking
# the Dreamworld

## By MICHAEL A. BURSTEIN

I USED to build sets for the Dreamworld.

It's a good afterlife, although like you I was told that it was only temporary and that eventually I would get to move onto the next phase, whatever that might be. When I first arrived here, I learned that everything I had been told about the world to come wasn't quite right.

"Dreaming is a taste of the afterlife," my original guide, Ruyah, had told me. "Those of you who have just died, well, we need you to work in the Dreamworld."

I wasn't ready for this. I was young, only 25, but cancer had eaten away my insides and I couldn't go on anymore. I died in a hospital and woke up, if that's what I should call it, sitting in a library with Ruyah. I hadn't been religious and expected nothing after I died.

The library, which turned out to be just a set in the Dreamworld, was a small room lined with bookcases overflowing with old books. I still remember the smell of musty paper filling my nostrils. The room was illuminated with a soft, white light, but I couldn't spot a light source. Ruyah had been sitting right across from me, both of us in hard, wooden chairs. I felt a soft rug underneath my feet. It took me a moment to realize that the room was in black and white, and then it suddenly flickered into color.

It felt—and there is no other word I can use to say this—dreamlike.

"Who are you?" I asked. "What's going on?"

"My name is Ruyah, John," she said. She had piercing blue eyes and a friendly face. "I hoped that this set would be relaxing for you. I understand that you loved libraries."

"I did—I mean, I do," I said. "Only I don't recall being in a library recently."

"Well, technically, you're not. This is just a set, as I said."

"A set?"

"Yes, like in a play or movie." She stood up, walked over to one of the bookcases, removed a book from a shelf, and handed it to me. "Here, take a look."

Puzzled, I took the book from her as gently as I could, since it looked old. I opened it up; the pages were blank.

"If we don't expect anyone to be reading the books, then we don't need to fill the pages with

*Illustration by Daerick Gross*

words," she explained.

I nodded slowly and passed the book back to her. She grabbed it, reshelved it, and sat down again. "Welcome to the Dreamworld."

"The Dreamworld," I echoed.

"Yes. The Dreamworld. You know how every night you would visit the Dreamworld and then be forced to leave it the next morning? Well, now you're here and you don't have to leave for a long time to come."

I nodded, trying to think of how to respond. Finally, I said, "So the Dreamworld is the place where I went when I was dreaming."

"Exactly. It's where everyone on Earth goes when they're dreaming."

"And now I live here?"

She frowned for just a moment. "Not exactly. At least, those aren't the words you should use."

"What words?"

"Well, the word 'live,' for one. How do I explain this to you? You're dead. You're a soul now."

Oddly, I didn't feel scared or confused by that information. I simply nodded and said, "That's what I figured."

"Don't you want to know what happens now?"

"Do I?" I felt apprehensive; my stomach tensed up almost as bad as it had when I developed the cancer.

She laughed. "It's not as bad as you think. It never is. Everyone who dies, well, they don't get to move on right away. We need people to run the Dreamworld. There

are sets to be built, costumes to be designed and sewn, roles to be played…"

"You mean, everyone I ever talked to in a dream was an actor?"

"Yes. And everything you saw, someone had to create it." And that is when she told me the rest. Three different types of entities dwelled in the Dreamworld: dreamers, souls, and guides. The dreamers, of course, are the people who are still alive, who only visit when they're dreaming. The souls are those of us who have died and work in the Dreamworld. And the guides are, well, the guides. They're in charge of what the souls have to do.

And so we talked about what I would do, as a soul, while I waited to be allowed to enter the next phase. And that was being a set builder. Not a designer, as designs and scripts for dreams were given to the souls by Ruyah and the other guides. They never told us where they got the designs and scripts from, but we souls figured that either the guides came up with them on their own or got them from, well, you know.

So, anyway. That was my afterlife. I got into the habit of helping to build sets along with other souls who up until now had been total strangers to me. Ruyah would give us the designs and my team, which included two other souls named Shawn McHenry and Gail Morse, would build the set. Set builders usually didn't hang around afterward to watch the show, especially as we weren't the departed souls that had been selected as the directors or the improv actors for the dreams, but there was no particular rule against it, and I found myself interested enough that I would stick around for the actual dreams. I saw a lot of people from all over the world, people I assumed were still alive, entering the dreams I had built for them and then exiting again.

And then one night, I saw someone I knew.

THE first time I saw her was when I had built a set for a rather typical dream. Ruyah had instructed Shawn, Gail, and me to build one of those narrow, spiraling staircases that seem to go up forever. I remembered a staircase like that from having climbed to the top of the Statue of Liberty, and I knew it would evoke both acrophobia and claustrophobia in many dreamers. Presumably, this was meant as a nightmare for the woman who would be arriving tonight in the Dreamworld. So we had built it to specifications, including its composition of a shiny silvery metal sheen, and when Shawn and Gail left, I stuck around.

As always, when I wanted to watch a dream play out, I had to sit in one of the chairs that was available in the few rows of chairs that were in the Dark. The Dark was the place just outside the dreams but still part of the Dreamworld. Dreamers couldn't see into the Dark, which is how it got the name, but souls could see it just fine. I sat among the actors and the director, a soul named Lynda Kay, and she let me look at a copy of the script. As always, the script had some lines for the actors but also a lot of guidance for improvisation, since we never knew exactly what a dreamer would do or say during a dream.

I was partly right about the nightmare aspect of this dream. The staircase wasn't a nightmare, exactly, but it was supposed to be an unsettling dream, representing unfinished business that the dreamer was trying to complete in her life. I've never been sure why certain things in the Dreamworld represent things in the Realworld—why a staircase?—but mine was not to reason why, mine was but to build sets.

The air around the staircase turned hazy and then the dreamer appeared.

She was at the bottom of the staircase, and her face was turned away from me, so I didn't recognize her at first. But as she started to climb the staircase, unsteady on her feet and clinging to the railing, she turned in our direction. I knew her instantly.

Mom.

I don't know how I knew it was her, or why I knew that, or what she was doing in this particular dream, but that was my mother on the staircase. I mean, yes, I recognized her, but I had not known any of the other dreamers I had ever seen, and I suppose I had assumed at this point that the guides would keep souls from ever encountering dreamers we knew from the Realworld. Maybe I recognized her because of the way everybody in the afterlife keeps changing their appearance, to look younger or older depending on what they want to do that particular moment, and yet we always recognize everyone. She looked a little older, and her brown hair had started to turn gray in a few places.

I stood up quickly and Lynda said, "What are you doing?"

"I have to go talk to her." I needed to let her know that I was okay.

Lynda frowned. "You can't go talk to her." She pointed at two of the other souls sitting in the Dark. "Tommy, Jesse, you're up. Go climb the staircase with the dreamer."

Tommy Kachru and Jesse Dobson stood up and headed over to the set. I began to follow but stopped short as Lynda grabbed my arm.

"John, stop," she said. "What do you think you are doing?"

"I—" I suddenly realized I couldn't tell her the truth. I tried for a weak lie. "I wanted to try acting," I said.

You know the rules," Lynda said. "When you got here, you were assigned to one role, and one only. You're a set builder, not an actor."

"Maybe I should be an actor," I said as I sat down again.

Lynda sighed and let go of my arm. "You're not trained for it and that's not your call. That's not my call, either. Now, do you want to keep watching or do you want to go?"

"I'll keep watching."

Lynda and I continued to sit as we watched my mom try to climb the staircase. Tommy and Jesse had morphed into other people as they crowded my mom on the staircase. It was clear that she was getting more and more upset and scared as she tried to climb down, to presumed safety, but Tommy and Jesse blocked her, as the script called for.

She couldn't go down on the staircase, and Tommy and Jesse threatened her, so she turned around and climbed up to get away from them. But then the trick we had installed in the staircase kicked in; it became even narrower and steeper, harder and harder for anyone to climb. She darted her head around, back and forth, a frightened expression on her face, and then shouted something that I thought sounded like my name.

I jumped up and ran toward the set.

"John, stop!" Lynda shouted at me, but I ignored her. I ran to the staircase, climbed up it, and reached out to pull Tommy and Jesse away from Mom. By now, Tommy and Jesse had morphed into some sort of weird combination of animal and person, but I knew it was still them.

Unfortunately, the moment I reached them, with their shouts of "What the hell?" and "John, get back!" my mother had disappeared.

She had woken up.

I MANAGED to convince Lynda, Tommy, and Jesse not to say anything to the guides. I didn't know what kind of trouble I could get into for this; Mom's dream was apparently intended to go on for a bit longer, and my actions had obviously disrupted that. But Lynda, Tommy, and Jesse were fellow souls, and after I explained that I had just had a sudden urge to act and I couldn't fight it, they forgave me and said they wouldn't report my indiscretion.

"But, John," Lynda added, "you need to go talk to a guide if you want to change roles. And in the meantime, I'm not letting you watch any more dreams."

I accepted that since I had little choice but decided that after some time I would ask Lynda again if I could watch one of the dreams. Also, Lynda was not the only soul working as a director, and I was hoping that she—and Tommy and Jesse—wouldn't tell the other directors and actors what I had done.

In the meantime, I had sets to build with Shawn and Gail. Some of these sets were standard and familiar: trains that went nowhere, doorways that opened up into gardens, classrooms from long ago. You know, the kind of sets that made me wonder why the Dreamworld didn't just keep a collection of standing sets around for dreamers. It's not like we lacked for space. But I asked Ruyah that question once, and she said something about each set needing to be crafted specifically for each dreamer, so I just let it be.

It was maybe a month later—time flows strangely in the Dreamworld, even for us souls—that Shawn, Gail, and I were given another set to build that really piqued my interest. Ruyah had given the design to Shawn, and he had brought it over to Gail and me. As Shawn laid the plans out on the table I studied the blue lines that covered the white paper. The shapes seemed rather familiar, almost like a map, but I couldn't quite place it.

"What is it?" I asked Shawn.

"It's a playground."

I took another look. Now I could see what we had been instructed to build. Over here would be the swings, over there the sandbox, on that end a climbing structure, there was a fence and a row of benches—

It was the exact layout of the playground I had played in as a kid. The one two blocks from my house, where my mom took me until I was about six years old.

"John, are you all right?" Gail asked. "You look pale." She shrugged. "Well, paler than usual, for a soul."

"It's nothing," I said quickly. "The set looks...daunting, that's all."

Shawn shrugged. "It's not that hard to build any of these sets using dreamstuff."

Shawn was right; it wasn't hard to build anything using dreamstuff as long as three souls worked together; otherwise, the dreamstuff would refuse to mold. Since I didn't really have a good response for him, I stayed quiet as we began to mold the dreamstuff into the pieces of the playground. Shawn and Gail chose rather generic shapes for the playground equipment and didn't really seem to care about the colors. But I knew this playground to the depths of my—well, my soul, so I suppose, myself. So although I started working with them by building the basics just as they were doing, pretty soon I started to modify the swings and benches they had already made.

"John, what are you doing?" Gail asked as I hovered over a large plastic climbing rock, changing its color multiple times from dark black to light gray.

"I'm trying to get this just right."

"Just right? It's a plastic rock. It'll probably be in the background of the dream, fuzzed out by the dreamer. She'll probably not even remember it when she wakes up."

"You know the dreamer will be a woman?" I asked.

"No, but what does it matter? And how would I know who the dreamer is? We don't get that information in the designs."

Shawn walked over to us from where he had built the baby swings. "John, Gail, everything OK?"

"Yeah," I said, before Gail could answer. "Everything's fine."

Gail and Shawn exchanged a glance but didn't say anything—or at least, they didn't say anything in front of me. We continued to work on the set for the rest of the—well, I guess "day" is the word for it. And I continued to make little touches here and there that neither Shawn nor Gail understood, but that made the playground closer to the way I recalled my own childhood playground. The sand in the sandbox had to be the right consistency, not too loose, but not too packed, either. The benches had to be a particular type of metal. And the swings, well, I made sure the one on the left was broken, as it had always been when I was a kid.

Finally, when the set was complete, Shawn, Gail, and I stepped into the Dark to examine our handiwork. We were usually proud of what we accomplished, despite how ephemeral the sets were.

"Looks good," Shawn said.

Gail nodded. "Shall we go get something to drink?"

"You two go ahead," I said. "I want to check something."

Shawn and Gail glanced at each other, shrugged, and headed off.

As for me? I hid.

Souls don't need to eat, or drink, or sleep; we're dead, after all. But whoever built the Dreamworld assumed that we would want to adjust to the afterlife, so they allowed us to keep up the pretense as much as we wanted. But we didn't have to. If we didn't eat, we didn't get hungry. If we didn't drink, we didn't get thirsty. And if we didn't sleep, we didn't get tired.

So instead of going back to my usual routines, I hid. I hid in the Dark, for I don't know how long, until the seats appeared and the director and actors showed up to play the dream.

It's a good thing I hid and stayed hidden, because the director was Lynda Kay again. She had a much larger cast of actors with her this time, actors playing parents and children for the playground set. Tommy and Jesse were there again, but there were many other souls I didn't know as well and some I only knew casually. If it had been another troupe I might have chanced sitting among them and pretending to be an actor, but with souls who knew me, my only option was to stay hidden.

The air around the playground turned hazy and then the dreamer appeared.

I popped out of hiding behind the seats just to take a quick look and my hopes and fears were met. My mom sat on the bench in the playground closest to the swings.

"Places, everyone," Lynda said, and the souls who were acting all converged onto the set that Shawn, Gail, and I had built. I didn't dare join them, or even move out of hiding, but I watched very carefully. Five of the souls I knew casually—Will, Steve, Ryan, Erica, and Derek—morphed themselves into squirrels and ran onto the set to provide an air of verisimilitude. The other souls morphed into parents and children and moved into positions.

Except for Tommy, who morphed into a four-year-old child that looked vaguely familiar, who wore a shirt of red and white stripes and blue pants. Tommy ran straight toward my mother.

"Mommy, Mommy!" he cried out. "I hurt myself."

My mom, like all dreamers, went from motionless to suddenly... well, "awake" isn't the word for it, but conscious, I suppose. She looked at Tommy and grabbed him in a tight embrace.

"John! John!" she shouted.

I now realized why the child looked so familiar. Tommy had morphed into me. That striped shirt had been one of my favorites.

I knew exactly where this was leading. This was going to be an anxiety dream of some sort. I'm sure Mom was still devastated from my death and dreaming of seeing me again, as a young child—that couldn't possibly be good for her.

I steadied myself as I decided that I had to come out of hiding and run to my mom before the dream progressed any further. I took one step out from behind the rows of chairs—

And then stopped. If I ran out into this dream, Lynda would probably stop it immediately. I might save my mother from a nightmare, but that would be all. And Lynda had said that she would report me if she saw me watching as she directed another dream again. I didn't know what kind of extra trouble I would get into if she reported me, but I would ruin my chances of connecting with my mother again.

On the other hand, I couldn't just stay there and watch my mother go through whatever dream she was being forced to experience. So I did something that to me felt both brave and cowardly at the same time. I slinked off deeper into the Dark and thought about my next move.

SHAWN, Gail, and I sat in a construct, a sort of café that existed for souls. I can't explain it better than that, so just imagine a set of round tables on an outdoor patio and a store that served drinks. Other souls were sitting at other tables.

"So," I began, and I reached into my satchel and pulled out a blueprint. "I have the plans for the next set we've been asked to build."

Shawn raised an eyebrow. "*You* have the plans? Ruyah always gives them to me."

"I went to see her yesterday." The lie I had prepared came easily to me. "Since I was with her anyway, she gave me the plans. Said we should start on these today."

Gail reached out for the blueprint and spread it out on the table. "It's a kitchen," she said.

I nodded.

"Should be easy to mold the dreamstuff for this," she continued. "All one level, a small room… We can knock this out in no time."

Shawn arched an eyebrow at me and pulled the blueprint closer to him. He studied it intently. I felt myself begin to sweat, even as a soul, and no, I still didn't understand. But that's how it seemed.

Finally, Shawn looked up at me, frowning. "John, what's going on?"

"What do you mean?"

"This doesn't make sense. The blueprints are always more carefully drawn, less haphazard. These plans look fake."

"Fake?" I squeaked out.

Shawn stood up. "I'd better go check with Ruyah."

"No!" I tried to grab the plans out of his hands but he held them firmly.

Gail tilted her head. "John? Is Shawn right?"

I looked back and decided I had to trust them. "Okay, the truth is that Ruyah didn't give me these plans. I drew them up myself."

"You wanted us to build a set that the guides didn't assign?" Shawn asked.

"Yes."

"Why?" Gail asked.

I cleared my throat and looked down at my hands. "So I could see my mom again."

"Huh," Shawn said. "Explain."

So I did. I told them. They already knew of my bizarre habit of hanging out to watch the dreams even after our job was done. But then I told them about what had happened with the staircase dream. They were as surprised to hear about my seeing my mom as I had been when it happened.

"I would have thought that the guides wouldn't let that happen," Gail said. "Having us see dreamers that we knew from when we were alive."

"My guess," Shawn said, "was that they didn't expect any set builders to be watching the dreams. John's the only one I know who's ever done that."

"Still," Gail said, "having John assigned to build a set for his own mother's dream?"

Shawn pushed his lips together and looked thoughtful. "Well, it doesn't matter. John, did you really think you could get away with this?"

"Why not?" I asked.

"Because—" Shawn began, but then cut off.

"No one ever checks in on us afterwards," I said. "And even if they did, it would be after."

"Wouldn't we get in trouble?" Gail asked.

"Would we?" I countered. "Has any soul ever gotten into trouble in Dreamworld? What could that possibly mean?"

Shawn and Gail looked at each other for a moment.

"I'm not sure," Shawn said, "but I wouldn't want to ruin our chances of moving on."

I nodded. "Okay. I understand that I'd be asking you to take an unknown risk for me. But think of what it would mean for you to get to see your parents again."

"That's just it, John," Gail said. "My mom died before I did, the usual thing. But she's not in the Dreamworld. I—I am hoping to see her again one day." She leaned back. "If building a fake set for you would ruin that…"

"We don't know if it would."

"We also don't know for sure that if we build your set that your mom will appear," Shawn said.

"I—I have a feeling."

"I'm not sure a feeling is enough," Gail said.

Shawn nodded. "I'm sorry, John, but I don't think we can help."

"Please," I said. "You know none of us can build a set on our own. The dreamstuff needs all three of us."

Shawn clasped his hands together and leaned forward. "John, can I ask you something? What about your dad?"

"I—I didn't know my dad. Still don't know who he was."

"Ah," Shawn said. He and Gail glanced at each other again. And I could tell they had made their decision.

Shawn stood up, and Gail followed suit. "Well," Gail said, "let's get started."

I stood up. "Thank you. Thank you both."

WE built the kitchen set I had designed. To the best of my memory, it looked like the kitchen of the home I had grown up in. The entrance to it from the dining room led to the middle of the wall, but of course we didn't build that wall. However, to the left stood the stove, to the right I could see the cabinets, and just across from where the entrance would have been sat the sink. In addition, a small breakfast table sat in the middle, covered by a blue tablecloth that matched the color of the walls. Two chairs were on either side. And a clock with pictures of birds on it hung on the wall.

Just in case my mom decided to do more than just walk about, we also built some of the things found in the drawers and cabinets, such as the pots, pans, and silverware. But the last thing I built was a plush toy. My old teddy bear, whom I called Beary. I knew that even if my mom wasn't drawn in by the set, she would be held back by this prop. And for all of my life, even after I had outgrown it, that bear, with a sweet smile on its face, had a place of honor sitting on the far corner of one of the kitchen counters.

Once we had finished building the set, the three of us backed up a distance and studied our handiwork.

"Looks good," Shawn said. "But do you think it will work?"

Suddenly, rows of chairs appeared in the Dark, directly between us and the set.

I smiled and gestured at the chairs. "Yeah, I think it'll work. You're welcome to stay if you want."

Gail glanced at Shawn. "No," she said. "This is for you. But do let us know how it turns out."

My two friends retreated. I watched them walk off into the distance and then I sat in the middle of the front row of chairs and waited.

However long I waited, it felt like it was both too quick and too long. But eventually, or suddenly, or finally...

The air around the kitchen turned hazy and then my mom appeared.

She stood at the stove, a spatula in one hand and a pan in the other, which she held over a gas flame. She used the spatula to reach into the pan and flip something over.

Pancakes. Mom was making

her famous pancakes. I could smell them, a sweet scent wafting through the dream.

I took a deep breath and walked onto the set.

"Mom," I said.

Mom paused just as she was about to flip a pancake again. She turned and looked at me. "John?"

I smiled. "Yes, it's me."

"But you died."

"You remember."

Mom furrowed her brow and spun around slowly. "This kitchen. I had it remodeled."

"Did you? I had no way of knowing."

"This must be a dream."

"It is a dream. You're in the Dreamworld. And I don't want you to wake up."

My mom took a sudden deep breath; she looked alarmed. "What are you saying?"

"I'm saying that I've seen you here a few times. You always wake up."

"Because I'm dreaming?"

"Well, yes. Because you're dreaming. But you wake up too soon. I want to spend more time with you."

Mom looked thoughtful for a moment, then went back to making the pancakes. "If we're going to spend some time together, you should eat something. Let me finish these."

"Okay." I hesitated, then went over to the corner of the far counter and grabbed Beary.

Mom finished the pancakes in a few minutes and while she was cooking I made us some coffee. Just before Mom finished, I pulled silverware and plates out of the drawers and cabinets and set the table. We sat down and began to eat.

"So," Mom said. "I'm dreaming."

"Yes."

"This is a dream."

"Yes."

"Why am I dreaming about breakfast?"

"Maybe you're hungry?"

She gave me a look even as she ate a forkful of pancake.

"Okay, sorry," I said. "It's my fault. I needed to build a set that would attract you, and I thought the kitchen would work best."

"Build a set?"

"Yeah. After we die, we hang out in the Dreamworld for a while. We have to work in dreams for the living. I build sets." I paused. "Dreamers, souls, and guides. That's who exists here. I'm a soul. Guides assign us our tasks, such as set building or acting, and the dreamers are those who are still alive. I saw you in a dream and then in another dream. I figured a set that looked like your kitchen would, well, bring you here."

She nodded. "I do like to cook, and it would give us a chance to talk."

"Exactly. I'm glad you understand."

She shook her head. "But I don't understand. I'm dreaming about you building a kitchen to summon me? Does this make sense?"

"It's a dream, Mom. Is it supposed to make sense?"

"Maybe it's making too much sense," she said.

"I don't understand."

She sighed. "I miss you, John. I've missed you since the day you died."

I held back tears. "I've missed you too."

"And I've dreamed about you. As a little boy and as the older man you never got to be."

"That's—okay."

"But I don't think I've ever had a dream quite like this one before."

"What do you mean?"

"You've brought me here. So why?"

"Just to talk."

"Is there something specific you wanted to say?"

Again, I fought back tears. "I wanted you to know that I'm okay."

"You're okay? Even though you're dead, you're okay?"

"I'm as okay as a dead person can be."

Mom leaned back. "I don't think so. You're clearly not okay."

"What do you mean?"

Mom paused, leaned forward, and then gently stroked my cheek with her hand. I finally broke into tears. She held my hand until I finished crying.

"If you're really here, John, you must know that I've moved on with my life. I've had to. I had no other choice. I had to make peace with losing you long ago."

"Well, I—I'm glad you moved on with your life, Mom," I said, and I meant it. "I wouldn't want you to have gotten stuck."

"But that's just it, John. If you're living—well, existing—in this Dreamworld, and you've got a job but you're ignoring it because of me—then, you're the one who needs to move on."

"Me?"

"Yes, you, John. You're the one who left. I've accepted that. And now you have to accept it as well."

She was right. My idea of keeping her in the Dreamworld—it made no logical sense. What would it mean for her in the Realworld, after all? Would she be half-alive, but half-dead? In a coma forever? I had no idea.

"I understand. I am glad I got to see you again."

"Well," she said, swinging her arm around, "if all this is real, then you'll get to see me again later on, I suppose." She shook her head. "I think this must be my own mind reminding me that although I moved on, you'll always be a part of me. So thank you for that."

With that, she vanished. I knew somehow that when she awoke in the Realworld, she wouldn't remember this dream. But I also knew that the feelings would remain.

The chair beneath me suddenly felt intangible, and I stood up before it could disappear entirely. The kitchen set faded back into dreamstuff and the rows of chairs vanished as suddenly as they had appeared. I was once again in the Dark.

And then in the distance I saw a woman walking toward me: my guide, Ruyah.

"John, are you okay?" she asked once she was only a short distance away.

"No," I said. "I'm not."

"Many say that souls should not interact with dreamers they knew when they were alive," Ruyah said. She knew exactly what I had been up to.

"I'm sorry."

She put a hand on my shoulder. "It's okay, John. I follow a different theory. Are you all set now?"

"What do you mean?"

"I mean, it's time. You're ready for the next phase. You're done with the Dreamworld"

And finally, I understood. "The dead and the living. We all have to move on. The souls that exist here—we're learning to move on."

She nodded. "That's it exactly. None of the souls in Dreamworld are able to accept that they are dead. It is only with that acceptance that a soul can move on."

"And I couldn't accept it until I knew my mom had."

"Yes."

I looked into Ruyah's blue eyes, nodded, and said, "Let's go."

# Lost Gold and Quicksilver

## By WILLIAM LEISNER

THE biplane's engine screamed from exertion as the little craft pushed against gravity, her pilot aiming for the gray underbelly of the cumulus cloudbank above. Casey Flynn gave *Acanthis* the full throttle and pulled the stick back so hard she was sure it would splinter in her hand. She could sense their pursuer gaining, but she knew she could shake him if only she could just gain a few seconds of cover.

Dark bullet holes suddenly appeared on the yellow canvas of the upper wing like dark blossoms. "Sweet Jesus!" Alice Ames shouted from the forward cockpit. "Why are they shooting at us?!"

"The usual reason, I suppose," Flynn said, fighting to keep control of the shimmying aircraft. "They want us out of the sky." Flynn watched the other craft skirt the edge of the clouds, glinting in the sunlight as it executed an impossibly tight 180-degree turn and came back at them. "Let's just hope they'll let us reach the ground at our own pace."

Alice yelped as the two planes, seemingly on a collision course, narrowly missed. Flynn cursed herself again for letting a groundling

wind up in a situation like this. Every town she visited had at least one Alice Ames. Flynn would drop down from her cruising altitude, engine roaring like a jungle cat announcing its presence, and execute a low, close pass of a prominent grain silo or water tower before landing in some farmer's fallow field. She'd quickly be swarmed by saucer-eyed country kids—and adults—marveling at the magnificent flying machine. She'd spend the rest of the daylight hours giving fifteen-minute rides at two dollars a head, circling the same patch of featureless west Kansas prairie, to the delight of the local yokels.

Come dusk, after she'd secured a place to spend the night, the boldest youngsters would linger to ask about her itinerary, hinting not so subtly at their desire to live the life she did. Most were easy enough to brush off. A few she gruffly advised that the circus freak shows were more accepting of runaways.

That particular morning, though, when she returned to the barn where she'd left *Acanthis* overnight, she saw a slight young woman leaning against the entrance, looking as if she had been waiting there all night. When Flynn appeared, she jumped to her feet, clutching a thread-worn carpetbag to her chest. "Miss Flynn! I heard you were fixing to leave this morning!"

"Mm-hmm," she said, otherwise ignoring her. She started her pre-flight inspection, examining every square inch of canvas skin and testing the tautness of every wire.

Alice followed closely, waiting for some of that attention to be granted to her. "Umm...Miss Flynn, I...I was wondering...I wanted to ask you...I..."

"You ought to finish one sentence before trying to start another," Flynn said.

"I-I want to go with you!"

Flynn sighed, and finally deigned to look at the girl. "What's your name?"

"Alice Ames," she said, beaming and offering her right hand.

"I'm not a passenger service, Alice," she told her. "That's what trains are for."

"I wouldn't make it halfway to the closest train station before they came after me."

"They who?" Flynn asked, against her better judgment.

"The Weavers. My husband's family."

Flynn raised an eyebrow. "And where's your husband in all this?"

"He's dead," Alice said. "He hanged himself right after I lost our baby."

Flynn blanched. "That's awful. I'm sorry." She then quickly turned away and knelt, pretending to examine her landing wheels while hiding her reaction.

"His parents blame me," Alice continued. "They say they don't, but the hatred they show me! I just can't stay here any longer!"

"I really am sorry," Flynn muttered into the furred collar of her flight jacket, not daring to look the poor girl in the eye.

"I can pay you!"

That got Flynn to turn. Alice reached into her carpetbag and withdrew a small porcelain jewelry box, white with gilded paint decorating the lid and edges. This, Flynn suspected, was the main reason Alice feared the Weavers would chase her to the train depot.

She studied the girl's expression, a cross between sincerity and desperation. "Get aboard," she sighed, and Alice practically bounced into the forward cockpit. Flynn felt far less gleeful, but she consoled herself with the thought, as she spun the propeller and brought the engine to life, that she and Alice would part ways soon enough.

THE sun had fully risen by the time Flynn had landed at Bivins Field, just north of Amarillo. The aerodrome's ground crew waved to her in warm welcome as she taxied off the runway to the cluster of hangars and offices. Waldo Royhill was out the door before the propeller had spun to a stop. "Hey, hey, K.C.!" he called out, flashing a smile she couldn't help but return. "I figured you were 'bout due for an appearance 'round here. How's ol' *Acanthis* holding up?"

Flynn jumped down from the cockpit. "Just fine, but I'm sure she'd appreciate a little of your tender attentions, Wally."

The mechanic nodded, and glanced over Flynn's shoulder. "Who's your friend?" he asked, pointing at the tuft of brown hair poking up from the lip of the forward cockpit, where Alice Ames was soundly sleeping.

"'Friend' is a strong term, Wally," she muttered.

Waldo chuckled. "Another stray puppy, K.C.?"

Flynn answered with a scowl. "I'll be in the canteen," she said. "Let her sleep if you can; she was up half the night. If she does wake, just tell her how to get to the train depot from here."

"And if she asks where you are?" Waldo asked, but Flynn, already walking away, pretended not to hear. She expected Alice Ames would prefer a quick uncomplicated parting of ways as much as she would.

As it turned out, Alice found Flynn before she was halfway through her ham and eggs. "Miss Flynn?" she said as she approached her table, clutching her bag to her chest. "Is it all right if I join you?"

Flynn bit back a tart retort, and kicked the chair opposite her out from under the table. "Welcome to Texas," she said as Alice sat. "I

trust this is far enough from the Weavers to satisfy you?"

"Oh yes! I really can't thank you enough!"

Flynn chuckled into her coffee mug. "Oh, you can't, huh?"

Alice looked panic-stricken. "No... I mean...I am so very grateful..."

"I know. Listen, Alice, let me make this easier on you. I ain't never been the type for diamonds and pearls, and I figure someone in your circumstance needs all she's got to get by. So..." She flicked a hand at her in dismissal. "You're welcome."

Alice stayed seated, looking at Flynn with surprise and, Flynn thought, a bit of disappointment? "You're saying you don't want to be paid?"

"Don't tell the whole world, huh? Just...make the most of this fresh start as you can."

Now it was definitely disappointment radiating off her. "Well...I..."

"What?" Flynn asked.

"I was going to pay you...with this." Alice placed the jewelry box on the table and lifted the lid. It was empty, save for a single folded piece of brittle brown paper, which Alice withdrew and unfolded slowly to keep it from falling apart at the creases.

Little surprised Flynn anymore, but this young woman had managed it. "You were planning to pay me with a stinking *treasure map*?"

Alice quailed, but answered calmly. "My grandfather made this map. He was a driver for Wells

Fargo, riding the route between San Francisco and St. Louis for over thirty years. On his last run, he was carrying a huge shipment of government gold—more than two thousand dollars' worth!—when his stage was ambushed by banditos. His partner was killed, but he was able to get away and escape into the wilderness. He knew he'd need to ride light if he was going to make it back to civilization, so he hid the gold and made this map."

"But you don't even know what this map shows, so you figured if you could search from the air and find it that way." Flynn shook her head as she looked at the map. To her eye, it was no more than the scribblings of a drunkard. Even the *N* pointing the way north was written backwards. "How old were you when he told you this fairy tale?"

"It's not a fairy tale," Alice said, her voice quiet but sharp. "My grandfather was an honest man."

Flynn chuckled softly. "Even honest men, the few of them there are in this world, enjoy telling tall tales to impressionable children."

"No! Look!" Alice grabbed the polished napkin dispenser sitting between them and laid it lengthwise across the map. "See that?"

Flynn looked at the reflective surface, and then did see. The *N* was the right way now, and what had looked like meaningless scratches resolved into symbols. A letter *V* framed by a pair of curlicues became a mountain labeled *p.p.* "Pike's Peak?"

Alice nodded. "Yes! That's what I think, too! And then..." She repositioned the dispenser, making a line between a pair of dots Flynn now noticed on the map's borders. "Here's the Santa Fe Railroad. See? It's like a picture puzzle done upside-down and backwards. And this lake that's shaped like a heart, this is where he hid the gold!"

Flynn felt flabbergasted. This was a hell of a lot of effort to put into a bedtime story, she had to admit. Still, it would be plain foolish to go hunting for Grampa Ames' treasure. The "Wild West" was long gone, and hundreds of cattlemen, prospectors and settlers must have trodden over every square foot of that land over the past forty years. She looked up at Alice, and saw the look of absolute determination and unshakable faith on her face. Then looking past her, she saw a pair of local flyboys roll into the canteen, loudly exchanging boasts of their latest exploits as they poured coffee from a steel urn. If Flynn did refuse to help her, it'd be a simple matter to find another pilot here at Bivins, most of whom would have no qualms about taking advantage of the young woman, in any variety of ways.

"All right," she said. "Show me what other mirror tricks this map has. If we're going to go looking a needle, let's make the haystack as small as possible."

ACCORDING to the *National Geographic Atlas* Waldo kept

in his office, the southeast corner of Colorado was classified as a "semi-arid region." While not technically a desert, the area saw minimal rainfall, and what little moisture it did get tended to evaporate quickly. As such, the map showed no lakes anywhere near where Grandpa Ames indicated, heart-shaped or otherwise.

"It must just be too small," Alice said, refusing to be discouraged. "Or maybe it goes dry in the summer, and that's why they missed it."

Flynn shrugged. She never expected the search to be this simple, and was prepared for a long day of flying wider and wider circles over empty wildland. *Acanthis* was loaded with provisions, including a cheap Brownie camera and a dozen rolls of film. "There's a hatch under your feet there," she told Alice, strapped into the trainee's seat. "Just put the lens directly over it. You can't use the viewfinder at the same time, but you'll get the hang of it."

And that she did. Alice spent the first two hours of their flight bent over in her seat, snapping shot after shot of brown lifeless earth. The terrain was heavily creased and cracked with long canyons, the remnants of an ancient geological past when a great network of rivers carved the land. But as for any recent signs of water, there were none to be found. Flynn raised her eyes from the barren landscape to check on Alice. She was still hunched over, out of sight. There

was no way of knowing if she was still taking photos, or had her head buried in her arms in despair.

A flash at the edge of her vision derailed that train of thought. Flynn's head whipped sharply to the left, a dark part of her memory warning that a squadron of Fokkers were about to swoop down on her. The reasonable part of her mind tried to tell her it was probably just Venus, but then it reappeared, blinking as it passed behind breaks in the clouds.

Flynn broke off from her search pattern, pulling the stick back and rising to meet the unidentified object above. In response, the thing abandoned the cover of the clouds and moved to an intercept course.

Flynn could see now it was another airplane, but not like any she had ever seen before. It was only half the length of her Jenny, with a single pair of stumpy wings and a skin of some highly polished metal. It looked like nothing so much as a bullet with a propeller and fins.

Its resemblance to a bullet didn't stop with its appearance, either. By instinct Flynn pushed into a sharp dive, just as the other plane shot through the space she'd occupied just seconds before, at what had to be nearly one hundred miles an hour! No man-made machine could fly that fast!

"Wow!" Alice Ames had popped her head up to watch the streak of silver recede behind them. The

Brownie was pressed to her eye, and she was snapping the shutter and twisting the winding knob as quickly as she could.

"*Get down!*" Flynn screamed as she gunned the engine. Instinct took over as she tried to shake their tail. The rigging wires visibly vibrated as the horizon went vertical, then slipped away so that nothing but earth filled her forward vision. Teeth gritted, she silently counted off the seconds as the plane started to spiral, and pulled out of the dive and leveled off. For a brief moment, it seemed they lost their mysterious pursuer.

Then the real bullets started to fly.

As *Acanthis* slowed and shed altitude, the other craft slid into formation beside her, wings inches apart. The cockpit was covered by a transparent bubble, allowing the pilot to forgo aviator goggles, and show Flynn his bare, infuriated face. He gestured for her to follow him, and given little other choice, she nodded and allowed him to maneuver in front and lead her to what she could only hope was a safe landing spot. She had her concerns about how safe they'd be wherever he was bringing them, but that was a worry for later.

Thankfully, the faint lines of a long straight dirt road appeared, running roughly parallel to a forebodingly dark canyon. Flynn landed, rolling to a halt in front of a small tin shack with the letters "G.A.B." painted above the door. That door slammed open and a

trio of armed men burst though, rifles raised and pointed at the airplane's occupants.

Flynn stood and lifted her goggles over her forehead. "And who the hell are you oafs?" she demanded.

The jaw of the lead guard dropped. "You're vimmen?"

Flynn laughed humorlessly at his confusion, but before she could say anything else, she was cut off by a high-pitched buzzing from above. Flynn raised her head to watch her airborne antagonist come in for a landing. Except he wasn't aiming for the dirt rut she had used.

He was flying *into the canyon.*

Flynn leapt to the ground and, heedless of the weapons trained on her, rushed to the lip of the chasm. The other craft passed right before her as it descended in a great gust of wind below ground level. Following with her eyes, it appeared to be swallowed into the guts of the earth, but as her vision adjusted to the shadows, what she saw was even more fantastic.

The hidden aerodrome wasn't as big as Bivins Field—that would have been impossible in such a narrow space. But in spite of the site's physical restrictions, it appeared just as functional as any airbase she had seen throughout her flying career. A strange sense of vertigo swept over her, taking in such a view while her boots were on solid ground.

The guards took advantage of her disorientation, grabbing her by both arms before she knew what was happening. The crack of a rifle butt to the back of her skull sent her tumbling into her own crevasse of darkness.

SHE came to with the taste of blood in her mouth and a throbbing drumbeat inside of her skull. She groaned and tried to rub the goose egg on the back of her head, only to find her wrists bound behind her back.

"Casey?" a voice hissed. "Are you awake? Can you hear me?"

Flynn cracked her eyes open, and found herself still in the dark. She was sitting on a cold concrete, back against a rough, splinter-riddled wood plank wall. "Yeah, Alice," she answered, then coughed. "Do you know where we are?"

"We're down at the bottom of the canyon," she told her. "Those men took us into the shack, down an elevator, then into a hangar and locked us in this closet." Alice was clearly scared out of her wits, but making an admirable effort to keep her voice steady. "Who are they? What do they want with us?"

"I'm not sure," Flynn said. "Did they say anything to you? Ask you any questions?"

"No. But they did take my grandfather's map," she said, the hint of a sob escaping her. "The camera, too, and the film I shot. God, I'm so sorry I got you into this!"

"Regrets are wasted energy. We both just need to keep level heads if we're going to get out of here with our hides intact. And your

grandfather's lost treasure is the least of the things to be concerned about right now."

She heard Alice take a halting breath. "You're right. The photos will all be in black and white, anyhow."

Flynn was about to ask what that meant, but just then the door was thrown open. The tiny space flooded with light, save for the silhouette of a goliath standing in the doorframe. He grabbed Flynn by the collar of her flight jacket, and dragged her out roughly. Alice only managed a tiny squeak before the door slammed shut again. He marched Flynn down a featureless corridor, ignoring her efforts to resist, and through another door that opened into the main body of the cavernous hangar.

And there it was.

Grounded and motionless, the stubby little airplane looked as aerodynamic as a hippopotamus, even though she had seen it fly like the fiercest of nature's winged predators. For the first time, she noticed the red script painted on the prow: *Quicksilver II*.

"She is something to behold, isn't she?"

Flynn turned to see the man who had been at *Quicksilver*'s controls earlier ambling her way. He had changed into a natty suit, and his dark hair was freshly oiled and combed. He fixed her with a smile that sent a chill through every nerve in her body. "Yes, she is," she answered. "I'm a bit surprised that you're giving me this close-up look now, considering how hard you tried not to be spotted before."

The pilot shrugged. "What's done is done. Now that you have seen it, I see no reason not to allow you the chance to appreciate it. And judging from your considerable skills in the cockpit, I feel certain you can appreciate *Quicksilver* as much as I do. She's ten years ahead of anything any other aircraft designer has even dreamt of!" He beamed with hubristic pride as he admired the ugly little warplane, then turned again to Flynn. "So, madam. I imagine you have as many questions for me as I do for you, eh?"

"Yes," Flynn said. "The first one is, *Was zur Hölle ist hier los?*"

The pilot's smile faltered, but just for a moment. "Ah, but you already have some answers, *ja, Fräulein* Flynn?"

"Some, yes. Though you still have the advantage of me, *Herr...?*"

"Major Heinrich Ochs," he said with a cordial bow. "And you are the enigmatic Casey Flynn of the Lafayette Flying Corps. We always wondered why there was so little information to be found about you. We never suspected that, even at their most desperate, the French would allow women to fly."

Officially, they didn't, which was still a sore spot for Flynn, but she wasn't going to let herself be sidetracked into that discussion. "So, the German government really is using the German American

Brotherhood as cover to rebuild their military here in the States."

Ochs shrugged. "What choice do we have, with the League of Nations keeping their tyrannical thumb pressed down over the Fatherland? The question now is, what we are to do with you and your companion now that you've discovered us?"

Flynn felt her guts twist into a knot. "Hold up! Do what you want with me, but leave Alice out of it. She knows nothing about any of this."

"Very valiant of you. However, she was the one taking these." Ochs brought his left hand out from behind his back, holding up a fuzzy photograph showing *Quicksilver* in flight. "Who are the two of you working for, *Fräulein?* Who tipped them off about us?"

"No one. It was my dumb luck spotting you up there."

The major shook his head. "I was watching you long before you spotted me. You were searching for something. If not for this base, then what?"

"I don't owe you any explanations," she said. She was certain he'd laugh in her face if she told him the truth.

Instead, he shook his head sadly. "You were most impressive during our brief skirmish, especially considering how outclassed you were in that flimsy Curtiss trainer. Pilots of your ability are a rarity. Your death will be a tragic one."

Ochs gestured to the soldier,

who once again took hold of Flynn and dragged her back the way they'd come. The bruiser tossed her into the closet with one hand, while grabbing Alice with the other. "No! Let go!" she shouted as she futilely kicked him.

"It'll be okay, Alice! Just keep a cool head!" Flynn shouted just before the door slammed shut and the deadbolt slid into place. She regretted her words instantly; there was no reason to believe things would turn out okay. God only knew how Ochs would respond when Alice also refused to admit to espionage, then started to retell her grandfather's bedside story. No matter how bad it was for her in Kansas, it would have been far preferable to than this!

*Regrets are wasted energy.* She repeated those words to herself over and over and she took a deep breath, held it for a ten-count, then pushed the air out in a long whoosh. She did this several more times, willing both her heartbeat and her mind to decelerate. When she reopened her eyes, they had adjusted enough that she could make out shapes amongst the shadows. It was time to focus her energies in a useful direction. She just hoped she had enough time.

HOURS passed.
   Flynn had no idea how long she had waited before she heard the door being unlocked again. But she was immediately alert and ready when the light flooded in

and Goliath hooked a hand under her armpit. "Where's Alice?" she demanded as he dragged her back down the same corridor as before. "Hey! I asked you a question. Are you too stupid to answer?" The guard pretended to ignore her taunt, and Flynn added, "Well, you're obviously stupid, since you didn't even check if my wrists were tied tight."

That caused him to lose a half-step off his precise martial pace. Flynn used that moment to drop the roughly worn rope she'd been holding together in her left hand, and swing her unrestrained right arm around. Her fist opened, and a clump of powdered hand soap exploded against Goliath's face. Before his hands made it to his burning eyes, Flynn drove her shoulder into his bread basket, sending him staggering backwards and crashing into and through one of the hallway's anonymous unmarked doors lining the hallway. She snatched the guard's sidearm from his hip holster before closing the door behind them.

She found herself in a large and comfortably outfitted office, plainly belonging to Major Ochs. To the left, a picture window looked out into the main hangar, allowing him to watch over his project. To the right was a large wooden desk, half covered by photographs.

Meanwhile, Goliath had splayed himself across a stuffed sofa, covering his face and whimpering in pain. Now that she didn't have to stare up at him, Flynn realized he couldn't have been more than eighteen. She poked him with the muzzle of his own gun and asked, "All right, what have you done with Alice?"

The guard spat residual Boraxo from his mouth. "The Major. He took her."

"Took her?" She looked out into the main hangar again, this time noticing that *Quicksilver II* was no longer there. "Took her where?"

"I don't know! He said they were going to go picnicking by the lake?"

*Damn*, Flynn thought. So Alice told Ochs what they had been searching for, probably explained the map to him, and he...believed her? And also believed the lost treasure was real? If that was the case, what would he do to Alice if their gold rush turned to a bust?

But that made no sense. Ochs was more familiar with the surrounding area than she was. What would make him believe there was some undiscovered heart-like lake somewhere out there?

She paced as she pondered, and found herself looking at the photo prints again. They were all mostly unremarkable, just like the landscape they depicted. A small stack of prints on the corner of the desk were all of *Quicksilver II* in flight. Then there was another stack, all nearly identical...

Her thoughts were cut off by the sound of pounding on glass. Goliath was on his feet again, and drumming his fists on the window, trying to draw the attention of whoever was in the hangar bay.

Flynn raised the gun behind him and pulled the trigger. The shot flew inches wide of Goliath's head, creating a sunburst of jagged cracks in the window. At the same time, she charged the guard at full speed, using him as a shield as she sent shards of glass, and both their bodies, flying through the pane.

Luckily, the hangar was populated by mechanics rather than armed soldiers, and they were content to freeze in place and stare at the strange gun-wielding woman. But the alarm bell they'd triggered outside would soon bring a small army she'd have to fight alone. She looked quickly around the hangar, and spotted what she was hoping to find on the far side, half covered with a tarp. She ran, then leapt onto the wing, dove underneath the heavy canvas, and pulled herself into the cockpit of the original *Quicksilver*.

With a single push of a button to the electric starter, the propeller disappeared into a circular blur. Flynn grinned wildly as she opened the throttle, pushing the airplane forward and maneuvering it toward the line of guards now forming at the mouth of the hangar. Flynn found the machine gun trigger and gave it a tight squeeze. There was no ammunition, but the weapon's loud staccato chattering was enough to get the men to scatter and give Flynn a clear path to the subterranean aerodrome's runway.

The plane taxied slowly, dragging the tarp behind it like a toddler with a blanket. A handful of guards ran to keep pace, firing shots that ricocheted off the metal skin. Then the pitch of the engine rose sharply and the aircraft shot forward, the cloth cover finally ripping loose. It barreled down the length of the canyon, picking up speed, but remaining stubbornly on the ground.

Then one wing dipped, and the plane swerved. It wobbled a bit, and almost regained equilibrium, but the wall was too close. The explosion shook the ground, and sent a roiling fireball up and beyond the lip of the canyon. Every man in the base went running to bear witness to the horrible devastation.

No one noticed Flynn as she crawled out from under the crumpled canvas, nor when she boarded the elevator. The explosion had drawn away the guards posted in the topside shack as well, so she was able to go completely unobserved until *Acanthis* was already in the sky. She gave those few witnesses a jaunty wing waggle before banking and heading after Ochs and Alice.

F LYNN surprised herself by spotting Grandpa Ames' lake first, before even catching the glint of sunlight off *Quicksilver II*'s metal skin. It helped that she now understood Alice's self-comforting comment about her photographs being in black and white: the body of water that had been here in ancient times had left behind a wide depression covered with rich dark-red clay—a heart-*shaded* lake!

She landed at the top of a gentle slope into the basin, and stopped about thirty yards away from the other plane. She approached cautiously, slipped underneath the shadow of the wing, and pressed her hand to the engine cowling. After getting a small taste of controlling a machine like this, a part of her ached to actually fly one.

She unlatched the small panel accessing the oversized engine's oil pan and removed the draining plug. With her pinkie, she shoved a corner of a handkerchief into the open hole, slowing but not entirely stopping the evacuation of lubricant. As the dangling end of the cloth became saturated, she reached into her trousers pocket to fish out a book of paper matches...

The *ping* of a bullet bouncing off the plane's metal skin seemed to reverberate through the entire airframe. "What are you doing, *Fräulein* Flynn?" Ochs shouted. "Come out where we can see you!"

*Damn it!* Flynn raised her hands as she emerged from under the plane's belly. Ochs was climbing up the incline, gun in hand, and guiding Alice by her elbow. Flynn had her attention focused on the major's gun, but she couldn't help but notice the the that Alice was carrying a wooden strongbox, bleached by the sun, but with the *W* of *Wells Fargo* still faintly legible. "Alice, are you all right?"

"She's perfectly fine," Ochs answered, "which is more than can be said of you if you do not step away from there now."

"Major, no!" Alice yelled. "You said if I showed you this place—"

"I said if there was gold here, I would consider letting you both go, as a gesture of gratitude."

"But we know the gold really was here!" Alice said, hefting her discovery for emphasis.

Ochs grabbed the chest, tore it from her hands, and dashed it against the hard ground. "'Was' doesn't mean a damn, stupid girl!" he sneered. Alice, horrified, fell to her hands and knees, gathering up the broken pieces of the artifact of her grandfather's adventure.

"To think I thought you were federal agents!" Ochs shook his head ruefully, then fixed his gaze on Flynn. "I was going to have my men stage an elaborate crash for your superiors to find. Someplace far from our operation. But now knowing that no one will come looking for you," he said, point the gun at Flynn's head, "I can keep your deaths simple."

Ochs squeezed the trigger, but at the very same moment, Alice used one of the splintered wood planks like a sword, jamming it into the major's thigh. He shrieked as his shot flew wild, and Flynn used the diversion to pull her stolen gun

from her jacket and fire back at the German. "Alice, run!"

Alice did as told, making a beeline for *Acanthis*, while Flynn retreated back underneath *Quicksilver II*. There were more shots, some ricocheting off the metal fuselage, some kicking up dirt inches from Flynn's feet. Gun still in her right hand, she fumbled her matchbook in the left. The handkerchief was now dripping wet; there would be precious little time for her to get a safe distance away before the airplane went up like a Roman candle.

"Think what you're about to do, *Fräulein* Flynn!" Ochs shouted. Was he engaging her because he had run out of bullets? Or because he was reloading and wanted to get her off her guard. "I know you appreciate what an achievement *Quicksilver* is. I can't believe you could so cavalierly destroy it."

"It's easier the second time around," she shouted back as she got a flame lit, and touched off her handmade fuse. The fire leapt like a living thing, climbing up and inside the engine before Flynn had the chance to turn.

The short distance between planes felt like miles. Bullets started flying again, and behind her she heard the *whoosh* of oxygen being sucked up by the growing fire. She needed to be in the air *now*.

Almost as if it understood the urgency, *Acanthis* started into motion, rolling away from the imminent explosion. Flynn suspected her eyes were playing tricks, but then she spotted Alice climbing onto the wing and into the plane. She put on an extra burst of speed, ignoring the bullets still buzzing past her head, leapt, grabbed the lip of the rear cockpit and swung her leg over. Even before her backside hit the seat she was goosing the throttle, and *Acanthis* surged forward, launching skyward just as the first boom sounded behind them.

"Alice!" Flynn shouted over the noise, "You swung the propeller? Yourself?"

She turned back over her shoulder and yelled back, "Yeah! I've seen how you do it. I figured the faster we got going, the better!"

"That's really dangerous if you don't know what you're doing!"

Alice's eyes widened like some moving picture damsel's. "Oh goodness! I'd hate to think we were ever in any danger!"

Flynn laughed harder than she remembered ever laughing before.

THE airfield at La Junta, Colorado was a dinky affair. But it was closer than Bivins, and it also hosted a division of the Colorado Rangers. Flynn told them she'd seen the wreckage of a crash while flying in from Denver, and since there was no more pressing business in La Junta, a pair of Rangers saddled up and rode off to take a look. With luck, Ochs had managed not to get caught in the explosion and would be well enough to help the lawmen find his secret base.

Coming back from the Ranger station, Flynn bought half a dozen sandwiches from a lunch wagon, and brought three of them to Alice. She held the few pieces of the strongbox she'd been able to rescue across her lap like a tray, from which she practically inhaled the first sandwich and half of the second. Between slower bites, she turned to Flynn and asked, "Now what?"

"Now? Whatever. I am sorry you didn't find more of your grandfather's treasure than that. There's not going to be a chance to look around the lake anymore once the Rangers start poking around."

"No matter. There's nothing there to find." Alice smiled as she set her last sandwich to the side, as well as the smaller pieces of wood. The largest piece, the thick bottom panel of the strongbox, she flipped upside down, and with a nail she pulled from her pocket, she pried the board apart, revealing what had been the chest's false bottom. She handed the thin cover to Flynn, showing her what was scratched and hidden on its underside.

"Oh," Flynn said, followed by a long silence. Then, she mirrored Alice's smile. "Well, I have been meaning to get back to San Francisco..."

DS·21

# Man-Bait
# for the Devil Snake

### BY PAUL KUPPERBERG

THE first thing you've got to know is, I hate snakes. And, of course, when I say "hate," what I really mean is "scared." And I also "hate" heights. To the tune of once getting a case of vertigo watching a TV documentary about some tightrope walking goof crossing the Grand Canyon on a piece of dental floss. I'm just lucky that I never grew to be taller than five foot seven or I'd probably be getting lightheaded every time I looked down at my shoes.

Normally, as an inhabitant of New York City, the snake thing is pretty much never a problem, and I can deal with the height issue as long as I stay off of balconies and away from windows.

In the jungles of Peru, on the other hand, things get trickier.

And trickier still when you're fleeing for your life from a 60-foot long Devil Snake with fangs the length of my now never-more-regretfully scrawny arms and the only path open to you is a 200-foot rope bridge sagging across a 150-foot deep gorge above a raging river. With, I might add, a tribe of angry spear-wielding, blow-dart shooting indigenous people behind me and a gang of heavily armed women air pirates waiting on the far side of the bridge.

And me with the sacred Gemstone of Eternity clutched in my sweaty little palms.

It was the likelihood of something precisely like this happening that had made me try to argue my editor, Rob Greenberg, out of sending me here in the first damn place.

MY name is Leo Persky. I'm more popularly known as Terrance Strange, my byline in the *Weekly World News*, the tabloid newspaper next to the other tabloids at the supermarket checkout. Most people assume that because of our subject matter— the unusual, the supernatural, extraterrestrials et al—that we're being ironic with the slogan, "The World's Only Reliable Newspaper." Ironically, it's all really, if weirdly, true. Well, except for my byline. And the photo of the handsome, square-jawed adventurer that goes with it. Those came from my grandfather, Jacob, the foremost monster hunter of his day, who thought "Strange" sounded better in his line of work than Persky. So did the *News*.

"Don't we have a stringer in

*Illustration by Dan Schkade*

Peru we can use instead of flying me halfway around the world?" I asked. Whined.

"If you'd rather," Rob responded in the tone of voice he uses when he's about to delight in telling me the even more repulsive alternative he's got planned, "it is possible to *drive* from New York City..."

"No."

"...*by bus*, to Peru, a total of about 12, 13,000 miles, through South American..."

"Jesus, Rob," I moaned.

"...across the 90-miles of roadless swamps and rainforests called the Darien Gap that stretches to the tip of Columbia and..."

I threw my up my hands. "I surrender."

"You're getting easy in your old age," he grinned, exposing the prominent canines that helped fuel the rumors I'd started that he was a vampire. "So. Peru. Up until last week, a country known to be home to 51 indigenous tribes. Now there are 52, thanks to a group discovered high in the mountains of northern Peru by remote mapping drones."

"And we care...why?"

Rob sailed a photographic print across his desk.

It was a snake.

"It's a snake," I said. "I hate snakes."

"Funny. They speak well of you. Check out the lower left of the shot. See that bundle about halfway down the length of the snake's body?"

I brought the print closer and squinted at the indicated item. Between the bird's eye angle and some shadows on the jungle floor, it was hard to make out very many details.

"That's a man," Rob said.

"What is? *This*?" I took a second, even closer look. "Was this taken at some weird angle or with a long lens? Because from this perspective, if that's a human being, then this snake..."

"...Yeah, factoring in the average height of other indigenous folk in the region, that would make it about 50 to 60 feet long."

"Holy crap! Amazing, but, you know, cryptozoology isn't exactly my jam, boss. There's gotta be somebody better qualified to handle this than..."

He raised a finger to silence me and said, "But, wait! There's more," and slid a second photo across the desk to me.

Ten hours and 3,700 *air* miles later, I was in Peru.

THERE were permits and arrangements and bribes and all sorts of shenanigans once I hit the ground at Capitán FAP Carlos Martínez de Pinillos International Airport in Trujillo, Peru, but Rob had everything sorted and organized for me in advance with the help of a local fixer and guide, all of which eventually led me to an old hanger at the far end of the airport where I was greeted by the arrival of a Korean War era Bell-47 helicopter that dropped out of the sky a few dozen yards in front of me on the tarmac in a roar of sound and blast of wind.

The pilot hopped out and snarled in my direction.

"You Persky?"

I blinked the tears from my eyes and stared at the form in khaki cargo shorts, white sleeveless t-shirt, and heavy-duty work boots, a holstered .45 strapped to her hip, and suddenly felt a little better about the assignment.

S HE said to call her Pancho. I said she didn't look like a "Pancho" and asked her what her real name was, and she said, in accented English, "Pancho. And...Leo? This is yours?"

I nodded.

"*Sí*. You look like a," and here her lips turned up in a throwaway sneer, "Leo. Are you ready to go?"

Pancho had about five inches of height and magnitudes of beauty on me, the former putting her at a solid six feet tall, the latter making my previously gritty eyeballs sweat. She was, to put a writerly turn to it, a knockout. Enough so that I let the implied insult pass and followed her tall, perfectly proportioned and tanned form to the copter, a goofy grin plastered uncomfortably on my face.

She was beautiful. So beautiful that I was shamed into silence about my fear of riding in the bubble-domed *doorless* machine. She climbed back aboard and

started playing with her switches. I swallowed hard, tossed my carry on behind the passenger seat, and hauled myself up with all the grace of a senior citizen trying to climb into the top bunkbed.

"Are you okay?" Pancho said, glancing over as I tried to fasten my seatbelt with trembling hands.

"Me? Yeah. Sure." I swallowed again, this time to keep down whatever was left of the Peruvian Airlines economy class dinner I'd eaten three or four hours earlier.

"If you're going to be sick, tell me, yes. You *vómito* in my chopper and I'll toss you out that door, *entiende usted*?"

Not trusting myself to speak, I gave her a queasy smile and a shaky thumbs up.

Shaking her head, Pancho snapped, "This had better be worth it." Then the whirling blades grabbed hold of the air and yanked us straight up into the sky.

I can't be sure, but I might have screamed.

N OWHERE near soon enough, Pancho found the open patch in the jungle she had apparently been searching for and aimed the chopper at it. We had been in the air for over an hour, following the contours of the ripe, green mountains. We hadn't been able to speak over the pounding thrum of the rotors.

But now, as we headed in for a landing, she reached behind her seat and produced two sets of headphones, tossing one to me.

"What the hell?" I said once I had them situated over my cap.

"I didn't want to have to listen to you moan and complain the whole trip."

"Fair point. Where are we?"

"A few dozen klicks from the village," she said, her voice crackling in my ears. "They call themselves the Hytabita. The lumber and mining interests were not pleased to find them and tried to keep this discovery to themselves. If no one knew the Hytabitans existed, no one would know their village had been razed to give *los corporaciones* access to the timber and whatever it is that's buried beneath their feet."

"So, what happened?"

Pancho slid me the side-eye and a piece of a knowing smile. "The object which you have been sent to retrieve for yourself happened. The Gemstone of Eternity."

"Hold on there, *hermana*, I'm not here for anything except a story and some pictures."

"Of course. Your newspaper went to the expense of sending you all the way down here for some photographs?" She gave a small shake of her long, dark tresses and turned her eyes back to guiding us in for a landing, and said, "Whatever you say, *jefe*."

THE clearing was recent, an ad hoc bulldozed landing pad built for much larger equipment than our little Bell-47. And from the hard, packed, sun baked ground and dried in tire and tread tracks, it appeared the area had seen plenty of heavy metal pass over it. Paths had been bashed through the surrounding tree line, disappearing in several directions into the dense foliage. A small hill of empty metal fuel barrels that had been hidden by the trees from above rose at the perimeter.

"You could land a Chinook here," I said in disbelief.

"Two," she said. "With bulldozers, jeeps, and thirty mercenaries. They went in six days ago and haven't been heard from since."

"Modern-day mercenaries against, what? Half-naked guys with spears, arrows, and blowguns? And you think indigenous cunning somehow won the day?"

"And the Gemstone."

"So, you buy into the mumbo-jumbo."

Pancho shrugged. "Truth is truth whether I believe it or not."

"Well, the last report of the Gemstone before now was in Spain in 1528, right around the time Francisco Pizarro was back home from Panama to beg the king to let him take stab number three at conquering Peru."

She nodded. "*Sí*. And its presence in Panama City would explain the disaster that struck *La Reina Pirata* in the bay on Christmas Eve, 1530, as she prepared to set sail just days ahead of Pizarro to Peru."

"Was that a ship? *La Reina...*

the Pirate Queen? Never heard of her."

"You would not. And she wasn't only a ship," Pancho said, then stuck her fingers in her mouth and emitted a loud, piercing whistle. From all around us, from the dark undergrowth, came the sudden roar of engines and a chorus of shouts and shrill yells.

I looked at Pancho. She looked at me and smiled, timing her words to coincide with the appearance of the first of the jeeps to spring into the clearing with their respective contingents of tan and khaki-clad women pirates waving an impressive assortment of high-caliber military-grade hardware.

"¡La reina pirata era...mi abuela!"

EN route, Pancho told her story: About four centuries ago, her however-many-greats grandma cut the throat of the dastardly villain who had abducted and ravished her and took command of his pirate crew. In time, the ruthless *La Reina* had attracted a virtual flotilla of female followers and began to dream of bigger things for them, including a country of her own. Word reached Pizarro that she intended to carve one out in Peru, the object of his own affection, and suddenly, grandma's entire fleet but one went under on a perfectly calm, Southern Hemisphere summer Christmas Eve. The survivors, including her *abuela*, were apparently so traumatized, they fled the

Southern Pacific and never again sailed below the Equator.

"I am the twentieth Pirate Queen," Queen Pancho proclaimed proudly as we bumped along the rough jungle road in the lead jeep. She was at the wheel and, other than me, the only lady pirate passenger not pointing an AK-something-or-other in the general direction of my skull. "And like those who came before, I have pledged my life to reclaiming the honor of *la primera reina de los piratas*."

"How you planning on making that happen? You gonna finally conquer Peru for her?"

"*Sí*," she said.

AND here's the funny thing. With the Gemstone of Eternity and the knowledge of how to tap into its magical energies, conquering Peru was probably well within the realm of possibility. I could fill a volume with its history and legend, but for the sake of brevity: First mentioned in ancient Sumerian texts around 3900 B.C.E. Built kings up. Tore kings down. Conquered empires, wiped others from the memory of history. It has punished sinners, rewarded tyrants, and mislead fools. It has been variously lost, stolen, ransomed, hidden, and displayed. For those of you who like lists, it would make the Top Five of *any* "Most Dangerous Things Ever" list.

So, yeah. Conquer Peru? No prob.

Of course, that did beg the question:

"Why am I here? You ladies seem to have the situation under control."

"Because we need *un hombre*."

"*¿Por qué?*"

"*Por qué*," she said with a sneer of contempt, "the Gemstone of Eternity was created by one."

PANCHO and her pirate gang would surround the Hytabita village, pick off a few of the locals with their thunder sticks, maybe blow up a hut or two, to establish their seriousness and superiority, and then demand they hand over the Gemstone of Eternity. That's the part where I came in. The same patriarchal He-man Woman Hater's Club in charge today was even more so back then, and to make sure the gals kept their mitts off their magic, this particular object was crafted to *literally* keep it out of the hands of women. Specifically, the older, smarter sister of the king who had it created it to save his throne from her.

We left the vehicles in a clearing a few hundred meters upwind of the village and went the rest of the way on foot. The pirate crew consisted of twenty women of varying ages, ethnicities, sizes, and—within a healthy parameter of body types required for this kind of work—shapes. But no doubt they were to the last one, hardened soldiers of fortune.

"We are close," Pancho said quietly.

City boy though I was, I'd already picked up on faint cooking odors wafting towards us. It was a sense I'd honed up in the city, in fact, refining my sense of smell to be able to track down food trucks by cuisine. At least my oversized schnoz served some use.

"Mm. Pork." I sniffled, my nostrils swirling the flavor molecules around. "Green onions. Beans. And…" I took in another nose full and said, in full voice. "And that's…oregano…nutmeg…something spicy, peppery…"

"Keep your voice down!" Pancho growled.

"Sue me," I shouted. "I'm hungry! I haven't eaten since…"

Sure, it was a dumb thing to do, trying to raise a ruckus and give the Hytabitans a heads-up, but I didn't have a plan B. Besides, Pancho needed me alive, so I didn't think there was much of a chance she'd shoot me.

I was right.

But she did punch my lights out.

WHEN I came to, my hands were tied behind my back and a gag was shoved into my mouth. Also, my nose hurt like a son of a bitch and I could taste blood in the back of my throat. I found myself sprawled slumped against a tree, opening my eyes to the sight Pancho's sun-tanned legs and booted feet. I followed them up to her face.

"Can you stand?" she said. "Are you ready to cooperate?"

I said, "Go to hell, sister, I'm not helping you!"

What she heard through the gag was, "Gggahllllsss!"

Pancho gestured and two of her pirates stepped forward, each grabbing me by an arm and hauling me to my feet.

She turned on her heels and marched off. The rest of us followed. But we didn't have far to go, and soon *la reina pirata* was signaling to her crew to spread out, going left and right to ring the small village of thatched roof huts with their firepower and throw a little 21st century shock and awe into the primitives.

They were good. They moved like the breeze, merging into the underbrush with barely a ripple of foliage, and then Pancho grabbed me by the shoulder and, .45 automatic in hand, raised her finger to her lips to remind me that silence was golden. She pushed me ahead, whispering in my ear, "You go as soon as we hear the first explosion, *lo entiendes*?"

"Bite me," I said, which came out as "Bmmmeem!"

The jungle boomed suddenly and from every direction with the deafening blast of a ring of flash/

bang grenades going off at virtually the same instant.

"Go!" Pancho roared over the concussive pounding and shoved me forward.

I immediately caught my foot on a tree root and went down on my face. Pancho lost her balance and came down on top of me, knocking whatever breathe I had left from me.

The good news was, the first wave of poison arrows flew right over our heads.

The bad news, we were sitting ducks when the Hytabitans dropped from the trees and landed on top of us.

THERE was a lot of yelling and war cries and gunfire, but I didn't get to see any of the action as Pancho and I were dragged by our feet through the underbrush into the village. For the same reason I couldn't get a good look at our captors, but the general impression they gave was one of an angry indigenous people with their backs up and their ceremonial face and body paintings on. Apparently, us non-indigenous folk and our weaponry didn't spook them in the least, but then they'd already faced that once, quite successfully from the look of the overturned and burnt-out jeep we were dragged past at the edge of the village clearing.

The Hytabitans dumped Pancho and me between the large communal cooking fire and the altar made from tree trunks and palm fronds tied together with braided vine rope. The altar was the tallest structure in the village, twice the height and almost as long as the huts.

And there, mounted atop that sacred structure, the Gemstone of Eternity. Eight inches in diameter, cut into 100 facets, it glowed a deep, throbbing purple in the afternoon sun.

More Hytabitans were returning from the underbrush, many with members of Pancho's pirate brigade at spear point or being dragged in behind them. And they were singing, all of them. Something bouncy and rhythmic, in what I assumed was their native tongue. It was quite a pleasant tune and if I didn't suspect that it was actually an incantation or summoning ceremony of some sort, I might have even enjoyed the show.

The warriors handed the other prisoners off to the women and children, who herded them into a hut with spears and sharpened sticks.

Meanwhile, the guys were drawing closer around Pancho and me, dancing and singing their song. The fact that the ground under my back was starting to tremble with increasing ferocity only added fuel to my suspicion that this was a summoning ceremony.

The Hytabita warriors danced around us in a circle, then two of them swooped in and pulled

Pancho, struggling, outside the circle while the rest continued chanting loudly and kicking their feet.

I heard Pancho shout, "Oh, *mierda!*" and when I looked at what she was looking at I shouted, "Oh *mierda!*" too.

Because the Gemstone of Eternity was pulsating, which, believe me, is never a good sign when it comes to *objets de magie.* Case in point: said pulsations were accompanied by rumbling of the ground and crashing of trees in the nearby jungle and then the singing reached its crescendo and the men fell silent and to their knees as the sound of several tons of ginormous snake rolled through the jungle towards us...

Okay, yeah, anacondas can grow to be 25, 30 feet, maybe a foot in diameter, weighing in at 500 pounds or more. But this one— let's just call it Devil Snake— dwarfed them all. Sixty feet, on the conservative side, and about as thick around as a VW Minibus. And fangs. Venom-dripping ones at that.

Even on my feet and given a head start I couldn't have outrun the scaly beast. It's hard to tell with those dead, glass snake eyes, but I knew I was Devil Snake's primary target. I don't know why they were singling me out. Probably because I was the man and that made me the boss in their eyes.

I was only guessing, of course, but, in the end, thank goodness

for Hytabitan male chauvinism, because while they were watching me, the women were kicking their asses.

I didn't realize it until my view of Devil Snake was suddenly blocked by Pancho, who appeared as if by magic, wild-eyed and bloodied, brandishing a six-inch matte black serrated ceramic combat knife and screaming in my face, "Turn the hell over!" While I was turning, one of the warriors tried jumping her, but she whirled and slashed at him and he went away with a gurgle and a spray of blood. With an impatient snarl, she wrenched me over onto my stomach and cut my ropes, taking a little bit of skin at the same time. I didn't complain.

Then Pancho was hauling me to my feet and yelling, "Get the Gemstone!"

The Gemstone was mounted 20 feet up in the air and on the other side of a Devil Snake that wanted to eat me. And what the hell was she going to do while I was at it? Hold off the entire tribe single-handedly?

I finally got the idea when the explosions and small arms fire started going off in the hut where the rest of the pirates had been taken. The Hytabitans didn't know the difference between a decorative bauble and a hand grenade, the same way they hadn't known to search Pancho and the others for knives or guns they'd have hidden under their clothes.

As soon as Pancho leapt back

into the fight and I could pull myself upright, I turned to find Devil Snake rearing up a good ten yards above me, its' great big jaws open more than wide enough to gobble me up in one bite. It hissed. Loud. I could feel as well as smell the hot, fetid snake breath and knew there was no escape once it decided to strike.

Just then, the pirates came bursting out of the hut right behind the grenade that blew out the roof and side wall, as well as several of their captors. Fortunately, they had enough explosives left to throw at Devil Snake as well, which seemed to irritate more than harm it, but it was just the diversion I needed to make a run for it.

I didn't relish the idea of climbing that altar, but that was the fastest route to the Gemstone.

Pardon me. *Second* fastest. First was apparently to roll a grenade against the corner support of the whole set up and blow it, bringing the whole shebang down with a bang. I glanced over and saw Pancho, who gave me a wink and thumbs up before she shot a Hytabitan charging her with a spear.

Suddenly remembering the kids who had been in that hut with the pirates, I had moment of nauseating fear, until I spotted a trio of pirates herding the frightened children towards the jungle and safety. Then, I went for the wrecked altar and the Gemstone.

It was still pulsing and glowing. I made sure to test it for heat before I grabbed it and wrenched it from the wooden wreath it had been mounted on to the altar by some gooey natural resin. It was cool to the touch but scary as hell.

"Leo!"

Pancho's voice, behind me. I whirled, but before I saw her, I saw the locals charging me. Then I heard my name again and spotted her, on the far side of a clump of warriors. She had her hands up, waving them over her head.

I threw the Gemstone, my life depending on the schoolyard game of "keep away," a cruelty to which I was usually the victim rather than the perpetrator. But score one for fear and desperation, because the purple bauble flew over the heads of the warriors and into Pancho's hands, as if drawn to them by magic.

The warriors stopped in mid-charge and, their eyes on the flying Gemstone, immediately reversed course.

I ran, making for a clearing at the edge of the village that looked as though it led into a jungle path.

Pancho screamed. Loud. Not in anger. In agony.

Thinking she'd been nailed by a spear or something, I risked a quick glance back over my shoulder. It wasn't a spear. It was the Gemstone, which had erupted into a blazing ruby red light, burning into her flesh.

Right! The long-ago Mesopotamian king who'd had this thing

built had installed a "no girls allowed" default into it.

I screamed her name a few times before she heard me, but as soon as she spotted me in the clear, my hands up in the air, she was happy to let the Gemstone go. It flew over my head and landed with a thud in the dirt behind me, at the mouth of the path.

"That way!" she yelled. "The rest of my crew...that way!"

Well, *d'uh*!

I should have known Pancho was too smart an operator to put all her eggs in one basket. She'd left herself a back way out. And, while they weren't my first choice to run into on a dark jungle path, they were preferable to Devil Snakes and angry tribesmen. Could I keep the Gemstone out of their hands? I figured I'd cross that bridge when I came to it.

OF course, I meant an idiomatic bridge, but, all of a sudden, there was a real one.

Now, when I say bridge, you likely think towering, majestic *solid* structures, like the Brooklyn or the Golden Gate. This wasn't even a structure. This was an... *ornament*, braided vine ropes and roughhewn planks strung between two cliff sides, a couple of hundred feet apart. A hundred and fifty feet above a narrow, raging white water river.

And me at the precipice.

It was days like this that taught a man a thing or two about himself, and on this one, I learned that I was apparently just enough more afraid of heights than of snakes that even facing the literal gaping maw of death, I couldn't make myself step out onto that shoestring with delusions of grandeur.

Instead, I turned and faced my second-greatest fear.

But when I saw it rearing up, coiling to strike, close enough to count the scales on its belly, I panicked and with no thought whatsoever, reared back myself and heaved the Gemstone of Eternity right at it.

Devil Snake gobbled it up like an enchanted Tic Tac, and when that was gone, returned its attention to me. But only for a second, because without warning, it suddenly went stiff and reared up almost its full length onto its tail, leveraging 40 or 50 feet of snake straight up into the air, and then smoke started wafting from its open mouth.

It trembled and hissed with a sound like a diesel locomotive being dragged across a football field of sewer gratings. Then it started thrashing its head back and forth as its skin erupted in manhole-cover sized glowing boils.

And then I got it.

"Pancho," I screamed. "Devil Snake's a girl!"

The pirate queen was at the head of a phalanx of her pirates shooting and stabbing their way through the locals to reach me and the Gemstone. Which was burning Devil Snake from the inside out the same way it had burned Pancho's hands when she had briefly touched it.

Pancho did not look happy that I'd fed her key to the kingdom of Peru to Devil Snake. In retrospect, it might not have been the best idea because while it *was* causing the mutant reptile lethal distress, said distress was also blocking my escape and left me nowhere to be but under her when the monster came tumbling down.

You know the scene in *Butch Cassiday and the Sundance Kid* where they're trapped at the edge of a cliff over a not too dissimilar raging river, and their only escape is to jump, so they psyche themselves up by screaming, "Oh, oh, oh, shit!" before taking the plunge?

I didn't do that.

I did yell, "Oh, oh, oh, shit!" but I didn't plunge. I went totally counterintuitive and charged straight at the thrashing monster. I figured with her guts being consumed by eldritch fire, Devil Snake had better things to worry about than me.

I was right, because the next thing I knew, Devil Snake erupted into a writhing tower of flame and toppled. I dove to the left. She went to the right. The ground trembled as she hit, falling half onto the rope bridge and sending it tumbling into the deep gorge below. Still burning, the rest of Devil Snake slid over the edge and fell after it.

Everything went suddenly quiet in the jungle. Too quiet.

I turned to Pancho and the others, all frozen in place, watching me. Pancho and her pirates were pissed. The Hytabitans were... well, I'm not sure. Something between awe and confusion.

"What?" I said.

"*¡Vamonos!*" Pancho said from between clenched teeth. "For the moment, they cannot believe a nerd like you could kill their Devil Snake, but there is no telling how long before they snap out of their stupor and attack."

We vamoosed, hustling back along the path to the clearing, where the pirates wasted no time filling their jeeps and taking off into the jungle.

When I tried climbing into the chopper with Pancho, she pulled her .45 from her waistband and pointed it at my nose, saying, "*Lo siento*, Leo. I fear we must here part company."

I cross-eyed the barrel and quipped, "Huh?"

"You have already cost me the Gemstone once. I can't trust you not to interfere with my plans to recover it now."

"Me? Interfere? You really don't know who you're talking to, do you lady? I'm not the Justice League. I'm just a reporter, an observer."

She favored me with an indulgent smile and said, "You use cowardice as a cover, *amigo*, but a coward could not have faced what you did today."

"Because the only alternative was crossing that damned bridge."

Pancho gestured with the gun barrel for me to step back, away from helicopter as she fired up its engine.

"You're not really leaving me here in the middle of the jungle?" I shouted in disbelief.

Pancho shrugged and smiled in regret. "I am a pirate, after all. Farewell, Leo. Perhaps we shall meet again."

And with that she did whatever she did to make the chopper go up, circle the clearing twice, then fly away.

I sighed.

It looked like that horse pill-sized pellet containing a GPS tracking chip Rob Greenberg made me swallow before I left was going to come in handy. The sudden memory of Rob (and having to swallow that pill) made me wince. I had gotten the story he had sent me for, but circumstances being what they were, I hadn't been able to get any pictures.

That was bad.

Bad enough that even as I heard the approaching thrum of the rescue helicopter coming for me following the ingested GPS, I considered going back and begging the Hytabitans for sanctuary.

# *Protocol 23*

## *By* DAYTON WARD & KEVIN DILMORE

*O*ne. One. Two. One. Two. Two. The cadence repeated in Veronica Faust's head as she stepped into every punch, driving her gloved fists with alternating strikes to the training dummy. Moving her feet in a similar rhythm, she shifted her body to put maximum power behind each attack. With every blow she landed, one of the highlighted circles on the man-shaped dummy flashed red. It wasn't the same as the sparring she did with her boss, but it still provided a decent workout. She was in the zone now, continuing to beat her helpless adversary even as the timer on her nearby tablet signaled the end of this round.

When the tablet sounded again, it was with an alert tone Ronnie knew she couldn't ignore. Sighing, she turned from the training dummy and removed her grappling gloves. She took a few deep breaths to bring down her respiration, running one hand through the auburn hair she kept cut in a short, bob style. Her tablet lay on a nearby bench, its screen flashing a status message she'd been expecting.

*Flight landed 15:43 local time. Proceeding to temporary staging area for final prep and rest. Will contact you 07:00 your time with instructions and tech check.*

Brief and to the point, as was normally the case with such communications. Ronnie's employer didn't like wasting time with pleasantries when she was on the job. That was simply not how "the Wraith" operated.

*The Wraith.*

Ronnie smiled at the thought of her enigmatic benefactor's chosen moniker. She'd worked for the Wraith for five years in an operational and technical support role and knew nothing about the woman who paid her very well for the work she did. What she did know was the woman behind the mask applied significant time and resources to hunting and capturing criminals of a particular breed: those who commanded a great deal of power and who used it to evade the long arm of justice. Their wealth and global influence made them all but untouchable to conventional law enforcement, but also attracted the Wraith for reasons she chose not to share.

Something drove her, Ronnie knew, but no hints or clues had ever been offered. Perhaps one day she would learn such secrets, but she'd seen enough to be certain the Wraith was committed to

*Illustration by Kerry Callen*

her personal mission. In the years since she'd answered an intriguing listing on a job search website, Ronnie had witnessed her employer bringing all manner of white-collar criminals to justice. Then there were the darker, more sinister individuals: terrorists, human traffickers, weapons merchants, and drug kingpins. Indeed, it was this last category into which the Wraith's current target fell. It was why she'd flown to....

Her tablet pinged again, this time emitting a shrill tone demanding immediate attention.

"What the hell?"

Grabbing the tablet from the bench, Ronnie saw the device launching an internal security schematic of the Bunker. Red indicators all along the diagram showed doors closing and locking on every floor. Every access point to the building's ground level was secure which by itself was standard operating procedure. What was unusual was the closing of stairwells and deactivation of elevators linking the complex's four subterranean levels. It was something that should never happen except in those few emergency scenarios necessitating a total lockdown.

Her fingers moving with practiced ease, Ronnie navigated the security system's multiple status screens. Was it a glitch? She and the tech support staff had been chasing problems following a software upgrade two weeks earlier, but those were isolated issues rather than systemwide failures.

*No,* she decided. *This was something else.*

"**D**AMN, I *hate* those guys!"

Carrying snacks in each hand, Bryce heard the complaint as he entered the operations center. His eyes took a moment to adjust to the glow from the video monitors covering the front wall and upsetting the room's otherwise subdued illumination. A variety of data—text reports, security camera feeds, satellite and weather information along with local and national broadcast outlets—filled every screen.

"Cliff?" called Bryce. It took him an extra second to see his friend hunched over one of the computer workstations. A bit overweight compared to Bryce's own slender physique, Cliff was dressed in sweatpants, sandals, and a faded *Star Wars* shirt. "What, they changed the password again?"

"Again." Cliff scowled. "There's no question it's deliberate. Beta Shift sucks."

Dressed in well-worn jeans, running shoes, and a simple black hooded sweatshirt, Bryce dropped into the seat at the adjoining workstation. He opened one of the snack bags before offering it to Cliff.

"Is that cheesy popcorn?" asked Cliff.

Bryce shrugged. "Is tonight the *Golden Girls* marathon on the Hallmark Channel?"

Returning his attention to the keyboard, Cliff started typing again. "Not unless I get around this password. I mean, *damn*. It's the only app they mess with be—"

"Because it's the only app *we* watch," Bryce finished.

"They insist on denying us even the simplest of pleasures." Cliff stabbed once more at the keyboard, and the monitor abruptly presented a menu of video offerings. "Boom!"

Around a mouthful of popcorn, Bryce asked, "So, what was the password?"

Cliff sighed. "'Gamma Shift sucks' but with a number one for the 'i.' They don't even try, really."

"We'll get them back later. Pass the bowls and—"

A loud, metallic clack rang through the room, interrupting Bryce and giving him an abrupt uncertain feeling.

"Magnetic locks," the two said in unison.

Then the power went out.

"Give it a second," Cliff said as they sat in the utter blackness. Then the workstations and screens flickered back to life and air surged once again through the room's overhead vents. "Good to know the backup generators work like they should."

"You don't think Beta—"

"Beta Shift?" Cliff shook his head. "They wouldn't jack with us like this. Could be the whole grid failed."

A flashing alert on a nearby screen caught Bryce's attention. "A power grid failure doesn't worm through a system firewall."

Forgetting popcorn or TV, both men went to work at their respective stations. As they raced through several test commands and other diagnostic requests, random monitors blinked or just went dark.

"External security cameras are out," Cliff called out.

"Internet's down." Bryce pointed to his screen. "Fiber connection's gone."

Cliff grimaced. "This isn't just a hack. They know exactly what they're doing. We have to iso—"

"Isolate systems before we lose them," replied Bryce. His typed as fast as his fingers would move. "If external cameras are out—"

"Then someone wants in."

"SOMEBODY'S hacking *us*? Son of a *bitch*."

Whoever they were, Ronnie conceded they were good. They'd managed to worm their way past multiple firewalls and into the core system before tripping the first alarm. According to all the specs, it should be all but impossible for anyone to gain access via an external connection without proper authentication.

That left only one explanation.

"They're inside. Whoever it is, they're *inside the damned building*."

Pulling up her system toolkit, she launched her own diagnostic program. She'd created it to hunt ways around the existing security protocols. Finding and addressing these made the system stronger and safer, but it also provided Ronnie with an unparalleled knowledge of the code responsible for maintaining the Wraith's security and secrecy.

*And I still don't know her real name. Go figure.*

A few minutes of digging into the communications and surveillance protocols rewarded Ronnie with an array of video images supplied by cameras installed throughout the bunker. It didn't take long for her to find what she now expected to see: people she didn't know, skulking through the corridors and rooms of her second home.

"Damn."

This was the nightmare scenario. The entire staff ran drills for a variety of external physical assaults on the Bunker, but the complex was fitted with countermeasures for such eventualities including a generator farm on the lowest level and a contained air circulation system protected from outside intrusion. Even more improbable was the idea someone could be inside, undetected, long enough to hijack the computer system running everything. Whoever was attacking them had gotten close enough to the building without notice, long enough to tap one of the very few hard lines connecting the Bunker to the outside world. This person was no slouch, and they had a lot of friends working their way

through the complex.

Ronnie wasn't a slouch, either.

One of the camera feeds showed movement in the ops center. She enlarged that window and breathed a sigh of relief. It was Bryce and Cliff; her Gamma Shift colleagues. Though she'd only worked with them on infrequent occasions when scheduling required any of them to substitute for other staff members, she knew they were good at their jobs. She also knew they tended to act like something of a shared consciousness; finishing each other's sentences and sometimes talking as though with a language only they understood. From how they were hovering over one of the workstations, Ronnie decided they'd surmised at least some of the current situation. At least now she wasn't alone. She tapped the control to open a line.

"Guys, it's me."

On the screen, she watched them look around the room before Cliff pointed to the camera and waved.

*"Hey, Veronica. You okay?"*

She nodded even though they couldn't see her. "I'm fine. We've got trouble."

*"Tell us about it,"* replied Bryce. *"We've been hacked."*

"I know." She gave them a quick rundown of what she was seeing on the camera feeds. "Right now, they've got the run of the place, but if I can work my way back into the system, I can bypass some of these lockouts and maybe seal off the really sensitive areas. Ops, weapons and tech, and the garage are the big ones, but I'm locked out."

Bryce's eyes widened. "*Hang on. There's something else that might work.*"

Watching as Bryce returned to the workstation behind him, Ronnie saw his finger moved across the keyboard. Rows of text she couldn't read scrolled by on station's screen before he slapped the Enter key. As though in response, Ronnie's tablet chirped, and she pulled up a status window.

"You activated the magnetic door locks in those areas," she said. "How the hell did you do that?"

"*Protocol 51,*" said Cliff as he and Bryce exchanged high fives. "*It's the old emergency protocols from the previous setup, before your time and before Wraith upgraded everything.*"

Bryce added, "*We kept it around while we worked out all the bugs with the new system, and then...I guess we just forgot about it. Totally on its own server and everything. If you don't know to look, it'd be easy to miss.*"

"*It's also where we keep the digital movie library,*" said Cliff.

Bryce glared at him. "*Dude. Protocol 34.*"

"*On second thought,*" Cliff said, "*pretend you didn't hear that.*"

"*Yeah. Nothing there.*" Bryce cleared his throat. "*At all.*"

Ronnie rolled her eyes. What was *with* these idiots? "Shut up, okay? I don't care. Look, we need to get somewhere we can plan our next move."

"*Sublevel Two,*" suggested Cliff. "*Computer servers.*"

"I like it," Ronnie said, swiping through screens on her tablet. "I've almost got a bypass ready, but I'm stuck in the gym. Can you help with that?" Her tablet beeped again, and she gasped at what she saw. "Guys, a couple of goons are heading for Ops."

"*Time for us to slide out of here,*" said Bryce, who looked to Cliff. "*Proto—*"

"*Protocol 14,*" Cliff finished.

Checking the other cameras, her stomach lurched as she found the feed for the corridor outside the gym. Two figures in masks and dark clothing—both men, judging by height and physique—stood at the door. One man held a weapon she didn't recognize, while his partner worked with the door's keypad. He'd removed its faceplate and was fiddling with the internal wiring.

Then she heard the door's lock deactivating.

*Move!*

Fueled by instinct and training received from her employer, Ronnie was reacting before the door began opening. Lunging across the room, she grabbed two five-pound, cast iron dumbbells. Her movements masked by the door as it opened, she waited before cocking her right arm until the first intruder entered. By the time she flung the dumbbell he was in the room and the weight caught him in the side of the head. He collapsed with a whimper, dropping limp to the carpeted floor.

With the other dumbbell in her left hand, Ronnie charged the door, forcing it closed just as the man's companion entered the room. The door slammed into him and his weapon fell from his hands. As he moved to retrieve it, she swung the dumbbell, catching him under the chin. The man yelped in surprise and pain and she hit him again for good measure. This time he sagged against the wall, unconscious before he slid to the floor.

Retrieving her tablet, Ronnie pulled up the Ops video feed. "Bryce. Cliff. You okay?"

The room was empty.

"Guys, what the hell is Protocol 14?"

ON his back and with his hands braced against the underside of the floor panel, Bryce slowly pushed upward. The panel's seal gave way with a slight popping sound and he paused. If someone else heard it, their crawl through the ventilation system from Ops to here would be for nothing.

*And we'll be dead.*

Rising from the subfloor, he peered through the narrow gap between the panel and the floor. Satisfied the server room above them was empty, Bryce slid the panel aside and pulled himself to

his feet before turning and offering a hand up to Cliff.

"Thanks, man," Cliff said, making a futile effort to brush away some of the grime now covering his clothes.

After replacing the floor panel, he and Bryce moved to one of the racks of headless servers packing the room. Bryce grabbed a drawer and slid it out, folding up a flatscreen display and activating the slim keyboard now before him. "Ronnie's bypass worked. I'm in."

Cliff said, "Security cameras are online. I think I can get to the primary security system and override the door locks, too."

"We need to shut down Ops," said Bryce. A check of the cameras told him there were at least a dozen and probably more intruders spreading out through the Bunker. "Now that they're inside we can't let them have direct acc—"

Cliff cut him off. "Access to the system. Veronica was right. There are two in Ops right now. Protocol 6." He keyed in a series of commands. "Locking the doors."

"Rerouting control to us," Bryce said. "Wham. It's ours. Ops is a brick."

"Let Beta Shift fix it," replied Cliff. "And it's not a total brick. I left the TVs on."

"Confirming," said Bryce as he reviewed the camera feeds. On his screen, he saw the entire wall of Ops video screens now linked to display a single image. "*Golden*

*Girls.* Nice. Which one is it?"

Cliff said, "Buzz the old boy-friend."

"Ah. 'Twice in a Lifetime.'"

"Fifth season."

"Too bad we didn't snag the pop-corn." Bryce clicked on another icon. "Hang on. I'm looking for Ronnie."

"Oh, it's *Ronnie* now?"

Ignoring his friend, Bryce kept scanning until something caught his eye and he backed up to a pre-vious feed. "Got her. Sector One, Camera Four." Donning a wireless headset from a hook next to the server, he tapped its microphone. "Base to Jumper."

A voice crackled in his earpiece. "*What?*"

"*Jumper*, this is *Base*. No uncoded transmissions during a security breach," Bryce said. "Protoc—"

"Protocol 9," Cliff finished with him.

"*Both of you, just...shut up,*" said Ronnie. "*Did you make it to the server room?*"

Bryce turned to exchange a silent glance with Cliff. No one spoke.

"*Hello? Are you there? Talk to me!*"

Cliff said, "The shut-up thing? We thought that—"

"Was an order," Bryce finished.

"*What? No! Good god...okay, look. Just tell me where they are, and where I can go.*"

After a minute, Cliff said, "I've got four in Sector Two, near the main conference room."

Struck by an idea, Bryce opened the Bunker's intercom system. "Base to Jumper," he said, his voice now sounding over every speaker in the complex. "Stay in the main conference room. They're moving away."

"*Hot mic! Hot mic!*" Ronnie screamed into Bryce's ear, and he made sure that carried over the open intercom.

On the screen, four figures in black fatigues and masks with weapons at the ready turned and ran toward the meeting room. Bryce waited until the first pair approached its open doorway before killing the room's lights. That was enough to send all four intruders charging into the room. Waiting until they were clear of the entrance, Bryce tapped another control and the door swung closed.

"Magnetic lock engaged," Cliff said into his headset as he looked at Bryce. "Four intruders detained."

"*What?*" Ronnie's voice sounded incredulous in Bryce's headset. "*What the hell did you guys just do?*"

"Protocol 17," Bryce and Cliff answered together.

L EANING against the back wall of the cramped, dark closet, Ronnie blew out her breath.

"I can't believe that worked."

She couldn't decide if Bryce and Cliff were going to get her killed, drive her to drink, or compel her to surrender to the intruders. Still, she had to hand it to them.

Nothing either of them said had anything to do with any of the Bunker's established procedures. Was it their own code? Ronnie had no idea.

Sighing, she swiped through screens on her tablet. "I'm not making it to you. There are still bad guys wandering around, and I've got to find a way to lock this hacker out of the system."

Cliff replied, "*We count eight out of commission including the two you took down in the gym. I think that leaves eight, but we've got a few ideas for them.*"

"Hang on." Ronnie paused, checking the camera feeds. One image depicted four intruders emerging from a stairwell onto Sublevel Three. "I've got eyes on some of them. They're down on the maintenance level." She noted three of the figures carried weapons while one walked with a more deliberate pace, hands in the pockets of his black jacket. Though dressed like his companions, he wore no mask. Enlarging the image, Ronnie tapped the screen to increase the image resolution. "I'll be damned."

"What is it?" asked Bryce.

Ronnie replied, "It's him. He's here. Stewart."

"*Harrison Stewart?*" Cliff's voice seemed to rise an octave. "*Are you sure?*"

There could be no mistaking the man's identity, given the Wraith had been tracking him for months. An international drug supplier, he was suspected of distributing a host of designer drugs for clientele who could afford exorbitant prices. He occupied a place of distinction on the most-wanted lists of law enforcement agencies around the world, but his depth of financial resources and influence over any number of corrupted agents and elected officials made pinning real charges to him a difficult proposition.

Then the Wraith took an interest in him. After months of building her file on him, she managed to disrupt a big piece of his operation two week ago when she swept into a warehouse near the port and seized what she estimated to be more than ten million dollars of a unique product: one half of a "binary drug." Harmless by itself, it was extremely potent when matched with another compound which triggered the substances pleasurable effects. That surely had been enough to anger Stewart, and it was the reason the Wraith was currently out of the country. She'd found the source for the binary drug's second component, and her investigation convinced her she might be able to capture Stewart himself on this latest operation.

*Obviously, that's not going to happen.*

Then, it all made sense.

"Oh, damn," said Ronnie. "That's why Stewart's here. The drugs the Wraith took from him." The compound she'd seized, though worthless on its own, was just part of the case the Wraith was building against Stewart, with plans to deliver the whole package to the police once she'd secured the other ingredient and the man himself.

"*While Wraith was searching for him,*" said Bryce, "*he was hunting her.*"

Cliff said, "*Is it too late to ask for vacation days?*"

"Later," replied Ronnie. "We have to stop him, right now." In addition to retrieving his lost property, there was everything else the Wraith stored in the Bunker and the very real possibility something here might aid him in hunting his nemesis and perhaps even revealing her true identity.

"*Protocol 66,*" said Bryce. "*Defend the Batcave.*"

"**R**ONNIE'S moving," Cliff said.

"I see that," Bryce said, toggling on his headset. "Base to Jumper. You're moving."

Ronnie snapped, "*Will you stop with that already?*"

"*Sorry. I think I've got a line on our hacker. There's a hardwired connection at a hub in Sector Two on Sublevel Three.*"

Cliff's hands worked his keyboard. "Checking cameras. Ronnie, they're in the tech closet next to HVAC."

"Oooh, yeah, that's where I would have gone," said Bryce. "Why didn't we look there sooner?"

"I've been a little busy over here, Bry."

"Not too busy to stream *Golden Girls* into—"

"*Shut up and clear me a path!*"

"Protocol 12," Bryce and Cliff said in harmony as they each turned to their keyboards.

Opening the intercom again, Bryce spoke into his headset, "Attention, all personnel." He smiled at his voice echoing across the Bunker's public-address speakers. "Defense Plan Alpha initiated. Nerve gas release on Sublevel Three. Repeat, nerve gas release in Sublevel Three."

"*You're kidding me?*" Alarm was clear in Ronnie's voice as Bryce glanced at a camera feed and saw her skid to a halt in the corridor.

Switching off his patch into the intercom, Bryce said. "Keep going. Trust us."

"That wasn't coded," said Cliff. "You broke protocol."

Bryce shrugged. "I'll put a dollar in the jar later. Tell me what you see."

"Four guys on the run," replied Cliff. "Including the one in the tech closet."

"Perfect." Bryce grinned. "Activating corridor fire-suppression systems." He watched as foam and water sprayed from overhead fixtures, drenching the floors. One by one, the masked intruders slipped and fell to the floor, none of them gracefully.

"Woof. You see that one dude?" Cliff asked, pointing to his monitor.

"Hope Stewart has a dental plan."

Before Bryce could reply, he saw Ronnie appeared in the corridor. She was carrying what looked like a rifle which she aimed at the closest of the intruders.

"Holy—"

Bryce stopped, almost gasping in horror until he realized Ronnie had grabbed a tactical stun gun from the weapons room. Each round was its own self-contained electroshock dart, packing enough energy in its single use cartridge to incapacitate a rampaging bull. The first man's body jolted with the charge coursing through his body before he fell back into the foam, but Ronnie was already taking aim at her next target. Bryce and Cliff watched as she dispatched the other three intruders within seconds.

"Ronnie," said Cliff. "That was…amazing."

Waving toward the closest camera, Ronnie said, "*Where are the others?*"

Cliff replied, "I've got an alarm on Sublevel Four. Someone's breached security measures there." On the screen, Ronnie was already running back the way she'd come.

"Wait a minute," said Bryce, beginning to feel uneasy. "Something's wrong. Cameras on Sublevel Four just went down. Stairwells, too."

Cliff swore something Bryce couldn't hear, then added, "They're all going. "I think they're on—"

"Onto us," Bryce finished before tapping his earpiece. "Jumper this is—Ronnie, we lost your visual. We can't see anything."

With his own headset, Cliff called out, "Ronnie, come in." He grimaced. "Nothing."

"Same here." Bryce pushed away from the server rack. "We've got to go."

His eyes narrowing, Cliff asked, "Go?"

"She might need help. Come on."

"And do what exactly?"

Bryce glared at his friend. "Dude, I don't *know*. We find a way to storage without being seen, we assess, and we improvise."

Cliff nodded. "Protocol 27."

"Protocol 27," said Bryce as they ran for the door.

RONNIE fought every step of the way as the two masked goons pulled her from the stairwell and into the storage level's main corridor. She came down here only occasionally, but she was familiar with the layout. The corridor branched off to two shorter aisles, but this was the level's main passage, flanked on each side by partitioned units such as those at a self-storage warehouse. Each door was large enough to allow forklifts and other vehicles and featured its own keypad, though Ronnie knew any door could be accessed remotely through the security system provided one had the proper authorization codes. None of the doors in this aisle were open, leading her to hope the intruders lacked that information.

The goon holding her right arm chose that moment to loosen his grip and Ronnie seized the opportunity. Yanking free, she lashed out and caught him in the throat with the edge of her hand. He coughed and sputtered, stumbling away as he reached for his neck, but Ronnie was already swinging toward his partner. Anticipating the attack, the other man blocked her before smacking her across the face. She forced herself to ignore the stinging pain, punching at his stomach. It was far from an effective blow but still enough to elicit a surprised grunt from the goon, who balled his fist and cocked his arm.

"Stop!"

The voice echoed in the corridor, freezing Ronnie and the goon in their tracks. Looking up the corridor, she saw the dark clad figure standing beneath one of the lights suspended from the ceiling: Harrison Stewart.

"Don't harm her," he said as the goon with the damaged throat moved toward her. "We may need her before we're done here."

The goon leaned close. "Don't think I'm not getting payback."

Without bothering to look at him, Ronnie replied, "Better bring your whole checkbook."

Stewart stepped closer. "Let's not waste any more time than your employer has already cost me. I'm here for what she took from me.

My only interest in you and any other minions crawling around here is what you can tell me about the woman who pays you. Please understand you can live or die, right here and now, and I won't care either way."

"She took something from you?" Even as she asked the question, the question rang hollow in Ronnie's ears. Stewart appeared equally unconvinced. Instead of replying, he removed his right hand from his jacket pocket, revealing a cellular phone.

"A tracking device installed within the lining of each of the containers the Wraith stole from me. You likely missed it because they weren't activated at that time." He waved the phone in the air before him as though gesturing toward the ceiling. They only have a short range, so it took my people time to search the city until they got close enough for their activation signal to work. From there, it was a simple process of elimination. Once we found you, the trackers acted as a signal booster for me to access your systems."

"Wait," said Ronnie. "So, *you* broke in?" She gave him a frank appraisal. "You don't strike me as a hacker."

Stewart chuckled. "My dear, I was infiltrating computer systems before you were born. Changing my grades in high school, accessing banks and siphoning funds to offshore banks, the usual amusements." His smile turned into a leer. "Don't even get me started on the Pentagon."

Pleased with himself, Stewart aimed the phone with great flourish toward one of the doors. "So, you see there's no point going through the usual denials. My people will see to the reclaiming of my product, after which you and I will begin what I imagine to be a very long conversation about your benefactor."

He pressed an icon on his phone and Ronnie heard the door's keypad click. At Stewart's direction one of the goon's reached for the door's handle, lifting so the door slid up its tracks and out of the way.

Inside, the storage unit was empty save for a pair of small blinking devices. Trackers. Along the compartment's rear wall, Ronnie noted the ventilation grate was missing.

*What the hell…?*

"Where is it?" Stewart clamored. "What hap—"

Bryce and Cliff appeared from either side of the doorway, covered in grime and looking like they had crawled through every chimney in the city. They held short-barreled tactical shotguns.

"Hey," said Cliff. "You're not the maid." Aiming the shotgun at the closest goon, he fired into the man's right leg. Only then did Ronnie realize the shotgun had to be loaded with flexible baton rounds. At such close range, the non-lethal "beanbag" packed enough punch to knock the goon's feet out from under him and he faceplanted on the floor.

Right behind him, Bryce turned and fired at the goon still guarding Ronnie. The beanbag slammed into the man's shoulder, spinning him around until he fell against another storage unit. Turning to look up the corridor, Ronnie saw Stewart running away and gestured toward Bryce.

"Gun!"

Bryce tossed her the shotgun and Ronnie snatched it. With an easy, practiced movement she pulled the weapon's stock into her shoulder and racked the slide. Taking aim at Stewart's back, she fired once and the round struck him between the shoulder blades, pushing him off balance and sending him sliding along the floor.

"Sweet," said Cliff.

Surveying the trio of immobilized bad guys, Ronnie returned the shotgun to Bryce. "Not that I'm complaining, but what the hell do you call that idea?"

"Protocol 88," replied Bryce. "*Die Hard.*"

"I thought it was *Home Alone.*" Cliff frowned. "Protocol 90."

Ronnie rolled her eyes. "Kill me now."

"*T*hat's some serious work very nicely done, you three."

The operations center's forward wall of video screens all linked to form a single giant image of the Wraith. As Ronnie expected, she still wore her black leather costume including a fabric mask concealing her entire head save for a pair of darkly mirrored lenses over her eyes. She'd removed the hooded cloak that completed the ensemble, and now reclined in one of the overstuffed recliners in her private jet's passenger cabin.

"Thanks, boss," said Bryce. "Definitely not what we planned for the evening."

With the assistance of one of the Wraith's trusted contacts within the police department, Harrison Stewart and his goons were now in custody along with the component for the binary drug and other evidence the Wraith had collected. The rest of it was on her plane and would be delivered upon her arrival.

Ronnie added, "We're just sorry it happened in the first place." She'd already begun a full diagnostic on the Bunker's systems to make sure Stewart left behind nothing of his hacking efforts. There would be a top-down review of everything inside the complex. Something like this wasn't going to happen again on her watch.

"Don't beat yourself up too much about it," said the Wraith. "Stewart is very good at what he does, but even I didn't think he'd ever manage something like this."

Ronnie gestured to Bryce and Cliff. "A lot of the credit goes to these two. I admit I thought you both were idiots at first, but I was completely wrong. If not

for you, Stewart would've gotten away with..." She remembered his threat. "With everything." She cleared her throat. "I have to ask: what in the world made you think to leave the trackers while you moved the drugs somewhere else?"

On the screen, the Wraith shifted to regard Bryce and Cliff. "Protocol 23?"

Bryce and Cliff pointed to the screen and in unison shouted, "Protocol 23!" before high fiving each other.

Unable to stifle a laugh, Ronnie shook her head. "You guys really need to give me a list."

# The First Dance

## By Aaron Rosenberg

**B**ELLE was standing by the rail, overseeing the transfer of goods when a shout shattered the calm sea air. "Cap'n!" It was Isaac Longstaff, up in the crow's nest on lookout. "Sails!"

"Where away?" she replied, already hoisting herself up onto the rigging and beginning to climb.

"Port and aft!" the lad replied, his voice cracking.

Scowling, Belle hooked one arm through the ropes halfway up, snatched up her spyglass, and yanked it open even as she raised it to one eye, squinting to focus where he was gesturing. Sure enough, a speck of white against the green and blue suddenly leapt into larger view, resolving into an array of sailcloth, all full near to bursting from the wind off the English shore. It was a good-sized ship, too, its three full masts and squared sails marking it as a frigate, which could only mean one thing. "Royal Navy!" she hollered, slamming the spyglass into her other hand to collapse it and then stuff it back into its leather holster at her belt as she half-shimmied, half-dropped back down to the deck. "Quince! Finish up and let's be gone!"

"Aye, aye, Cap'n!" her first mate responded, then turned to the rest of the crew still over on the merchant ship with him. "You heard, lads!" he bellowed. "Step lively, lest you're wanting to explain to the Navy why we're out here nicking these bales and barrels and crates!"

That jolt of fear added a kick to everyone's steps, and a short time later Quince and the others were leaping back across to the *Deadshot* and hauling the gangplank after them. The whole while, Belle had kept one eye on the proceedings and the other toward the shore, where that frigate had loomed larger with each passing second. It had just come hull up as they cast off lines and shoved away from the now-emptied merchant vessel, and she was able to make out its flag, with its tell-tale red cross quartering white and the Union Jack a splash of color in the upper left quadrant. The fact that she could make out the ensign with the naked eye meant her own flag—the Jolly Roger, but with crossed cannon rather than bones—must now be visible to the approaching ship as well. Bother. "Lay on the sailcloth!" she shouted. "Put our back to the wind and let's haul ass!"

The crew cheered and set to work with a will, no more eager

*Illustration by Jeff Weigel*

to face a sea court than her. It was a rare thing for "Cannon" Belle Pearcy to run from a fight, but this was one she knew she couldn't win—a standard frigate might have as many as forty cannon, though they could hold up to fifty, whereas the *Deadshot* with her dozen was still more heavily armed than most schooners. Nor were hers as heavy as the frigate's. But even with two sails to three, and riding low in the water from their fresh cargo, Belle's ship was the faster of the two, provided she had the wind on her side, and she was counting on that to get them all away safely.

The frigate was clearly making for them now, its prow aimed right at their stern, but as the minutes marched on Belle was relieved to see that it was no longer gaining. And then, little by little, it fell back, dwindling in size so slowly she worried that might only be wishful thinking. She was finally convinced when she could no longer make out the ensign's design, and then not even its colors. It was only once the frigate was again a mere spot on the ocean, though, that she turned to her crew and smiled.

"Well done, lads," she told them all. "I'm sure they thought they had us, but it'd take a sharper crew than that to catch us, eh?" They cheered. "Now let's make for home. We'll take the long way round, just to be sure, and then it's shore and celebration and

drinks for all!" That brought even more cheering, and the deck was a lively place as they tacked sail and brought the ship around in a long arc that would point them well away from where they'd found that merchant, and where the frigate might still be waiting.

One crew member was not whistling and singing and laughing, however, and he sidled up to her as she stood near Gregor at the wheel, his customary scowl upon his face. "First time we've seen a Naval vessel this close in," he commented, his long blond hair ruffling in the breeze. "Least since we chased that last one off."

"It is that," she agreed, not at all put off by his manner, for she knew Quince to be trustworthy as well as competent. Every captain should have a first mate willing to ask them the hard questions, if only to make sure they did not forget to ask those themselves. "Must be that one you mentioned, sent by London to track us down."

"Must be." He frowned, rubbing at his chin, which he kept scrupulously bare perhaps in defiance of the typical image of a bearded pirate. "What was his name again? I've clean forgot it."

*I have not,* Belle thought but did not say, for she saw no reason to tempt the fates by uttering it aloud. The name rang in her head, though, clear as a bell—or a warning trumpet.

BELLA stepped down out of the carriage and bit back a curse as her dress hem snagged on the runner, tangling about her legs and nearly spilling her out upon the muddy ground. Blazes, but she forgot how hard it was to move in all this fabric! Give her back her velvet trousers any day! If only she had not needed to come into town today, giving her a little time to get her land legs once more, but yet again her father had overspent and she was forced to meet with their solicitor to discuss the situation. She managed to keep from falling, but in doing so dropped her reticule. Damn and blast! She lurged forward, trying to catch it before it struck the dirt—or worse—and growled as the heavy velvet bag slipped through her fingers—

—only to watch a larger, more weathered hand catch it an inch above the ground.

"Oh!" She straightened to find a man rising to stand before her, the bag in his hands. And this was quite the man! Tall, broad-shouldered but trim-waisted, those attributes well-displayed by the fitted navy blue jacket with its gold edging hanging open over a white waistcoat and breeches, his dark hair tugged back beneath his bicorn to show off a strong, handsome face with noble features and dark eyes alight with interest. The hint of a smile tugged at his lips, and his bare cheeks were slightly weathered from sun and sea.

"I believe this to be yours, madam," he stated, presenting the bag with a slight bow. The single epaulet on his left shoulder proclaimed his identity as clearly as a card, yet Bella pretended not to know it, for they had not yet been introduced. Still, she smiled and curtseyed as she accepted the reticule back, her gloved hands almost but not quite brushing his bare ones.

"Thank you so much, kind sir," she told him, careful not to let herself simper, for she hated such behavior. She did reward him with a warm smile, however. "I do appreciate it."

He answered with a deeper bow, sweeping the hat off his head and revealing that his dark hair had a tendency to curl about the ears, which she struggled not to find charming. "Nicholas Reid, at your service, if I may be so bold."

"Isabella Parsons, a pleasure," she answered. Daniel had stepped out from behind the coach door to present himself at her side, a silent but visible chaperone, and Bella quickly introduced him as well. She was pleased to see that her new acquaintance did not behave as so many gentlemen would have, acknowledging the coachman with a nod but without a glance as he was not of their social class. Instead Reid turned and met Daniel's gaze and even offered his hand, which was accepted with some surprise.

"Are you new to the area, Captain?" Bella asked, and was quietly amused to see Reid frown and nearly sigh. "Only, I do not recall seeing you before."

"I am only lately arrived, yes," he returned gamely enough. "This past month or two, my crew and I have been quartered at the docks in Seamont." That was a smaller town only a short ride from Hillington but right on the water and thus the location of the region's Royal Naval barracks, which had been in disuse for as long as Bella could remember. "And it is only Commander, I am afraid," he could not resist adding, though he at least managed to do so without visible rancor.

"Oh, I apologize!" she said, pressing a hand to her mouth and not missing the way his eyes followed that gesture, lingering a moment there before flashing up to her eyes and then away. Well, now! "But surely you must come to the ball tomorrow night!" she urged. "It is here in town at Barrage Hall, of course, as all our simple country entertainments are. There you will have a chance to meet all your new neighbors—and I daresay you will garner much attention, both for your novelty and for the smartness of your uniform."

He laughed. "It is good to know what qualities I have to offer," he said, his eyes lively and that hint of a smile tugging at those lips again. This man was dangerous! Especially since he followed that with a tilt of his head and added, "I hope that, if you are also in attendance, as you seem to be suggesting might

be the case, you will reserve for me at least one dance?"

How could she respond to that but to nod and say, "It would be my pleasure, Commander."

"Excellent!" His smile broadened and he offered a final bow before clapping his hat back onto his head. "Until tomorrow eve, then." He turned on his heel and was gone, long, strong strides carrying him down the street without haste but still at a good, steady clip.

Bella watched him go, admiring the way his figure filled out the back of those breeches. Dangerous, indeed!

BELLA had barely stepped through the doors of Barrage Hall when she was accosted—but not by a tall figure in Navy blue. Rather, it was a shorter, softer form swathed in peach and topped with dark curls who rushed her so close her first instinct was to reach for her cutlass. Good thing she had come to the ball unarmed, or she might have run her dearest friend through before realizing it!

"Isabella, there you are!" Abigail engulfed her in a quick hug, her head only reaching Bella's shoulder, then stepped back to study her at arm's length. "Let me look at you! I do declare, it is utterly unacceptable—you grow more lovely every time you go away!"

Bella laughed. "That is only your own fondness coloring your perceptions," she replied. "But I thank you for it." There were others trying to enter behind her so she moved off to one side, Abigail gliding along beside her. Together they sought out a pair of seats with a good view of the floor, not so close to refreshments as to risk being spilled upon but not so far away as to make resupplying a chore, and with an easy avenue of escape if someone unpleasant approached. *Listen to me*, Bella thought, biting back a laugh. *I'm approaching a ball as if it were a naval engagement!* Still, the two certainly had their commonalities.

Not the least of which was the officer now descending upon them, his path as unwavering as his ship had been mere days before.

"Miss Parsons," he proclaimed, sweeping into a deep, formal bow. "I am happy to see you are a woman of your word. And I do not believe I have had the pleasure of meeting your charming companion?" Though he was alone, here in the presence of so many onlookers it was allowed to introduce oneself to a young lady without being thought reprehensible or, worse, ill-mannered.

"Commander Reid, may I introduce Miss Abigail Montrose," Bella replied. "Abigail, this is Commander Nicholas Reid of His Majesty's Royal Navy."

"Delighted, Miss Montrose," Reid told her, bowing over her hand, but his eyes immediately returned to Bella's. "Miss Parsons, I believe I was promised a dance

tonight. Might I be so bold as to lay claim to it now, before you are no doubt assailed by others demanding your attention?"

She laughed and rose to her feet, setting her reticule on the seat to hold her place. "How could I refuse such a noble and considerate offer, Commander?" She turned to Abigail. "I hope you will excuse me for a moment, Abigail."

Her best friend feigned a pout, though her eyes sparkled. "I will be forlorn, of course," Abigail sniffed, "but somehow I shall endure." She winked. "Especially if you return with punch."

"Consider it done." Bella let Commander Reid lead the way out to the floor, her hand resting lightly upon his, and then turned to face him as they settled in among the many other pairs assembling for the first dance of the evening. "Are you always so daring, sir?" she asked as the music began and they stepped toward and around each other, twirling in time, their hands still held gently between them, connecting them yet also maintaining the proper distance required by decorum.

"When I have an objective in sight, certainly," he replied with a small grin. "I hope you will forgive me my forwardness. I am a military man, and accustomed to the need for swift and decisive action."

"There are many who would say such behavior was antithetical to social niceties," she pointed out, able to focus her attention on him as her body went through the familiar steps of the dance all on its own. It did not surprise her at all that the commander was light and sure on his feet, his steps graceful and smooth. She suspected he would be deadly with a blade, especially with the way his eyes remained focused on her face the whole time, sharp and intent.

"And are you one of those?" he asked now. "For if so, I will endeavor to moderate my behavior."

That drew a laugh from her, and his own smile broadened, his eyes crinkling in pleasure. "Am I? Not at all! No, I applaud anyone who knows what they want, what they must do, and sets their sights on achieving it." As she had done when she had made the rather strange decision to turn to piracy. Not that she'd had a choice at the time! It had literally been "do or die" then, or at least "do or be ravished or ransomed or some other horrendous fate," and she had determined to accept none of those. Instead she had laid her own course, unconventional as it might be, and had turned what could have been a torment into a triumph.

Commander Reid was studying her, and Bella realized with a start that her chin had risen and her lips had firmed into a thin line. She forced herself back to the present, back to Barrage Hall and the ball, and back to her previous smile. "How are you finding Hillington and its environs?" she asked as

sweetly—and demurely—as she could manage.

A rapid blink of the eye was the only indication that he had noticed her sudden shift. "Most agreeable," he answered easily, bowing as the dance ended and they returned to their starting positions. "Especially the company."

"You flatter me, good sir," she told him, curtseying. "Thank you most kindly for the dance. Now I believe I promised my friend refreshments as recompense for abandoning her."

"Well, we cannot have you go back on your promise," he stated, and offered her his arm. "Would you permit me to accompany you?"

"Of course." Together they quit the floor, allowing other couples to take their place, and headed back toward the edge of the room, veering away from where Abigail waited and angling toward the nearest refreshment table instead. There Bella's companion insisted upon pouring two crystal cups full of punch and then carrying them as they returned to their seats, where he presented one to an appreciative Abigail.

"But you did not get one for yourself!" she pointed out. "You must rectify that, and then join us!"

"It would be my honor," the commander stated, bowing. "I shall return momentarily."

No sooner had he stepped out of earshot than Abigail turned to

Bella, eyes sharp as a hawk's but smile bright as the sun. "Spill, my dear," her friend whispered. "Do we like the handsome Commander? Because you certainly seemed all smiles just now, and he could barely tear his eyes away from you! Trust me, the room is already abuzz about it!"

Yes, Bella had felt some of those eyes upon her as they had danced, and not all of them as friendly as Abigail's. Hillington was not a large community, and thus there was a dearth of eligible young men to be had. For her to have already claimed some attention from the newest—and most appealing—would seem a coup to many, and an injustice to others. For now she merely allowed herself a small, smug smile. "He is acceptable thus far."

"Acceptable!" Abigail swatted her friend's shoulder with her closed fan. "If that is all, step aside and allow me to take a turn! I'm sure he'll be far more than *acceptable* to me!" She was laughing as she said it, but Bella knew there was some truth behind the jest as well. Which was why, when the commander returned, she favored him with an expression of feigned concern.

"Abigail was just lamenting the lack of suitable dance partners," she informed him after giving him barely enough time to take a sip from his cup. "And I believe I hear the musicians gearing up for the next dance."

Her hint was not subtle, nor was he slow to apprehend—or to rise to the occasion. "Then perhaps, Miss Montrose, you would allow me the pleasure of this dance?" he told a beaming Abigail, handing his mostly untouched cup to a passing manservant and bowing to her as he offered his hand. The dip of his head to Bella, however, made it clear that this was being done more as a favor to her than out of real interest on his part, and she acknowledged that with a nod and a smile a touch warmer than she had originally intended.

The two departed for the dance and Bella watched them go, though her mind quickly wandered. She exchanged polite greetings with other neighbors and acquaintances as they strolled by, pleased at least to not have to deal with the Tremont sisters, who were away visiting an elderly relative for a fortnight. There was no question that Barrage Hall was pleasant, with its high ceilings lit by glittering chandeliers and its tall windows framed by lacy curtains and its vast rooms filled with happy, laughing people. Yet Bella found her heart yearned for the salt tang of the sea and the wide open space of the glittering blue water, and the gentle roll of the *Deadshot*'s deck beneath her feet. At least she had re-acclimated to dry land! It would have been terribly embarrassing to have tripped over her own feet during the dance because she was still adjusting her footing to the imagined sway of deck at high tide!

When Abigail returned after the dance, she was alone—and fuming. "That Penelope Sinclair!" she declared, flopping down in her seat. "Can you believe the nerve! The dance had only just ended— the music still hung in the air!— when she declared, loudly, 'Oh, if only I had someone to dance with! But all the good men are spoken for, or else not willing to attend me!' So of course your dashing Commander—"

"He is hardly *my* anything," Bella interrupted, only to be tutted at as if by a spinster aunt.

"Oh, I think he is, Isabella," her friend confided, her dimple showing as she smiled. "He might have been dancing with me, but I am not blind—I saw how it was done for your approval and nothing more." She pouted, though only for an instant, for Abigail never could hold anger for long. It was one of the things Bella treasured about her. "I would be severely put out if I did not love you so." This was accompanied by a fond pat to her hand. "So, anyway, your dashing Commander of course immediately offered his services— though he made sure to glance my way for permission first. And"— she lowered her voice even more, as if they were discussing deep secrets rather than ball gossip— "he bade me request that you reserve the last dance for him."

Bella smiled at that, despite herself. First *and* last dance! Partiality indeed! "Then he shall have it," she declared, and raised her cup to toast and seal the matter. Abigail giggled and did likewise, and the two of them settled back in to people-watch and gossip and poke gentle fun at their peers, which was often far more fun than the dancing itself.

"YOU have been rather popular this evening," Bella said as she faced "her" commander once more. It was the final dance of the evening, and he had indeed made good on his request, appearing beside her to offer his hand.

"I apologize," he told her, with a quick grimace that vanished almost as soon as it had appeared. "Such was not my intent." He glanced about them before leaning in and adding, in a softer tone, "I had not realized there would be so many ladies in desperate need of a dance partner."

"Oh, yes, you have landed in a veritable garden of unwed young women," she answered with a smile. "We are all of us available, and thus all desperate to find a good man."

That earned her a calculating gaze whose frankness made her flush slightly. "You do not strike me as desperate at all," he told her as the music began and they fell into step. "Quite the contrary. You seem very self-possessed, as if you could take or leave such things. Which," he added, smiling, "I find extraordinarily appealing."

"Do you now?" Bella laughed. "That is good to know, for it is true that I have been said to be head-strong and proud. 'Accustomed to having my own way,' is I believe the popular term." She swept around him, her skirts swishing to the motion, and he matched her step by step.

"I have yet to see any pride beyond what must be considered justified," he responded. "Nor have you seemed headstrong, only confident." He grinned, and the expression made his eyes crinkle again. "But we have only just met."

"Indeed." Bella grinned in return. "And yet I feel a bout of such willfulness coming on."

She deliberately increased her pace, still keeping her general motions in time to the music but upping her own tempo, adding an extra step, an extra twirl. Reid raised an eyebrow but echoed her, staying in time with her move-ments. They were still in their place in line, yet Bella saw some of the other dancers looking their way, and a few faltered as they muddled their own steps, unsure if they should be pacing her or the music or both.

That only urged her on. She sped up yet again, now stepping twice to the other pairs' once, twirling in between, and yet still Reid kept up. Good. She liked a challenge.

Dancing was normally warm-ing, under all the layers and lights.

Now she was positively aglow, her skin damp from perspiration, only the recent shortening of her curls preventing them from becoming a sticky mass atop her head. Yet Bella felt more alive than she had all night, and she laughed aloud as they spun together, her and Reid, out of synch and yet still in step with those around them. That felt like her whole life described right there, outwardly still in line but inwardly moving to her own beat, refusing to be constrained by the rest yet somehow still fitting in, and she was flushed but grinning when the music finally ended and they came to a stop, her heart beating wildly as she curtsied to her partner.

Commander Reid was breath-ing heavily as well, and his face was shiny with sweat, but his eyes were alive and still dancing as he bowed. "A fine, spirited way to end the ball," he told her, offer-ing his arm to escort her back to where Abigail waited. "Thank you, Miss Parsons, for a most pleasant evening, and a welcome relief from the norm."

"Thank you, Commander Reid," she replied as they reached her friend and disengaged. "Some-times, you simply have to let the lady lead." She could already see from Abigail's expression—half shock and half glee—that the gossiping had also accelerated to reflect her own feverish pace. "I fear I must now bid you good night."

"Of course." He bowed to them both, then turned and disappeared back into the crowd, which was already beginning to disperse. He did not do so with the haste of a man trying to distance himself from a dangerous reputation, at least not to Bella's eye, but who could be sure? Only time would tell.

For now, she patted Abigail on the arm. "Come, we will find our coaches," she suggested, leading the way toward the door and enjoying how the crowd parted for her, much like the sea before her ship's prow. "Best to depart now, so they can talk about me in peace."

ABIGAIL was still laughing about it the next morning. "La, the whole room practically erupted!" she crowed, accepting the cup of tea Bella had poured her and stealing one of the small sandwiches Margaret had prepared exactly how she liked them. Bella had invited her friend over for morning tea and they were comfortably ensconced in the sitting room, just the pair of them. "Dame Sarah was near to apoplexy! 'Does she imagine this to be a race?' I heard her say. 'Men are not interested in women who can outpace them!'" She tittered as she imitated the county's most venerable—and most crotchety—widow, her brown curls dancing about her head.

Bella laughed as well, eschewing the sandwiches in favor of a small apricot tart. "Yes, well, who says women are interested in slow men?" she retorted, making her friend quake with laughter. But she shook her head. "Ah, Abigail, I fear I am becoming a bad influence on you," she warned. "You should take care lest my bad reputation rub off on you." She said that only half in jest, for in truth she worried about her effect on her friend, and not just from her behavior at the ball. What if her other identity, her occupation, were to be somehow revealed? Would Abigail be censured as well, for their close association? Bella hoped not. Though of course she hoped never to get discovered for her own sake as well.

"Pah, as if I care what those old fusspots have to say!" Abigail protested. She grinned. "Besides, while they might have been scandalized I heard a few closer to our age say they admired your spirit—and more than one gentleman mutter that he'd be happy to have a go at keeping up with you!"

"Hmph. They can but try." There was only one gentleman whose opinion Bella was concerned about at the moment. She suspected it would be some days before she knew whether he had in truth been as unaffected by her behavior as he'd claimed, and cursed herself for caring so much.

Still, her heart skipped a beat when, after a discreet knock, Geoffrey entered. The family butler was carrying a silver tray, the worked metal circle all but disappearing beneath his enormous hands, and on the tray was a single letter, addressed to her.

"Ooh, mysterious!" Abigail declared, rising from her seat to plop down beside Bella instead as she accepted the small, tidily addressed missive. "Who is it from, and what do they say?"

Bella unfolded it and read aloud, for she had only one secret she kept from her closest friend. "My dear Miss Parsons," she began. "I hope you do not consider me overbold in stating again how much I enjoyed your company last night. Never have I had a dance so invigorating, and only partially from the pace. If it pleases you, I would very much like to call upon you and your father at some point in the near future. Yours cordially and with great spirit, Nicholas Reid, Commander."

"Oh, very nice!" her friend stated after the recitation was done. "Not at all afraid to tell you he likes you, that's certain! And 'you and your father'—he's been asking after you! Considerate, too—if your father is present, there's no question of impropriety." She tapped Bella on the arm with her fan. "*He*'s up for a little racing, hey?"

Bella laughed. "Now I *know* I am rubbing off on you," she said, "for surely you were never so coarse before." But she found she was beaming, too. Yes, there was no question of his interest, and she

had to admit that she returned it in full. But how much more complicated that made everything!

Still, where was the fun in life without a few complications?

THE letter—and its reply, which she had sent that afternoon, returning the compliment about their time together and extending an invitation to dine with her and father a week hence—was still on Belle's mind two days later, only gone now were cushions and tea sandwiches and Empire dresses, replaced by oiled wooden railings and hard tack and trousers. Though she missed Abigail's sunny company, Belle had to admit she preferred the scenery here on the *Deadshot*'s deck—especially now, with a fat merchant ship floundering in their sights.

"Ahoy, the ship!" she heard Quince shout as they pulled up alongside the *Mother of Pearl*, their warning shot having snuffed out any fight the poor traders and sailors might have possessed. "Stand down and prepare to be boarded, or suffer the consequences!"

A tall, skinny man with a high forehead and a long face, presumably the captain, stomped over to the railing, hands raised to show them empty. "We surrender," he called back. "We offer no resistance, and ask only for mercy."

"And mercy ye shall have," Belle announced, wrapping one hand around a line and swinging up onto the railing to face her fellow captain across the narrow gap. "Behave, do as you're told, and you'll all be free to go soon enough, and unharmed."

The captain nodded and gestured his men back as the grappling lines were tossed across and made fast. The gangplank followed, and soon her crew was over and beginning to haul goods up from the hold.

They had only brought a handful of items across, however, when Belle heard the cry she'd been half-expecting. "Sails!" shouted Isaac from the crow's nest. "Three-master, to starboard!" That was out at sea, and she cursed as she yanked free her spyglass and scanned the horizon. There! It was a frigate, sure enough, and she did not think it her imagination that its ensign was white quartered by red. Damn! How had he found her again, and so quickly!

Quince was already hurrying up to join her near the rail. "It's that commander again, has to be," he agreed to her unspoken question. "And this time he's got the wind at his back, driving him on. No chance to outrun him, or dart past toward the open water. We'll have to go shoreward, but he'll be here afore we can get safely away, even if we cut ties now."

Her first mate had already turned and taken a deep breath, preparing to give that order, when Belle stopped him. "No," she said, her mind racing. "You're right, we can't outrun him, not this time.

So we'll outthink him instead." Quickly she outlined what she had in mind, and Quince's sour face split into a rare smile.

"Aye, that might do the trick," he said. "And if not, well, at least we'll have given it a rum go!" Then he was leaping over to the *Mother of Pearl*, calling the rest of their men over there to him as he went. Belle grinned and turned her attention to the merchant captain, who had since identified himself as one Alan Brava and who was watching the commotion with a bemused look upon his long face. "I must beg your patience a while longer, good sir," she told him, making sure her voice carried across the water. "But I assure you, we still intend to leave you and yours in peace—only a little later than originally planned."

That seemed to satisfy Brava, at least, for he did not interfere as Quince took command of the other ship's wheel and the men scaled the riggings and began playing out the sails. A handful of others continued the work of unloading, only now they were doing so across two moving vessels instead of two anchored ones. The two ships ground against each other, scraping both hulls, but thanks to echoed commands they were able to keep both sails trimmed to match, and though the lines strained, they held.

The *Mother of Pearl* was not a particularly fast ship—which was how the *Deadshot* had caught her in the first place—and so even at her swiftest pace they had not advanced far before the frigate pulled up within hail on the merchant's far side. "Ahoy!" came the shout from that vessel, in a voice Belle had already begun to know well. "This is Commander Reid of His Majesty's *Diligent*. Yield the ship and surrender yourself for judgment!"

"No thanks!" Belle shouted back, perching high up on the *Deadshot*'s rail so that she could make out Reid on his own deck beyond the *Mother of Pearl*'s She took care to keep her voice as deep and rough as possible, and was glad the wind was strong enough to send her black braid whipping about her head. They were near enough that she saw his eyes narrow in recognition, but trusted that it was merely the famed pirate Cannon Belle he saw, and not his recent dance partner.

He seemed surprised by her open defiance. "Surrender," he insisted again. "Or—"

"Or what?" she retorted. "You'll open fire through innocents? I think not."

When he visibly fumed she threw her head back and laughed. It had worked! She had thought that a Naval man, and especially one as honorable as Reid, would not be willing to fire upon a civilian ship. Which was why, rather than doing the expected and cutting their target loose so they could run, she had instead ordered the *Mother of Pearl* hauled in close. The two ships were sailing as one now—and as long as they continued this way, with the *Diligent* on their far side, the merchant acted as a shield, keeping the *Deadshot* safe.

"I ask you to reconsider putting these good people in harm's way," Reid tried again, clearly exasperated by this strange turn of events. "It is highly dishonorable."

"More or less so than piracy?" Belle countered. "And I am not putting them in harm's way, for I am not the one threatening them. You are."

That caused "her commander" to jam his bicorn down more firmly on his head and turn away from her to spit orders to his crew. A moment later, the *Diligent* let her sails fill again and the frigate leaped forward, racing ahead of the paired ships.

Her crew cheered at this, but Belle silenced them with a gesture. "We've not won free yet, lads," she warned. "That was just the first step. There's more to come."

Sure enough, the *Diligent* heeled about, jibing to swing wide and circle around in front of them so that it could approach the *Deadshot* from its unprotected side. The frigate's square rigging was not ideal for such maneuvers, however, and it was going from windward to leeward, making such a turn a slow and cumbersome process.

At the same time, Belle signaled Quince, who nodded and swung the rudder over a notch, Gregor matching him so the *Deadshot* and the *Mother of Pearl* both jibed as well, wearing ship to angle farther toward the shore. This forced the *Diligent* to widen its arc, lest the paired bowsprits pierce it broadsides before it could complete the turn.

But while the *Diligent* was describing a wide arc, the *Deadshot* and the *Mother of Pearl* were executing a much tighter circle, using the *Deadshot*'s hastily dropped anchor to help hold them in place as they wheeled about together. It did not hurt that even the *Mother of Pearl* was smaller than the frigate now trying to loop around them.

Still, Belle held her breath, gauging her own ship's position and speed against that of the frigate. She had the weather gauge but it would be a near thing indeed.

At last the *Diligent* completed her semi-circle. Now she was facing them and on their shoreward side. But the frigate soon discovered that it had another problem, or at least the same problem as before—thanks to her own maneuvering, Belle had kept the *Mother of Pearl* between herself and the Reid's vessel. All three ships were now more or less in a row and facing into the wind, with the *Deadshot* on the seaward side and the *Diligent* caught between the merchant ship and land.

That, of course, was what Belle had been hoping for. Of course, if she ran the frigate would give

chase—except she had a plan for that as well. "Now!" she shouted. Quince and the boys leaped back across, tossing the grappling lines over first and tugging the gangplank after. Then Gregor spun the wheel and the *Deadshot* turned, falling behind its two escorts as its sails no longer caught the wind— and then tacking hard across the wind, toward the shore.

Which ran the pirate ship straight behind the backside of the frigate that had been pursuing it.

Quince glanced her way, a question evident on his sour face, but Belle shook her head. Even with their smaller guns a solid broadside from them now, straight up the *Diligent*'s unprotected stern, would devastate the Naval vessel. She could not bring herself to do it, however, and told herself it had nothing to do with Reid being aboard the ship. No, she just didn't believe in butchery, or unnecessary violence. Yes, that was the only reason.

As they passed behind the frigate she saw her helmsman haul on the wheel, trying to bring the *Diligent* about, and tensed. If they managed the turn they'd be in a position to fire a full broadside at the *Deadshot*, and at this range there was no way they would survive such an onslaught.

But the *Diligent* had been too focused on her prey. She had not paid attention to other details—like how close they'd drifted to shore, or the depth of water. Belle winced instinctively when she heard the crunch of a hull grinding against sand and rock, but then had to repress the urge to cheer. This was why she'd angled them so close to shore. She'd known there were shallows laying in wait here.

A pity Reid had not.

With its shallower keel, the *Deadshot* skipped easily across those same shallows, gliding past the *Diligent* close enough they could almost touch. The marines rushed to the stern and opened fire with their muskets, and their commanding officer followed behind, claiming a space along the taffrail. Despite the hail of bullets Belle hopped up on the rail and grinned as she passed Reid, who had the decency to call to his men, "Belay firing!" Then, as the firing ceased, he tipped his hat. "Well played, madam," he called out. "Your reputation for boldness is well deserved."

"You are too kind, commander,"

she shouted back, and swept off her hat in a bow—though carefully, so that her long black wig remained in place. "Thank you for the dance!" Then they were clear and the *Deadshot* continued on, leaving the *Mother of Pearl* to slowly correct its course and the *Diligent* to carefully kedge off the shoal, using small anchors on boats to pull itself out of the shallows and back to deeper waters.

The crew all let out a cheer then. "Here's to Cannon Belle," Quince shouted. "Cleverest captain in all the Atlantic!"

Belle bowed and spun about. "Thanks, boys!" she told them all. "Now let's be off before the good commander comes looking for another round!"

There'll be time enough for that, she told herself. After all, Reid had made it clear he was up for a race. And as long as he let her lead, she was optimistic about her odds of coming in first.

# *Quake*

## *By* PAIGE DANIELS

SHE swore that only Armageddon itself would see her back at this place. As she surveyed the ruins strewn around her, she figured this was close enough. In the early hours of April 18th 1906 a violent quake hit San Francisco and in a matter of minutes the city that served as Molly Maloy's childhood home was reduced to rubble and flame. Molly thought of how she remembered her home. The Queen of West, a vibrant humming metropolis brimming with life and activity. But now it stood in flames and rubble in stark contrast from the royalty it once was.

Molly strolled along the streets; heart heavy. She came here to check on her mother after hearing about the quake, but her mother would not see her. Molly's mother's caretakers told Molly that her mother was given to foul moods, forgetful spells, and bouts of malaise. This was not the Mary Malcy who could charm the most elite of San Francisco socialites with her conversation, who would had enough energy to plan fund raisers and cotillions. Molly knew her mother was in the evening of her life, and she hoped she could patch things with her. But she knew it would not be the way of things.

Molly shook those thoughts from her head and focused on the scene before her. There wasn't a building in sight that didn't suffer from some sort of damage. It was truly hell on earth. However, for all the carnage the community did seem to be in good spirits. Most were optimistic about their future. They were confident they could rebuild and start again. The streets were bustling with people cleaning, building, and generally trying to get their lives back together.

As Molly made a turn down Grant Avenue, the memories started to flood back. Chinatown. This is where her brother met his end and her life changed forever. Henry was the best of her whole family. He was handsome, smart, charming, and genuinely friendly. Most thought of her of as a strange chubby redhead with her nose permanently affixed to a book. Henry encouraged her imagination and never once made her feel as though she was strange. Part of her died when Henry died. On the night Henry passed, she came to Chinatown to prove that he was murdered for uncovering a land grab scheme by Michael Murphy, an esteemed businessman in the city, and not by the poor Chinese woman implicated for his death. Although she was unsuccessful,

*Illustration by Peter Krause*

that night she met someone who changed her life forever.

Reality and her thoughts collided; she could hardly believe what was before her eyes. It couldn't be. She walked closer to a group of men who seemed to be in a heated debate. The closer she got the more confident she grew.

"Bo? I mean, Mr. Fan. Is that you?"

A man with a kind round face turned and narrowed his eyes at her. His skin was darker and lined since she saw him last and his jet black hair was speckled with gray, but it was the eyes. They were dark and welcoming. That same boy who tried to help her two decades ago to find her brother's real killer and prove his mother's innocence.

The man smiled politely and sauntered over to her cane in hand. "I beg your pardon, ma'am, you seem to know me but I don't have the pleasure of making your acquaintance."

"It's me, Molly." Her stomach sunk thinking that she just made a fool of herself. How could he possibly remember her? It was just one night they had together. She cleared her throat. "I'm sorry, sir. I didn't mean to interrupt your conversation. I'll be on my way."

As she walked away, a hand gently touched her shoulder. "How could I forget you?" He asked as a smile came over his face. He turned to the crowd of men and spoke something in what Molly assumed was Chinese then lead her a few feet away.

Molly returned his smile. "What are you doing here, Bo? I thought they made you and your mother go to China."

"My mother died a few years after we went to China."

"Oh my, I'm ever so sorry," Molly gasped.

"That was many years ago. I never did grow accustomed to life there. San Francisco is my home. So I came back and they couldn't stop me because I was born here and never charged with crime. When I came back, I found out that you had left. Why did you come back?"

"My mother isn't well. I have paid caretakers to look after her, but with all of this," she said with a flourish of her hands, "I felt I needed to come back and look in on her myself."

"How long will you be staying?"

"I'm afraid not terribly long. My mother does not care for me." Molly's mouth drew down and she sighed. "I knew that my mother never approved of me, but hoped that maybe we could put our differences aside. I'm afraid that mother is more concerned with holding on to past wrongs rather than mending the present. As soon as I can find passage out of here, I will be leaving."

Voices from the crowd of men broke through their conversation. Bo turned and said something unintelligible to Molly that almost sounded like he was telling the men to be patient. Molly narrowed her eyes. "Is everything okay?"

"No, it is not. There has been a group of town officials that have been trying for years to move Chinatown to the outskirts of town. Mind you, they don't want to move out of San Francisco—"

Molly finished his thought. "Heaven sakes no, how would they still make money off you then?"

"You are bright one, Miss Maloy," Bo said with a chuckle. He continued, "You're correct they want to move us to the mud flats at the southern edge of the city. Still in the city to get revenue from us, but far enough away that they don't have to look at us."

"That is reprehensible. What are you going to do?"

"We have a plan." His face fell and he continued, "At least we had a plan. Mr. Eli Tin Look is a venerable business man here. He established a bank that allowed me and many other of these people to grow very successful businesses. Everything was set for an agreement to be signed with Chinese governmental backers, the Chinese Consolidated Benevolent Association, and even some of the white business men in town to rebuild Chinatown better than it has ever been."

"That is wonderful!" Molly looked at Bo then his group off in the distance. "But something happened, didn't it?"

"Yes, Mr. Look has gone missing. There is a big ceremonial signing of this agreement later tonight. While everything could be okay if he doesn't show, it will not instill much confidence of the backers if Mr. Look doesn't show up to the very deal that he created." Bo shifted nervously, "I would love to talk with you much longer, but I have to figure out what we are going to do about this."

"Yes, yes, I agree. This is a troublesome situation you have found yourself in. It was good seeing you."

Bo nodded. "Yes, you too."

As Molly turned to go, the wheels in her brain started to churn and a smile crept on her face. She yelled, "Unless, you would like to solve another mystery together...for old time's sake."

Bo stopped dead in his tracks and turned to face Molly. "You don't mean...?"

"Of course. Let your group ruminate on how to save face if Mr. Look isn't able to make the ceremony. We will concentrate on finding him."

"It does sound like fun, but I have responsibilities here and I am much too old to do these kind of things," He said holding his cane as if emphasizing his point.

Molly waved her hand. "Balderdash! You look like you are in very good health. You're only too old if you think you are." She gestured to the group of men and said, "How many men does it really take to think of strategy to cover your conundrum? We will find Mr. Look and have him back before the ceremony."

Bo shook his head and laughed. "How can I say no to that? Let's go solve a mystery."

AFTER a long discussion with the group of business men Molly and Bo finally were on their way. Molly looked over at Bo and he made his way quickly through the disheveled streets. She didn't know Bo's exact age, but she figured he had to be close to her age, mid-forties. Despite this, he was hardly winded as he made his way through difficult territory of the street his cane didn't even seem to impede him much. His tailored suit told the tale of his success of as a businessman. She shook her head before her mind wondered to more inappropriate areas.

Molly focused on the task at hand and asked, "Where are we going, Mr. Fan?"

"Just a few blocks ahead is Mr. Look's house. I thought we could start there by asking his wife some questions."

"Has no one questioned her?"

"No, that was actually our next step. I told our group that I would take on this task. We'll see where this leads us and go from there."

After a few minutes of walking, they happened on tent with a woman whose eyes were filled with worry and fear. When she saw Bo her face relaxed a bit into a sad smile. She bowed her head slightly and said, "Mr. Fan, thank you for coming," her questioning eyes met Molly's. "And I do not believe we have met."

Molly extended a hand. "Molly Maloy, pleased to meet you. Mr. Fan and I are old friends and I

have agreed to help him find out what happened to your husband. Can you tell us the last thing you remember?"

Mrs. Look's eyes knitted in worry. "They barged into our tent," she said pointing to her makeshift house. She took a deep breath and continued, "They grabbed him and said if I screamed they would hurt our children."

Bo patted her shoulder and said quietly, "Did they say what they wanted?"

She shook her head. "No, they just said that if we did as we were told then no one would get hurt."

Bo asked almost in a whisper, "Can you tell us what they looked like?"

She shook her head. "No, it was dark and they were masked. They just blended into the night. I don't know if I will see him again."

Molly gave Mrs. Look a reassuring smile then asked, "Do you mind if I look around your tent, ma'am?"

Not waiting for an answer Molly was off. She crouched down in the dirt looking over every square inch, careful not to miss minute details. She stopped when she found something and waived her friend and Mrs. Look over. She pointed at few boot prints. "See here, there appears to be two of them by the boot prints. One is rather large. The other is not as big. Also, from the tread I can tell these are worn workmen's boots. The men who took your husband are most definitely under the employ of someone, if they did not give you monetary demands up front." Molly stood and brushed off her skirt. Both Bo and Mrs. Look stared at her in amazement. Molly cleared her throat. "Solving mysteries is a bit of a hobby of mine. If my gut is right, I do believe that your husband will not be harmed. He is worth far more alive than dead. But it seems that someone wants their cake and eat it too."

"What do you mean?" Bo asked.

"What if they could put doubt in the minds' of the backers, especially the white business men, as to Mr. Look's capabilities to implement his plan. If you lose backers, then you'll be pushed to the outskirts of town and they get their prime real estate. But with Mr. Look still alive, you will certainly still be prosperous. So they get the prime real estate and all the revenue—"

Before she could finish she was cut off by a gruff familiar voice. "Molly Maloy. What on earth could have brought you here?"

Molly took a deep breath and gnashed her teeth. She let the breath out in clipped measures so as not to say anything regrettable to Mr. Michael Murphy. "When I heard of the disaster, I wanted to check on Mother right away."

Michael gave Bo the once over and then took Molly by the elbow. "Come, dear, I am sure your mother is worried sick about you and you don't need to keep company such as—" he stopped mid-sentences and glared at Bo. "You, you're the boy who stole away with

Molly years ago. Didn't we ship you back to your country?"

"No, sir, this is my country. You shipped me to China which is not my country," Bo said with practiced calm.

Bo's face had no trace of anger. On the other hand, Michael's red face betrayed his aggravation. He yanked on Molly's elbow as he said, "Come now, dear. The people will talk more than they already do."

In that instant Molly felt small like she was that insignificant teenager again. Then the feelings of inadequacy turned to anger that burned bright in her belly. She yanked her arm free and glared at Michael. "Thank you kindly for your offer, Mr. Murphy, but I am just fine with Mr. Fan." Bo gave a half smile and offered his elbow to Molly and she took it and they strolled down the street.

AS soon as Michael Murphy was out of sight Molly giggled despite herself and put a hand to her mouth. "I haven't felt that free in years. It will probably be the closest I come to telling that man what I really think of him." She laughed again and glanced at Bo who seemed to be deep in thought. "I'm sorry, Mr. Fan. I know we have far more pressing issues to think of than an old grudge, but Mr. Murphy has been a thorn in my side for years. I just wish we could bring him to justice many years ago."

Bo nodded. "It probably would not come as a surprise to you that he is one of the biggest proponents of moving Chinatown."

Molly folded her arms and shook her head. "Very greedy that one. I don't know why—" she paused and held her breath for two heartbeats. "Oh, my stars. It was Michael Murphy."

Bo narrowed his eyes. "What do you mean?"

"You said it yourself that he's a leading proponent for moving Chinatown. It's him, it has to be, he has the most to gain."

Bo paced in the street. He stopped and ran his hands through his hair. "Then we are at his mercy. There is no one in Chinatown with the clout that Mr. Murphy has."

"Fiddlesticks! Our goal is to find Mr. Look. If we can implicate Mr. Murphy that would be ideal, but not required. I need to think where he would hide Mr. Look." She paced and mumbled under her breath of all the scenarios that she could think of then she stopped in her tracks. "My father's mine!"

"I'm not following, Miss Maloy."

"My father's mine went barren a number of years ago. Michael Murphy knows nobody goes there. He would not risk holding Mr. Look in town. No one would go to the mine, they're too busy here to go to there. It's just an hour's ride from town. I'm sure of it, Mr. Fan."

"Well then, what are we waiting for?"

AS their horses trotted to the mine, the scents of pines, eucalyptus, and cypress trees filled the air. It was a welcome departure from the fetid smells of the city. Molly forgot how beautiful it was on the outskirts of town. Her parents rarely let her venture further than the city limits. The freedom she felt when she took trips with her brother to their father's mine was one of the few good memories from her childhood. Sadness tugged at her heart remembering her brother and how he would never get to see the success she had become.

"So, I see you took my advice to heart," Bo said breaking Molly's concentration.

"What do you mean?"

"Remember when we last saw each other, I told you to write stories?"

Molly's eyes went wide. "I didn't tell anyone that it was me writing those stories except for mother. That was a momentary lapse of reason though, I thought she would be proud of me. She wouldn't dare tell anyone it was me for fear of dying of embarrassment. How did you know it was me? I have a pen name."

Bo chuckled. "It doesn't take a great detective like your characters, Henrietta or Bo, to suss out you were responsible for those stories. Especially your first story about the rich businessman who killed Henrietta's brother. Only we didn't get to go off and solve mysteries together."

Molly sighed, "I fear not, but that is why they call it fiction, Mr. Fan."

"Indeed. If your other stories followed your life as closely, it seems that you had a very adventurous couple of decades. Did you solve all of those mysteries?"

"I did. It started innocently enough. After I left home, I knew my meager personal savings would not go very far, so I scanned the classifieds for employment. Then I happened on an ad looking for information about a missing child. It was a handsome reward. Unfortunately, they only wanted a man to help. So I hired a man to be "Henry Ashe" and for a goodly cut of the reward fee he was willing to play the part while I did all the work. So I went from town to town solving mysteries and writing about them as "Henry Ashe". My name got around and soon people were writing to me asking me to solve their mysteries. I'm due in Patagonia in the next month." She looked excitedly at Bo. "You should join me!"

"Miss Maloy—"

Molly's cheeks burned. Why must her mouth engage before her brain? "I'm dreadfully sorry, Mr. Fan. That was very gauche of me. I'm sure you have family and many responsibilities here. Please forgive me."

"Miss Maloy, I am not at all offended by your offer. I do not have any family. I suppose I was too focused on building my business. I swore I would not raise a child in the squalor I was raised in. So, by the time I was successful I felt it was too late to start a family." He sighed, "Lately, I have thought about seeing the world and taking

time I never did as a young man."

"Well, I'd say this is the perfect time. Not to make light of your situation, as I am sure losing your business in this disaster is truly gut wrenching, but maybe this is a good time to see the world. Who better to do it with than an old friend?"

"Miss Maloy, people would surely talk."

"Mr. Fan, I'm an unmarried overweight red-headed woman who is known to spontaneously speak her mind at random times. I am well accustomed to people talking about me. You should come to Patagonia with me. I've been to the region once before and it's ruggedly beautiful. Jagged mountains that jut up from the ground, lakes so clear and turquoise they don't look like they're of this earth. Oh and the massive icebergs. You really must see it!"

"I see what you mean about spontaneously speaking your mind." Molly's face fell. Bo's eyes went wide. "No, I like it. It wasn't meant as an insult. I love your passion. I just don't know. I'm old and—"

"As I told you before, you are not old. One piece of advice, if you think you're going to kick yourself for an opportunity not taken then you should probably take it."

Bo pulled back on the reigns of his horse and Molly followed suit. He stared in her eyes for what felt like an eternity. His eyes were as if he was mulling all the possibilities. Molly's heart flitted hoping the impossible. Bo gave a sad smile.

"There are so many regrets, but knowing I have helped make my community better does lessen the sting." He pointed ahead. "Speaking of which, is that the mine there?"

Reality tugged Molly back to the present. "As a matter of fact, it is. Now we need to sneak in. Any ideas?"

"I do have a few."

"**P**LEASE do tell, Mr. Fan." "In my younger days, I did a fair amount of work in mines around here. It was how I accumulated money enough to start my business and how I got this cane. All mines have cross cuts in them to let air in," he said as he pointed at the mine. "We can ride around the mine and crawl into one of the crosscuts and see how many we have to go up against."

"Brilliant!"

They made their up a steep hill that led to the mine, the rocky surface below their feet made the ascent difficult. Once they were near a crosscut, Bo put his finger to his mouth and motioned for them to stop. The air was still the only thing they heard was the cool wind whistling between them. The hill was nothing more than loose rock making sitting in one place difficult. Molly fidgeted to get better positioned and without warning gravel tumbled down the hill breaking the silence.

"Did you hear that?" a gruff man's voice wafted from the mine. "I'm tellin' ya someone is here. He told us we wouldn't get caught. It ain't worth it if we get caught."

Another voice responded, "Cut it out. We just gotta hold this guy here for another few hours and we're scot-free. Stop imagining things."

Bo motioned for Molly to follow him to the crosscut. Slowly, they made their way to opening then peered through. There was a dim light coming through, but they could make out two burly men both wearing bowlers and a handkerchief across their faces on their faces. They were flanking a Chinese man, presumably Mr. Look, in his pajamas. Molly gestured for both of them to go back down the hill.

After they were a ways from the opening Molly said, "There appears to only be two of them. Seeing as they weren't expecting anyone to find them, they probably aren't very heavily armed. So I will go tease them out and—"

Bo waved his hands. "No, I can't allow you to do that. It's much too dangerous."

"It's all dangerous. But it makes more sense for me to tease them out. It's my father's mine. I can say that I was in town and I'm just here to reminisce. While I was here I can say that I twisted my ankle or some such nonsense that will make them feel manly to help little ol' me," she said as she batted her eyes.

Bo frowned. "I still don't like it."

"I know, but we don't have time to go back to town and get reinforcements. We need to do this now or risk losing everything." Bo nodded reluctantly. "Okay then. While I have the men out with me, you will need to find a way to get Mr. Look out. I dare say that coming out of the front will not be an option."

"No it will not. There is some rope over there," Bo said motioning to a pile of old mining equipment. "I'll drop a rope down to Mr. Look. Hopefully, he'll be able to climb out with my help."

Molly held her breath then slowly let it out. "It's as good as plan as any. Let's do this before we both come to our senses."

"OH dear me. I do believe I've gotten myself into a pickle." Molly sat at the entrance of the mine holding her ankle. "Of all the luck. I can't believe this would happen to me."

The mouth of the mine was filled with the sounds of footsteps bumbling forth and men arguing. In a matter of minutes Molly was darkened by shadows of two men towering over her. She batted her eyelashes and grinned. "I...I seem to be in a bit of trouble here."

The men now had their handkerchiefs around their necks instead of their faces. One of the men was tall blond and lanky, the other was a bit shorter and stockier with red hair. They both pointed their guns at Molly and she raised her hands.

Molly's voice quivered. "Oh my. This is my father's mine. I was in town after a long absence and I wanted see it before I left. And

then clumsy ol' me fell on some of the loose gravel. This mine is of no account to anyone. If you want to stay here it doesn't matter to me."

"Are you are alright, ma'am?" The shorter man asked as he lowered his gun.

The blond man kept his gun trained on Molly and narrowed his eyes. "Why in the world would a woman want to see a mine?"

His eyes seared through her. Molly decided to play to the shorter man, it was clear that the blond man wasn't going to yield. She looked at the shorter man and bit her lower lip then winced in fake pain. "I told you this was my father, Bryan Maloy's mine. I am Molly Maloy," she held out her hand in greeting.

The smaller man took her hand and said, "Pleased to meet you, ma'am."

The blond man pulled him back from Molly and whispered harshly. Molly could make out just a few of the words they were saying. It sounded like the shorter man wanted to help Molly so as not to draw attention to them, but the blond man wanted to dispose of Molly. Molly's stomach churned hoping that she could keep the men occupied until Bo freed Mr. Look. She looked over the arguing men to see Bo at the crosscut lowering a rope down.

AS he lowered himself down the rope, Bo wondered why in the world he went along with this plan. He shook his head and smiled.

Molly had a way about her. He only knew her a very short time as a boy, but through their adventure she made him believe that he was capable of nearly anything. Bo would be the first in line to buy her penny dreadfuls. It wasn't just that her stories were fun and engaging, but it was almost like being able to spend more time with Molly every time he read them. He didn't know how he could miss someone he knew for such a short time.

A voice dragged him from his thoughts. "Who goes there?"

Bo held a finger to his lips and motioned to the rope. Then he whispered, "Do you think you can make it up, Mr. Look?"

The man in pajamas nodded and headed for the rope and made a slow ascent out of the cave. Bo looked out the mouth of the mine to see Molly holding her ankle and two men arguing. His first instinct was to go help his friend, but he knew if went out there then their whole plan would go awry. He looked up and Mr. Look was at the mouth of the crosscut. Bo took a deep breath hoping Molly was right about him still being an able bodied man.

THE men's argument dissolved into a shoving match. Molly stood silent as she watched Mr. Look emerge from the crosscut and then Bo.

"Gentlemen, there's no reason to fight. I am sure there will be enough reward for both of you to split."

The two men stopped mid-shout and slowly turned to Molly and said in unison, "Reward?"

Molly smiled and shook her head. "Yes, quite. I told you that my father owned this mine. He passed a few years back leaving his wealth to my mother and me. Mother will ensure that you're handsomely rewarded for my safe return."

The shorter man stepped forward and smiled sweetly. "Ma'am, I'd be pleased to get you back home."

The blond man pushed the other aside. "You'll stay here. I'll take—" he stopped mid-sentence and turned toward a moving figure. "Wait a minute..."

*Drat*, Molly thought.

The blond man turned to the shorter man, "The Chinaman, he got out." The shorter man ran off and then the blond man turned to Molly and said, "What are you really doing here?"

"Sir, I...I...wasn't lying," Molly said as she inched away from him and put her hand in her skirt pocket.

"I don't believe you."

In an instant he went for his gun, but Molly was quicker on the draw and pulled her derringer out of her skirt pocket and shot the man in the knee. He landed with a thud to the ground. Molly stood over him and kicked his gun out of the way and picked it up. In two heartbeats, she ran in the direction of Bo. She would never forgive herself if he was harmed. She was stopped dead in her tracks by a man lying unconscious in the dirt. She looked up and Bo was holding his cane over his shoulder grinning ear to ear.

"I told Mr. Look to head to the meeting and that we would catch up with him."

Molly smiled and they both sauntered over to the tall blond man who was screaming and writhing in pain.

"We're not going to harm you or your friend any further, but we are going to restrain you and tell the authorities where you are. I suggest that you tell them who paid you to do this and they will go easier on you," Molly lectured.

The blond man grumbled, "I ain't goin' down for Michael Murphy."

MOLLY stared out at the steamer on dock that would be taking her to her next destination. As she waited, she thought about the events over the last few days. The expression on Michael Murphy's face when Mr. Look came into the signing ceremony was like receiving a gift that she anticipated for the last twenty years. The last she heard the police were taking Michael Murphy in for questioning. Although she was doubtful he would face the charges he was due, she was happy that his reputation would be sullied in the community and her friend would be able to see his home rebuilt. Molly sighed thinking of her friend. She realized it was foolhardy to think that he would come with her, but her heart still felt empty. She took refuge in the

thought that she would be back here after her latest adventure and they promised to write each other while she was gone. It wasn't the same though.

A man's voice echoed through the shipyard calling the ten minute warning until boarding. Molly checked her pocket watch, grabbed her luggage, and headed toward the steamer.

"Excuse me, ma'am, can you tell me where I find the ship bound for Panama City?"

Molly's breath caught and she slowly turned. A smile involuntarily spread across her face. "I... I...It's over—" she lunged and wrapped her arms around Bo and he returned her embrace. "Are you really coming along?" She whispered in his ear.

Bo disentangled himself from her and held her hands. "If you'll have me." A few onlookers mumbled in disapproval of the public display. "And if you think you can handle sentiment such as that."

Molly patted her eyes. "Oh well, that's nothing. Have I told you of the time that I found myself in the middle of the Boer War in South Africa?" Bo shook his head and extended his elbow for Molly. "Well, yes, I hadn't planned on going to South Africa, but I got word there was woman there in need of extraction to her home in Britain and..."

They strolled toward ship both nervous and excited for the adventure that awaited them.

# *Fiasco*

## By DAVID MACK

MARCH 1956

**I**'M six whiskeys into a Friday night at The Blue Moon, basking in the club's nicotine fog and grooving to a jazz sax that sounds like a rusty hinge, when two apes with crew cuts and cheap suits step in front of my table and block my view of the band.

One of them shows me his badge. "Detective Jack Halligan?"

I take a drag off my Lucky. "Y'askin' me? Or tellin' me?"

His pal brushes open his suit coat, casually, and rests his hand on the grip of his holstered revolver. The one doing the talking leans down and fills my face with his sour-milk breath. "I'm Walker. He's Morris. Internal Affairs. You need to come with us."

I hoist my drink and my half-finished coffin nail. "I'm busy."

Walker snatches my Lucky, snuffs it in my rye. "You're *done*. Get up."

*So much for professional courtesy.* I drop a sawbuck on the table and nod at my waiter as I follow the rat squad dicks outside.

It's a cool night, dry as a bone. Somewhere above downtown Los Angeles the stars are shining, but good luck seeing them through this ceiling of pink smog. Walker and Morris march me back to my car, which is guarded by a pair of patrolmen. The passenger-side window has been smashed in, and the glove compartment is open. Lying on the passenger seat is a brick of heroin that I've never seen before in my life.

Morris points at the kilo and looks at me. "Care to explain *that?*"

"If you're too dumb to know a frame-up when you see it, I can't help you."

Walker steps toward me. Jabs my chest with his meaty index finger. "Wise up, Halligan. That brick's just one of three that went missing from Hollywood Station's evidence lockup two days ago. Where are the other two?"

"With whoever's framing me would be my guess...you fuckin' mook."

I never see the punch that sends a sickening jolt through my right kidney. All I know is one second I'm standing, the next I'm on my knees in the gutter, seeing purple and tasting sour bile. I take a few deep breaths and fight to keep my shit together as I get back on my feet.

Walker tells the patrolmen, "Bag and tag the brick, have the car towed."

Morris pushes me back against

*Illustration by Daniele Sera*

my car. "Jack Halligan, you're under arrest for theft of evidence and possession of narcotics. We'll need your badge and your weapon."

As I reach inside my jacket, Walker adds, "Slowly."

I hand Morris my badge. Then I use two fingers to remove my Smith & Wesson .38 from its holster. As I hand the pistol to Walker, I do a sleight-of-hand trick a skel once taught me, and with a flick of my wrist I open the revolver's cylinder.

All six bullets fall out. The bright sound of brass on pavement is like music.

Walker bends down to retrieve my bullets. I knee him in the face.

Blood pours from Walker's broken nose as he sprawls on the sidewalk.

Morris reaches for his weapon. I still have my empty .38, so I clock him in the temple with it. He hits the street like a 230-pound sack of flour.

On the other side of my car, one of the uniforms clumsily starts to draw his sidearm. I throw my empty roscoe at him. It smacks him in the forehead as his steel clears leather, and he fires a wild shot—into his partner's foot.

I run like my ass is on fire. I'm half a block away when the stunned rookie opens fire. He hits a store window and a random citizen on the sidewalk before he puts a slug through the bulge of fat beneath my ribs. I press my hand

over the bleeding exit wound and lunge onward.

Distracted by the burning pain on my right side, I dart down Skid Row side streets. Weave through a dark trash-strewn alley where scabby hookers blow their johns against brick walls, hidden behind garbage bins that reek of rotten fish and a hundred things far worse. At the far end of this urban slice of hell, I pay a bum twenty bucks for his tattered gray overcoat, which smells like he's been using it to wipe his ass for a year, and I snatch a grease-stained beige trilby from a pile of trash behind a Chinese restaurant.

Wrapped in my disguise of filth, I stagger onto San Pedro as a fleet of LAPD radio cars races past, lights flashing and sirens screaming. None of the cops in those cars spares me even half a look. I've rendered myself invisible to their eyes. To them, I'm just one more bum in the night, another ghost in the City of Angels.

Time's against me now. Doing my best not to look like a man on the run, I keep my head down and my hand over my wound as I turn my steps toward a place I used to call home.

THE fleshy side of my fist goes numb after a minute of pounding on the bungalow's side door.

It's dark inside, but through the door's curtained window I see a shadow moving closer. Exhaustion takes over, so I give my hand a rest and slump against the door jamb.

A hand pushes the curtain open from the side. Nadine stands at the door in her gauzy nightgown, with curlers in her auburn hair and contempt in her jade-green eyes. Her stare turns cold at the sight of me, and she raises her voice to be heard through the closed door. "You can't be here, Jack. Judge said so."

"C'mon, honey."

"Don't call me that."

I lean back to show her the blood stain on my shirt, the crimson stain fresh and warm on my hand. *"Please,* Nadine. I've been *shot."*

*"Pfft.* So? Go to your slut girlfriend."

"That's over. History. Kaput." Every word of that is true, but the real reason I came here is that my ex-squeeze wasn't a nurse. Nadine is. She has a first aid kit and knows how to use it.

But she's not having my bullshit. "Not my problem. Go to a hospital."

"I can't. They'll be looking for me there."

"Who will?"

I nod toward the back of the kitchen, behind her. "Please, I just need the first-aid kit."

"There's an all-night pharmacy up the street. Get some Band-aids and a motel room."

"If I had any money, I would." I'm tempted to mumble something about her divorce lawyer being the reason I'm broke, but I keep my mouth shut; right now I'd rather stanch my bleeding than score a rhetorical point. "Look, I'm too tired to go anyplace else. You don't have to let me in, but unless you loan me the first-aid kit, I'm gonna die here on your steps."

She cocks an eyebrow in disdain. "Promises, promises."

I have the perfect sarcastic retort, but I fade out before I get to say it. When I snap back to consciousness, I'm slumped against the bottom of the door, and Nadine has one side of her face pressed to the window so she can see me. "Jack? Are you all right?"

"Nothing a blood transfusion won't fix."

I hear guilt in her voice. "I'll unlock the door, but you have to leave your gun outside."

"I'm unarmed. IAB took my weapon an hour ago."

She's quiet for a second. Then I hear the door's locks being undone.

Nadine opens the door, and I collapse into her kitchen as a bleeding, putrid mess. "Thanks, beautiful. Gimme some gauze and a spritz of Bactine, and I'll be out of your hair."

She towers over me, looking down with pity and reproach. "What a mess." She walks toward the cabinet where the first-aid kit lives. "Drag your ass to the living room, you stupid bastard. I'll be right behind you."

**M**Y favorite armchair swallows me like quicksand. Nadine has dimmed the lights in the living room and planted me in the spot that used to be mine. She squats next to the chair and patiently stitches shut the wound in my flank while I sip from a half-empty doubles glass that she filled to the rim with my peatiest scotch. The jab of the needle through my flesh is dulled, and everything feels soft and far away. I look her way, and my head almost falls onto my shoulder.

"How's it goin'?"

"Just stay still." She loops steel and silk through the bloody mess left by the rookie's lucky shot. "What the fuck did you do this time, Jack?"

My words come out slow and slurred. "Fucked if I know." I search my memory, but everything's gone foggy. "They said they found horse in my glove compartment, but that's bullshit. Somebody's setting me up."

"Who'd want to do that?"

I lift my increasingly heavy glass and down a swig of Laphroaig. "Who knows? Not like I haven't made enemies, pissed people off. Politicians. Gangsters. Judges.... Long list."

"Maybe it was IAB."

I fill my mouth with smoky whisky, and then I swallow. "Maybe. But it doesn't add up. I had no beef with them."

"Right. Because you're Mister Lovable." Nadine wipes clean both the entrance and exit wounds, and then she preps some bandages.

I turn the facts over in my head, but none of the angles work. "Had to be an inside job. That smack only came in a week ago." I down another swallow of liquid heat. My head swims as I fight to make one-plus-one equal two. "Who had access? The clerk? One of the uniforms?" My eyelids are as heavy as lead. "A detective?...I just can't buy it."

Nadine slaps a final strip of tape on my bandage, and then her voice takes a sharp turn. "You *should*."

She's a blur now, a soft-focus spectre in the dark, standing over me. I feel like I should know what's going on, but all I feel is confusion. Then the golden heat moving through my body becomes beautiful but strange. I know what whisky-drunk feels like. This ain't it.

When I look at my glass, it's surrounded by a halo.

My voice is flat and weak. "This wasn't just whisky."

"Correct. It was four parts scotch, one part heroin."

I want to curse her name, but the room's paltry light fades to black as I sink into my favorite chair's suddenly bottomless abyss.

**T**HE sting of a million needles hits me in the face and shocks me conscious.

I wince against a blinding light, then shake off the pain. My head is sopping with ice water. Freezing droplets snake down my back, under my shirt. I try to reach up to wipe my face, but my hands are bound to the arms of a wooden chair. My ankles are tied to its front legs.

A few hard blinks and my eyes adjust to the glare of the naked bulb hanging above my face. I'm in what used to be my garage. Nadine stands in front of me, her arms crossed, all her weight on one leg while she stretches the other to one side.

Next to her, holding the now-empty bucket, is my partner, Dan Kostelec.

I'm drugged, I'm hurting, and it's been a long night. It takes me a few seconds to recognize what's staring me in the face. I look at Dan. "She told ya, didn't she?"

"That you've been fucking my wife? Yeah. It came up."

Nadine looks pleased with herself. "My lawyer hired a private dick. Got me photos of you and Sarah." She shakes her head. "You even lied about what you lied about."

Dan cracks his meaty knuckles. "You called my Sarah your floozy?"

"C'mon, man, it wasn't—" His punch snaps my head to the left, sends a tooth flying.

Blood fills my mouth. I spit it out, grimace at the coppery aftertaste. "Dan, let's—"

He sinks his fist into my gut. I try to breathe but I can't inhale. Dan doesn't wait for me to catch

my wind. He lands one blow after another. Splits my lip, cracks my nose, tears open my brow. For the longest half minute of my life, he uses me for a punching bag— slamming his knuckles into my ribs, my jaw, my balls. He winds up for a big finish. Lands a right cross so hard it knocks me and my chair over sideways.

I land on the cold cement floor; it stinks of mold and motor oil— and now, my blood.

Dan reaches down, rolls me and the chair so I'm on my back. "How ya' doin', asshole?"

"I've had better nights."

"I'm sure you have—with my *wife*, you sonofabitch." He pulls a handkerchief from his trouser pocket, wipes my blood off his hands. "But don't worry. That's why I've been balling your ex. I figure that makes us *almost* even."

"Almost?"

He stomps on my gut, and I nearly vomit. "I ain't done with you, pal. You or Sarah."

Hearing him say her name turns my dread to rage. "What've you done to Sarah?"

"Nothin'. Yet." Dan pulls a pack of Camels from his jacket. He lights one with a match, sharpening the air with a bite of sulfur. He squats next to me. Blows smoke in my face. "But don't worry—she'll get hers." He puts out his cigarette on my chest. I scream as it burns through my shirt. He stuffs his kerchief into my mouth, muffling my howls as his Camel blackens a tiny spot of my flesh. The prick can't help but grin while I squirm. "Right after I finish with you."

AFTER getting tobacco-branded, I lose track of time. Dan gets creative, uses some of my old tools to work me over. The ropes on my ankles and wrists are too tight for me to pull free, so there's nothing I can do but take the beating until, at last, he loses his stamina or his interest and stops.

The garage goes quiet. The naked bulb above me swings like a pendulum. My face is wet with my own blood, and I can't think of a single part of my body that doesn't hurt. I keep my breathing shallow. If Dan thinks I'm out cold, maybe he won't go back to kicking my ass.

He sounds winded as he says to Nadine, "Get me that big blanket."

Her voice is pointed. "What for?"

"So he doesn't bleed all over the trunk of my car."

"Oh, for Christ's sake." I recognize this tone in her voice. I've heard it a million times: she's losing patience with Dan. "Just finish him here—wash the blood down the drain."

"That's not the plan."

"The plan?" Nadine heaves a sigh of irritation. "That went down the shitter the moment Jack landed on my doorstep. You said he'd go to

jail and get knifed, or get shot trying to escape. Now he's back home, bleeding in my garage."

I hear heavy footsteps; must be his.

A flutter of heavy fabric: the blanket unfolding.

Dan tries to sound comforting. "Look, sweetheart, you did great. Kept him calm. And doping his drink? Genius. When they find his body, the smack in his blood'll make him look like an addict—and that'll back up the story that Jack stole the drugs."

"I don't care about your frame-up. I just want this done." She summons her most seductive voice. "Can't you just blow his brains out right here?"

"Are you fuckin' crazy? Ever heard a gunshot in a closed room? S'louder than you think. It'll wake your neighbors for sure."

I feel a tug on the rope around my right ankle. Dan starts untying me. I play dead.

Dan frees my right foot. "Besides, the blood spatter gets into places you wouldn't think possible." He unties my left ankle. "And I bet you this cement floor is porous. Blood'll get deep down in there. You'll never get it out, not with all the fuckin' bleach in the world." The rope around my left wrist tightens, then goes slack. "Trust me, you don't want that kind of evidence left behind in here. Not when we've got the perfect setup waiting to go."

"Fine, whatever you say. Let's

just get this over with."

The rope falls away from my right wrist.

I let them pull me out of the chair, onto the waiting blanket.

They roll me up like a burrito full of raw hamburger.

I hear the garage door clatter open. Cool air floods into the garage from outside, washing away the sultry atmosphere of exertion and the ferric tang of blood. Then come the clicks of a key in a lock, of tumblers turning...and the hollow sound of a car's trunk being opened.

They both grunt with effort as they hoist me into the trunk.

I struggle not to groan or betray my lingering consciousness while they force my body to fold and twist in painful ways.

Dan's voice quakes with excitement. "This'll work, sweetie. We'll meet Sarah, snuff her and Jack at the same time, and then we're free and clear."

As ever, Nadine sounds skeptical. "The rest of the drugs?"

"In my satchel, ready to sell when we hit Mexico. With the cash we took from our joint accounts, we'll be in Acapulco before anyone knows we're gone."

"Sounds dreamy. So let's get to it."

"Anything you say, baby. Anything you say."

Dan slams the trunk shut.

I count to three and let myself exhale—slowly, softly. Can't let them hear me.

The car's engine rumbles to life. I have no idea where we're going, or how long until we get there. All I know for sure is that I'm being driven to my own execution—and Sarah's.

THE road hum is hypnotic—or maybe it's the car's exhaust fumes that are making me lightheaded. Smothered inside the heavy wool blanket, I find it hard to stay awake. My body wants to quit. It needs to rest. But I know better. I need to get free. To fight, before it's too late.

A hard jolt jostles me, bangs my head off the trunk's door. We must have hit a pothole, a deep one from the feel of it.

I welcome the pain. It sharpens my senses, wakes me up.

Almost as soon as I regain focus, I regret it. Every part of me aches from Dan's savage beating, and my brain is still half-clouded with heroin thanks to Nadine. I want to gasp for air, but I'm gagged.

Fighting free of the heavy wool blanket is harder than I expect. I have no room to move, and I'm trying not to make too much noise, so my options are limited.

I twist and roll until the edge of the blanket catches on something. So far so good. I keep turning until my death shroud unwinds and sets me free. I pull the gag from my mouth and gulp in a few greedy breaths. That helps clear my head, just a bit.

The steady roar of asphalt beneath the tires changes to a gritty crackling, like exploding popcorn. We've left the highway; we're on a dirt road now.

I hear Dan and Nadine in the passenger compartment.

She's anxious: "How much farther?"

Dan's as cool as ever. "Not far. Trust me."

With caution I roll over to see a beam of pale moonlight spear into the trunk through a fist-sized hole in the car's backseat. We're in Dan's beat-to-shit '49 Studebaker Champion. A bandito's shotgun made this hole five years ago, during the Mexicali phase of Dan's bachelor party. He's never had it fixed, because he loves telling people how close I came to getting killed over a bottle of tequila. But that's a story for another time.

I paw the floor of the trunk. My palm finds the claw-teeth of the tire iron that snagged the blanket. I dig it free and hold it close to me. It's the only weapon I've got, so I clutch it for dear life. With one hand I drape the blanket over me. If I'm lucky, when Dan or Nadine opens the trunk, all they'll see at first is the blanket's texture. And by the time they realize it ain't rolled up anymore, I'll be out of the trunk, swingin' like DiMaggio and crushin' skulls.

Or I'll be eating a bullet. Either way beats being executed. Trust me—I know.

As the car slows down, I'm grateful for the blanket. We're in the desert somewhere outside Los Angeles, and the night air has a frigid bite, even in the car's trunk.

I steal a peek through the hole in the backseat. We pull up to a single-engine plane that looks like a winged shoebox held together with spit, prayer, and bailing wire. Dan's soft-spoken wife Sarah stands on the dirt runway next to the scuffed Cessna, clutching her suitcase in both hands. Apparently, she thinks she and Dan are taking a trip. I wish I could warn her of what's coming, but it's too late for that now.

Dan stops the car.

Sarah raises one hand to shield her eyes from the headlights. "Dan?"

He opens his door and gets out, feigning good cheer: "Hi, honey!"

The sharp crack of a gunshot echoes in the night. Sarah drops her suitcase and stumbles backward, a scarlet stain spreading fast across the front of her yellow dress. She lands on her back and lies bleeding in the dust.

Smoke curls from the barrel of Dan's pistol as Nadine gets out of the car. "One down," she says. "One to go."

They parallel each other as they walk toward the back of the car, out of my line of sight. Inside the trunk I tense beneath the blanket. I white-knuckle the tire iron when I hear the key in the trunk's lock. I'll only get one chance at this—

Dan opens the trunk. Cold air rushes in—and I spring up and out.

I keep the tire iron in front of me. It hits Dan in his chest, and my momentum takes us both down in a tangle. He rolls away from me, tries to aim his pistol while lying on his back. I swat the weapon from his hand with a hard but clumsy sweep of the iron.

I try to get up and take another swing, but Dan tackles me. We wrestle for the iron, and it ends up between us. Each of us fights to push the bar toward the other guy's throat—

Another gunshot stops us cold.

We both look at Nadine. She holds Dan's pistol, its barrel aimed skyward. "First shot was a warning. Next one won't be." She looks at Dan and waves the pistol. "Get up. Take the iron."

Dan wrenches the metal tool from my hands and stands up. Nadine has me covered, so I stay on the ground. He moves toward her. "Great work, baby. Great—"

"That's close enough." Nadine cocks the revolver. "Lose the iron. Now."

"Baby, what're you—"

She fires, puts a bullet in the dirt between his feet. "Now."

"All right, baby. All right." Dan heaves the iron into the dark.

My ex looks at me. "Up." Once I'm on my feet, she nods toward the car. "Both of you, over there. Dan, get the heroin—but leave the cash in the car."

Nadine keeps us both covered while Dan reaches inside the car to retrieve two bricks of smack from the backseat. He holds one in each hand as he steps back from the car. "Now what?"

"Both of you back up, slow. Toward the plane."

We do as she says. But poor Dan can't seem to get his head around what's happening.

"Baby? What're you doing?"

Her scowl of condescension is a work of art. "What does it *look* like I'm doing, you clod? I'm taking your cash and leaving the three of you with the drugs I helped you steal."

Dan, deluded fool extraordinaire, still doesn't get it. "But what about *us?*"

She shoots him high in the gut. As he falls, I dive toward the front of the car.

Nadine pivots, fires, and puts a bullet in my ribs. I land hard in the dirt between the car's blinding headlights, clutching the burning-hot wound my side and fighting to breathe.

I hear footsteps drawing near. From under the car I see Nadine's feet. She steps past the car to get a clear shot at me.

From the other side of the car comes the *click* of a small revolver's hammer. Nadine spins toward the sound—then comes a *pop*, like a firecracker.

Her left ear is blown to bits, and she screams like a banshee.

Dan, mortally wounded and still

on the ground, steadies his .22-caliber backup piece, the one he keeps in an ankle holster. Nadine aims his stolen .38 back at him.

Their shots pass each other in flight.

Hers pulps the top of his head.

His rips her throat into salsa.

A mournful howl of wind coats us all in grit, and then the desert goes still.

Bleeding, in agony, I crawl over rocky ground, flanked by the car's headlamp beams, to the plane. As I pass Sarah, I hear a soft rasp from her blood-filled mouth. She's still breathing.

It takes all my strength to pull myself up to the pilot's door of the shitty little plane. Blood surges over my hand clasping my side as I stretch to reach the plane's radio. I switch it on and grab the mic. My voice is like sandpaper as I send out a mayday and hope someone hears it.

My hail Mary pass thrown, I slump to the ground beside the plane.

I don't expect to live long enough to see rescue.

But even if I do, I'm not sure I deserve to.

TWELVE years of my life fits in a cardboard box. A dozen years on the job, and all I have to show for it are a couple of commendations, a bunch of notebooks, and a few knickknacks.

The rest of the squad is conspicuously silent as I pack up my desk. I've never heard Hollywood Station so quiet, not even on the overnight. My ex-brothers in blue pretended not to eavesdrop while the captain took my shield and my piece, and they averted their eyes when he gave me a check to buy me out of the pension plan.

As I carry my box out of the station, escorted every step of the way by a pair of uniformed officers, my former squad acts like I'm going to the gallows.

But all things considered, I'm getting off easy. Sarah lived to tell the D.A. that she heard Nadine's confession at the airfield, and that I'd done all I could to save her. Her testimony, plus the fact that they found Dan and Nadine's fingerprints all over the drugs and money—and none of mine—put the blame for this mess where it belonged. Mostly.

So the D.A. didn't charge me with anything, but the brass doesn't care. I was cleared of stealing the drugs, but apparently banging your partner's wife and getting him and your own spouse killed in a "domestic spat gone wrong" is the kind of thing that can get you fired from the new "modern" LAPD. Chief Parker's gotta draw the line somewhere, I guess.

I step out the door into the swelter of the parking lot, squint against the late-afternoon sun, and grimace at the stink of garbage rotting in the bins behind the station. As I walk to my car, I feel the squad's eyes on my back, but I keep my face forward.

My box of crap I put in my car's trunk. Then I slump into the driver's seat and light a Lucky. Savor a few puffs while I start the engine and listen to it purr. I want the guys to think I have places to be and things to do, so I put my baby into gear and drive to the gate.

I pause to let traffic pass on Wilcox. While I wait, I wonder what to do next. I'm too old to learn new tricks, but too young to call it quits. So what's my play?

Seeing a break in the line of cars, I pull out and tell myself not to worry. This is L.A. There's gotta be work for an ex-cop somewhere.

A bail bondsman in need of a bounty hunter.

A movie star in need of protection.

A lawyer in need of a snoop.

Whatever it is, I'll find it.

But until then...I'm just another ghost in the City of Angels.

THE
SURREY
SAMSON

★ HELD OVER ★

# The Problem
# of the Surrey Samson
## By WILL MURRAY

MR. Sherlock Holmes had been in one of his most disagreeable moods for nearly a week. I could do nothing with him. He was without distraction or entertainment. No case could be found to occupy his mind, which was a finely-tuned machine that required continual productive operation in order to avoid going out of kilter and seizing up altogether.

He had been in a foul humor on the night of March 3, 1882 and I noticed him looking longingly in the direction of the mantle piece, where rested a small bottle and Morocco case dedicated to the injection of cocaine. I did not think Holmes was quite to the point of surrendering to the impulse, but ennui had seized hold of his brain rather firmly.

"I am off to catch a remarkable performance in Piccadilly," I announced after dinner. "All of London is talking about it. Would you care to join me?"

"I would not," Holmes said brusquely. "Go without me."

"Thank you for stating it so unequivocally."

"I mean you no offense, Watson. It is only that I am in a frank mood."

"I would not use the word 'frank' to describe your mood. But you are the master of your tongue and no other. Have things your way. There is a rather remarkable strongman giving a performance at the Egyptian Hall. I mean to take it in."

"No doubt he bends horseshoes in his hands, snaps chains with his expanded chest, and performs other muscular wonders. No, no, I decline. There is nothing for me to take hold of, mentally. I must have a challenge."

"It is my fervent hope that one arrives soon. Good night, Holmes."

Sherlock Holmes did not deign to respond. And so I went down the stairs and got on my way.

I will not describe in detail the exhibition that took place at the Egyptian Hall, other than to record that my astonishment at the performance of the colorful fellow who called himself the Surrey Samson was profound.

Hurrying back to Baker Street, I found Sherlock Holmes still seated in his comfortable armchair by the fire. I expected him to be smoking. But he was not. His chin was sunk deeply in one hand and his sharp eyes were

*Illustration by Gary Carbon*

fixed on nothing that I could see.

"I bring good news, my dear Holmes," I greeted.

"I would welcome any tidings that dispel my infernal boredom."

"I have in the nature of a challenge for your mental powers. I took in the performance of one Mr. Jack Marvell, otherwise the known as Surrey Samson. And it was one of the most remarkable displays of manly might I have ever beheld."

"Bah! I do not find strongman to be particularly interesting. The application of muscular power to physical tasks is a rather dull subject, Watson. Dull and dreary."

"Perhaps in a general way it is, Holmes. But in this particular performance, the fellow appears to do the impossible."

"I duly note your use of the word 'appears.'"

"To all outward appearances," I continued, "the impossible is accomplished. Mr. Marvell looks healthy enough, but I think he could hardly weigh ten stone. Yet he is able to crawl under a safe believed to weigh a quarter ton and through impressive contortions and exertions lift it up over his head through a Herculean effort that I daresay would daunt a much larger individual."

"I also note the use of the word 'said.'"

"I am only reporting what the fellow asserted, but the safe was of a prodigious size and built of steel by W. E. Brain & Company of Birmingham, according to the manufacturer's plate visible on the front. And I would imagine that two if not more men of average size could be squeezed into its confines."

"Were any number of men crammed into the safe before it was lifted?"

"No, for the safe contained odd bits of scrap iron, adding to the weight of the safe."

"Was this demonstrated?"

"Not directly, no. But six men were invited onto the stage and invited to lift it as a group. They failed miserably. They could barely budge it. In fact, the entirety of their efforts resulted only in the safe shifting slightly on its ponderous legs. But they could not lift even a solitary leg off the platform stage. It was astounding, Holmes. I wish that you had been present to see it with your own eyes."

As I spoke, the languor began going out of Sherlock Holmes' ill manner. He reached for his pipe, charging it with black shag. His head lifted and a gleam of interest leaped into his keen eyes.

"Tell me more, Watson. Pray begin from the portion of the performance where this Surrey Strongman produced his miracle."

I felt rather like a fisherman who had gotten a tug on his line. Holmes was interested. I proceeded to reel him in, as it were.

"After the six sturdy men failed in their endeavors, they were returned to their seats and Mr.

Marvell proceeded to lecture us on the nature and force of the human will. The upshot of it was that a man with sufficient conviction in his innermost powers could perform feats that other men employing mere brute strength could not accomplish."

"Did he say where he learned to do this?"

"There was talk of having visited Java and other such places. He hinted more than he explained."

"Naturally," murmured Holmes dryly. "Go on, Watson."

"Mr. Marvell concluded his lecture by drinking from a bottle a concoction he claimed was of his own devising. He did not explain the precise ingredients, other than to speak of exotic herbs and roots and other such sundries. Again, he invoked a visit to Java."

Holmes mused, "There are stimulants which, as you know, can briefly empower a man beyond his natural abilities."

"I know this," I remarked, thinking of my friend's ready solution of cocaine. "But there were limits, Holmes. And this man exceeded them beyond all bounds."

Holmes finished lighting his pipe. "I am listening."

"Having imbibed this potion, Mr. Marvell then proceeded to lift an assortment of dumbbells and barbells that had been set on the stage. These he at first hefted with evident difficulty, progressing from the short dumbbells to the great elongated barbells, which

latter required all of his might. The more he endeavored to lift them, the greater his strength seemed to become. He appeared to be building up towards the main event."

"Intriguing showmanship," Holmes remarked.

"It was a very convincing display," I agreed. "By the time he dropped the last barbell to the floor, his muscles appeared to be visibly larger."

"Purchasing time, I imagine," muttered Holmes. "But toward what end?"

"I beg your pardon?"

Rather than replying, Holmes asked, "How did he manage to lift this prodigious safe?"

"By crawling under it and working himself into contorted positions whereby he lifted the safe in stages."

"He made no other preparation?"

"Nothing other than to take hold of one corner and restore the box to the position the six sturdy men had jogged it from."

"Ah-ha!" exclaimed Holmes. "While that effort would seem to be superfluous, I imagine that it was key."

"He appeared to be a fastidious fellow; it might have merely been a quirk of his personality."

"You have my interest, Watson. Do not fumble it. Continue."

"Mr. Marvell crawled under the safe, whose legs were sufficiently high enough to permit this. He lay on his belly for some time and then commenced to arch his back. Gradually, he gathered himself, turning over until he was up on hands and knees, and there began the laborious process of lifting the safe."

"This took some time?"

"Ten minutes, if not longer. He was very careful to position himself and work his body into the proper posture. Gradually, he began to lift the safe on his back and as he did so, endeavoring to balance it, he managed to bring himself erect in stages, until he was standing in full view of the audience, holding the massive steel safe over his head in the palms of both hands. At that, the audience jumped to their feet and broke into thunderous applause."

"What happened next?"

"Stage hands rushed out and secured the safe with rope and tackle, and it was lifted higher so that Mr. Marvell could take a grateful bow with the massive thing suspended over his head. Once the audience applause died down, the safe was lowered onto the stage, and Mr. Marvell, the Surrey Strongman, made his final bow to the acclaim of all."

"I see."

"So I put it to you, Holmes: however did he do it?"

Sherlock Holmes did not immediately reply. His pipe by now was fulminating. And the cast of his features had become fixed and firm.

"I do not think, Watson, that the secret lies in the man and his muscles, but in the safe itself, and its contents."

"If it was too heavy for six man to lift, how could one slender fellow accomplish it not twenty minutes later?"

"I do not yet know, Watson. But I am convinced that watching Mr. Marvell perform his act will lead me to a satisfactory answer."

I smiled with delight. "I would not at all mind watching the performance again. It was one of the most extraordinary I've ever seen on the London stage."

"The Surrey Samson sounds less like a strongman than a showman," Holmes murmured, almost to himself. "If this is an act, it is a very clever one."

With that, Sherlock Holmes lapsed into a grim and stony silence. I knew from previous experience that further conversation would be pointless. He was turning the problem over in his mind. A seer looking into a crystal ball could not be more self-absorbed in his focus.

Satisfied that I had broken the stubborn spell of ennui, I retired for the evening, confident that my good friend would leave his solution of cocaine alone for the nonce.

THE following afternoon, Sherlock Holmes purchased five-shilling tickets for us both. We took front row seats at the Hall, just slightly to the left of center, where we would have an excellent view of the show.

Mr. Jack Marvell stepped out to a smattering of welcoming applause. He presented himself unannounced, for by this time his fame had permeated all of London.

On the previous occasion, the lean and limber fellow was attired in a rather garish purple-and-gold cotton leotard. But tonight he outdid himself, for he was in scarlet trimmed with black. Black pointed mustaches slanted in parallel with his exotic eyebrows gave his triangular features a decidedly Luciferian cast.

I thought to myself that the garish outfit accentuated his absence of musculature, but it made no difference, for his arms were entirely bare, leaving the facts in the matter unadorned, as it were.

Sherlock Holmes made no comment as the man made his own introductions. They were essentially the same as the night before. The Surrey Strongman extolled the powers of the human will, augmented by certain practices which included a rigorous diet and imbibing juice of certain botanical rarities that could only be found in Java and similar rarely-travelled environments.

"To demonstrate my prowess," he announced to the packed house, "I call upon six husky individuals to take the stage and attempt to move or lift the great safe that you see placed there."

The curtain was drawn aside to reveal the safe. Possibly a small horse could have stood inside it. It faced the audience, its handle and keyhole visible.

The box itself was painted black, but it had the appearance of stout formidability.

To my surprise, Sherlock Holmes left his seat and mounted the steps, becoming one of the six men who had volunteered to pit their might against the great obdurate thing.

Jack Marvell greeted them all warmly, saying, "Between you six gentlemen, I imagine you weigh over 300 stone. The box you see before you has been filled with scrap iron and other odds and ends. I have never weighed it, but I would venture to suggest it would come to between a quarter and a half ton of steel and iron. For the entirety of the box is forged from steel of the finest craftsmanship, and manufactured by W. E. Brain & Company of Birmingham, as you can see from the manufacturer's plate adorning the front."

Even seated in the front row, I could barely make out the manufacturer's plate, but I knew Brain was a reputable firm.

Sherlock Holmes made a circuit of the safe, and using the stem of his pipe, he tapped the steel sides at various points, placing one ear to the metal each time.

"And what are you doing, my good fellow?" asked Jack Marvell after he noticed this.

"Testing to learn if the walls are hollow."

"Ah! I see. And what is your conclusion, good sir?"

"They ring as if solid. But I do not think the walls are very thick."

"I beg to differ. For they are quite thick."

"Is there any reason we cannot have a look inside the box?"

"Only one," replied Marvell. "I do not wish the scrap iron to come tumbling out, for it is very heavy. And restoring it would delay the performance."

"How do we know that it is filled with iron then?" countered Holmes.

To this, the Surrey Strongman laughed loudly, his pointed mustaches leaping about.

"Why, it could be filled with cold butter and it would make no difference. If you and the other five members of the audience cannot budge it in any direction, what difference would it make?"

"I take your point," said Sherlock Holmes.

He was looking at the round legs of the stupendous box. They were naturally stout and high, not only to support the whole of the contrivance, but to permit Jack Marvell to crawl beneath it and exhibit his tremendous prowess.

"It is not bolted to the floor?" asked Holmes.

"You can prove to yourself that it is not. So far, no group of men have lifted the safe, but a few have managed to jostle it around ever so slightly. You may prove this to your own satisfaction any time you are prepared to do so."

"Thank you," said Holmes. "I think it is time that we begin."

Setting a shoulder to one corner of the safe, Sherlock Holmes attempted to budge the great safe. The others fell in where they could, and a concerted effort was made to move the safe in the direction of the rear curtain.

Considerable straining and pushing and exerting, accompanied by grunting and perspiring, followed. Through a concerted effort led by Sherlock Holmes, the safe shifted ever so slightly. Perhaps by an inch, perhaps an inch and a half. But move it did.

The end result was that all six men had expended their energy. Leaving off the unfinished task, the group straightened and began mopping their moist faces with their handkerchiefs. None showed an appetite to attempt to lift the great safe upward.

Jack Marvell smiled broadly, and I thought his teeth a trifle too white to be natural. "Are you gentlemen satisfied that the safe is too heavy to be lifted by a group of ordinary men?"

Exhausted comments of agreement were given; Sherlock Holmes said nothing. He was studying the floorboards of the stage. His expression was intent, his eyes as alive as I have ever seen them.

"In that case, gentleman," announced Jack Marvell, "you may

reclaim your seats. For the show will now proceed in a way I think you'll find most astounding."

The small upright table was brought out and on it reposed a glass bottle of juice that appeared to be deeply purple.

Smiling broadly, Marvell stated, "I have extolled the virtues of the elixir of Java, which I show to you now. Permit me to drink a dram. Only one swallow, for it is exceedingly potent."

Without benefit of drinking glass, Jack Marvell removed the stopper and brought the neck to his lips. He drank slowly. When he was done, he closed up the bottle and replaced it on the taboret.

"This elixir takes some time to work its magic upon the human constitution," he continued. "But even as I am speaking to you now, it is revitalizing my brain, sharpening my focus while my beating heart pumps its power through my circulatory system."

Stage hands brought out a number of dumbbells and barbells, setting them heavily upon the stage, which resounded with their weight. Mr. Marvell did some preliminary stretching and preening, and then proclaimed, "In order to build up to the superhuman feat I am about to attempt, I must limber up in various ways."

Picking up the lightest the dumbbells, he began pumping them in the air, one in each fist, in regular alternation. When he was finished, Marvell moved to the next set, and minute by minute worked his way up to the largest weights.

I confess that the speed with which he progressed impressed me once more. It really did seem as if he was growing stronger with each exercise.

Beside me, Sherlock Holmes remarked dryly, "This fellow is a veritable wizard."

I took that to be a compliment. "He is very impressive," I allowed.

"My dear Watson, this fellow is no strongman. He is an illusionist. All eyes are upon him and are growing impressed by his performance. But the secret is not in the bottle. Nor is it in his constitution. It lies elsewhere."

"Truly?"

"As with every illusionist, every word, movement and gesture is calculated. All have hidden significance and operate in furtherance of the illusion. Watch, and you will see."

Having completed his routine of exercises, Jack Marvell went over to the great safe, walked around it once, studying its legs and then, grasping one corner, bent his back into one side, laborious shifting the steel box around until the door faced the audience as squarely as before.

"Pardon any slight delay," Marvell told his audience. "This unique safe was constructed expressly for this purpose, and the manufacturer rightly insists that their name be prominently displayed. I am sure many in this audience know of their good reputation."

Holmes whispered to me, "I had expected this, Watson."

"I beg your pardon?"

"This last gesture is the most telling of all. I daresay he does not give a performance without straightening out the safe to his satisfaction. Such elaborate fussiness has nothing to do with the manufacturer's plate."

"So it is a trick then?"

"An illusion. This man is schooled in the ancient art of misdirection. He is trying to convince the audience that he owns nearly supernatural physical prowess, and doing a convincing job of it. But nothing could be further than the truth."

"You don't say!"

"Examine the problem, Watson, and the solution will become obvious to you."

But it was not. I watched with growing fascination as Jack Marvell wiggled himself under the steel safe, inserting himself into position. He did this from the side, so that we could see him in full profile, the better to display his struggle.

And struggle he apparently did. For he got on his hands and knees, and began to exert himself upward. Wonder of wonders, the safe began to work around under his upward pressure, one steel foot clearly separating from the floor before long.

In the beginning, the struggle was so convincing that perspiration streamed from his forehead. And I could not see how that was accomplished, other than by actual physical effort.

"He struggles at his task," I noted.

Holmes undertoned, "It is all part of the act. But the struggle is real. The safe is too heavy for him to lift. But soon that will change."

True enough, for several minutes passed. Abruptly, as if his body had been fully infused by the powerful drink, Jack Marvell brought his body increasingly erect, pausing on one knee as he transferred the palms of his hands to the bottom of the safe, raising it easily and perfectly over his perspiration-bathed head as he straightened his entire body.

Then he turned about so that he faced the audience.

As before, the audience jumped to their feet and cheered as if the Duke of Wellington himself had appeared, triumphant from the plains of Waterloo.

"He has done it again!" I cried out. "Wondrous man, he has achieved the impossible."

"Nonsense, Watson. The safe is empty now. A child could lift it."

"But what of the contents?"

"Evacuated. The strongbox is a void. This is incontrovertible. When I and my fellow audience members undertook to elevate the safe, the task was beyond our combined powers. When Jack Marvell first attempted to do the same, it was initially beyond his. But during the period when he was on his hands and knees, slowly and steadily this changed."

"But how? I fail to divine it."

The applause was beginning to die down.

"Think, Watson. Think! There is a logical and practical explanation. You need only disrobe the problem of all fanciful possibilities and that which remains stands unclothed as the truth."

"Could there be a powerful magnet under the stage, holding the safe down until the proper time for release?"

Sherlock Holmes made a dismissive noise deep in his throat.

"I doubt that such a powerful magnet could be created. Perhaps some future generation might achieve such a thing. No, no magnet lies beneath the stage. You may rest assured on that point."

"Then I must confess to my utter bafflement."

"It would do little good to tell you, Watson. Perhaps we can demonstrate it for all to see."

Burly stage hands were endeavoring to capture the suspended safe with stout rope and tackle, and got it under control, permitting Jack Marvell to step forward and take his bows.

Another wave of applause washed over him. The Surrey Strongman was beaming. It was clear that he enjoyed every moment of his triumph.

Audience members were shouting to him, asking where the miraculous juice could be purchased.

"Unfortunately," he returned in a voice pitched to be heard over their acclaim, "the supply is meager, because the ingredients are so rare. Perhaps one day it can be manufactured for the public general public, but for the moment, I possess the only sample."

Sherlock Holmes stood up and said loudly, "I congratulate you on your performance. You are a superior illusionist."

"I beg your pardon?" asked Marvell, gazing down at him.

"Permit me to introduce myself. I am Sherlock Holmes."

The broad smile on Jack Marvell's face wavered. He struggled to replenish it, and half succeeded.

"Why," he said magnanimously, "everyone has heard of Mr. Sherlock Holmes of London. I trust you enjoyed the performance, good sir."

"It held my interest from start to finish. But it has left me with many unanswered questions."

"Such as?"

"If the safe in question is too heavy for six men to lift, how is it that three stage hands with only a block and tackle are managing it even as we speak?"

"Why, because the equipment is of professional quality and the three men understand the necessary physics."

The safe was slowly lowered and

brought to rest upon the floor-boards. The sound its legs made was modest.

"I note the absence of a jar that would normally accompany a heavily-weighted object returning to the stage," remarked Holmes casually.

"My assistants are quite adept at not damaging the exhibition halls in which we are pleased to perform, thank you very much." Marvell's voice contained a distinct chill.

The Surrey Strongman turned his attention back to the audience, but Sherlock Holmes would have none of it.

"If I were to speculate," Holmes said crisply. "I would speculate the safe is now empty."

"Nonsense! It is full of scrap iron and other weights."

"Have you the key?"

"Not on my person, I fear," remarked Marvell, his voice showing a tinge of irritation.

"Pity."

Sherlock Holmes was mounting the stage and fell to examining the huge black safe once more. His pipe was in his hand and he was tapping at the walls on one side and at the back with the bowl.

"Whatever are you doing?" demanded Marvell.

"The sound is different now, if I am not mistaken. The steel rings hollow."

"Sir, those walls are three inches thick."

"I doubt it," said Holmes. He was looking at the rear legs, particularly the one on the right.

"Remarkable," he said.

Jack Marvell joined him, demanding, "What do you find remarkable?"

"I thought I would discover water pooling around his leg, but I see none."

"Water?"

Holmes walked over to another spot and examined the floor-boards. "Could you tell me what this signifies?"

He pointed downward with his unlit pipe.

Jack Marvell hardly glanced down, but his lean face lost some of its reddening color. "I haven't the faintest notion. I did not build this stage. Now sir, the performance has concluded. Would you kindly leave the stage?"

"I noted that when you restored the safe to its original position, you made certain that this particular leg made contact with this unusual aperture in the floor-boards whose flange I perceive surrounds a hole drilled into the wood."

Removing a handkerchief from his pocket, Sherlock Holmes knelt down and pressed it upon the spot. When he brought the cloth up again, it was limp with moisture.

"As I suspected. A slim pipe. One should not be surprised, I suppose, for I see from the door plate that the manufacturer is W. E. *Drain*. I know of no such concern, unless they are by trade *plumbers.*"

"Sir, I beg of you! The performance is at an end!" Jack Marvell began snapping his fingers in the direction of the stage hands. And they converged upon my friend with the intention of removing him from the stage forthwith.

Sherlock Holmes was either oblivious to them or entirely unconcerned, for he continued speaking in a casual tone of voice.

"The problem of the safe is easily understood as one of hydraulics. The safe was full when the six audience members attempted to move it, and it was empty when you succeeded in lifting it over your head. In between, it was in a state of flux."

Marvell stared blankly. He was quite pale now.

"I asked myself whatever could be in flux?" continued Holmes. "Only one substance can to be made to flow in and out of enclosed spaces, unseen and unsuspected. And that is water, common $H_2O$. I daresay if we were to open the safe door, there would be no scrap metal inside. Only emptiness. I also imagine that the inner walls of the safe would be quite moist to the touch."

"What are you doing, Mr. Holmes?" demanded Marvell heatedly.

"I am merely musing out loud. Speculating, as it were. Since you do not have the key at hand, we have no means to prove my theory.

But my belief is this: when the curtain opened, the safe was full of water and this included the hollow walls of all four sides and possibly the top as well. This volume of water would add up to a considerable weight, a weight roughly equivalent to scrap iron. No ordinary man could move such a thing. Nor, if the safe was sufficiently water-tight, could its true contents be suspected."

"Nonsense!"

"So you assert. But as I cast my eyes in the direction of your bottle of elixir, it's coloration reminds me of common prune juice. It is all very droll. Again, I complement you, Mr. Marvell. Once you had repositioned the rear leg so that it was connected to the drainage pipe, water commenced flowing into the reservoir that no doubt rests beneath this stage. A simple mechanical valve would effectuate the transfer. This would take some considerable time. During which time, you kept the audience occupied with your conversation and your exercises. The timing was wonderful. Your attempt to lift a sealed safe while it was still partially filled with water, made for a convincing show of exertion. During the latter phase of the operation, the last of the water would be draining out and you would be able to lift the entirety of the box over your head, given that its hollow walls are very thin, but substantial enough to contain the liquid contents and make plausible your final feat of exertion."

"The very devil!" muttered Jack Marvell, turning pale.

This exchange was made in the normal of voices of both men, and so reached the front rows only. But those who heard it, passed it on to others, and soon the entire hall was alive with news of the preposterous imposture.

There came complaints, catcalls and other forms of verbal abuse. The stage hands who were so intent upon laying hands upon Sherlock Holmes stood around, looking dumb and helpless, not knowing what to do.

Realizing that the audience was turning against him, Jack Marvell made a final quick bow and exited, stage left.

It was good that he did this, for the audience became increasingly restive and abusive.

Sherlock Holmes drove his point home when he got down upon one knee and using both hands, endeavored to lift the massive safe from the front.

He could not quite lift it more than a few feet, but he showed that it could be done. Lowering the box, he hastened off the stage, pausing only to acknowledge the cheers and jeers of the crowd.

Saying, "You know, this is an opportune time to be on our way, Watson," Sherlock Holmes pulled me out the side exit and into the blustery winds of Piccadilly.

As we hastened away, I remarked, "I suppose that will prove to be the last of Jack Marvell's performances in London."

"I imagine so, for news travels rapidly in the metropolis. Fleet Street will have the story before long, and that will be that."

As we sauntered in the direction of Baker Street, I remarked, "Well, you must admit that it was quite a performance."

"Indeed, Watson, I do. And I am greatly appreciative that you lured me out of my funk to see it. For this evening of entertainment has made a profound alteration in my mood. I regret spoiling Mr. Marvell's future engagements, but I do believe he laid it on rather thick."

"Very thick," I agreed.

"I do not care very much for strongmen, though I appreciate a good illusionist. But a man who is one and pretends to be the other, well, he is an imposter and deserves exposure. Still, the clever fellow is no criminal. We must not think too poorly of Mr. Marvell."

"I do not think badly of the man at all. Why, the pleasure of watching a trick being performed is the willingness to accept it as real."

"I imagine so," said Sherlock Holmes dryly. "Regrettably, I am a man whose fascination with tricks and schemes lies entirely in the unraveling of them. Perhaps I became carried away, ruining Mr. Marvell's act. It was harmless enough. He was not selling his elixir. He was not bilking the public. He was bamboozling them, which is in the fine tradition of those who ply the time-honored practice of misdirection. Much less of an offense, I suppose. Yet still I am somehow offended."

"Perhaps your disappointment lies with the intelligence of the general public, and not in the audacity of Mr. Jack Marvell."

"I do believe there is something in what you say, Watson." Holmes's pace quickened. "Come along, now. Let us seek a good restaurant. Now that I have put this minor challenge behind me, I feel that I must fortify myself in the certain hope that other, more worthy, challenges lie just around the corner, which is how I prefer daily life to be."

# The Jeweled Cobra Affair

### By RICHARD C. WHITE

ANOTHER typical day was winding down at the Chase and Blackthorne Agency. Loosely translated, that meant no clients all day. To make matters worse, my partner, Ze'eva Blackthorne was out of town, so I couldn't even distract myself with conversation. The sunbeam I'd been observing finished inching across the floor and began working its way up the wall when Kyra, my secretary, stuck her head through the door to the inner office.

"Theron, why don't you call it a day and go home?"

"What? And deny my adoring public the chance to come see me?"

Even though Kyra was only 4'3" in heels, she could pack the attitude of an ogre into one look. She flipped her gossamer wings at me and walked back to her desk, leaving the connecting door between our offices open. She was right, though; my bed was softer than this chair. I'd just taken my feet off the desk when the outer door banged open. Kyra let out a startled shriek as a man stumbled past her—his face ashen and his eyes staring straight ahead. Laboriously, he worked his way to my desk, his feet barely rising off the floor. I noticed he was holding a package against his stomach with both hands.

"Y-you're Theron Chase, right?"

I rushed around the desk and grabbed him by the shoulders. "Here. Let me help you."

His eyes glanced everywhere and nowhere as he shook me off. "No time. No time. They're right behind me. You gotta take this package. Don't let them get it."

"We'll deal with the package later. Kyra, call a doctor."

He grabbed my arm in a vice-like grip. "No doctor. No time. Take the package. Hide it. Don't let them have it."

"Don't let who have it?"

His eyes were glazing over. "His men...everywhere. Thought I'd gotten away... they found me. Hide...package. Keep...it...safe."

"Who found...?" My question remained unasked because the man suddenly went limp and sprawled on the floor. The package slipped from his fingers onto my office floor. That's when I noticed the large red blotch on his stomach. He'd been pressing the package against a gunshot wound. I checked, but there was

*Illustration by Jeff Weigel*

no pulse. Whoever this was, he wouldn't be worrying about packages any longer.

While Kyra was phoning the doctor, I checked him for identification. When I didn't find anything, I picked up the package. It felt like a simple box beneath the brown packing paper and strings. An unremarkable package, but whatever it was, the bloodstains proved someone wanted it bad enough to kill. *What have you gotten into this time, Chase?*

He'd mentioned being followed, so I secured the package in the floor safe underneath the desk. I was setting the boards back in place when Kyra came in. "The doctor's on his way, Theron."

I stepped around the desk and stood next to the body. "Doc won't be much help, Kyra. Get Captain Corvinus on the phone. He's going to have a lot of questions I can't answer. But bad news doesn't get better with age."

A strange voice came from the door to my office. "Now, that would be a very bad idea, Chase."

Two thugs stood in the entryway. The one who'd spoken was your regular street thug—flashy clothes, big attitude, and a gun to match. His partner worried me more. One, he was a minotaur, a rare customer even in Calasia. Two, he looked more intelligent than his partner.

"Welcome, gentlemen. What can I do for you?"

The flashy mug stepped forward, his .38 revolver never wavering

from my belly button. "I like this guy, Clyde. He's got manners. Not like your regular shamus."

"We like to keep our customers happy. Also, the landlord complains when he has to patch bullet holes more than once a month."

The minotaur's bass voice reminded me of a landslide, "He talks too much. Ask the questions, so we can get the stuff and go."

"You heard Clyde, shamus. What did our pal there tell you?"

"Nothing. He collapsed as soon as he came in. We've already called for a doctor. I suspect the constables will be right behind them."

The gunsel cocked his head to one side. "No sirens yet. We got time. Now, where's the package?"

I eased onto the corner of my desk between Kyra and the two thugs. "Package? The only thing this man was holding was his guts with both hands."

"Pretty neat trick, seein' there ain't no blood on his hands." There was a quick blur of motion and then the thug's gun barrel caught me right above my eyebrow. "Don't get smart. He had a package when he entered this building. He didn't have time to go nowhere else. So, what'd you do with it?"

I heard Kyra moving, but I signaled her to wait a moment longer. "Search the office if it'll make you happy. You'll just waste a lot of time and probably my blood. I never saw a package. Hell, I never saw that guy until he walked in and I wish I'd never seen him."

"Truer words were never spoken, shamus."

The gunsel started to swing again, but I stepped forward, blocking his swing with my left arm and catching him with a right to the chin. He went one direction and his revolver went the other. The minotaur took two steps toward me when a whirlwind caught him, slamming him into the ceiling and then down against the floor, knocking the breath out of him. He tried to push off the floor when Kyra stepped out from behind me, her green eyes blazing. Her whirlwind slammed the minotaur against one of the walls and then back down to the floor, pinning him there.

My buddy leapt for his gun in the confusion. I went after him and the two of us wrestled for the gun. I forced him to drop it as his knee hit my nether regions. My stomach heaved, but before he could do anything else, there was a commotion in the outer room and two constables rushed in. My playmate snarled and dove through the window onto the fire escape. One of the constables followed him through the shattered window. I heard clanging footsteps receding down the metal stairs.

"What the devil is going on here, Chase?" Officer Michael Lain asked.

"You tell me and we'll both know, Officer," I wheezed. I pointed to the body and then the gun on the floor.

"That guy came in with a gunshot wound, probably from that gun. You should find smudged fingerprints of mine and that gunsel's your boy is chasing. The big guy Kyra is holding is named Clyde. I suspect he knows what's happening, but I also suspect he won't say much."

"Oh, I've met Clyde a time or two, haven't I, bucko?"

The minotaur's head slowly turned so he could look up. "And you're as big a pain-in-the-ass as always, Lain. Now, will you get the witch to turn me loose? I'm about to bust a couple of ribs."

Kyra glanced at Officer Lain and me. I grabbed my .45 automatic from the desk and nodded. Normally, I would have relied on my hickory head-knocker, but even enchanted wood might splinter on Clyde's thick skull.

It was obvious, Clyde had done this before. Claimed he was coming to see me, and the other man, whom he had *never* seen before, was already here. In fact, he tried to help when my secretary, (who barely came up to his waist), viscously attacked him without provocation. Officer Lain dutifully took down Clyde's statement without snickering, and asked Kyra and me to swing by the Citadel later to give our versions of the story. A bit later, the doctor and the crime scene guys filled up my office taking pictures and asking questions no one seemed to be able to answer.

After a long while, everyone filed out and Kyra called the building manager. He said he'd take care of stuff later. Once we were certain things had settled down, we called it a night and I retrieved the package from the floor safe. Something told me I should keep it with me after all this.

AROUND eight that evening, there was a knock on my door. I thought about ignoring it, but the rising volume suggested my unwanted visitor was not going away. I glanced over at my liquor cabinet where I had secured the package in the hidden drawer where I kept my very best scotch. I hoped it would keep both secrets well.

I eased the door open and the tallest and skinniest man I'd ever met stood outside. His voice was as cultured as his appearance was odd. "Good evening, Mr. Chase. Might I come in?"

I stepped back as he bent forward to slip beneath the door's mantel. "Good evening, Mister..." I let the unasked question trail off.

"Thaddeus Green," the giant said. I took his coat and to my amazement, he couldn't have weighed more than 150 pounds dripping wet, yet stood well over seven feet tall. He sat in my easy chair and I took the corner of the bed. "Let me come to the point, Mr. Chase. You have the cobra. I want it. I'm willing to pay a sizeable finder's fee if you will hand it

over with a modicum of fuss and bother."

"The cobra?" I could feel the wrinkles forming on my forehead. "I'm afraid you have me at a disadvantage, Mr. Green. If you'd care to explain?"

Mr. Green's smile dimmed as he leaned closer. "Mr. Chase, there's no need to bargain. I am fully aware of the cobra's value. Now, name your price and we'll get on with this."

"Sir, I would love to oblige. Trust me, my bookie and my landlord would appreciate it also, but I have no clue what you're talking about." I had a rising suspicion I did, but since I hadn't opened the package, I wasn't lying...really.

His heavy sigh almost echoed in the silence. "I had *so* hoped you'd be reasonable. Oh, Wilbur."

Before I could reach for the pistol hidden under my pillow, the door opened and the gunsel from this afternoon came in, a new pistol in hand. "Good to see you again, shamus."

"I see Calasia's finest were as efficient as usual."

"I got a little exercise after I left your place. Nothing I couldn't handle."

The thin giant stood up. "You see, Mr. Chase, we followed Lance to your office building. Lance left your building under a sheet, but neither he nor the officers had the package. Neither did your secretary. By the way, how *did* you ever convince that lovely sylph to work for you? Well, anyway, the law of logic tells me if no one else has the cobra, then you must."

"That's a lovely theory, but I've never seen any cobra, couldn't describe it to save my life, and simply can't help you."

"Save your life? Oh how droll, Mr. Chase. That's *exactly* what you should be doing, but very well." He turned to the thug who was staying out of range. "Wilber, I'm afraid Mr. Chase is being most recalcitrant. Perhaps you could persuade him to help?"

Wilber got a big grin on his face and moved in front of me after Mr. Green tied me to a chair. As Wilber started, Mr. Green turned on my radio, inching the volume up with each blow. The first five or six punches didn't hurt too much because Wilber was trying to ensure I stayed awake. When my protests failed to convince them, Wilbur began using the barrel of his gun. Somewhere around eight or nine, my eyes rolled up and darkness swept over me like fog coming in off the bay.

"M R. Chase. Mr. Chase. Wake up."

The voice sounded like it was coming through a mile-long pipe, soft and distorted, but that could have been everything still rattling around inside my head. I felt myself lifted off the floor and sat in a chair. My benefactor seemed to be holding me in place, which was good since everything swam

in front of me. At least the voice was becoming clearer.

"Mr. Chase. Are you awake now?"

"If not, I'm doing a great job of sleepwalking. Who're you?"

"If you can joke, then you will live. You may call me Chantar. I need to ask you some questions."

My head lolled to one side before it was pushed back into position. "Great. My office opens at nine. I'll be there by noon."

The voice grew sharper and I felt my chest constrict. "Mr. Chase, tomorrow will be too late for both of us. *Do* you have the cobra?"

I groaned. *Oh, no. Not this again.* "I can't see straight yet. Has the room been searched?"

The voice remained calm. "Oh, yes. Quite thoroughly."

"Before I answer your question, can you answer one of mine?"

My visitor had an odd accent I couldn't place. I blamed that on Wilber's tender ministrations. "Acceptable, but do not press your good fortune. You were lucky to even wake up."

*Yeah, that's not ominous at all.* "What is your interest in...the cobra, I think you said."

"The Jeweled Cobra is my people's most sacred relic, Mr. Chase. It was stolen recently. We've traced it to this city. We believe the gentleman who smuggled it into Calasia died in your office today."

"A man did die in my office today. Who he was is still a mystery." My vision was clearing, but I couldn't spot my benefactor. Someone was still holding me upright in the chair though. A low-grade tornado couldn't have done more damage to my room. I couldn't see the liquor cabinet but I couldn't imagine them missing that. "Given the condition of my room, *if* the cobra was here, then Thaddeus Green and associates undoubtedly have it."

The voice darkened and I realized something was pinning my arms to my sides. "That is most unfortunate. His yacht will unquestionably sail when the fog rolls in tonight. Thank you for the information. Now, you must die."

"Wait, what?"

Something started squeezing my chest and I realized I was encircled by large black coils, mottled in white. The air slowly was being forced out of my lungs. I did everything I could think of to get loose, but nothing helped. The coils just kept squeezing...and squeezing... and...

As tunnel vision started setting in, there was a violent pounding on my door. I couldn't make out what was happening, but, suddenly, the coils loosened and wonderful oxygen filled my lungs. I fell forward gasping for breath as something slithered across the floor and out my window.

Seconds later, the door burst open, and Captain Corvinus and two officers rushed in.

"Dammit, Chase, why don't you answer your phone? We need you down at..." he bellowed before he saw me lying among the rubble of my own apartment. I waved feebly at the window and the constables rushed over. They shined lights over the courtyard, but Chantar had made a clean get-away. Par for the course.

Corvinus turned my easy chair upright and helped me into it. Two glasses of water and a shot of scotch later, I began to feel like myself. He took notes while I clued him in on the day's events.

"You *were* right, Chase—that gun *was* the murder weapon. Now, at least we have a name for the killer and his boss, but catching them will be tough. I'm certain they didn't register this yacht under their real names."

"Did you get anything out of Clyde?"

"Hasn't said a word since leaving your office. We did find out about your visitor though. His name is Lance Merlain, a steward aboard the *S.S. Dawn Runner*, recently arrived from the Pagolin Islands. Had a clean record up 'til now."

"That makes sense. He was smuggling the cobra into Calasia and either got cold feet or was double-crossed."

"Either way, it ended with him dead in your office...wait! What cobra?"

"Why, the Jeweled Cobra. Didn't I mention that?"

Corvinus pushed his hat back to scratch his forehead. "And just what is a Jeweled Cobra?"

I patted him on the shoulder. "I haven't got a clue. Whatever it is, Thaddeus Green probably has it and this Chantar is after him. So, I'm going after both."

Corvinus brushed my hand off his shoulder and snorted. "In your condition?"

"Captain, someone came into my apartment and slapped me around. And then someone else tried to crush me. What kind of detective would I be if I didn't get to the bottom of this?"

"Chase, I've got an entire force of constables. We can track down these killers. You should get to the hospital."

"I'll take that under advisement. Unless you're planning on arresting me, Corvinus, I'm going."

He started to say something, but I guess the look on my face convinced him otherwise. "All right, Chase. Anything you want me to say at your funeral?"

I tucked my .45 auto into my shoulder holster and dabbed some medicine on my face to hide with the worst of it after Corvinus and his boys left. The mirror confirmed Wilbur's work would be pretty evident tomorrow. After another shot to fortify myself, I grabbed my trench coat, secured my head knocker, and headed out. From the way the fog was coiling in the courtyard, I knew it was going to be a miserable night tonight.

ALL I had to go on was Chantar mentioning Green's yacht. I knew few yachts berthed at the East Docks—too pedestrian. The South Docks cater exclusively to merchant ships. Besides, Green looked well-heeled enough to afford the fees at the North Hills Marina. So, while Corvinus and his men went to check on information about the S.S. Dawn Runner, I caught a cab for the ritzier part of town.

Luckily, the yacht club's offices were still open. Once the young lady working at the office quit staring at Wilbur's handiwork, some quick patter, a little flirting, and twenty crowns got me the break I needed. Thaddeus Green had been bold enough to register under his own name. Probably hadn't expected to be in town long enough for it to matter.

Once out of sight from the office, I prayed my magical jinx wouldn't hit tonight and activated a black gem to turn me invisible. Sneaking past several guards, I got into the North Hills Marina and made my way out onto the slip. Green's yacht, the Sea Sparrow, was still at its docking buoy. It was hard to make out details in the foggy darkness, but it was easy to see it was built for speed. If he got into open water, the Coast Guard would have a hell of a time catching him. No one seemed to be preparing for departure from here, but I knew Green would sail the second the tide changed.

An old dock hand agreed to row me out to the *Sea Sparrow* for a small fee. No one seemed to notice our approach. I grabbed the ladder and gave the sailor a couple of crowns extra and told him to call Corvinus and tell him where I was. I crept up onto the deck and slipped into the nearest shadows. I didn't know if the ship's crew was aware of Green's activities, but no reason to alert them if I could avoid it.

I soon realized the crew was the least of my worries. I found a sailor laying sprawled in a gangway, his eyes bulging and his lips blue. A quick check confirmed he'd been crushed to death. I realized I wasn't the only uninvited guest this evening. On the bridge, I found two other sailors there. One had been crushed, but the other had two nasty puncture wounds in his shoulder. Given the blackness radiating from them, I guessed he'd been poisoned, but by what? The bite marks, if that's what they were, were a good five inches apart.

Tightening the grip on my .45, I moved deeper into the ship, checking the cabins and holds for any sign of life. Finally, near the front of the ship, I found a huge cabin with the lights on inside. Thaddeus Green lay groaning on one of the couches near a well-stocked bar, holding his side. On the floor nearby, Wilbur lay staring up at the ceiling not seeing anything.

Surprised to find Green still alive, I rushed to his side. I opened his shirt and saw the black lines still spreading across his body from the bite there. It was only a matter of time.

His eyes fluttered open. "The wages of greed, Mr. Chase. Apparently my sins have caught up with me."

"Don't talk, Green. I'll summon the Harbor Patrol. They can get a doctor here quick."

Green laboriously raised his head. "Don't bother. I've never heard of anyone surviving a naga's bite..." he coughed before continuing, "...and I don't expect to be the first."

"A naga?" Suddenly, a few things fell into place. "Chantar stopped by my apartment after you left. I see he wasted no time getting here."

"He didn't introduce himself. Most ungracious fellow. Wilbur didn't even get a chance to scream. I think his windpipe was crushed instantly. I tried to flee, but he was too quick."

"Did Chantar get the Jeweled Cobra?"

"And you said you didn't know about it."

"All I know is Chantar told me it was a sacred relic."

"Oh quite, although they themselves did not forge the cobra. No, they stole it from a more ancient race. To be honest, Mr. Chase, my interest in the cobra was a tad more worldly. The jewels alone are worth an emperor's ransom, but as a whole, it would bring any price to the right collector."

"Such as yourself?"

Green allowed himself a small laugh in-between wincing. "No, Mr. Chase, I only collect coin of the realm. Wilbur acquired the cobra in the Pagolin Islands and we arranged for Lance Merlain to bring it ashore—the customs agents don't search crewmembers as thoroughly as passengers. However, he learned the nagai had sent a Night Naga to recover the cobra—assassins of the highest caliber, Mr. Chase, make no mistake—and, panic-stricken, he decided to dispose of the cobra. We caught up with him momentarily, but he escaped and eventually wound up in your office. Whether it was blind luck or he knew of you is of no matter."

Green's eyes closed before he slid to the floor. Whether he had simply fainted or had died, I couldn't tell. His pulse was barely perceptible. I picked up the microphone to notify the Harbor Patrol on the ship's radio when I heard a soft voice behind me. "Please, put the microphone down, Mr. Chase."

A huge snake-like creature with a human face rose from behind the bar. Its scales were black with intricate white splotches almost forming constellations and its cold reptilian eyes bore into mine. "You should have recognized your great fortune at escaping my coils and retired from the field of battle, Mr.

Chase. Now, your pursuit of the cobra leads you to your death."

I set the microphone down, resting it so the transmit button was open in a vain hope someone would be listening. Chantar slithered from behind the bar, keeping the front third of his body erect, eerily indifferent to the .45 in my hand. As he passed Green's body, I saw Thaddeus raise his head slightly and then lower it again. I had no clue what he might be up to, so I decided to keep Chantar's focus on me.

"Honestly, I was after Green and Wilbur for killing Merlain. When I found the bodies above deck, I thought you and the cobra were long gone. Wouldn't you want to return the cobra to your homeland as quickly as possible?"

"All in due time, Mr. Chase. Green intended to flee on this yacht to meet his buyer. I will follow his strategy and use my enemy's own yacht to reach my homeland. This will help avoid dealing with nosy custom agents. The changing tides will ensure I slip through the bumbling Calasian constables' fingers. However, when I saw a rowboat disappearing into the fog near the yacht, I knew someone must have come aboard. I decided to wait to see who and now I have the entire story thanks to our departed host."

He inched closer. "As I see it, you are the only loose end left to tie up. I'll give you a choice, Mr.

Chase—the coils or the venom?"

"I vote neither. You're forgetting I'm armed."

"A trifle." He barked a command and a large dark-skinned man came through the door behind me, carrying a nasty-looking pistol. He motioned for me to toss my gun aside and then frisked me, tossing my head knocker aside. The man bowed to the naga and slowly backed out of the room.

"You were wise to remain still. I personally trained Kasan, one of the few humans ever inducted into my cult. Normally I need no help, but sometimes I find having arms comes in handy. Now, Mr. Chase, I believe you were about to make a choice?"

I couldn't see Green any longer, but I still had to stall to give him as much time as possible. "So, what exactly does this Jeweled Cobra do?"

A small smile crossed Chantar's face. "Do? Does it have to do anything, Mr. Chase? It is a symbol—a symbol of my cult and a symbol of my power. It normally resides in a temple in my compound, a venerable relic from an earlier time. Perhaps once it had magic, perhaps it still does, but the magic of belief enthralls the nagai into doing my bidding. That is powerful enough magic for me." He rose even higher as he advanced toward me. "And now, Mr. Chase, the time for talk is over. Your death rises to meet you."

A shot rang out behind him

and I saw him stiffen. He wheeled around and Wilbur's revolver spoke again and again before Chantur struck Green with a vicious bite. I dove to the side and grabbed my own automatic and pumped three shots into Chantur's head while he was still fastened to Green. Chantur's body whipped around the room in his death throes as I dove to one side to avoid him. I heard running feet and when Kasan rushed in, I fired once, dropping him before he ever spotted me.

An ominous stillness settled on the room. Green weakly raised his head to speak. "And now the book is closed. Chase, promise me something."

"If I can."

"Destroy the cobra. As long as it exists, another Chantur may come to claim it."

I nodded as a harsh rattle came from his throat and his head slumped, leaving me alone on the boat until the Harbor Patrol showed up along with Captain Corvinus.

AS the sun rose, I had Corvinus drop me off at Markham's Emporium of the Ancients. I was tired, unshaven, and unkempt, and didn't care. I pushed right past the concierge and made my way back to Theo Markam's office. Along with being a brilliant businessman, Theo was one of the empire's greatest wizards, and more importantly he was a good friend. Theo immediately poured me a glass of scotch and a cup of coffee.

"Theron, you've looked worse, but I can't remember when."

"Good to see you too, Theo. Got a little disposal job for you."

He sat down behind his desk. "What magical deviltry did you bring me this time?"

"Ever heard of the Jeweled Cobra?"

I've never seen Theo go pale before. "You have that? Here?"

I eased the still-wrapped package on his desk. "Promised someone I'd destroy it, but I haven't a clue how."

Theo bolted from his desk and locked his office door, and pulled the shade. "Did you touch it?"

"Haven't even opened it. Thought I'd leave that up to you."

"Ze'eva's good sense must be rubbing off on you. Anyway, if that's the real thing, you can't destroy it. Even your magical jinx won't affect it."

"Suggestions? Comments? Critiques?"

Theo waved his hands and a blue light surrounded the package, quickly turning black. Sweating, profusely, Theo pulled something from a safe behind him. and withdrew an obsidian casket. After more words I couldn't understand, he closed the package inside an obsidian casket. He summoned a swirling black spot on his office wall and stepped through. I used the time he was gone to work on the coffee and the scotch. Three refills later, he reappeared, tugging at his collar as if his tie was tight.

"Theron Chase, *would* you warn me the next time you decide to bring a ticking bomb into my office"

"Theo, I wouldn't if I didn't have to. What'd you do with the cobra?"

He gave a worried glance at the wall. "It's in storage. A representative from the Imperial College of Wizards will retrieve it tomorrow. I don't know what you got paid but I hope they made it worth your while."

I hadn't made a cent, but I'd never admit that to Theo. "Let's just say, this affair had a satisfying conclusion. And now, my friend, I'm going home and going to bed."

Mike Collins '88

# The Man Cut in Half

## By LESTER DENT

*Illustration by Mike Collins*

**M**EET Feder. And his flowers! Operative Nat Feder of the Tri-State Detective Agency, his license said. Maybe he'd been called this some. But that was at first. He was Feder-and-a-Flower now, or the Blossom Sleuth, or the Columbine Clewsman, or the Hollyhock Hawk, or the Foxglove Fox, or the Wisteria Wizard, or whatever else newspaper reporters could grab a dictionary and cogitate up.

It was always Feder and some kind of a flower, though. Nobody'd ever seen him without a bloom of one sort or another in his lapel, or his hand, or his desk, car, apartment, office. He had them everywhere. Nobody quite understood why. Feder didn't tell them. Neither did Old Man Jon Sutton, who owned the Tri-State. It was their secret. "It's a secret that'll make you, with a little more experience, the greatest in this business ever to live," Old Jon had told Feder.

Feder sat in the Tri-State offices now, playing with a big red rose and listening to Old Jon Sutton tell about Claussen.

"Claussen is dead—the town constable of Garnet phoned the word a minute ago," Old Jon said

slowly. Old Jon's ropy hands, shaking a little, betrayed his grief. He was getting awfully old to hide his feelings. Old Jon had been thirty years on the force before he founded the Tri-State Detective Agency, and that was twenty years ago. He continued, "Garnet is a little place out on Long Island."

"I know where Garnet is," Nat Feder said, and put the rose in a vase on his desk and took out a couple of long-stemmed violets. Old Jon still looked like a cop. Feder didn't. Feder had stepped from a university criminology course to the Tri-State Detective Agency. You'd call him a career man in the detective business.

"The constable knew it was Milt Claussen by the agency cards in Claussen's pocket." Old Jon put his shaking hands under the desk, as though ashamed of them. "Somebody happened on the body about an hour ago. Claussen had been dead about half an hour. He was still smashed under the car. The doctor said he positively had died when the car skidded over the bank. It had been raining hard. Claussen was alone in the car."

"Whose car?" Feder asked, fingering the violets.

"It was stolen off a Garnet street this afternoon. The constable said Claussen's death was absolutely an accident."

Feder said coldly, "Somebody made a mistake." Feder was under thirty, tall, could carry twenty pounds more flesh without being too heavy. Around his eyes was the aged look of a man who has worked his brain a little too hard.

"You know why Claussen was at Garnet?" asked Old Jon.

"No. I wasn't aware he was away from the office."' Feder changed the violets for snapdragons.

"This morning, a Sir Bernard Bredhame gave us a ring," explained Old Jon. "He said a friend of his named Scofield, a guest at his house, had missed a wallet with two thousand dollars in it. He said it looked like someone in the house had taken it, and he didn't want to notify the police because they'd give it to the newspapers. He asked for a man and I sent Claussen."

"Claussen had not reported since reaching Sir Bernard's?"

"No." Old Jon tied his ropy hands together on his desk. It was a long minute before he queried, "Did I ever tell you how Claussen got that twisted foot of his?"

Feder shook his nose among the snapdragons.

"It was fifteen years ago, the first time Claussen ever got behind the wheel of an automobile," Old Jon said. "Claussen hit another car. Claussen got that twisted foot

in the wreck and a little girl in the other car was killed. It wasn't Claussen's fault, but he was taking his first driving lesson when it happened and he always felt that if it had not been for that, the little girl would be alive."

Feder said into the flower, "They said Claussen drove that car over the bank tonight."

"And Claussen couldn't drive a car," said Old Jon. "He would never learn."

Feder stood up, tall, serious, studious, putting a carnation in his lapel. He went over to the water cooler and drank.

"I'm off for Garnet," he said.

THE village of Garnet was strewn along one of the small bays that nicked the hilly north shore of Long Island. A few houses were cocked on the precipitous sloping terrain that enwalled the bay. The highway descended to the town in serpentine curves. Feder's car was in the shop, so he took a taxi out instead of a Long Island train. Feder disliked trains. And a lot of flowers blossomed along the roads at this time of year. It was night, of course, but their aroma was in the air.

Feder stopped at the Garnet morgue to look at Claussen's body. Claussen had been a man about the age of Old Jon, and he had been Old Jon's dearest friend.

The body had indeed been crushed under the car, the head especially. To tell what sort of a blow had first made Claussen unconscious would be impossible.

Feder went over Claussen's clothing and few personal affects. He tarried longest over a gaberdine topcoat, still moist from the evening shower.

"One of the murderers had old-fashioned catarrh[1]," he muttered.

"What say?" asked the Garnet constable, who was present. The constable didn't know anything about the death being murder. But then, had he known, he'd have been incredulous. Even a microscope couldn't have shown a clue that pointed at anybody having catarrh.

"It doesn't matter," Feder shrugged. "Where is Sir Bernard Bredhame's home, and where was Claussen found?"

The constable replied to the two questions. Claussen had been discovered about half a mile from Sir Bernard Bredhame's place.

Feder telephoned Sir Bernard's residence, said he was from the Tri-State agency, but nothing more, and asked if a car could come to Garnet for him, since he'd dismissed his taxi.

"Righto," said Sir Bernard. "I shall send my chauffeur, Kaff, at

---

[1] **Editor's Note:** According to NHS. uk, "catarrh" is a build-up of mucus in an airway or cavity of the body. It usually affects the back of the nose, the throat or the sinuses. It's often temporary, but some people experience it for months or years. This is known as chronic catarrh. The term has been around since the 1500s but not commonly used today.

once." Sir Bernard had a strong British accent.

Feder talked flower culture with the Garnet constable while he waited. The constable had heard of Detective Feder and his flowers, and had also been a florist by trade back when foreign bonds were considered an investment.

The car arrived in fifteen minutes. It was a black Rolls, probably five years old. The driver, Kaff, was a compactly built little man who interspersed his talk with seafaring lingo. He looked rather pale.

"Some shower we had about eight bells, sir," he offered by way of conversation. He spoke in a listless voice, as though he felt ill.

Feder said it'd sweeten up the vegetation, then asked, "You're not afflicted with catarrh, I hope?"

"Keelhaul me, no," said Kaff. It was a full minute later when he added, "I never knew anyone who had it, sir."

Feder didn't seem interested, except in a nice greenhouse they'd passed.

Sir Bernard Bredhame's home was palatial, vast, Colonial in architecture. It sat like a white sailor cap on the tree-furred head of a round hill. The grounds were neat, grass clipped, shrubbery manicured. Feder liked the tulip beds especially.

SIR Bernard Bredhame was about what one would expect. Average in height, well-knit, he needed only a monocle to make him the stage Englishman. And the wide starey look of his left eye indicated he might have worn something of the sort a lot.

"Jove, I'm a bit taken," Sir Bernard murmured. "I already have one of your Tri-State chaps around somewhere. Name of Claussen." He produced an English-made cigarette, took one, offered the pack. They smelled like good, unblended tobacco.

Feder eyed some roses basketed by a telephone, said he'd take one of those if it was all the same, then asked, "You don't know Claussen is dead, then?"

"Now I say!" ejaculated Sir Bernard, and threw his cigarette away without lighting it. "Is that right? I thought he was still here somewhere."

"He was found in a car that had crashed over a bank." Feder, tall, somberly attired, looked like an undertaker with his rose.

"An accident, eh?" Sir Bernard fingered absently in a vest pocket, brought out what Feder at first thought was a monocle, but later saw was a compact loupe of the sort jewelers wear pinched in their eye.

Feder didn't tell him it was no accident. He said slowly, "I'd like to talk to the man who lost the wallet. Scofield was his name, I believe."

Sir Bernard put his eye-scope away. "Deuced neat service you give, taking up this affair where Claussen left off. But I say—ah, hm-m-m." He hesitated. "I'll call Scofield."

Feder let it pass that was hunting a wallet thief instead of a murderer. No use stirring things up.

Scofield—Ervin J. Scofield by Sir Bernard's introduction—was big, burly, angular withal, and finely dressed. He gave somewhat the impression of a bull in silks.

"My wallet contained two thousand dollars with which I intended to purchase a car," he explained. "It was taken from my clothing while I slept."

"We thought the thief might be one of my servants," Sir Bernard added. "Only they knew Scofield was carrying the money."

Feder had put the fresh rose in his lapel. He asked, "Any of your servants suffer from catarrh?"

"I think not," Sir Bernard replied.

"I'm afraid you're mistaken," Feder said shortly. "I wish you would question them on that point at once. I shall return later."

He glanced incuriously at Scofield, added, "Wool clothing is rather annoying when it gets wet, isn't it?"

"Huh?" said Scofield.

Feder didn't elaborate. He swung out, pursued by the puzzled stares of Sir Bernard and Scofield. Feder was a new one on them. But then, Feder and his flowers had been a new one to a lot of people.

Feder carried a flashlight, a five-cell article, one of the most powerful made. He found a path that led through a wood toward the spot where Claussen had been found mutilated under the car. Here was a clean freshness to the night air. Lots of nice blooming plants along the path, too. For Feder, that walk was almost a stroll in Heaven, except for a hunch that something savoring very much of Hell would break before the night was over.

THE rain of the evening had washed sandy Long Island soil across the path at spots where the ground was low. Feder used his flash to avoid these.

He made a discovery. Claussen's footprints in the soft sand, headed the same way Feder was going! There was no mistaking them. The twisted foot Claussen had received in that automobile accident of long ago made his trail distinctive.

Feder quickened his pace. Ahead, he heard a car drum past, and knew he was nearing the road where Claussen had been found.

A hundred feet from the road, Feder halted for no visible reason at all. Standing in one spot, he turned slowly around, twice. He stepped off the trail to the right, then, slamming through high shrubs, played the flash beam.

The crushed-down condition of grass and weeds there showed where men had lain in ambush. Sodden tobacco ash was plentiful. There was none of the dottle that would be present had it been pipe ash. But neither was there cigarette butts.

"Put the nubs in their pockets," Feder mused to himself. "Two of them waited here. The one with the catarrh is troubled badly with it.

And the other was our friend of the lost wallet, Scofield."

An onlooker would have called the deductions black magic. To the human eye there was no clue discernible, absolutely none, to indicate what Feder had learned.

Feder returned to the path, casting the flash beam about incessantly. He retraced his route along the trail. A rod or so back, he found a spot where a man had walked straight into the brush and straight out again. The soggy leaves held no definite track; there were no bits of cloth or the usual clues clinging to the brush.

But Feder said mentally, "The catarrh-man went in here. He probably got something and came right out again. It was probably something Claussen threw in here when he discovered their ambush. They made him tell where he threw it."

Not without reason had a reporter, watching Feder perform, once dubbed him the Wisteria Wizard.

Down the path to the road, Feder followed the jumping flash beam. He found a spot there, in the mud beside the pavement, where Claussen had been knocked down, probably before they put him in the murder car.

A roadster came singing along the pavement, passed with a gush of headlights. Feder scrutinized the pave in the headlight glare, then ran down the slab a few score yards to where he had seen wet paper.

He picked up an envelope. Soggy,

it bore no address. It was empty. Feder ascertained the envelope had been sealed, but soaking had loosened the flap mucilage. The glue which held the thing together was still sodden.

Hurriedly, Feder pulled the joined paper apart, spread the whole of the envelope out flat. He looked at the inside. A break!

THE envelope had evidently contained a single sheet of paper, unfolded, and had lain a while in the rain before being opened. The soaking had slightly dissolved ink which had been on the sheet of paper inside. The penned letters were outlined in vague, reversed form on the envelope interior. There was one sentence. It ended in a small cross instead of the conventional dot period.

*Thirty-seven stored at Old Oyster Farm+*

He stowed the envelope away, hurried down the road to where Claussen had gone over the bank. A wrecker crew was removing the car. It was a touring, top down, now a ruin. Feder went over it—spending most of his time on the wheel. There were no fingerprints.

But on the wheel, which was worn bare of enamel, was a mottled faint, brownish stain.

Feder asked the wreckers if they had ever heard of a place called the Old Oyster Farm.

"Must be that old seafood dining room down the road," he was told. "But it played out two or three years ago and has been locked up tight since."

Feder asked for the exact location of the place, got it, and took his departure.

It was a mile and a half to the Old Oyster Farm. Feder walked it. He was avid about this clean country air, sweetened by the earlier rain.

The Old Oyster Farm proved to be a rambling barn of a thing. The building was scabby with peeling paint, forlorn looking, but solid for all that.

Feder tried to peer through cracks in the boarded windows. Inside was dark and silent. The place had an odor of a thing long disused. Its atmosphere was vaguely sinister, what with the tall weeds about and the scratching noises rats made inside.

There appeared to be only one means of ingress—the front door. Feder hammered a fist on it. No answer. He had hardly expected one. He turned the flashlight on the door. A padlock securing it had been freshly torn off.

Feder stared at the door intently. There was nothing unusual about it, except the torn lock. Feder reluctantly discarded some goldenrod he had gathered, shifted the light to his left hand, took a blue revolver from a speed holster under his left arm.

"Somebody in there—was cut or stabbed," he grunted.

And that was another deduction that would have sent a bystander off talking to himself, swearing there was no way of noticing such things. He'd have been wrong, of course. But it did smack of looking into a crystal ball.

Feder bothered the door open with a toe, saw a narrow passage, popped his light into it.

No dead or wounded man lay there. But a lot of blood had spilled on the dusty plank floor.

WITHOUT going in, Feder eyed the weapon which had drawn the blood. A sword! A monster thing with a blade near seven feet long, wide, heavy. The cutting edges were feathered to the keenness of a razor. The hilt was wrought of an entwining of silver and gold and steel.

"English broadsword, early Sixteenth Century," Feder decided. "Rather a rare piece."

No magic about that. Anyone who had studied ancient history could have told.

The broadsword hilt was affixed to the ceiling by a crude hinge. A thin thread stretching a foot above the floor, now broken, had been rigged to a catch overhead. Whoever had come in had snapped the thread, causing the razor-edged, huge blade to swing down. A death trap!

Feder was a tall, darksome ghost of a figure as he eased inside. He picked up a pipe which lay against the passage wall. The pipe was a wreck. The descending sword blade had apparently caught it at the joint between stem and bowl-piece. Had

the razored steel bit anywhere else, it would have sheared through, but there was a heavy aluminum nicotine trap at the joint. As it was, the edge of the broadsword had sliced almost through the aluminum.

"Somebody was blamed lucky when he came in here with that pipe in his mouth, Feder decided.

He wandered deeper into the ancient structure. The floor creaked underfoot. Scampering rats gave him feelings like buckshot rolling down his back. The first room he peered into was empty. So was the next. So were they all.

Dust of years reposed everywhere, undisturbed except for rat tracks that looked like lace, and queer patterns where the roof had leaked rainwater. It was a ghostly place.

Feder was turning back from the rearmost room when he had another of his previsions. He suddenly saw something—how he knew it bordered on the inexplicable. He eased the flash off, hefted his revolver.

"The man with catarrh just came in!" He didn't speak aloud. He was just telling himself.

He waited; faculties strained. After a while, there was a creak in the corridor outside the room. Someone was creeping there.

"Who is it?" Feder called sharply. No answer.

Feder deliberately fired his gun twice into the room wall, careful to aim high enough to miss whoever was in the corridor.

*Wham! Wham! Wham!* Three times the prowler in the corridor returned bullets. Lead banged through the wall, tossing gusts of plaster. Feder felt the chill of a slug passing his face. But he stood perfectly still. The man outside, firing at random, was not likely to put two bullets in the same spot.

While echoes still bawled, the man in the corridor fled, running wildly. It seemed that he paused momentarily near the entrance, then went on.

Feder didn't rush in pursuit. He never worked that way; he had a not unreasonable wish to die of old age. Anyway, his chances of catching that man who had catarrh were slim.

The great, finely-wrought broadsword was gone from its devilish suspensory just inside the door.

Feder did one more thing before he left. He inspected the pipe which had, partially at least, stopped the death-trap drop of the sword. He went over it with microscopic care, using the lens of his flashlight for a magnifier.

The pipe bowl, around the rim, was scarred where it had been knocked against things to dislodge dottle. Imbedded in those pits was what looked like a brownish dye.

Exiting, Feder retrieved his posy of goldenrod from where he had discarded it.

FEDER returned to Sir Bernard Bredhame's white house on the hill by a roundabout course. Nearing the place, he went silently and did not play his flash beam. His shoes were wet from dew, somewhat muddy.

He approached the garage, a long white matchbox of a building with room for half a dozen cars below and chauffeur's quarters above. A lighted window glowed there, on the side away from the house.

Feder tried to find a ladder, had no luck. He cleaned mud from his shoes, entered the garage, and in one of the cars there, located a jointed fishing pole. He connected it, removed the rearview mirror from the car, lashed it to the pole, and with this improvised periscope went out and looked in the chauffeur's quarters.

Kaff, the compactly built driver who talked sailor lingo, sat on a bed. He had drawn the shade of the window that faced the house. He was stripped above the waist.

Pale, trembling with pain, he was dressing a terrible vertical cut on the upper right side of his chest.

Satisfied, Feder replaced the fishing rod and mirror. Before he left the garage, he looked in the front seat of the black Rolls. A pair of Kaff's brown leather driving gloves were there. They were wet. When Feder rubbed a thumb on them, brown dye came off which exactly matched the faint traces on the bowl rim of the pipe he had picked up in the Old Oyster Farm. Kaff had beat the pipe against his damp gloves to knock dottle out.

And Kaff was the near-victim of the broadsword trap.

"Hm-m-m," Feder reflected, face buried in his goldenrod. "Scofield and the catarrh-man waylaid Claussen. Kaff was waiting on the road in that car that they ran Claussen over the bank in. His brown glove-stain was on the wheel of the car."

Feder discarded the goldenrod for good, entered the house. He made little noise. There seemed to be no one downstairs. But on the second floor voices murmured faintly.

Feder went to the telephone half hidden behind the basketed roses. He called a New York number.

"Worldwide Clipping Bureau," a feminine voice said finally.

"Look in your file of clippings from English papers," Feder requested. "The stuff you keep filed for antique collectors. I want anything on an early Sixteenth Century broadsword, gold and silver wrought hilt. Rather a rare piece. I'll hold the wire."

He waited, caressing the roses. He put a fresh bud in his lapel.

The Worldwide was one of the largest newspaper clipping bureaus in the city. They kept clippings on every subject, from newspapers of every country and every language. They did a tremendous business. They remained open all night, because they were always getting calls from New York newspapers and from theatrical people. The Worldwide was an encyclopedia of current events.

"Such a broadsword was a part of a theft of antiques in England, six weeks ago," said the clipping bureau attendant finally. "There has been a series of antique thefts over there recently, but this is the only mention of a broadsword."

Feder breathed his thanks and hung up. He walked to the foot of the stairs, called loudly, "Hello!"

Sir Bernard Bredhame popped into view above. He was white. His eyes were staring. He had his jeweler's loupe clenched tightly in his fist.

"My god, come up here!" he wailed. "We've been waiting for you. Poor Scofield has been murdered! Cut completely in half!"

UNFORTUNATE Scofield lay in a bedroom, on a bed, the two halves of him. Apparently he had been napping on the bed when his end arrived. Feder took only the shortest of glances. He wasn't inured to such gore. If he'd been thirty years a cop, now, like Old Jon Sutton, it might not have affected him so.

The broadsword lay on the floor. The same broadsword, gold-silver wrought hilt and all, which had been the death trap at the Old Oyster Farm.

A tall man whose shoulders were like the cross-arms on a scarecrow, so bony were they, stood to one side. He wore a butler's livery. His head was long, a sallow pink like an orange somebody had taken in their hands and squeezed. He had wet, bubbly eyes.

"He is my butler, Jim," Sir Bernard Bredhame explained. "He was downstairs when I found the—the body. He is the only servant here, except Kaff, my chauffeur. The others are off for the night."

Feder started to look for fingerprints on the broadsword hilt. Then he didn't—for the simple reason there was no need. He knew who wielded the huge thing.

Jim, the butler, had sniffed. Jim the butler had catarrh. And it was a man with catarrh who had helped kill poor Claussen, and who had taken that broadsword from the Old Oyster Farm not many minutes ago.

"What shall we do?" moaned Sir Bernard. "By Jove, this is beastly! A horrible ballyhoo for the newspapers. My family name swabbed in the gutters and all that!"

Jim, the butler, took a cigarette from a pocket, lighted it. The smoke he drew in and expelled through his nostrils impregnated the room with the strong, biting odor of a chemical-treated tobacco catarrh sufferers smoke to ease irritation.

Feder touched the rose in his lapel. "Do you know whether Scofield had ever been a newspaperman?"

Feder was thinking of the cross which had served as a period on that message he had found inside the damp envelope. Newspaperman commonly employed such little crosses for periods.

"Why, yes." Sir Bernard seemed uncertain. "He was London correspondent for an American news association at one time. It was there I met him." He hesitated, continued, "Shall I call the police? I imagine they shall give me a raking for delaying this long. But I thought—I hoped—you could do something."

Feder put a palm over the rose, as though to protect it from something. "Wait a bit," he said absently. In Feder's brain, puzzle pieces were clicking into place. They just about made the whole pattern. But there was one piece yet to go.

Feder glanced at the halved body of Scofield, something that was hard to do. But he had thought of a possibility and wanted to make sure. He got a start. Scofield's left hand was more muscular than his right. Usually, it is the other way around; Sir Bernard's hands for example.

That note had been written by a right-handed man.

"Was Scofield left-handed?" Feder asked.

"Righto," said Sir Bernard. "He was."

Feder hesitated, tall, somber, the aged look around his eyes more pronounced than ever. "Were you a newspaperman, Sir Bernard?"

"Righto again. I met Scofield while serving in that capacity."

Feder gazed at Sir Bernard, his too-old eyes dreamy. The soles of Sir Bernard's shoes were leaving faint grayish tracks when he moved about, tracks so vague they had escaped Feder's notice before.

Feder shut his eyes. He had it all, now. The whole dirty plot! The puzzle pieces were assembled; they needed just one stroke to smooth them out, to pretty-up the picture.

"Wait here," Feder said, "while I go downstairs a moment."

IN the hallway below, Feder drew his revolver and flashlight. He descended to the basement. Again and again he raced the glaring rod of his flash beam across the basement floor. Finally, he found where Sir Bernard's grayish tracks started near one wall.

The basement walls were of solid concrete, but divided in panels like a sidewalk turned on edge. It was no trouble to find the secret door, get it open. Feder merely shoved against the top and a panel of the wall folded down, eased by counterbalancing weights.

Beyond was a room the size of a village grocery store, but low-ceilinged. The floor was gray with cement dust. The place must extend out under the lawn. Feder calculated. It must reach the garage. There was a trapdoor in the ceiling of the far side. Evidently that opened through the garage floor, making simpler the storing of stuff there.

The place was filled with what an unschooled chap might have called plain junk. But a closer look would have shown differently. The stuff was all old, but of priceless workmanship. Mantels, chairs, tables, queer armor—the newest had probably been made two hundred years ago. Antiques! Antiques of a fabulous value!

Feder lunged ahead, darksome in his almost black suit, gangling as a daddy-long legs. There was a cleared spot to one side, the only place where nothing stood against the wall.

Rapidly, Feder walked to the open place. He removed his speed holster from under his arm, tossed it behind an exquisite old armchair.

The ceiling was made of concrete set atop I-beams. Near the wall, Feder reached up and placed his revolver on the lower flange of an I-beam. It would rest there.

He pulled down his coat, drew deep of the aroma of the lapel rose, and returned to the center of the room to wait. His face looked drawn. His hands shook a bit. He had deliberately put himself in a spot, and he knew it.

It required about four minutes for Sir Bernard to appear. He came through the hidden door with an abrupt lunge. He had a revolver ready-pointed.

"Don't move, you nosey bloke!" he snarled. He was a very different Sir Bernard. The devil was cropping all over him.

Feder swept up his hands. It was no trouble for him to look scared. His upraised arms tugged his coat up until the sweetness of the rose was almost under his nostrils.

"I was afraid you would tumble in here!" Sir Bernard gritted.

He turned to close the secret

door. But Jim, the butler, defeated his purpose. Jim had come skulking after sir Bernard. Jim's eyes were ugly in their bath of dampness as he strode inside. He sniffed with his catarrh, then called loudly, "Kaff! Kaff!"

After a moment, Kaff also came in. He had donned his chauffeur's uniform. The military coat bulged some over the bandage he had put on his chest cut.

"Well, keelhaul me!" he croaked when he saw the antiques.

"Surprises you, eh?" Feder said softly. "None of you, except Sir Bernard, know where the stuff was hidden."

SIR Bernard threw Feder a violent, surprised glare.

Feder backed slowly to the space cleared along the wall. When he was against the wall, his upraised hands were not two inches from his revolver on the I-beam.

"You're a gang of international thieves trafficking in antiques stolen in England," he said.

"Stow that gab, matey!" rapped the nautical Kaff.

Feder hesitated. His breath stirred the petals of the rose. "Better let me go on. It will interest you. The part concerning that cut on your chest, especially."

Sir Bernard stiffened.

Feder kept his eyes on Sir Bernard's gun, went on, "Scofield's stolen wallet was a myth, of course. It was a story concocted to bring Claussen here so Sir Bernard could

send him with a note which all of you were led to believe held the location of these antiques. Actually, the note was to decoy into a trap somebody Sir Bernard knew was double-crossing him. He didn't know who it was, though. And Sir Bernard didn't give a damn what happened to Claussen."

Emotion—astonishment—flickered on the faces of all three of the men before him.

Feder blew on the rose again. "It was Sir Bernard who sent the note after all."

Jim and Kaff wet their lips simultaneously.

"You thought it was that way at first, when Scofield told you about the note," Feder informed them. "You were all double-crossing Sir Bernard, instead of one of you. But after Kaff was nearly killed by that sword, you figured Scofield had set the trap at Sir Bernard's suggestion. So Jim went after the sword and used it to cut Scofield in two pieces."

"He's lying his bally head off!" sneered Sir Bernard. "Trying to preserve his neck, he is!" He was uneasy now, tardily realizing all his men had been conspiring against him. He tried to divide his attention between Jim and Kaff and Feder.

"How'd you harpoon all this information, matey?" asked Kaff, studying Feder, but also trying to watch Sir Bernard. The chafferer evidently had an idea what Sir Bernard would do to traitors.

Feder never took his eyes from Sir Bernard's gun. He wouldn't tell them, of course. He never expected to tell anybody how he solved his cases. That was his secret, the one Old Jon Sutton of the Tri-State Agency said would make Feder the greatest detective of all time, if he lived to get a little more experience.

No, he wouldn't disclose the fact that nature had endowed him in excess of other men. Some men had unusual eyesight, saw like eagles. Some men had great vocal cords, like Caruso. Some were handsome. Some were ugly as apes.

Feder's particular ability was his sense of smell. It was phenomenally keen. Old Jon Sutton said he'd never heard of anything like it.

Feder breathed deeply of the rose aroma. That was why he liked flowers; he had an appreciation of them beyond other men.

SIR Bernard, Jim, and Kaff were watching each other more, and Feder less. They were like a capped, too-hot volcano, the three of them.

Feder waited. He wouldn't need to tell them how he'd learned things. How he'd detected on murdered Claussen the odor of those strong chemically-treated cigarettes Jim smoked for his catarrh, and which had evidently clung to Claussen from the moment Jim helped lift his unconscious body in the death car.

Scofield needn't know, either, that Feder had detected the odor of wet wool about Scofield and had deduced the man had been out in the rain in a wool suit. Wool suits had a strong tang when they got wet. The odor had been at the spot where they ambushed poor Claussen, together with the smell of Claussen's catarrh cigarettes. Then, at the Old Oyster Farm, there had been blood, and Kaff's cigarettes again.

The three were almost ignoring Feder now.

"Can't you see he's going to kill you two?" Feder asked Jim and Kaff sharply.

That uncapped the volcano. Sir Bernard jabbed his revolver at Kaff, murder in his eyes. But Jim lunged, bent the gun up, and Sir Bernard lost the weapon. It gyrated across the treasure room, fell amid a set of priceless chairs which had probably a few months ago graced an English castle.

Jim and Kaff closed with Sir Bernard. Blows cracked. Sir Bernard's eye-scope—no doubt he used it to examine antiques—flew upward. The three shrieked curses, accusations, threats.

Feder listened, gathering tidbits of information he could tell on the witness stand. When he knew he had enough to hang them for Claussen's murder, he picked his revolver off the I-beam, ran over to the infuriated pile.

"All right!" he barked.

They knew what to do when they looked into a gun barrel.

# Black Flames

## BY GREG COX

JARTINE needed money. The few gold pieces she'd received from selling that stolen horse had not lasted long in Port Loqais, where temptations were many and the living as high as the prices. "Bane's bile," she swore under her breath, wishing that she'd pinched a more valuable steed to reach the celebrated City of Vice.

Turquoise hair and eyes betrayed her roots in the untamed forests of Kaggia, nearly a continent away from what most city-dwellers considered civilization, while her eclectic attire testified to her wide-ranging travels over the years: a shirt of light Dakeesh mail over a burgundy silk blouse straight from a Tifflan bazaar, buckskin trousers from the Southern frontier, and a pair of fine leather boots she'd won off a pirate queen in the Amber Sea. Kaggians were more than scarce in these parts, but her sullen expression discouraged the curious, as did the cutlass resting against her hip. A hardwood baton tucked into her belt and a dagger in her boot also awaited anyone who tested her patience too far. Brass rings added punch to her fists.

She sat at the bar of a squalid tavern in one of the city's less salubrious districts, nursing a flagon of watery ale as she perched upon a rickety stool. The pungent atmosphere reeked of smoke, sweat, and spilled drinks, while bad singing and worse jokes echoed off the crudely-plastered walls. Lewd doodles, carved into a creaky wooden counter, added character to the furnishings, albeit of a disreputable sort. The grubby surroundings reflected the lightness of her purse. Who knew carousing could be so expensive? Still, Port Loqais surely held prizes to plundered. She simply had to be alert to opportunity.

Brushing untidy blue bangs away from her eyes, she swept her gaze over the bustling tavern and its patrons. It lingered briefly on a heated game of tiles going on at a nearby table, before moving onto a solitary figure drinking alone in a shadowy corner of the tavern. Pallid white flesh and eerie red eyes pegged him as a Vesari, as did his somber black frock coat and saturnine expression. A tonsured pate, with dark hair growing back in, suggested that he'd recently belonged to a monastic order from which he had fallen away. The man peered dolefully into his cup, seemingly

*Illustration by Luke McDonnell*

oblivious to the rowdy merriment nearby, while keeping one hand draped protectively over a package wrapped in a black velvet cloth.

Something valuable?

Jartine's interest was piqued. Abandoning her stool, she strolled across the tavern and, without waiting for an invitation, sat down across from the stranger. "You got a name, Vesari? What brings one of your kind to these parts?"

"Leave me, savage." He drew his bundle closer to him. "I seek no company."

"Suit yourself," she said with a shrug. With any luck, the man would leave the safety of the tavern soon enough; then she'd find out just how precious an item he guarded. She hoped it would be worth her trouble.

Retreating to the bar, she waited impatiently for her quarry to stir. In time, although not soon enough for Jartine, he finished his drink and exited the tavern, seeking perhaps quieter lodgings. She quietly followed him into the murky streets beyond. She moved with practiced stealth, honed by hunting beasts and men in the primeval wilderness that birthed her, yet her silent tread and ability to blend with the shadows seemed almost wasted on the former monk, who appeared preoccupied with his own concerns.

*All the better for me,* she thought. Her conscience did not trouble her, and not merely because of the man's bad manners. She'd once found herself stranded for a time in Vesara, a gray, dreary land of craggy mountains, crumbling ruins, and desolate villages that had offered little in the way of entertainment or employment for a fugitive rover who had worn out her welcome elsewhere. Positively infested with necromancers, revenants, ghouls, and bodysnatchers, Vesara also housed a cowed, fearful populace who barely crawled out from beneath their covers after the sun went down. There'd been no night life to speak of and the wine had been weaker than the villagers' spines. Jartine had been so bored that it had practically come as a relief when that half-crazed alchemist had tried to steal her soul, prior to her divesting him of his bowels. The way she saw it, Vesara owed her and she aimed to collect... with interest.

Drizzly weather kept most others indoors, although lights, laughter and the occasional wayfarer spilled out of the bars and brothels lining a maze of narrow streets and alleys. She stalked the Vesari as he made his way to a desolate stretch of derelict buildings, many of them burntout, that looked to have been abandoned for years. Jartine wondered what long-ago plague or fire had emptied this part of town—and whether it was said to be haunted.

*Who but a Vesari would venture here?*

She appreciated the lack of witnesses, though. Closing in on her prey, she drew the baton from her belt. Before she could strike, however, three vicious-looking ruffians emerged from beneath an arched doorway, blocking the Vesari's path. Scars, broken noses, and missing teeth attested to violent doings. The Vesari gasped in shock, then slowly exhaled, as though relieved that he was *only* being accosted by common street trash. The men fanned out to surround him as Jartine scowled at the interruption.

*Find your own payday,* she fumed. *I saw him first!*

"Hand over your goods," the largest of the rowdies said, "or—"

She cut off his threat by bludgeoning him from behind with her baton. He collapsed at her feet as she grabbed the Vesari by the collar and snarled at the other two men.

"This one's mine, boys. Walk away."

The Vesari peered at her in confusion. "You?"

The remaining rowdies disregarded her advice. "These streets are ours, slag," a pock-marked bruiser said, which struck Jartine as a poor thing to be proud of. "You're going to pay for braining our friend."

Howling, he charged at her with his knife. Jartine shoved the Vesari to the ground as she drew her cutlass. "Stay down!"

Her attacker had more malice than skill. Jartine easily sidestepped his clumsy lunge, then swung her cutlass to much better effect. The man's knife-hand went flying into a nearby puddle, severed at the wrist. She silenced his screams with a swipe to his neck, then stepped back to avoid getting blood on her boots.

"You should have walked away," she muttered before glancing at the last ruffian standing. A murderous look dared him to avenge his comrade. "You next?"

The man turned tail and ran.

*Smart boy,* she thought.

She turned toward the Vesari, who climbed awkwardly to his feet. "Many thanks, Kaggian, for your timely—"

She punched him in the face, knocking him flat onto his back.

"I told you to stay down."

Jartine nudged the crumpled Vesari with the toe of her boot, eliciting only a feeble whimper in response. Confident he would not rise for some time, she relieved him of his bundle and eagerly unwrapped her prize.

"Let's see what we have here."

Swaddled within the black velvet was a hollow bulb, roughly the size of a wasp's nest, made of a smooth, translucent material unknown to her. Equally unfamiliar were the arcane symbols etched into the surface of the object; she grimaced at the sight of the markings which were oddly repellent. Even stranger were the unnatural ebony flames that flickered and smoldered within the bulb, producing a dark, unearthly glow that made Jartine's skin crawl. The object felt warm to the touch, almost like a living thing, and inexplicably slimy as well. Her very soul cringed at the sight and feel of it.

"Sorcery!" Her face curdled in disgust. "I should have guessed as much!"

A healthy distaste for the otherworldly discouraged her from holding onto the curio; no profit was worth trafficking in such foulness. Mentally kicking herself for wasting her time and sword, she flung the bulb away from her, lobbing it into the gutter of an overhanging eave, out of sight and mind. Leaving it with its fallen owner never crossed her mind. Anyone in possession of such a thing probably shouldn't have it.

She wiped her blade with the velvet cloth, then hurled the blood-stained rag to the pavement before leaving the moaning Vesari sprawled in the street alongside his would-be robbers, who might well have treated him far more lethally.

"You're welcome," she muttered.

A brisk walk brought her back to the tavern, where she was tempted to spend her last few coins on a strong drink. Instead she retired to a cramped attic room she had already paid for in advance. Come the morning she would need to find other lodgings, or else funds to procure another night, but that could wait. After her fruitless altercation in the street, she knew better than to tempt fate by trying to waylay another stranger, particularly in this grimy corner of the city. She didn't feel like risking her neck for a random wastrel's skimpy purse. Better to get a good night's rest while she could.

*Daylight will come soon enough.*

Sleep proved evasive, however. Raucous laughter and raised voices from the tavern below, defying any last calls from the bar, made her think that nameless Vesari had been right to seek repose elsewhere. She tossed restlessly atop a lumpy mattress, troubled by the lingering memory of eerie black flames and unholy writings, which writhed in the dark behind her eyelids. *Begone with you,* she grumped silently. *I tossed you away, remember?*

She was only just drifting off when the door to her room slammed open without warning. Rusty hinges shrieked and a feeble wooden bolt snapped as several members of the city guard forced their way into the chamber, armed with short swords and truncheons. Crimson cloaks and turbans vested them with authority. Stern expressions boded ill.

"That's her!" the tavernkeeper shouted from the hallway. "That's the woodlands wench I told you about!"

The captain of the guard nodded. He fixed a stern gaze on Jartine, backed up by at least three
subordinates. A fringed sash proclaimed his rank. "Come along,
Kaggian, or we'll spare the heads-
man some work."

Jartine sprang to her feet, snatch-
ing her cutlass from beneath her
pillow. Any trace of doziness evap-
orated instantly as her hot blood
rose to the occasion.

"If there's blood to be spilt, it
won't be mine alone!"

Clad only in a rumpled shift,
she lunged at the startled officer,
swinging her hungry blade with
all her strength and fury. Had it
not been for the quick reflexes
of the other men, who rushed to
defend their captain, he would
have been clutching a severed
throat before dropping to the
floor.

As was, steel clanged against
steel instead, striking sparks in the
unlit chamber. The close confines
of the room worked to Jartine's
advantage, impeding the men's
movements and causing them to
get in each other's way, but she
was still outnumbered. Worse yet,
these soldiers were no unschooled
rowdies like those bastards she'd
fought earlier tonight; she was
fighting uniformed guards trained
in the deadly art of combat. Hanging back, the captain shouted
harshly.

"Surrender, you lunatic barbarian! You can't overcome us all!"

"Care to wager on that?" she
shot back. "I could use the win-
nings."

Her bold words belied the fact
that the captain was not wrong
about the odds against her. Surrender was not in her nature,
but she was not above a prudent
retreat. Even as she parried the
guardsmen's swords, her gaze
darted to a curtained window
only a few yards away and then
to a ceramic chamber pot resting partway beneath the ramshackle cot she had occupied
only moments before. A sly smile
lifted her lips as she shoved the
cot aside with her hip, then kicked
the exposed pot towards her foes,
spilling its fetid contents onto
the floor. The men instinctively
backed away from the spreading filth, their noses wrinkling in
revulsion.

*Waste not the waste,* she thought,
even as the barkeep cried out in
dismay.

"My floor!"

Jartine wished she had a dagger to throw at him, but she had
neither the arms nor the time to
reward him for his loose tongue.
The guards' disgust bought her
the moment she needed to roll
across the bed and back onto the
floor, then dash for the window,
where she clambered out onto
a narrow stone ledge overlooking a dingy back alley two stories
below. Barefoot, she scrambled
nimbly along the ledge as easily
as she'd once traversed the sturdy
branches of the Kaggian forest.

She fled the irate shouts and curses of the guards, one of whom leaned his head and shoulders out of the window to hurl imprecations at her.

"Come back here, your feral bitch!"

*Like hell I will,* she thought, laughing out loud at the ludicrous command. A rusty lead drainpipe called out to her and she shimmied down it to land deftly on the uneven pavement below, still gripping her cutlass in her free hand. A heady rush of exhilaration accompanied her escape, despite her having been forced to leave her paltry belongings behind. As long as she had her sword and freedom, she could recoup her losses soon enough—perhaps from that backstabbing tavernkeeper?

"Don't think you've seen the last of me," she said. "By the dead gods' doom, you'll wish you never—"

A hard blow to the back of her skull left the rest of her oath unspoken. Stunned, she toppled forward toward the paving stones. Darkness swallowed her world even as she silently cursed the foresighted captain for stationing guardsmen in the streets surrounding the tavern…

S HE awoke in chains. Bleary eyes gradually made out the gloomy contours of a dungeon, lit only by the torchlight filtering through a barred metal gate. The back of her head throbbed like the devil and she reached to feel for a bump, only to find her wrists manacled together. Matching irons fettered her ankles, hobbling her. Finding herself sprawled on the cold stone floor of the cell, she managed to rise to a sitting position, although the effort made her head swim. Gritting her teeth against the pain, she let the world stop spinning before taking stock of her situation.

It wasn't good.

The dungeon made that rattrap of a tavern seem like an empress's palace. It was dank and cold and reeked like a sewer. Mold slimed the mortared stone walls, while the floor made her long for that overpriced mattress she'd been rudely awakened from. She shivered from the chill, the manacles making it difficult to hug herself to keep warm. Only anger at her circumstances heated her blood; she stoked it as best she could.

*Which capricious Fate did I piss off this time?*

Her sword was gone, naturally, and the bastards had even confiscated her rings, leaving her fingers bare. She clenched her fists anyway, if only to remind herself that she was never defenseless as long as her body and soul were still hers to command.

"If only my accursed head would stop pounding," she groused.

"You ought to be grateful you still have a head," a gruff voice taunted her from outside the cell. A paunchy jailor stepped into view on the other side of the bars. He took a swig from a bottle and wiped his lips before continuing. "You'll live…at least until the torturer gets you to reveal what you stole from that murdered Vesari."

Jartine blinked in confusion. "Murdered?"

"Don't play innocent. The barkeep saw you follow the Vesari into the streets. He also said the man had a bundle he never let out of his sight. Yet no sign of it was found near his charred remains."

"Charred?" Jartine's head was spinning in a different way now.

"That's how they found him all right, as you know full well. He was identified only by his garments, which survived the blaze somehow." He belched. "Come clean, what did you take from him…and where did you hide it?"

Jartine was perplexed. The Vesari had not perished at her hand, let alone been burned in any way. The ebony flames within his treasure rose up from her memory, but she held her tongue; she was more interested in preventing her own death than solving the riddle of another's.

"No need to wait for the torturer," she said. "I'll tell you exactly where to find the Vesari's prize…for a gulp of those spirits."

With any luck, she could overpower the jailor if she lured him close enough. If not, the wine might at least dull the pain from her bludgeoned skull.

"You mean that?" the man asked, sounding intrigued. "You're not just blowing smoke?"

"Damn thing's not doing me any good in this hole." She shifted her weight, testing her limbs to ensure they were ready to strike if the opportunity arose. "You're welcome to it if it will buy me a drink." She puckered her lips in distaste. "My mouth's dryer than the Joongau Wastes at high noon. I couldn't spit if I tried."

The jailor stroked the stubble on his jowls. "No tricks?"

"You won't find a better bargain anywhere in the city," she assured him. "Better move fast, though, if you want to beat the torturer."

"All right then." He unlocked the gate and entered the cell, but kept a safe distance from the shackled prisoner. He dangled the bottle before her, then yanked it back. "First, tell me what you stole from the Vesari. How valuable was it?"

"Come closer," she promised, "and I'll whisper it in your ear."

"Hah!" He laughed in her face. "You'll have to do better than that. Do I look like a fool?"

*Worth a try*, she thought. "That answer will cost you another swig."

"Don't waste my time, Kaggian." He tugged at his collar. "By the Rack, why's it so infernally hot in here?"

Was that supposed to be a jest? The clammy dungeon was anything but warm, as Jartine's goose pimples attested, and yet she saw that the man was indeed sweating profusely. Perspiration drenched his features as he wiped his brow and flushed as though feverish. Jartine scooted away from the man, backing up against rear wall of the cell. Her blue eyes widened in alarm.

*What plague or deviltry is this?*

"Divinities help me!" the jailor exclaimed. "I'm burning up!"

Anguish contorted his face as his obvious discomfort flared into agony. The bottle slipped from his fingers, crashing onto the floor, as he tore open his shirt to bare reddened flesh that blackened and burned before Jartine's eyes. Smoke billowed from his throat, choking him, as though he was being consumed from within by a volcanic heat he alone could feel. Black flames ignited across his skin, burning him alive even as his shredded clothing remained unsinged by an all too unnatural blaze.

Jartine shuddered. This was no fever; this was sorcery of the foulest sort.

The jailor's torment was mercifully brief. A charred corpse tumbled to the floor, only a few paces away from the prisoner. Flames rose from the carcass even though there appeared little left for them to feed upon. Spying the dead man's keys through the blaze, Jartine pondered reaching into the fire long enough to snatch them, but then the eldritch flames flared

up even more furiously, forcing to avert her eyes, before they died away to reveal five ominous figures in their place.

The newcomers were Vesari, clad in monastic robes of midnight black. Callously ignoring the smoldering ruin at their feet, they advanced on Jartine, led by a gaunt, cadaverous fellow that Jartine felt an instant aversion to. The rich fur trimming of his robe, which was conspicuously more ornate than that of his companions, gave Jartine a good idea who was the leader here. His sepulchral voice, when he spoke, was thickly-accented.

"Speak, woman. Where lies the Cage you took off the apostate?"

Jartine assumed he was referring to that slimy blub she had discarded earlier, but she chose her words carefully. She had no desire to end up like the jailor once these Vesari got what they wanted from her.

"Is that supposed to mean something to me?"

Blood-red eyes scrutinized her. "Understand, we seek no vengeance. Indeed, you did us a service by taking the Cage of the Nameless from the apostate, thereby depriving him of its protection. But along with punishing our former brother for his sacrilege, we are also duty bound to reclaim the Cage at all costs. Reveal its location or there shall be *two* burned bodies in this wretched hole."

Jartine bristled at the threat. She

did not respond well to ultima-
tums, no matter how diabolic their
source.

"Kill me, conjuror, and you'll
search for your filthy treasure
until the City of Vice becomes
famed for its virtue!" She glared
at the Vesari, unwilling to surrender her only bargaining chip.
"Why should I trust the likes of
you?"

"Because you have no alternative," the cult leader said, his
tone growing impatient. "Perhaps
a taste of perdition will convince
you."

Fixing his incarnadine gaze
upon her, he murmured an incantation unsuitable to any human
tongue. Despite her bravado, Jartine feared the worst as the chill
of the dungeon was swiftly dis-
pelled by a growing warmth that
spread outward from her core to
her skin. Within moments, she
felt as though she was staked
out in the desert beneath a blazing sun. Sweat soaked her, stinging her eyes and salting her lips,
as the unnatural heat grew more
unbearable by the heartbeat. She
clenched her jaws to keep from
crying out, while staring anxiously
at her chained fists, half-expecting
them to burst into flame at any
moment.

"Well," the gaunt man said, "are
you ready to speak?"

Jartine wavered, her stubborn
resolve faltering, but before her
parched lips could tell the Vesari what they wished to know,

footsteps echoed outside the cell.
Tonsured heads turned toward
the unmistakable sound of boots
descending a staircase toward
the dungeons. Muffled voices
indicated a party of individuals
approaching.

The torturer and his minions?

"Eldest," a female cultist addressed her leader. "Without the
Cage, we are diminished. We cannot risk an encounter with the
prison's defenders."

The gaunt man frowned, yet
nodded in assent. "You are correct, Sister. Our work is not for
the eyes of infidels." He plucked
the keys from the jailor's corpse
and flung them at Jartine. "Keep
yourself alive, thief, until we meet
again."

Raising his arms, he led his followers in a mystic recitation, summoning back the ebony flames,
which rapidly enveloped them,
whisking them away to whatever
unclean lair they hailed from. Jartine's hellish fever broke at once
and, gasping in relief, she wasted
no time applying the keys to her
shackles, racing against those
nearing her cell. To her surprise,
the iron keys were cool to the
touch, despite their proximity
to the burning corpse. Like the
jailor's clothing, they too seemed
untouched by the occult flames.

*Thank fortune for small favors,*
she thought.

Tendrils of gray smoke lingered
in the cell, along with the nauseating stench of burnt flesh. Jartine

tucked the keys beneath her and feigned unconsciousness, keeping the unlocked shackles in place as her latest visitors arrived to discover a shocking tableau: one chained prisoner, slumped against a wall, and a smoldering corpse.

"Fate's flail!" a voice blurted. "What's transpired here?"

Peering out through barely-open eyelids, she counted the torturer, recognizable by his stained leather apron and gloves, and two guardsmen to back him up. Jartine bided her time, while taking a moment to savor being cold once more. She had no idea why the cultists had not been able to take her with them when they vanished, but she could only assume that even sorcery had its rules and limitations. Perhaps the trick was reserved only to practitioners and not their prey?

"He's burned to a crisp!" a guard said, recoiling. "Just like that dead Vesari!"

The other guard regarded Jartine fearfully. "She must have done it, but how?"

"I'll get the truth from her," the torturer vowed, proving more devoted to his craft that Jartine would have preferred. He gestured at the prisoner in her cell. "Rouse her so that I can put her to the question!"

The men hesitated. "But, sir, you see what she did to Garff!"

"We don't know what she's done...yet," the torturer said. "Get in there and do your duty.

Are you truly afraid of one caged woman?"

*You should be,* Jartine thought. It galled her to be blamed for burning both the jailor and the murdered Vesari, but saw no advantage in protesting her innocence. *I'll give them something to tremble about.*

The guards approached her warily. She waited until they came within arm's reach, then sprang to her feet and shoved the nearest man over the dead jailor so that he fell backwards onto the damp stone floor, landing with a thud that knocked the breath from him.

"What the—" the second man blurted, gaping in surprise. "She's loose!"

*Obviously,* she thought.

Making use of what she had, she swung the unlocked manacles like a mace, smacking the second guard across the face with the sturdy iron cuff and dropping him to the ground. The first man tried to scramble to his feet, but, whirling like an Evajan dust-devil, she vaulted over the charred jailor and gave the dazed guard a taste of iron as well, taking the fight out of him. Jartine was unimpressed by their prowess.

"Not so easy when the prisoner's unchained, is it?"

That left the torturer, who was already turning to flee.

"Halt where you stand, pain-master," she shouted, "unless you want to burn like the others!"

The man froze at the base of

the stairs. "Please, for the mercy's sake."

"Fine words from one in your profession," she replied. "Turn around and get in here before I bake you to ashes!"

Falling for her bluff, the trembling inquisitor joined her in the cell, where she hastily donned a downed guard's tunic, trousers, boots, and weapons. The boots were not a perfect fit, but better than making her escape barefoot. The hilt of a dagger, on the other hand, fit her grip just fine.

"Listen closely, torturer." She tucked her wild blue hair under a crimson turban. "You're going to escort me out of this hole, all the way to the street. "Get me there in one piece and neither of us has to die tonight. Do you understand me?"

He swallowed hard. "Yes "

"Pleased to hear it." She prodded him with the dagger. "Lead the way."

Sweating for entirely natural reasons, her hostage guided her out of the jailhouse, where they attracted only a few casual glances. It seemed that few guardsmen were in a hurry to engage with the torturer, let alone challenge him.

*Can't imagine why,* she thought wryly.

For herself, she affected a confident stride until they passed through the outer gate into the slumbering streets beyond. Night still cloaked the sky, showing no sign of lightening. Jartine

estimated that she'd only been unconscious for a few hours at most as she walked her hostage briskly away from the gate.

"Please," the torturer whispered. "I did what you asked. Please let me go."'

"Fair enough." She had no sympathy for a man who made a career of torment, but gutting the official would doubtless create more difficulties for her on a night when she had a far more dire threat to contend with. "Pleasant dreams."

She brained him with the sturdy metal hilt of the dagger, then dragged his unconscious body into a doorway, propping him up so that he resembled a drunk sleeping off his cups. Next she turned the stolen tunic inside-out to disguise its origins, discarding the turban at the same time, and made her way back to the deserted street where she had left the Vesari apostate and his unholy treasure, the latter of which was now her best hope of escaping the cultists' sorcery. According to the Eldest of the sect, the Cage had protected the runaway Vesari from their wrath—until Jartine had taken it from him.

Now she needed that protection for herself.

Wasting nary a moment, she climbed to the overhanging gutter and groped through its soggy contents until she found the discarded object, whose eerie radiance made it all too easy to locate in the dark. She flinched at touching the vile thing again, yet saw no other choice. Recovering the Cage, she scrambled back down to the street.

No sooner had she set foot on the pavement, however, when a ring of dark flames erupted from the cobblestones, surrounding her. Jartine assumed a battle-ready stance as the flames receded to reveal the Vesari cultists.

"Keep back!" She held the Cage up like a talisman, attempting to ward off the sinister figures as she rotated to avoid being attacked from behind. "You're too late, ghouls. I have your precious Cage now, so you're no threat to me."

That they outnumbered her five to one did not worry her. It was only their sorcery she feared.

The Eldest laughed out loud.

"Ignorant savage! You may have the Cage of the Nameless, but do you truly expect us to believe that you know how to invoke its protection? Unlike the apostate, you cannot wield the power contained within the Cage, which will soon be ours once more."

To prove his point, he pointed a bony finger at Jartine and recited his incantation again. At once, she felt the infernal heat ignite within her as before, growing far too fast for comfort. Her fury erupted as well.

"Curse the Fates!" She spat at the Eldest. "You may take my life, but you'll not have what you seek!"

Her skin fairly sizzling, she hurled the bulb to the pavement,

where it shattered loudly, much to the horror of the Eldest and the other cultists.

"NO!" the gaunt man shouted in alarm. "You know not what you've done!"

All Jartine knew was that the deadly heat instantly abated. She grinned wolfishly. "That's what comes of hounding an 'ignorant savage,' you decrepit old skeleton!"

"But the Nameless is free at last…after untold eons!"

Truly enough, a terrifying presence rose from the shattered bulb. A pillar of black fire, with white-hot eyes and a gaping white maw, it roughly resembled a man in shape. Roaring in rage and exultation, it towered over the cowering cultists, who had apparently been holding it captive for only the oldest gods knew how long. The Eldest and his followers backed away, frantically chanting and making arcane motions with their hands, but to no avail; they all burst into flames, smoke billowing from their throats as they were incinerated.

*Good riddance,* Jartine thought.

Then the fiend turned its fiery gaze on her.

"Hold!" she cried out. "I'm not one of those ghouls. I'm the one who freed you, remember?"

She snatched a jagged shard from the street and waved it before the demon as a reminder, but the fragment only seemed to enrage the unearthly being. A hand of fire reached out for her; its steaming claws extended…

"To blazes with you then!"

She hurled the shard, made of the very substance that had contained the demon for well-nigh an eternity, at the heart of the creature. The missile plunged into the demon's flaming chest, piercing its inhuman form and eliciting a scream of anguish from the fiend, who desperately attempted to remove the fragment from its heart, but whose claws were repelled by the strange substance, which was seemingly beyond its power to touch. Jartine watched in wonder as, within moments, the fearsome entity crumpled into a pile of ash, joining the charred remains of the cultists who had held it prisoner—and harnessed its might?—for so long.

Jartine panted, surprised and relieved to find herself the last one standing after all she'd been through this night. She briefly considered looting the bodies of the fallen, in payment for her trials, but decided against it. Wanting no part of the cultists and their doings, she merely pocketed another pointy fragment of the Cage...just in case the demon had kin.

*Never hurts to be prepared.*

She'd had enough of Port Loqais as well. The sun was still hours from rising, but she intended to be far from the city before dawn broke. Surely there was profit and pleasure to be found in another port, another country.

She just needed to steal a better horse this time.

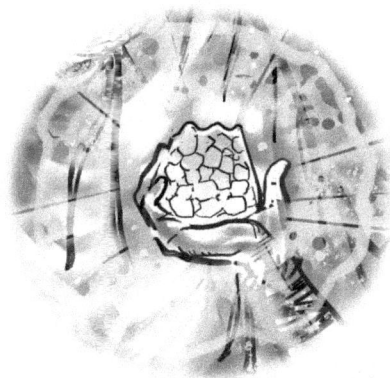

# Queen
# of the Violet Flame!

## By STUART MOORE

THE air hung hot and wet on the plains, raising thick sweat on the brow of Kurak Rush as he led his warriors cautiously out of the forest. Flies buzzed, swarming in angry clouds against the crimson light of the rising sun. Kurak's horse reared back, whinnying.

"Save your strength, my stallion," Kurak growled. "I fear we'll face worse than insects today."

Hercya, his finest warrior, was less patient with her steed. "Be still!" she cried, slapping its flank with her mailed hand. "Or I'll trade you in for a racing dog, next market time!"

Kurak opened his mouth to scold her, then smiled instead. Hercya's blood flowed fierce in her veins—too fierce, sometimes. Like the rest of his soldiers, her muscled arms and legs were pale white, bronzed slightly by the merciless summer sun. Kurak's own skin was dark, betraying his southern origins.

"You see, my lord?" Hercya asked, pointing ahead. "It is as I said."

Kurak followed her gaze, and the breath caught in his throat. A dozen warriors drew up behind them, pausing at the flat, open plain just beyond the treeline. Old Oengus, the Latic priest, came last, muttering and grousing at his horse. Kurak barely heard the words. He liked the priest, but sometimes the old man's complaints grated on his nerves.

And Kurak's attention was riveted by the sight before him. Ahead, beyond an expanse of low, burnt grass, a strange structure rose from the ground. It was dome-shaped, about the size of a large barn. Its surface shone smooth and unnaturally reflective, as if it were made of iron—but *not* of iron, at the same time.

"Aye, lass," Kurak said, "you spoke true. And you say it appeared all at once, three days past?"

"Yes, my lord." Hercya's hand tensed on her sword hilt. "I was scouting for game, when a blaze of fire shot down from the sky and shook the earth. When its fury passed, *this* remained."

"Sorcery!" the priest, Old Oengus, exclaimed. "And so close to our lands...a mere forty miles from the royal castle."

"Thirty-eight miles," Kurak murmured. "And a few odd feet." He spurred his horse forward a few steps, gesturing for the others

*Illustration by Mike Collins*

to stay back. Then he pulled up on the horse's reins, halting it again, and peered ahead.

The structure stood roughly one point two miles away. Kurak's vision was unparalleled at a distance; from here he could discern a strange symbol on the front of the otherwise featureless building. It looked like an inverted letter "V," or perhaps a primitive rendition of a hawk or eagle in flight, viewed head-on. As he stared at the symbol, Kurak felt a strange crumbling sensation, as if reality itself were falling away. He found himself drawn to this mystery, spurring his horse once more to action, its nimble hooves dodging patches of burnt, steaming grass.

Hercya and the priest exchanged worried glances, then moved to follow their king across the plain. The others fell in line behind them.

As the inverted V grew larger in Kurak's vision, its pull seemed to seize hold of him even more strongly. It called to him on some deep level, reminding him of something he'd known long ago, perhaps in another life. The thick air pressed down on him, and he felt as if he were falling, drawn down into an endless abyss filled with hidden, terrible truths.

"My lord!"

Kurak shook his head, the spell broken. His warriors surrounded him now, swords drawn for battle. Old Oengus drew up alongside, letting out a worried gasp.

"Bugger," the priest said.

Just ahead, between Kurak's host and the featureless citadel, stood an army of the undead, newly risen from holes in the ground. White tendons showed through torn clothing; their hands were naked bone, gray skin scraped clean away as they'd clawed their way out of unmarked graves. They advanced on Kurak's throng, slow but numerous in their advance.

"My lord?" Hercya called urgently.

Kurak tensed, drawing his broadsword.

"Attack!" he cried.

TWO things were whispered of Kurak, in the rat-strewn alleys and sodden beer halls of the Latic Kingdom. First was that he held an Object of Power, some unknown talisman that he consulted before battle, and that ensured his continued rule over his adopted subjects. For Kurak had not been born of the Latic people. His parents were slaves from the southern lands, viciously slain when they dared to speak out against unimaginably cruel masters. It was said that Kurak had witnessed this atrocity with his own eyes, when he was but seven years of age.

The second whisper spoke of a curse that lay on Kurak's head. No living soul knew the nature of this curse, nor the name of the mage or demon who had cast it upon him. But as long as it held sway, the rumors said, Kurak Rush would never know peace.

One thing was certain: Kurak's sword-arm was the swiftest in all of Latia. With it, and his near-unnatural cunning, he had conquered this land, slain the tyrant king Bushik and assumed the throne. And today, on this burnt plain before the strange reflective building, Kurak swung his sword with all the strength and skill that had raised a simple barbarian to the highest office in this land. His blade was a blur, slicing through a dozen undead necks in one blow, scattering brittle bones and flesh-tattered limbs to the four winds. Hercya and the others fought with admirable vigor, but no warrior downed half as many attackers as did their beloved monarch.

As his blade ground through undead bone, Kurak saw red, recalling the slavers who had slain his parents. That fire, that rage, spurred him ever forward, always on to the next conquest, the next righteous victory.

"To victory!" Hercya called, her sharp sword piercing the dry heart of a shadow-man twice her size. "These creatures are many, but slow. None shall stop the elite guard of Kurak!"

She pressed forward, flanked by two tall, broad warriors. A clutch of undead snapped and clawed at them, dropping low to nip at their horses' shins. As his guard moved to protect their king, Kurak's blood-fever ebbed, and he gestured for Oengus to draw closer. The old priest grimaced; he was long past fighting age, and had never been trained in the arts of combat in any case.

"They are many," Oengus said fearfully. "Should we retreat?"

Kurak glanced back at the forest, his mind whirling. The tree line stood zero point eight miles away. The king's steeds were the finest in all Latia; when properly spurred, they could assume a speed of thirty-nine miles per hour in an instant's time. Were Kurak to call a retreat, his host could achieve the trees in point zero two hours—roughly seventy-four seconds—

"MY LORD!"

Kurak whirled at Hercya's cry—too late. A blaze of violet fire seared past his face, grazing his cheek. Kurak gritted his teeth in pain, but made no sound. His horse let out a panicked cry and leapt to the side.

All at once, the battle stopped.

Kurak looked up to behold a remarkable sight. His warriors stood flanking him, swords ready and eager to taste dusty flesh. But their enemies, the shambling undead, had retreated, facing them in a line, bones twitching in a senseless mockery of human behavior. Carrion birds circled high and black in the sky, keeping their distance.

And before Kurak, between his warriors and the undead army, stood a most striking figure. Tall she was and long of limb, with pale skin draped in thin, reflective silks like nothing Kurak had ever seen.

Long hair flowed jet-black down her shoulders, like the endless depths of the Firmament itself.

Staring at that lovely face, Kurak felt once again the tug of something very old. Something deeper and more profound than himself, something no man nor woman could resist. Her eyes locked onto his, and she spoke in a voice as calm as the sea.

"I am Aura," she said, "the Queen of the Violet Flame."

She raised one hand and purple fire rose from her fingertips, sparking harmlessly in the air. Kurak touched his cheek, realizing it was she who had fired the bolt that had nearly felled him.

"Surrender, witch," he growled, "or we'll see if your *magic* can mend a severed head."

Hercya and the others moved forward in response. Aura eyed them calmly, her face unblemished by worry. The undead clacked and clattered, but made no move to defend their mistress.

Then Aura raised both arms above her sides. The undead shivered, rattled, and collapsed as one to dust, returning to the earth that had twice spawned them.

Hercya frowned, unsure. She looked over at the priest, who shrugged. But Kurak's gaze remained fixed on the sorceress Aura, who eyed him steadily. She stepped forward, heedless of the warriors closing ranks around their king.

Her eyes bored into his, her lips slowly curling into a knowing smile. Kurak was seized by the strangest feeling: that despite the unnatural citadel ahead, the presence of his guard, and the unquestioned stench of sorcery in this place, somehow he and the sorceress Aura inhabited a world, a realm, all their own.

"I yield," she whispered.

AURA, the self-titled Queen of the Violet Flame, said not a word on the long march back to the village. The uneven ground of the thick forest seemed not to hurt her sandaled feet, nor did the chains binding her wrists cause her any obvious discomfort. She trod at an even pace, flanked on horseback by Hercya and another warrior, staring straight ahead save for the occasional glance at Kurak, who led the procession. Only then did a glimmer of light enter her eyes, the hint of a smirk tease at the corners of her lips.

Kurak felt her gaze on his back, but he did not turn to look.

By the time they reached the guard tower, the sun hung low in the sky, threatening its nightly fall. As one, Kurak's warriors let up an exultant, victorious cry. They whooped and howled, proudly displaying their captive to the sentry and to the waiting children and elders, who cheered their warriors' return.

"Hail King Kurak!" Hercya cried. "Once more, he has prevailed over base sorcery!"

At the word "base," the Queen raised an eyebrow.

Old Oengus sidled his horse up alongside Kurak's. Ahead, the thatched roofs of the village jutted just above a low line of trees.

"Your subjects rejoice at this victory," the priest said, "yet you seem troubled."

"'Twas too easy," Kurak rumbled. "And we know nothing as yet of this 'Queen's' sorcery."

"She'll spend a night in the dungeon," Oengus smiled, "and then we'll learn all."

Kurak frowned. The priest was popular among his people, and Kurak valued his counsel. But Oengus's tone held a trace of sadism that Kurak found disquieting.

Kurak turned in his saddle. The Queen stood proud, staring curiously at him as Hercya's chain tugged her along. "Be gentle with her," he said, and jerked on the reins, urging his horse down a side path around the center of the village.

"You'll not join the celebration?" Oengus called. "There'll be mead aplenty in the town square. And lusty toasts to the King's victory."

"Another time," Kurak replied. "Drink a flagon for me."

"Would that my vows allowed!"

Kurak paused his steed, smiling. "My friend," he said, "is there a priestly vow I have *not* seen you break?"

Oengus let out a wheezing laugh. Kurak's eyes strayed once more to the Queen. She was definitely smiling now, eyeing him with undisguised interest. He had the strange feeling she could snap those chains at any moment, that she was playing some unknown, sorcerous game with him.

Kurak felt a strange, uncomfortable closeness, almost a sense of violation. He turned away and spurred his horse forward, allowing the trees to swallow them up. Behind him, the sounds of hoofbeats and revelry faded into the growing dark.

As he rounded a bend, the trees parted to reveal his castle, high on a ramparted mountain. It spread out low, rising at either end in a pair of square-cornered towers. Kurak shook his head ruefully. The square towers were a relic of an earlier time, an architectural style the Latics had favored some centuries ago. The old King, Bushik, had boasted of their beauty, not considering for a moment the easy target those broad walls made for catapults and other long-distance weapons. Small wonder Kurak had tricked old Bushik so easily, marching him off a cliff to the sea by the simple application of higher mathematics.

Kurak's thoughts drifted back darkly as his horse trudged up the winding path to the castle. Bushik had not been a popular king; his taxation policies in particular had driven the outlying farmers to near starvation. They had gladly accepted Kurak as their king in his place, despite Kurak's Congolian blood and dark skin. Old Oengus had played no small part in this. The priest had been a thorn in Kurak's side more than once these past years, but the Latic people revered their religious leaders, and the old man's common touch had made him a beloved figure throughout the kingdom.

Once inside the castle, Kurak dismissed his handmaidens, declaring he wanted to be alone. He felt the Curse drawing upon him, dark and weighty, inevitable as the fall of night. He hastened to his drawing room, pausing a moment in the shadows to be sure he was alone. Then he crossed to the far wall and leaned his shoulder against a huge carved statue, grunting and straining as he pushed it aside.

A heavy door slid open in the wall, gliding easily on a handmade system of pulleys and levers. Kurak did not pause to give this any thought, for he had designed the pulleys himself. He hastened through the door into the dark, elbowing the door closed behind him.

A flight of stairs led down, deep into the mountain. The narrow stairwell was dark, too dark even for Kurak's night-trained eyes; but he moved confidently, knowing each turn and depression in the stairs from long experience. His pulse quickened in anticipation as he approached the bottom, pausing to light a brazier mounted on the wall.

The chamber ahead stretched high and long, with torches set at intervals along the stone walls. These torch-mounts formed the only breaks in a huge row of shelves, lining the chamber from near side to far, from dusty floor to the vaulted ceiling high above. Each shelf, every surface along the walls, was filled with books: ancient tomes and newly pressed volumes, science texts and historical records and religious tracts, all arranged in an order that only Kurak knew.

And in the center of the room, atop a crude wooden table, lay a pile of charts, maps, and diagrams. These plans, hand-drawn and marked with charcoal, had consumed hours of Kurak's attention the day before. On them he had calculated the exact distance to the Queen's citadel, the thickness of the forest, the travel time the horses would require. In this same manner, Kurak had plotted every campaign, every war of conquest his people had carried out.

But the plans held no interest for him now. Crossing to the table, he swept them aside with a savage sweep of his strong arm. An ornate gold box sat revealed, now, in the center of the table. Within this box, secured deep in this underground chamber, nestled the fabled Object of Power of Kurak Rush.

Trembling, Kurak reached down gingerly, opened the box, and raised the Object to his eyes. He paused to flick dust off one lens, rubbed the other against his tunic, and then, adjusting the frame slightly, balanced the Object over the bridge of his nose.

Kurak's vision, as has been noted, was unparalleled at a distance. But only by employing the Object could he consult the vast library surrounding him, the greatest hidden accumulation of knowledge in all of Latia.

He squinted through the lenses, crossing to a dusty shelf holding volumes pertaining to ancient sorcery. In a crumbling tome called *Arcana Atlantia*, he found a passing reference to violet flame. In another, a plate showed an ancient temple, long lost beneath the sea, bedecked with a symbol similar to the inverted V on Aura's citadel. But neither volume provided any further illumination.

In a third, oddly colored tome, a passage caught his eye. Written in the old script, it spoke of the horrors of the Firmament, the terrors that lay beyond the sky itself. Reading it, Kurak felt a shiver pass through him, as if the chill of dark gods had descended briefly to touch his very blood.

He grunted, suddenly impatient. He pulled down one volume after another, thrusting them roughly into a heap on the floor. He felt maddeningly close to some mystery, some vast secret that might bring peace to his yearning intellect. Yet the answers he sought eluded him, as if some elder god were laughing at his frustration.

He felt a burning sensation, and raised a hand to his cheek. The Queen's eerie flame had left a mark, he knew, that yet lingered on his flesh.

"Hell's teeth," he hissed, feeling no closer to answers than before. He stalked, frustrated, to the far side of the chamber and kicked open a second, lower door. Ducking down, he hastened through it and commenced another descent down an even darker, more cramped stairwell. The air seemed heavier here, thick and foul, as if neither man nor demon had breathed its like for centuries.

But such was not the case. At the base of this stairwell lay the Pits, deep chambers built long ago, when the castle had been a fortress. When war, dark and foul, had spread across the Latic world, and huge dank gaols were built to house and torture unfortunate prisoners.

All that lay in the distant past. Upon assuming the throne, Kurak had closed the last of the Pits, sweeping it clear of bones and bending it to his own purposes. He reached the bottom stair, now, and fumbled with the brazier on the wall, his hands shaking as the flame ignited on its tip.

Before him lay a vast bowl-shaped chamber, circled by a narrow ledge looking down on the one-time Pit. The entire room, twice the size of a royal ballroom, was filled with a most strange and impressive display: a hanging model of the Heavens. At its outermost layer, near the high wall, a bright gourd hung on a hand-woven string. This was Saturnia, outermost of the planets. Several feet nearer to the center dangled dark Jovis, a swollen melon imported from the East. Then crimson Mars, and the bright Sun, whose overripe seeds threatened to break loose from its scarlet shell.

Kurak frowned; he would have to replace the Sun-gourd soon. He had built this entire display with his own hands, in secret. Not even Old Oengus knew of its existence.

He rounded the ledge until he came to a set of footholds notched into the wall. As he climbed, he studied the inner worlds. Within the Sun's orbit floated hazy emerald Venis, then tiny Mercuri, and then the cold grey stone that represented the Moon. And in the very center of the chamber, a humble plum dangled alone, dwarfed by the enormity of the dark gulfs all around. This, of course, was the Earth, birthplace of humankind and central orb of the Universe.

Kurak climbed halfway to the domed roof and paused within reach of the dangling Saturnia-gourd. Behind him, the words PRI-MUM MOBILE were scrawled on the wall in his own hand. He reached out and shoved Saturnia with all the strength in his good sword-arm. The ripe gourd wobbled, swung briefly back and forth, and then grew still again.

"You hang as you should," he hissed, glaring down at the model, "yet you do not move. You fail to *rotate*."

He clung to the wall, clenching one fist in anger. "Why?" he demanded, as he had done a hundred times before. "Why do you not work? What is *wrong* with the world?"

"So," a deep female voice said, "*this* is the fabled Curse of Kurak…"

He looked down sharply. Aura, the Queen of the Violet Flame, stood in the entrance to the chamber, staring up at him with calm, dark eyes. Her stance was confident, her wrists unbound by chains. As he watched, she raised both arms and rose up into the air, wafting easily into the midst of the hanging worlds.

"…curiosity," she finished.

"You," Kurak said, rage rising in him, "you *mock* me?"

And drawing his sword, he leaped into the abyss, toward the spot where the Queen hovered. She smiled slightly and seemed to *step* to one side, in midair. As Kurak hurtled past her, his sword severed the string holding small Mercuri. The gourd clattered to the floor of the Pit, cracking open to reveal dry, barren seeds.

Kurak landed hard on the stone floor and rolled quickly to his feet. His shoulder ached from the impact, but he paid it no mind. He raised his sword, adjusted the spectacles on his nose, and turned toward the Queen, who fired a burst of purple fire from her sleeve-arm.

When it struck Kurak's sword, the blade glowed bright. The hilt grew rapidly warmer, until it blazed with the heat of a thousand suns. Grunting in pain, he dropped it to the floor.

The Queen floated alongside the grey pitted Moon, her eyes darting from one world-fruit to another. Though she faced the finest swordsman in all of Latia, she seemed as calm as ever, displaying not the slightest sign of worry or discomfort.

"This..." She gestured around the room. "...is a good guess. A good start." She turned to stare straight down at him. "But perhaps you could use some help."

She waved both arms, and all around, the room seemed to swim into a dark haze. The planets wobbled and wavered, the letters scrawled on the roof blurred and vanished. Kurak blinked and shook his head, thinking: *Sorcery!*

When he opened his eyes, a remarkable vision lay spread out before him. It was as if he hung in the dark depths of Space itself, surrounded by all the wonders of the Firmament. The Sun was no overripe treefruit, but a blazing ball of primal fire. Jovis steamed and simmered in the distance, and the Moon's sharp craters cast deep shadows on stark powdered sands.

The Queen floated down, positioning herself between the stunned barbarian and the Earth itself. The mother world hung deep blue and clouded, in the exact center of the cosmos. Just as Kurak had been taught, just as the ancient texts averred.

"I am of Old Atlantis," the Queen proclaimed.

"Impossible," he scoffed. "Atlantis sank beneath the waves, thirty centuries ago."

"I was a scientist," she continued, "one of the finest in all my kingdom. Does that stun you? That a *woman* might bear such a distinguished position?"

Kurak shrugged. "My finest swordsman is a woman."

She nodded in approval, then continued. "When the Cataclysm drew near, we of Atlantis marshaled all our scientific knowledge in the cause of our survival. Some of our skills would appear to you as magic." She grinned, startlingly, and a burst of flame rose once again from her hand. "Some already have."

"The resurrected dead," he grumbled. "The violet flame at your command."

"Lasers," she shrugged. "Short-term biogalvanation. But all our skills, our mastery of nature, could not prevent the Fall. In the end, we were able to construct but one vessel, a single ship such as you, my lord, might once have traveled in your years as a buccaneer. But instead of the raging seas, this 'space-ship' was built to sail the Firmament itself."

She gestured around her. The planets, the Sun, the floating worlds began to quiver in place. Kurak stared from bright Venis to distant Saturnia, captivated despite himself.

"I was chosen to pilot the ship," the Queen said. "Alone. And now, at last, I have returned."

Kurak frowned, shaking his head to clear it. "The wonders of Atlantis are known," he said cautiously. "Your story may or may not ring true. But none of it explains how you yet live, three thousand years past your natural lifespan."

"As I sailed the stars," she continued, "time moved at a different rate for me. While many centuries flowed by here, a mere handful of years passed within my lonely vessel. It's called special relativity... I'll explain that later." She paused and smiled at him. "There will be time, I promise."

"Time," he echoed. He felt adrift in a void, faced with a yawning depth beyond his comprehension. Yet now, to his surprise, he felt no fear, only a hunger for knowledge and a tantalizing sense of anticipation.

"Time," she agreed. "But first, let's see if we can't lift your curse. Just a little."

She gestured again, and the worlds began to move. They swarmed and swirled, flashing through the firmament. Blue Earth receded, narrowly avoiding a collision with Venis and tiny Mercuri. When the bright Sun soared near to Kurak, he stepped back, unsure of what etheric substance he stood upon.

"You may trust me, King Kurak," the Queen said. "For I have witnessed the Firmament with my naked eyes. The wonders of which you speculate, I have *seen*."

She hung in the air, surrounded by sights undreamt by man. And yet, those dark eyes seemed to draw Kurak's gaze to her alone, promising secrets more beautiful, more personal. That, he knew, was no sorcery. The Queen had indeed cast a spell on him, but of the type that two people might often cast on each other, whether they be men or women; sorcerers, commoners, or kings.

She smiled as if she shared the emotions roiling through him. Once more she gestured, and the room shimmered before his eyes and returned to its previous state. Kurak and the Queen stood face to face in the center of the curved stone floor, where once men had been tortured and put to death in this chamber deep beneath the Earth.

Above them, the world-fruits hung once more in their orbits. But now the inner planets had assumed a far different configuration. Earth dangled between red Mars and emerald Venis, with the Sun-gourd now ripe and bursting at the room's center. Kurak had to squint to make out the Moon, now a tiny chip of stone hanging just off of the blue plum of the Earth.

"Kurak." The Queen stepped up to him, and a thrill ran through him as her pale hand grazed his cheek. "From the moment I saw you, I sensed your hidden depths. Your thirst for knowledge, your secret yearnings. The side of yourself that you must ever conceal, in order to rule over a barbarous, fallen people."

"They are *good* people," he replied, thinking of brash Hercya and Old Oengus. "But at times, it is difficult."

"Go on," Aura said, gesturing upward. "Try it."

He followed her gaze to a new world, a green-white melon hanging outside the radius of Saturnia. It hung tantalizingly close, almost within his reach. He drew his sword, pointed it up, and tapped the melon-world gently.

Slowly, wondrously, the worlds began to rotate around the Sun.

"Gods," Kurak breathed. He felt deeply moved, forever changed, as though some part of him had clicked firmly, finally, into place.

"There is much more to be learned," she said. "Even for a three-thousand-year-old woman."

She smiled at him, and for the first time he saw the hesitancy, the loneliness within her. The years of her journey might only have numbered a handful...but even a small span of years can be an eternity when one is alone.

This, Kurak knew all too well.

Above him, the worlds circled in a steady, graceful dance. Yet all he saw was her dark, lovely eyes.

"Perhaps," he said, "we share the same curse."

She nodded. "Then perhaps we might work on it together?"

He smiled in agreement.

Then, to his surprise, she stepped back and loosed a violet bolt up into the air. The flame seared through the string holding the Earth-plum, severing it from its supports. Aura reached out and caught the plum in one hand, then raised it lustily to her mouth and took a bite.

He rushed forward, closing the distance between them in a few quick steps. He felt drawn to her, to her beauty, her intellect, her quick wit and dark hair like the mysteries of the Firmament, begging to be sailed and explored. She drew closer to him in response, wiping the juice from her chin. Her scent was intoxicating, her hair soft as stardust where it brushed against his rough cheek.

"First step," she whispered, tossing the plum aside. "Let's *stop* thinking for a while, okay?"

# PARACHUTE PATROL
by Pat Powers

THESE STRAPPING YOUNG BUCKS ARE THE CREAM OF THEIR BRITISH BOARDING SCHOOL, AND THEY'RE DRIVING TO PUT EVERY INCH IN THEIR EFFORT TO BE SEEN BY MEN AS WORTHY OF THE EFFORT! THEY ARE SPENDING THE WAR AT AT LORD PHIL McCRAVIS'S ESTATE TO HELP WITH THE FARM ANIMALS WHEN ROUGH INVADERS PROBED THEIR DEFENSELESS DERRY AIR...

DICKIE   BLIMPO.   ROGER

WE HAVE DROPPED MASSIVE LOADS ON BRISTOL CITIES! NOW WE FLY TO RAID NATURE'S TREASURY AND CAPTURE BIG JOHN BULL!

YES, WELL KNOWN THAT YOU LOOKING FOR BULL FOR GOOD TIME! *

*TRANSLATED FROM THE ETHNIC —ED.

THE FOREIGN DEVILS LAND DEEP IN NATURE'S TERRITORY...

SIR, WHILE POKING AROUND THE BUSH, WE SWARTHY HEATHENS FOUND SOMETHING WRONG WITH OUR UNDERCARRIAGE!

BUT THE BOYS WERE PLAYING IN THE WOODS WHEN THEY CAME...

WE NEED LUBRICATING OIL. CAPTAIN ROSSO, YOU SPEAK ENGLISH..SEE IF YOU CAN GET US SOME!

BUT MY UNIFORM, MAJOR..

LOOK! THAT WOMAN OVER THERE WILL HELP US LUBRICATE OUR UNDERCARRIAGE! GET HER TO GIVE US A LUBE JOB!

BLIGHTLY GETS THE MESSAGE!

BLIMEY, SQUIRE! IT'S THE CHEEKY LADS FROM THE PARACHUTE PATROL I CHAT WITH AT NIGHT!

WHY ARE YOU ALWAYS TALKING TO YOUNG BOYS?

AFTER A REMINDER OF THAT WEEKEND IN LEEDS, BLIGHTY AGREES TO HELP...

THERE SHE BLOWS! LET'S GO DOWN ON HER!

THE STUPID ETHNICS MISTAKE THEM AS FRIENDS!

OH, GOODY! THEY'RE BACK AND THEY BROUGHT PLAYMATES!

A SAILOR OUT FOR A GOOD TIME PACKS THE SEAMEN IN A SMALLER VESSEL...

...AND THE BOYS FLY BACK TO THE CASTLE, NEVER USING PARACHUTES EVEN THOUGH THAT'S THE NAME OF THE STRIP!

PIP PIP, GOOD SHOW! YOU SAVED ENGLAND AND CAPTURED A NEW BUNCH OF WOGS TO WORK IN THE FACTORIES! THE SUN WILL NEVER SET ON THE BRITISH EMPIRE BECAUSE OF BOYS LIKE YOU-- GOD WON'T TRUST US IN THE DARK!

ANOTHER PARACHUTE PATROL STORY IN THE NEXT ISSUE OF WINGS COMICS

# Mustangs and Colts

## *By* SHERRI COOK WOOSLEY

THE wild mustangs gleamed in the stark morning sun, the light showing off the colors inherited from the original Spanish horses: dun, black, cinnabar. The herd picked up speed as they came down the mountain, hooves striking against stones before meeting the hardened ground at the base. Morgan's hand was on the rope hanging off her saddle, heels shoved down in the stirrups while she took her position on one side of the herd. This was the tricky part: keep enough speed that the herd wouldn't realize they were heading into a corral, but not so fast that they'd pile up inside of it. Henry was on the other side and, in the distance, a figure with gray hair opened the gate. Gus. He was getting too old for this, but insisted the owner should be part of everything that happened at Stony Pass Ranch.

Morgan adjusted her bandana against the dust and squeezed her legs around Mac, keeping pace with the herd and funneling them inside. Gus clanged the gate shut behind the last mare. Morgan exhaled in relief as she slapped Mac's neck. The herd circled inside, safely delivered. Good. It had been a long ride—over two hundred and fifty miles of driving them south from the Sand Wash Basin—but these ten horses would secure the future for Gus and the ranch.

Then the wild stallion's shrill whinny pierced the air.

Morgan turned in her saddle to see Skinny, the last cowboy, struggling with the rope holding the herd's stallion. Skinny was off-balance, trying to use his own strength against the power of the shaggy black-and-white mustang. She'd taken to calling the mustang "Woodrow" in her mind. He was a fine horse with a well-shaped head and a conspicuous movement to his hips that suggested smooth riding. She'd imagined being the one to break him, not like a broncobuster, but like her adopted father had taught her.

Now, though, Woodrow planted his feet and jerked.

Skinny flew through the air, falling hard to the ground with a thump.

Woodrow reared, his scream echoing off the mountain.

Morgan shifted her weight and clucked to Mac, her own stallion. Unlike the sturdy mustangs they'd penned, Mac was a 16-hand Quarter horse. She'd fallen in love the first time she'd seen him running in a local race, his chestnut coat gleaming as his neck stretched forward with his will to win. Buying him was the best thing she'd ever done.

Woodrow galloped toward Skinny,

*Illustration by June Brigman*

who'd managed to get to his hands and knees, but Mac was closing the distance toward the man.

"Stay down," Morgan yelled, leaning forward.

Mac launched over Skinny and then jogged to a stop, becoming an immovable object. Woodrow had to turn or collide.

The mustang darted to the right. Morgan used Mac's greater speed to cut off Woodrow and spin to face the runaway again. Feeling the gaze of the three men watching—Skinny and Henry had worked with her to wrangle the mustangs, and Gus, the ranch owner—Morgan knew she couldn't mess this up or her hard-won reputation would be ruined.

The stallions stared at one other, nostrils flared. Morgan watched the mustang's ears, the way he listened to the herd in the pen. He'd be torn now—wanting to get away and wanting to protect the mares already in the round pen.

Morgan urged Mac forward one step.

A panicked whinny from the corral.

Instinct to protect overcame the instinct to flee. The mustang wheeled around and sprinted toward the corral.

"Open," Morgan yelled, standing up in the stirrups to see better.

Gus wrenched open the gate to the second corral while Henry urged his gelding into position.

She urged Mac back toward Skinny, who'd managed to get to his feet. He knocked dust from his hat and glared at her.

"You jumped your horse over me," he accused. His face, always on the red side, was flushed with a mixture of anger and embarrassment.

Morgan understood the expression and its affects; humiliation made men dangerous. "I saved your life," she said.

"That mustang needs to be beat until he knows what's good for him. I'm going to do it right now."

"I guess you get paid for delivering the horses," Morgan said, her tone even. "Nothing more."

"You don't tell me what to do," Skinny exploded. Spittle flew from his mouth and he waved his hands in the air.

He'd meant to unseat Morgan, but Mac was too well-trained for that. He didn't like it, his ears went back, but he didn't move. Morgan slipped her hand under her duster and touched the cold steel of a 1851 Navy Colt. Touching the sidearm gave her confidence—and a reminder of the original owner, William "Bear" Barclay. He'd been many things before that day he met her at the train station: gunfighter, gambler, deputy. Now that he'd passed, she'd taken over the horse business, but that wasn't the only thing he'd taught her.

"Guess that mustang isn't your property now. He belongs to Gus."

Morgan nudged Mac and they rode past the corral of mares. Gus waved her over from his spot against the fence. His shoulders rounded a little more since the last time she'd seen him and he walked with a bit of a limp which meant his hip was hurting again, but, overall, he looked good.

Gus and Barclay had been friends for decades and Gus had become a benevolent uncle figure for Morgan. Now Gus and his wife had settled at this ranch and he'd been willing to pay her for cowboy work: this drive had been her first job. She ran a practiced eye over the wild mustangs. This was a solid group of animals. They'd need to be saddle broke soon enough and she wanted the job, but it had to be earned. She wouldn't accept charity.

"Any trouble?" Gus asked, holding out an envelope with her pay.

He could have meant with capturing or driving the herd. He could have meant with Skinny. Either way the answer was the same, "Nothing I can't handle."

Morgan took the envelope, touched the brim of her hat, and set off to town. She needed a drink.

Silverton was a mining town, nestled in the shadow of a range of mountains that looked like the tines of a queen's crown, snow where pearls should be. The past few years more and more people came, some looking for space, others looking for a new life. Most, though, came because mining companies made false promises to poor immigrants. Even the train had made it out here.

Mac allowed himself to be tied to the post outside the saloon and Morgan walked inside. It was early in the day, but there was a card game in the corner. Based on the empty glasses and hangdog expressions, it was still going rather than starting. Smoke hung in the air, an unwelcome smell compared to a natural perfume of leather and summer grass.

Morgan put money on the bar and took a seat. The bartender came closer and stopped, palms splayed on the bar. She didn't flinch or apologize, but was glad when he took the money and slid her a drink to wash away the taste of dust that she'd had for the past month.

"What are you, a Belle Star?" It was more a poke than a challenge, comparing her to the infamous woman horse thief and bootlegger. He was trying to figure out how to place her. Morgan wore canvas trousers and bound her breasts for easier management, but she had money. In a mining town where so much was on credit, that gave her status.

"What's your name?" Morgan asked in return.

"John Nacinovich."

"How about that drink, John Nacinovich."

He filled one and slid it to her. Morgan took a gulp and swished it around her mouth, washing away the taste of dust that she'd had for the past month.

The saloon doors creaked as Skinny and Henry walked in. She took a deep drink. They called out their orders and settled at a table away from the card game.

The bartender started a conversation, asking where they were coming from, where they were going. "Up near Craig?" he asked. "Did you hear about what happened at Grand Junction?"

"No," Skinny said. "What happened?"

In the distance, a train whistle shrieked that it was nearing the Silverton station, a sound that made Morgan grit her teeth. The sound was a call from the past, a memory of pain, and a distraction from her life now.

"Some kind of horse rustling ring. Money flying everywhere. Marshal was shot dead so it's a free-for-all until the new one arrives." The bartender shook his head. "Probably all those foreigners coming in."

Morgan kept her head down. He meant the immigrants coming west from Italy, Serbia, Wales. Shame burned through her and she took another drink. She didn't remember much about Boston. She'd been young when she was shipped out west on the "orphan train" because she was Irish. She had no memory of parents. Nothing before Barclay stepping up to be her adoptive father. Uncomfortable, Morgan drained the glass and paid for another.

John the bartender was smooth this time, swiping the cash and replacing the drink.

When the saloon doors squeaked open, Morgan didn't turn around. She didn't need any trouble. Then, everything stopped in the saloon. The bartender still had his hand inside a glass as he gaped at whatever was behind her. Even the constant shuffle of cards ceased.

Giving in, Morgan looked over her shoulder.

A young woman stood in front of the swinging doors dolled up in a hip-length blue traveling jacket over a skirt of the same color with a bustle in the back. She had blond hair in curls under a hat and held a flowered carpet bag that looked heavy by the way she gripped it with both hands.

"I wonder if someone could help me?" Her voice was like a candy Barclay had once bought Morgan from a company store in some no-name town. "My name's Josie McGuire. I need a guide to the town of Victor. I'm the new schoolteacher, but this is the last stop on the track."

One of the poker players stood up, knocking over his chair with a loud bang. "Big Jim," he announced, unsteady on his feet. "I'll take you wherever you want to go." He leered and stumbled into a table, making it screech as it slid to the side.

Big Jim's companions snickered and made comments that Morgan didn't try to hear. She was barely tolerated out here and she could prove herself with her horse, her Colt, and her cash. But, she wasn't looking for trouble.

"I have a trunk as well." Josie looked around with a slight smile as if this was all good fun. "Sitting at the train station."

Skinny stood up.

*Here we go*, thought Morgan, swiveling around on her seat.

"I can get you to Cimarron." Skinny sauntered over and stopped in front of the woman, looking her up and down before spitting to the side. "You'll have to rent a buckboard."

Josie set her carpet bag on a chair. "And you'll help me?"

*You were new once,* Morgan could practically hear Barclay say. *I took care of you. Pass it forward.*

"Well, then, pay me now and I'll find a buckboard," Skinny said. He reached out to touch the blue cloth on her arm with his dirty fingers. "I'll find us a place for tonight, too."

"That's not necessary," Josie said, shaking his arm away.

"Don't go with him," Big Jim shouted from his side of the bar. "I'm going to help you."

Skinny sneered at Big Jim. "Go sleep it off, you drunk."

"I'm not drunk! You're drunk." Big Jim made his way toward Skinny, but he stumbled again, and Skinny laughed before shoving him. Big Jim tottered and then fell back into a bar stool, knocking it over.

"Hey," a small man called from the card table. "That's my brother." He leaped up from the table, skirted the bar stools, and then shoved Skinny, who stumbled back. The three other card players stood up and moved into a half-circle around the small man and Skinny.

Meanwhile, Henry moved into position from his side of the room and when the small man passed in front of him, facing Skinny, Henry reached out from behind and hooked the man's throat with his left elbow. With his right hand, Henry pressed the muzzle of his pistol to the man's temple.

"This doesn't concern you," Henry said. "Go back to your game."

Skinny tipped his hat. "Thank you, kindly, sir."

No one was paying her any attention. Morgan moved around the room to force her way between Skinny and Josie. She grabbed Josie's sleeve with one hand and the carpet bag with the other and marched the young woman through the swinging doors to the porch outside.

"Where do you think you're going?" Skinny said, his eyes narrowed as he followed them outside.

"You're not stealing this woman's money." Morgan had the carpet bag in her left hand and her right hand on her Colt. "Or anything else your nasty mind imagined."

Skinny glared. Then he cocked his arm back and threw a punch.

Morgan ducked to the side and swung with the carpet bag, hitting him square in the ribs, the same place he'd landed on the ground earlier. Off-balance, Skinny fell, wheezing for breath.

Laughter broke out in the saloon.

Skinny writhed in pain, but he managed to say. "You are going to pay for this."

Morgan ignored him and untied Mac's reins.

Josie skipped forward to join her.

Looking down at the carpet bag, Morgan said, "What the hell is in here anyway?"

"Books." Josie touched her hat. "Thank you for helping me in there, but who are you?"

"Morgan Barclay." Morgan eyed Josie's dress outfit and then shrugged out of her duster. "Put this on. It'll keep you clean." She gestured at Josie's lower half. "Can you ride in that?"

"My bustle?" Josie asked. "It's more relevant that I've never ridden a horse at all than what is attached to my backside."

Biting back a curse, Morgan helped Josie onto Mac with the young woman sitting side saddle, one leg around the saddle horn. "Hold onto his mane. It won't hurt him." Morgan tied the carpet bag to her bedroll and then climbed behind Josie, using the reins to turn Mac towards Stony Pass Ranch.

Gus finished filling the water trough as they rode up. He wiped his forehead with a bandanna and stared.

"This is Josie McGuire." Morgan dismounted. "Mind if she stays in the bunkhouse with me tonight? And, we need to borrow your buckboard to take her to the train station tomorrow."

Josie made a sound as if to argue but she couldn't quite figure out how to dismount and Morgan wasn't going to help her.

"This place is always open to you and your friends." Gus shoved the bandana into his back pocket. He had a twinkle in his eye as he said, "I'll let the Missus know that you'll be joining us for supper, Miss McGuire. It'll be nice to have some civilized company for a change."

Morgan chose not to respond to his teasing. Instead, she led Mac over to the bunkhouse while Gus went back to the pastures.

Josie slid down the side of the horse, holding onto Mac for balance. Smoothing her skirt, Josie said, "Thank you for finding me a place to stay tonight, but I'm not leaving."

Morgan put the saddlebag in the bunkhouse and led Mac into the stable. He deserved a treat after driving the mustangs south. She checked the hay and water in the stall and put his saddle away.

Josie followed behind. "This is all new to me." She blocked the stable door so Morgan couldn't leave. "But I'm willing to learn. All I need is a chance."

A breeze blew through the stable making a moaning sound. Morgan ducked under Josie's arm. "Shut the door on your way out." This direction faced the town, but behind it were the mountains, a towering presence.

A headache formed in the front of Morgan's head and she wanted to be alone, but Josie followed her into the bunkhouse.

"Are you feeling alright?"

Morgan ignored her, shaking out her bedroll and placing it on a bottom bunk. She stretched out and closed her eyes. "Why do you want to be a teacher so bad?"

Floorboards creaked as Josie moved around the bunkhouse. "I've read so many books about the Wild West. I want to be part of it. I want to help people."

Morgan opened her eyes and

turned on her side. "Silverton's dangerous. Full of desperate men following the promise of gold so they can send money back to their families. This is no place for a lady."

"But Victor—"

"Will be the same," Morgan finished. "You should take the train home."

"Well," Josie sat up straighter. "What about you?"

"I'm no lady," Morgan snapped. "You have to be strong, to earn your way out here."

Morgan rapped against the bunk. "This isn't a forgiving place."

"You're like that man who grabbed me in the saloon, thinking that I don't belong out here. That I'm weak. And because of that you've decided that I should go home." Josie stood up and paced. "But I'm not going to. It wasn't easy to get an education, but I did it. I'm the oldest of five children and I was more a mother to them than our actual mother because she and my father had to work so hard. And it wasn't easy to save up the money for train fare, but my whole family sacrificed. I will not squander that."

Feeling guilty, Morgan said, "I'm not like Skinny—"

"I wasn't finished." Josie put her hands on her hips, looking how Morgan imagined a schoolteacher would. "I get to make my own decisions. Your only choice is whether to help me or not."

THE clanging bell was part of a dream before Morgan's eyes snapped open. She leaped out of bed and yanked open the bunkhouse door. False dawn lit the sky behind the mountains. Movement in the semi-darkness, horses screaming. Gus stood in the doorway of his house, light from his wife's lantern outlining him and the shotgun he held, pointed toward the pastures.

Pounding hooves. The mustangs were running.

"What happened?" Josie asked, pulling on the blue coat over her nightgown.

Morgan shoved her feet into boots.

"Who's out there?" Gus called.

"Where's Morgan?" It was Skinny's voice, coming from near the horses. "She owes me."

"Get off my property," Gus yelled, swinging around to point toward the voice's position.

A chill passed through Morgan as she remembered how angry Skinny had been. He was the kind of man to nurse hurt feelings. She opened her mouth to warn Gus to get inside, but before she could, a shot rang out. The acrid smell of gun smoke scented the air.

Then another shot.

Gus's body jerked in the doorway. He'd been a clear target with the light behind him. His wife screamed.

Morgan's heart jerked in her chest in mimicry. She cursed and ran to the shadow thrown by the stable, between the bunkhouse and the main house.

A figure on horseback appeared from the darkness—it had to be

Henry—a rope twirling above his head. "Ready!"

Skinny emerged from where he'd been hiding when he shot Gus and opened the gate. "Get the buckboard," he yelled to a third figure. Then he mounted his gelding, waving his hat and yelling to spook the excited horses.

The mustang herd thundered past where Morgan stood. She pressed back against the stable wall. Dust rose to coat everything.

"Help," Josie screamed from the porch of the bunkhouse.

Morgan's hand dropped to where her Colt should be, but it was still in the bunkhouse. She couldn't do anything as Skinny wrestled with Josie, finally picking the teacher up and throwing her across his gelding before mounting behind her.

The buckboard, pulled by a familiar looking grey gelding, rattled past. It was the animal more than the silhouette that helped Morgan recognize Big Jim from the saloon.

"Stop!" Morgan yelled to Skinny. "It's me you want."

Looking over his shoulder, Skinny yelled. "Not anymore. Your friend is dying and I've got the horses and the girl. I guess you could say that I win."

Skinny jerked the reins so that his horse reared up and then they galloped after Henry and the wild herd.

Morgan stood there, frozen.

*Life is tough,* Barclay's voice whispered, *but so are you.*

Morgan rushed to Gus. His wife had him laid out on the kitchen

floor with a cloth pressed to his shoulder. "They shot him clean through." Her expression was tight, scared. This was bad.

"You gotta let me up. I'm going after those bastards." Gus said, but his hands shook as he plucked at his wife and his face was paler than Morgan had ever seen. "All our money was tied up in the horses."

"Hold still, I'll take care of you." Gus's wife smiled down at her husband as she stroked his cheek. "Don't worry about a thing."

Morgan wanted to say that she was sorry, that this was her fault, but the words gummed up in her throat. She stood up.

"You're leaving?" Gus's wife said with an incredulous expression. She glanced at Gus and then back. Morgan understood the message that he might not make it through the night, but Morgan wasn't a doctor. Staying here wouldn't help. There was, however, something she could do.

"I'm going to get your horses back."

MORGAN urged Mac to move faster. The chestnut stallion wasn't happy about the situation, but it was all or nothing. She had Gus's shotgun as well as her Navy Colt. She needed to find the gang, rescue Josie, and bring back the unbranded mustangs or Gus and his wife would be bankrupt. So, she'd done the unthinkable. She'd lassoed the wild mustang stallion and tied the other end to Mac's saddle. Then she'd let Woodrow loose.

"Call your herd home," she encouraged him.

The mustang whinnied, an insistent high-pitched sound made to travel, a sound made for communication.

An answering sound traveled back to them and Morgan exhaled a breath she'd been holding since she left the ranch. She'd had to guess where Skinny would go and all she had to go on was the comment by the bartender about the horse rustling in Grand Junction. If she'd had a herd of unbranded mustangs that she had to offload, that's where she'd go. Fast. Before the new marshal arrived.

Clucking her tongue, Morgan urged Mac forward.

Suddenly, Woodrow whinnied again and lunged up the rocky path toward the crest of the mountain. The rope connecting the two horses pulled taut and Mac stumbled as the frenzied mustang thrashed in his frenzy to reach the herd.

Morgan lurched, only her years of riding experience keeping her in the saddle. "Hold, boy." She pulled out her knife and dismounted in a smooth motion. Her horse braced his feet against the powerful pull of the mustang, his shoulders bulging with the effort, his eyes rolling.

Keeping her hand on the rope, Morgan moved toward the mustang. She had to get close enough to cut him loose with the rope at a length where it wouldn't trail behind him. Otherwise it was a death trap, the rope catching between rocks or causing a panic if it looked like a snake.

"Calm," she soothed in the tone Barclay had taught her. "Steady." When she was as close as she could get without being kicked, she sawed at the rope.

The last string broke with a snapping sound. Free, Woodrow reared and then galloped along the crest instead of over, rocks scattering behind him. Morgan shook her head, unsure where the stallion was going.

Reaching the crest, Morgan dropped to her belly and peered over.

Henry was on horseback, keeping watch over the herd, who were drinking from a shallow stream. There was the buckboard. Big Jim was driving it and Josie sat beside him. Her eyes were swollen like she'd been crying, but she held her head up.

Skinny was horseback and had a rope around the head mare's neck attached to his saddle the way that she'd had Woodrow's.

Morgan folded her left arm and used it as a brace for her Colt. The problem was that if she shot then all the horses would run. Josie would be thrown from the wagon and Morgan would never be able to get the scattered herd back to the ranch. Reluctantly, she put it away.

Skinny's voice drifted up to Morgan, "Let's go to the cabin."

He and Henry moved the herd. Big Jim brought up the rear, driving through a cloud of dust. Josie let her hand drop over the side of the wagon and released a blue hair ribbon. Don't worry, Morgan wanted to say. She knew the abandoned cabin they meant—they'd stayed there when driving the mustangs to Gus's ranch.

Morgan climbed back up the hill to Mac and they were off.

Mac's hooves weren't as thick as the mustangs, but he had shoes on and that let Morgan pick out a more direct route down the mountain. The dust was easy to follow and Morgan rode right up alongside the buckboard. Big Jim had a slack expression, both hungover and eyes watering from dust. She dropped Mac's reins and jumped into the back of the wagon. Confused, Big Jim pulled the reins and then turned to look over his shoulder.

Morgan hit him on the side of the head with her Colt. The pistol connected with a satisfying thud and then the man's eyes rolled up into his head and he fell back.

"Morgan!" Josie turned around and her mouth fell open. "You came."

"Of course I did. Hold onto the reins so the horse doesn't take off."

Morgan pulled his inert body all the way into the wagon and then hogtied him.

"Do you know how to get back to the ranch? I've got to take care of the other two."

"I'm not leaving!" Josie shook her head. "Those criminals kidnapped me. They can't get away with that."

Morgan started to argue, but it would be a lot easier to bring back the herd with Josie's help. "Fine," Morgan said, hopping over the side of the wagon and mounting Mac. "I can get to the cabin faster by myself. Follow the herd and then you'll be in position to help me."

Josie nodded and picked up the reins.

Morgan leaned over to correct her grip and then clucked Mac into a ground-covering lope.

The abandoned cabin sat in the hot sun with a pen off to the side. Even Barclay hadn't known who'd built it. Someone who'd been beaten by the desert. Morgan tied Mac behind the cabin and took a position inside.

Soon the sound of hooves on rocks and a cloud of dust warned her they were coming. There was Skinny. And coming through the dust was... Josie. He must have gone back to check on the buckboard to see what was taking so long. He'd tied Josie's hands together and made her walk. Her blonde hair was bedraggled, dirt covered one cheek, and her blue coat had a rip in it. Morgan tightened her hand on the Colt.

Skinny dismounted and led the mares and colts into the ring, securing the gate with the rope he'd used on the lead mare.

Mac whinnied and Morgan turned from looking out the window just in time to see Henry sneaking up on the back of the cabin.

Morgan raised her Colt, sighted

the way Barclay had taught her, and pulled the trigger.

Henry's body jerked. His face had a shocked expression as he fell over. He would have killed her without a thought, but was surprised that she'd do the same.

"Morgan!" Josie screamed from in front of the cabin.

Morgan turned around to see that Skinny had Josie's body in front of him as a shield with a knife to her throat. He was such a coward. She raised her Colt, but she didn't dare shoot with Josie held in front.

"You in the cabin, girl?" Skinny called. "Come on out with your hands up where I can see them and both you gals might live." He spat to the side.

Morgan took a breath. She'd tried to avoid trouble, but trouble was here and it wasn't Josie's fault. She held her hands in the air and walked outside.

"Empty your gun and put it on the ground." He pressed the knife tip into Josie's skin so that she moaned.

Morgan obeyed, lowering the Colt to the ground.

A whinny ripped from the round pen rippled through the air. An answer echoed from nearby and then Woodrow galloped around the corner, running straight toward the pen.

"That beast." Afraid of being trampled, Skinny reached for his gun to shoot Woodrow.

While he was distracted, Josie stomped her foot hard on Skinny's boot and then twisted out of his grip.

Morgan charged forward, tackling the man so that they both hit the ground, her on top, her leg blocking him from pulling out the gun. She punched down and blood spurted from his broken nose. Then pain flared in her leg as Skinny sliced with the knife still gripped in his hand.

Morgan grabbed his right arm and wrestled it over his head. He bucked his hips to dislodge her and she let him wear himself out. If a bronco couldn't shake her, there was no way this man could.

She held his arm down with her left hand and punched him in the ribcage with her right again and again. Once for threatening to beat Woodrow, once for threatening the farm, once for kidnapping Josie. Then, she took the knife and cut his throat.

That was for shooting Gus.

Skinny's body convulsed. He put a hand to his throat and made gagging sounds. Red splashed. He kicked his feet and then was still.

Morgan watched Woodrow touching noses with his mare. "Ready to go home?"

Josie wrapped her arms around herself. "Are you talking to me or the horse?"

"Both."

"And home is...Stony Pass Ranch."

Morgan squinted at the sky. They could be back by dark. "I reckon so."

# Trouble on the Rails

### By JODY LYNN NYE

I SAT on the aisle in the middle of the rumbling train car, sending glances of apology out to everybody sitting around us. Next to me, my lady friend Kerrylynn Kuhn went on and on about what she could see out of the window, where we were going, and just about everything else that came into her head, which was plenty.

"There's a road that runs next to the rails!" she exclaimed, pulling me by the arm so I could look out and see it, too. I went, not because I wanted to exactly, but Kerrylynn is mighty strong for a girl. I looked out at the dusty stretch of road accompanying us over the sun-washed landscape. "I think it's been following us all the way from Center City! Aren't they clever to build it right there where it will be handy?"

"I think it was there first, Trouble," I said, doing my best to extricate myself from her grip. I stood a good six inches taller than her, had weighed forty pounds more than she did since I started shaving, and I wrangled horses, but I couldn't break free of it. "The workers must have run it out here so they could work on the rails."

She let go of me so abrupt I fell back into my seat with a thump.

"Well, you're right, Duncan Wrayburn!" she said. "What was I thinking?"

I'm pretty sure everyone else in the train car had exactly the same thought on their mind. They all looked everywhere but at the pretty girl in the voluminous ochre skirt and trim jacket with the tailored white shirtwaist underneath that showed off her tiny waist. I think that the big man in the severe black coat at the end of the car next to the sliding door wanted to laugh, but he kept himself under pretty tight control. I straightened my jacket, where Trouble's fingers had made a mass of wrinkles of my lapel. I was wearing my best blue Sunday suit, with a string tie and polished boots. Now I felt like I'd invaded a ladies' parlor in my cattle-wrangling clothes.

You'd never guess, to look at Trouble's big, wide blue eyes and that mass of long golden hair piled up that inside that beautiful head was a mighty good brain. In fact, except for her daddy, Denton Kuhn, she was probably the smartest person I had ever met in my life. Smart didn't mean the same thing as wise, though. Neither of them had the common sense that God gave a day-old

*Illustration by Karl Kesel*

chick. Denton, who invented things no one else had ever seen before, usually confined his investigations to the mysteries inside his la-BOR-a-tor-ee, but Trouble was wide-ranging, hence her name.

Her ma, Jo, who ran the local saloon, had come to me about a week before, worry on her face.

"Denton's got to go to Denver," she said, wringing my hand with both of hers. She was darned near as strong as her daughter, so it made quite an impression on me. "He's finished that there secret device for the Department of the Interior, and they want it as soon as he can get it to them."

"Should be no problem for him," I had said, working it out a little in my mind. "All he's got to do is load it onto the train and find his seat. Once the conductor says they reached Denver, he just has to remember to get off."

"He can do all that," Jo had said, "but Trouble is determined to go with him."

I knew what she was asking me, and my heart sank, but I couldn't inflict Trouble on the rest of the United States with a clear conscience.

"I'll go," I promised.

So, there I was. I had stood by as Denton Kuhn, in his shirt sleeves, his fair hair all askew, oversaw the loading of his invention into the luggage car at the rear of the six-car train. The secret device was so heavy that the car sank a little

as the wheeled cart rolled up the ramp. It kind of looked like a Civil War Gatling gun with a mass of big cylindrical barrels mounted flat on it, and ee-LEC-trick-el cables like thick ropes leading to a couple of massive planks made of metal behind it. Underneath the canvas tarpaulin on the rear, you couldn't see any details, but it had something that looked like two big scoops on either fork of an enormous slingshot. Denton made sure to tell everyone not to touch those at all. It must have been something really dangerous, because even Trouble wouldn't get near them.

Maneuvering the device in the baggage car didn't go easy. A couple of chests in the forward corner were chained to a cleat in the floor with padlocks on them. The uniformed conductor was apologetic about it, but he said he wasn't allowed to move them. The only way they could get the wagon into the car was for the barrel to face backward toward the caboose.

Once it was loaded, Denton sat himself on a pull-down seat and folded his arms. He wasn't leaving his invention alone for a minute. Trouble and I had went to our seats in the next car forward.

Most of the other passengers in our car belonged to a group of some kind. Men and ladies alike all wore the same sober, gray-colored clothes in a cut that spoke of Sunday-go-to-meeting. I wasn't

particular religious, but I showed
up in church one time a week
when I was expected to, but these
people looked as if they went all
the time, and liked it. About every
one of them had a leather-bound
Bible, either in a handy pocket,
for impromptu prayers, or in a
handbag or valise close by. The
big man in black who I thought
was their leader had his good
book right in his hand all the
time. His leatherbound copy had
the name "Holy Bible" stamped
right in gold on the cover and the
spine, which he turned so people
passing by in the aisle could see
it so they knew he was important.
Once in a while, he stood up in
the swaying car and addressed
his flock. They bent their heads
over their Bibles and murmured
in unison over a page or two as he
harrumphed a syllable or so out
loud, ending in a loud and echoing "Amen!" Once they had been
rendered suitably blessed for
the moment, he sat down again.
Except for that, Trouble was the
chief source of entertainment on
the train.

"Those government fellows
must have sent Daddy twenty tele-
grams asking about bringing the
drill starter to Denver," she said.
"They're in a powerful hurry!
He kept writing back to say the
mineral refinement for the linear
accelerator couldn't be rushed,
but they just didn't want to hear it.
He's done his best to oblige them.
But what could Daddy do?"

"Nothing, Miss Kerrylynn," I
said, politely, trying to figure out
how to get her to lower her voice.

"Exactly! So, Daddy asked me
to help him out with the projec-
tiles instead. I got every one of
them case hardened and sturdy
and mounted in that magazine,
just as pretty as you please. They
ought to be able to drive straight
into the South Pass of the Con-
tinental Divide and blow a hole
in it that can hold eight men
with pile drivers and pickaxes.
There'll be a straight railway tunnel underneath it in just about no
time. It's a lot more modern than
the old way they've had to do it all
these years." Trouble's expression
grew thoughtful. "Daddy still
hasn't been able to do anything
at all about that kickback. I think
all they'll be able to do is brace
it solid to take best advantage of
that forward thrust. That's what
I'd do."

"I guess so," I said. I never knew
what she was talking about when
she got onto the science she and
her Daddy did.

"Daddy wrote to the train company about having the baggage
car empty to accommodate the
accelerator," Trouble went on,
occasionally meeting the eyes and
smiling at people in the car who
glanced up at her. They seemed
powerful embarrassed to be eavesdropping, but they just couldn't
help themselves. "It's as heavy as a
whole building, but they did manage to bolt it down so it can't move

an inch. Lucky it fit in with all those valises, and those two heavy boxes chained to the floor. Wonder what's in those?"

"It don't help to speculate, Miss Kerrylynn," I pointed out. "It's none of our business."

"Aren't you just a little curious?" she asked, turning one of her winning expressions toward me. Those were pretty hard to resist, but when it came to right and wrong, I had to find the backbone.

"Well, I can be curious," I said. "Don't mean I plan to indulge myself."

Her big blue eyes widened, trying to draw me in. She sat up straighter and straighter as each new notion hit her.

"But it could be trade secrets! Jewels from India! Gold bullion from Sacramento! We're going to be pulling into Denver pretty soon. Isn't one of the mints right there?"

I waved a hand to drive away all her crazy ideas that were buzzing around my head like flies.

"If it was gold, there would be a dozen Pinkertons on board this train with us," I said, dropping my voice low.

"Well, it could be gold," Trouble insisted. "That's about the heaviest mineral there is."

"Thou shalt not covet thy neighbor's goods," one of the gray-clad women near us said, a stern expression on her wrinkled prune of a face. "That's a sin!"

Trouble was only momentarily cowed.

"Oh, I don't want to keep it, ma'am! I only want to see it. Don't you think it would be a sight to behold, gleaming and pretty?"

"I would not!" the woman protested.

"Lying's a sin, too," Trouble said, but so sweetly that the woman retired in confusion.

Some murmuring erupted among the rest of the parishioners. Their leader decided now would be a good time to get up and preach at them some more. He almost collided with the conductor, who appeared through the sliding door at the end of the car, letting in the deafening clatter of the train on the tracks. The conductor checked all our tickets and let his gaze rest on each of our faces in turn. If I didn't know better, I'd have said that he was memorizing all of us. I hadn't ever been on a long train ride before, so all the little customs and tasks were new to me.

As soon as the conductor left, a couple of burly men, one white and one black, both with their hair slicked back on top, wearing sharp white jackets and pressed black pants, rolled a rattling three-tiered cart into the car. Savory smells wafted from the two big platters covered with silver domes. A pile of plates and a cylinder full of cutlery sat beside stacked boxes of sandwiches, a bowl of cut up fruit like a jumbled rainbow, and a tiered server holding three whole pies. I had eaten a good breakfast, but that suddenly seemed a long time ago.

"May I buy you some lunch, Miss Kerrylynn?" I asked.

"Well, that would be downright generous of you, Duncan," she said, in delight.

We waited while the men served the preacher and the members of his flock. The servers pulled down little tables that looked like part of the wall and set small white tablecloths on them. They put real china plates down and served up whatever the diner asked for. The black man sliced ham off the bone with deft strokes of a wicked long knife. His companion scooped steaming, smooth-whipped potatoes and chunks of carrot and deposited them next to the meat. My mouth watered.

Trouble beamed at both men as they dished out her food and put a braided roll on the side of the plate with a pat of yellow butter on top.

"That looks delicious," she said. "You're all so nice! What kind of fuel do you use to cook all of this up?"

The two men looked at each other for a moment in bemusement.

"Wood-burnin' stove, ma'am," the white man said at last.

"Well, that takes a lot of refueling!" Trouble declared, and aimed a thumb toward the rear door that led to the baggage car. "You ought

to talk to my daddy about his new fuel system. It's about a hundred thousand times more efficient than wood fire. You could cook for every single person in *Kansas* with it...."

They looked even more confused, which is the general way people reacted to meeting Trouble for the first time.

I pulled on her arm. "Trouble, I don't think they need to hear about that. They've got people to serve. Thanks, gentlemen." I pulled my poke out of my pocket and put a couple of coins in the tray. They nodded their thanks to me and moved the cart down the aisle.

I started to cut a piece of ham, when I noticed Kerrylynn staring hard at me. Abashed, I dropped my hands into my lap. I recalled that I should always let a lady begin first.

"Daddy told me not to let anyone disturb him," she said. "Ma packed him a good lunch."

I glanced behind me. I hadn't even thought about it, but there were no more passengers in the seats between us and the baggage car. The porters were moving with some speed toward that rear door. I squeezed my way out from between the seat and the fixed table, and moved to intercept them.

"Gentlemen, you don't need to go in there," I said, putting my back against the door.

They both turned to smile at

me. I didn't quite like those smiles, but I couldn't say why.

"The lady said her daddy is back there," the black man said, moving the cart forward a little. It hit me in the thighs. "He might like some of this fine food."

"It's considerate of you, but he is provided for," I said, holding their gaze. "Thank you all the same."

With some resentment on their faces, they turned the cart and rolled it all the way back and out the forward door. I made my way to join Trouble, who had already tucked into her meal. I couldn't resist the aroma any longer, and set into mine.

"This fruit salad is as pretty to look at as it is to taste," Trouble said, having disposed handily of her main course and side dishes. She tapped the cut glass bowl with her spoon. "I've got to tell Ma about this, only I don't think most of the men in the saloon would appreciate it." She glanced up. "Look there, the waiters are shaking out tablecloths. Kind of strange that they're doing it where they can get whipped right out of their hands."

She pointed out the window. I leaned over and peered in that direction. The black porter was shaking a length of white linen vigorously off the back of the car ahead of us. We were coming out of a low canyon, where the train slowed as it strained up the gentle slope. We were heading for the foothills where the tracks turned from westbound to northbound on the way to Denver. I knew the details of our route from the small printed map that I had in my breast pocket. From there, Denton would be accompanying the Army Corps of Engineers up to Casper, Wyoming with his invention and start work on the mountainside. Once I escorted her on a tour of the big city, her ma hoped I could persuade Trouble to turn back and go home on the first train east.

I heard a loud, grating squeal come from the front of the train. Everyone in the car looked in that direction. The car shook hard and swayed from side to side.

"Is it the Apocalypse?" a woman in gray asked, clutching her hands over her Bible.

"No, Miz Pritchard," the preacher said, with a gentle smile. "The train is doing God's work trying to fight against the demon Gravity to deliver us safely to our destination."

"Gravity is God's work, too," Trouble pointed out. "Sir Isaac Newton wrote all about it, and he was a physicist and a theologian, both. You oughta read his treatises."

"Uh, yes, ma'am," the preacher replied, taken aback, but he reasserted his authoritative stance. "May I...?"

I pulled Trouble back.

"Let the man tend to his flock," I said.

"I hate to have anyone believing a lie," she began, then stopped. "We're nowhere near a town, are we?"

I fumbled for my map and unfolded it.

"Not for forty miles," I said, following the lines of to-PO-graph-ee. "That'll be where we're stopping for water. They say you can get a mighty fine view of Pike's Peak from there."

"Then where are those men coming from?" she asked.

"What men?" I looked up from my map.

"Them," Trouble said.

I followed her pointing finger, toward a rising cloud of dust a few miles away.

A couple dozen men on horseback were galloping down the road that ran alongside the tracks, headed in our direction. I could just barely hear the sound of their hooves hammering on the ground as they rode. I sprang up.

"Bandits!"

"Where? Where?" the other passengers demanded. I pointed. They sprang to the windows to look out.

"We got to tell the conductor," Trouble said, pushing me out into the aisle. "He's got to wire ahead to Denver." I scrambled to help her rise. "Hurry!"

Under my feet, the train lurched forward. The engineer and firemen must have seen the approaching bandits, and were trying to pour on steam. The locomotive moaned, as though it didn't like the idea. The gray-clad flock let out a collective squawk and held tight to their chairs. We started to hitch our way forward.

The door at the head of the coach slammed open.

"Nobody move!" It was the white porter. He held a couple of mean Colt .45s leveled at us. "All of you! Drop your guns! Get back in your seats!"

"Why, sir," the preacher said, rising up out of the seat like he was on springs, his face a thundercloud, "what is the meaning of all this!"

"Sit down!" the porter commanded. "Stay where you are, and no one gets hurt!" He glared at me. "Drop those hoglegs on the floor. Do it! Careful, now. I don't want no accidents!"

Gingerly, I picked my guns out of my belt and held them up with my thumbs and forefingers. I stooped slowly to the floor and set them down on the boards. The porter strode toward me.

"Back off! Unless you want to meet your God right quick!"

The preacher flipped to the back of his bible and withdrew from a hollow compartment a silver pistol a lot bigger and meaner-looking than the porter's. He aimed it at the man in white, his voice calm and low.

"The Lord helps those who helps themselves, son. I'm Mike Gonzales, a US Marshal. Now, you drop your weapon, and we'll just sit down quiet-like. Ma'am," he addressed Trouble, whose eyes were as wide as saucers, "you were gonna wire the sheriff in Denver. I suggest you go do that right now."

"Nossir," said the black porter, heaving into view. He held a shotgun on us. The barrel was trembling. We were in more danger from him than the white porter because he was too nervous to aim right. A shot from him could go anywhere. "Drop that, sir. I mean it!"

The preacher had no choice. He opened his hand and let the pistol fall to the floor. It bounced out of sight underneath a table. The black man moved up until his rifle barrel was in the middle of the preacher's back. His hands were shaking so much I feared for anyone in the range of his gun. I couldn't figure how the marshal stayed as calm as he did.

The white porter doubled the menace in his voice.

"Everybody sit down and be quiet with your hands up. We're gonna stop soon, just pick up a couple of things, and then everybody can be on their way."

"So, it is gold in those chests!" Trouble said. Behind her, the preacher's flock gasped.

The white porter sneered. "You're pretty smart, miss, but it won't do you no good."

"You won't get away with this," the marshal said.

"It's already done," the white porter said, an evil grin spreading over his face. "Conductor is one of our men. Two of them are in the engine compartment right now. Y'all cooperate, and we'll be on our way with no one any worse off."

The hammering of horse hooves grew louder as the sound of the train grew quieter. It was slowing down. The two men in white coats grinned at each other. The black man tilted his head toward Trouble.

"Her daddy's in the baggage car guardin' somethin' else valuable. Mebbe we oughta take it, too."

"You can't do that!" Trouble declared in alarm. The fire in her eyes meant that the men were in over their heads. They just didn't know it yet.

"You don't tell us what to do, miss," the white porter said, aiming one of his pistols at her heart. "Go sit down, now! I don't want to have to blow your pretty head off!" Trouble backpedaled a mite.

"Leave her alone!" I bellowed, shoving myself in between them. I reached for my sidearms, forgetting they were on the floor behind me.

Something hit me hard upside the head, and I went down. I looked up to see the black porter aiming his shotgun right between my eyes.

"You get back," he said. His dark eyes looked as mean as anything I had ever seen. I eased up off the ground and stood with my hands in the air. The side of my head was on fire with pain. "What Daddy has must be awful good. Let's go get it. He can't do nothing to two of us, and Brummel will be on board soon."

Brummel! Louis Brummel? I blanched, even though it made the throbbing in my head worse. The wanted posters in the Post Office called him the Master of the Rails. He had a gang the size of a city, so they said. It took a lot of robberies to pay them all and keep Brummel in the style he liked to affect.

"Good idea," the white porter said. He gestured with his guns. "You come with us. You, too," he ordered the marshal.

"No!" cried a narrow-faced, elderly woman in a lace cap. "He's our preacher! You can't take him!"

"Quiet down, ma'am," the white porter said, with a glare. "Go on, y'all. Move!"

"I can't!" Trouble said. She started to sway to and fro, letting her head drop back. Her straw hat fell off her fancy hairdo and fluttered away. "I think I'm going to faint! I'm swooning! I'm going down!"

The porters gawked at her; guns lowered. Trouble dropped backward into my arms with all the grace of an anvil. I caught her before she hit the floor, but she twisted in my grasp like a cat.

"Run for it, Duncan!" she shouted, flinging herself to her feet. "Help Daddy!"

The men gawked as she hurtled down the aisle toward the baggage car. I was a couple of steps behind her, trying to find my guns, when a bullet whistled over my head. It smacked into the wood paneling not two feet from me.

"Get down, Trouble!" I yelled. She glanced over her shoulder, then ducked through the sliding door. I spotted one of my pistols underneath the feet of a bald-headed man in a three-piece suit with a gold chain across his waistcoat, and snatched it up. I made it to the back of the car like a greyhound, and ducked through the door.

"You come back here!" the white bandit boomed. Another bullet sang out. It buried itself in a seat cushion. The other passengers screeched and ducked out of the way.

Before the door closed between us, I saw the marshal battling with the black porter for his shotgun. The other porter was hammering down the aisle toward us. I yanked the second door open and hurtled through it, panting. Another bullet sang through the air and cracked the glass in the passenger car door.

Trouble was on the other side, flailing at the handle.

"There's no lock on this door!" she shouted.

"What's going on, Kerrylynn?" Denton Kuhn demanded. "Duncan, you have blood on the side of your face. What's wrong?"

Trouble's daddy was on his feet. Like us, he had been enjoying his lunch. Napkin tucked into his collar, he had a roasted chicken leg in one hand and a bottle of beer in the other.

"Bandits, Daddy," Trouble said, out of breath. "They're trying to rob the train. Those chests are full of gold!" She pointed to the two strongboxes chained to the floor.

"Confound it," Denton said, his fair brows knitting together. "I told the railroad not to stow anything else in here with my accelerator! The government was supposed to back me up. What is this nation coming to?"

"They've got guns, Mr. Kuhn," I said urgently, trying to get him to focus on the real problem at hand. "It's the Brummel gang. Their confederates are in the engine compartment, making the train stop. There's two dozen men heading this way on horseback. We got to get out of this place and go somewhere safe!"

"I am not leaving my invention!" Denton Kuhn said.

"It could mean our lives!"

Loud screeching punctuated my remark, as the train continued to slow down on the upslope. Pretty soon, it'd come to a standstill, putting us all at the mercy of the Brummel gang.

We couldn't have been going more than a few miles an hour any more. The baggage car didn't have windows, so I couldn't see out. The car was lit by oil lamps bolted to the walls and the shifting light from the windows in the doors at each end.

Through the glass on the forward side, I saw the porter with the six-guns had made it to the door. The bandit holstered one gun and tried to pull the baggage door open, but I smacked him over the wrist with my one remaining pistol. He let out a howl and bent over in pain. The door slammed shut. That wouldn't buy us much time.

I looked around for a defensive position. All the valises, trunks and bags belonging to the other passengers had been lined up according to which stop they were getting off at. I handed my gun to Trouble, who braced herself against her daddy's invention, facing the baggage compartment door. I pushed all the soft cases to one side and started heaping the trunks up against the door.

"Good idea, son!" Denton said. He came over and hefted a trunk on top of the first row I had made. "Stagger them like bricks. That'll make it harder to push over."

I agreed. We built us a wall as fast as we could move. The bandit on the other side couldn't push the door inward by himself, but he wasn't alone.

"This won't hold them long," I said. "The preacher's really a US marshal, but his flock is no earthly good. I hope he's got some fellow agents in the other cars."

Another squawk of metal on

metal erupted, but instead of being the sound of the train slowing down, it was beside us. Even though we were still moving, someone was trying to break in through the big sliding doors. The train must have slowed down enough that horses could keep up with it.

"It won't be long now," Denton Kuhn said, his face a grim mask. "Confound it, we're all in danger if my invention gets into the hands of people who don't know what they're doing!"

We had the wall of trunks about chest high. Over the top of them, the bandit glared at me. He was still trying to fight his way in. I hoisted a big square red leather case up and blocked out the view of him.

Trouble let out a yell.

"They're coming through, Duncan!"

The sliding door let out a massive creak of protest. The edge of a pry bar appeared in the crack and widened it. The metal catch holding it shut strained. I abandoned the valises and ran to the door. Fingers appeared around the edge. Outside, I heard rough voices shouting.

"Bring up that ram!" a man shouted.

I brought up my boot and smashed the hands clinging to the edge. With a bellow, the owner yanked them out of the crack. I fumbled at the pry bar, trying to dislodge it. The metal nipped my fingers, but I kept on fighting with it. I thought I just about got it to where I could push it out of the door, when a big metal bar thrust through the space. It caught me in the chest. I stumbled and fell backward.

"Duncan!" Trouble shouted.

"I'm all right," I said. The metal strut started winching back and forth, widening the open space. "Mr. Kuhn, you and Kerrylynn take shelter. Shoot if anyone gets through!"

I looked around for a weapon. We didn't have much. Trouble had my only gun. Denton hardly ever went armed. This was supposed to be a peaceable journey. An arm in a dust-colored shirt got in between the door and the jamb. I ran over to the far edge and threw my shoulder against it. I pushed hard, but it was no use. Another arm, in a blue shirt, shoved inside, followed by a couple extra hands. I strained to shut them out. Before I knew it, the owner of the dust-colored shirt, a bearded man with greasy brown hair squeezed halfway in. Despite the jarring motion of the train and the door pinning him tight, he managed to draw a gun from the holster on his belt. He leveled it at me.

"You just back away, son. I can't miss at this range."

"Neither can I!" Trouble declared. A deafening bang made my ears ring as she fired my pistol. A bullet pinged off the sliding door right next to the man's right ear.

Trouble and her daddy were huddled behind the tarp covering Denton's invention. Just the top of her head and the barrel of the gun showed over the top. "That was a warning! Now you get out and go away!"

"What in the Sam Hill...?"

When his head swiveled to look at her, I threw myself at him. I grabbed his wrist in both of my hands and wrestled for his gun. He was strong, but he didn't have the leverage to resist me. I got the pistol away and aimed it at him. He sneered.

Unfortunately, moving like I did allowed his blue-shirted confederate to pry the door the rest of the way open. The two of them, followed by a Pawnee Indian in a buckskin shirt with hair clipped off his scalp except for a crest on top of his head, leaped up into the baggage car straight at me. I fired, palming the cocking lever, but I missed with my first shot. A second later, the Indian was sitting on my chest and the gun went spiraling out the door into the sun. He drew a long knife and held it to my throat. I struggled a little, but the sharp blade bit into my skin.

"We don't want no heroes here," the greasy-haired man said, as he unlimbered the Colt on his other hip. I had no doubt I was looking at Brummel himself. His eye lit on the chests. "There's my beauties! Rogers, get those unfastened. Any

of you got the key?" He kicked me in the side. I winced. "What about you?"

"No, sir," I said, trying not to move my jaw too much.

The banging on the other side of the wall of trunks attracted the attention of the leader. Rogers started pulling the cases down until the white-coated porter could burst inside.

"We got everything under control in there, Mr. Brummel," he said. He held up a chain of brass keys. "There's a US Marshal in there who was holdin' onto these. Carson is minding him right now."

"Good man, Lewis," Brummel said. "Unlock the chests, and let's get moving." Rogers took the key and bent over the first chest.

"Mr. Brummel, we got somethin' else valuable maybe," the porter said, pointing to the draped shape.

"Mebbe we'll take it along, too," Brummel said, perusing it with a grin. "The wagon'll be along shortly."

"That don't belong to you!" Trouble said, popping up over the side of her daddy's invention. She had the gun fixed on him. "You just leave it alone!"

"You don't have a lot of leverage here, missy," Brummel said, almost amused, turning his weapons on her. "Drop it! Drop it now, right here." Reluctantly, Trouble let my gun fall to the floor. "What's it do?"

The train screeched and swayed

hard then, making me slide almost all the way to the door. It had turned northward and was slowing down even more. Through the opening, I saw a dozen men on horseback pacing us up the slope, preparing to catch hold of the car. The Pawnee looked up, too. When his head shifted, I kicked up and caught him in the wrist with my boot. The knife went flying. I bounced to my feet and made for Brummel.

The Indian leaped for me, and I met his hurtling body square with my own. We wrestled together until a boom from a gun made us both jump.

"Stop gallivantin' around!" Brummel ordered, with his pistol pointed at the ceiling. It now had a hole in it letting in a pencil-thin beam of light. The Pawnee grabbed my right arm and hauled it up against my back. The train screeched some more, and another man jumped off his horse and into the baggage car. More of them weren't far behind. "We're slowing down now. In a moment, we're gonna stop. You all just act peaceable and let us take what we want. We'll move out, and no one will get hurt. Understand?"

I was pretty sure I didn't believe him. Brummel had a reputation as a stone-cold killer. If we slowed down, we were done for. Trouble, Denton Kuhn, and I all looked at each other. I saw a look in her eyes that I recognized with some alarm.

"We understand, sir," I said with some haste. "We got it like a Bible truth, sir. Right, Miss Kerrylynn?"

"Sure do," Trouble said, as sweet as pie. "You want to see what my daddy's invention does, Mr. Brummel?"

"I'd like that," the train robber said. He fixed an indulgent eye on the pretty girl and completely misinterpreted the innocent expression on her face, but he didn't know her like I did. I braced myself. She had something up her sleeve. "Don't try nothin' funny."

"Of *course* not!" Trouble said, brightly. She swept the tarpaulin off the top of the invention. It looked like a children's toy cobbled together from pieces out of the hardware store, only on a huge scale. Four big wheels with steel rims held up a solid wooden platform containing a couple of long steel rails that sloped upward between a forest of brass pistons to where the two arms of the slingshot held their half-spheres of gray metal. On top of the long barrel rested a painted metal hopper that resembled the magazine of a Gatling gun but was fifty times bigger. The whole thing had cloth-covered wires winding all over it like Granny's cat got into a hank of knitting yarn. She laid her hands on a lever that stuck out on one side of the framework. "Now, you know that Newton's second law says that force equals mass times acceleration, right?"

"Uh, I guess so," Brummel said, looking bemused. Another of his henchmen climbed aboard, grinning like the devil. Rogers was just undoing the chain on the first chest of gold bullion. One more lock, and they'd have it loose.

Trouble beamed at him. "Well, this is my daddy's invention to drive a metal rod straight into a mountain, so the Army Corps of Engineers can dig railroad tunnels. These uranium hemispheres are capable of generating more than half a million pounds of force, which is enough to make the rod go at least forty feet into solid stone. Maybe more!"

Brummel tipped back his hat with the barrel of his pistol. His eyes had dollar signs behind them. "That sounds mighty impressive, ma'am."

"Sure is! But, do you know what happens when the source of the force isn't bolted down to anything?"

"No...what?"

"This!"

Trouble pulled the lever. With a clank, one of the big metal rods dropped out of the hopper on the top of the device into the slot on the long barrel. The two gray hemispheres on the stalks flew toward each other like a child clapping his hands. When they met, lightning sprang out of them and run crackling down the long rails. The whole contraption glowed red for a second, then a boom of

thunder broke out. I sneezed on air that smelled hot and metallic like a thunderstorm. The world swept out from under my feet. Brummel, the Pawnee, and all the rest of us fell over. And there was a great big ragged hole at the rear of the car where the heavy rod had shot out the back of the train like a giant bullet. The carriage hurtled forward, bouncing and creaking, leaving the horsemen outside behind. They spurred, trying to catch up.

I didn't miss my opportunity. I grabbed the Indian with one arm and rolled him toward the open hatch. His body hit the legs of the man who had just climbed on board. Both of them disappeared out the door. Then the train swayed, and I almost went with them.

"Yahoo!" Trouble shouted, clinging to the lever.

I could hear shouting and screaming coming from the train car ahead of us. The passengers had been caught off guard by the sudden surge of speed. I held onto the door frame, praying that I wouldn't be thrown out onto the tracks. The train shimmied from side to side like it was as scared as the rest of us.

"What the devil did you do?" Brummel demanded. He got up to his hands and knees, fumbling for his gun. He braced himself against one of the gold chests and put a bullet in the wall over Trouble's head. They both flinched down behind the accelerator. "Make this goldarned train stop!"

They knew they couldn't. The moment we stopped, we were all dead.

"That isn't gonna last, Kerrylynn!" Denton Kuhn boomed at his daughter, hanging onto the frame of his device. "The acceleration won't be able to maintain the momentum going uphill!"

"How long's it going to last?" she shrieked back.

Denton being Denton, he reached into the pocket of his coat and came up with a stub of pencil and an envelope. The train hit a bump, and his calculating materials went flying.

"Never mind that!" I shouted, clinging to the door. The horsemen were now a couple hundred yards behind us and still falling back. "Keep it going!"

Trouble grabbed the lever and yanked it again. The two halves of the sphere separated, then clapped together again. Another pole dropped into the barrel and spewed out the hole in the wall. Boom! The train jerked a mite, then shot forward like it had a burr under its tail.

The porter and the two bandits had lost their guns, too. Only Brummel was armed, so I figured it was a safe enough fight. I let go of my handhold and rolled toward him.

Out of the corner of his eye, he saw me coming and blasted away at me. A splinter jumped up out of the floor of the car into my cheek, but I didn't let that discomfort stop me. Trouble and her daddy were in danger! I pried myself up and sprang at him.

Despite the unsteadiness of the train, we grappled together. He was older than me, thirty pounds lighter and a hand smaller. I got the gun out of his hand and threw it just anywhere. He squirmed like a snake. I gave him one punch in the gut, but he twisted and I hit his ribs instead.

"Help me! Knock this fool down!" Brummel coughed out.

His henchmen jumped in. One of them yanked my head back in his elbow and started pummeling me with the other. My face mashed against his stinking, unwashed sleeve and I almost gagged. I refused to let go. As long as we were still moving, we were safe. I only hoped someone would report the runaway train and get the local sheriffs involved.

The man holding me bellowed and his grip loosed suddenly. The cloth blocking my vision fell away. I saw Denton Kuhn swinging a lady's flowered cloth bag like the hammer of God. It must have had an anvil in it, because the man who had been holding me was on the floor clutching his head. I couldn't pay too much attention, because Brummel sank his teeth into my neck. I yelped and socked him hard in the kidneys. His face set in pain, he kicked out at me. The white porter put his shoulder down and charged at me. I twisted, but I found myself on the ground. Brummel and Lewis, the porter, sat on me. I kicked and thrashed, but the porter kept me down.

I felt the train start to drop back. Outside, I could hear shouts from the gunmen pursuing us. Trouble reached for the lever. Rogers came up from behind Denton Kuhn and put a gun to his head. The inventor held up his hands.

"Touch that and your daddy dies!" the bandit said to Trouble.

"Drop it!" a voice boomed from the door. "US Marshal!"

There in front of the broken glass stood the black-clad preacher, a pistol in one hand and his Bible in the other.

All of us were shocked into immobility for a moment. Then Trouble leaped for the lever and hauled it again. Clap! Bang! The train plunged forward. Disappointed shouts came from outside and got quieter and quieter as we sped away from the gang. The preacher jerked forward, then caught himself before he fell. I twisted out from underneath the train robbers and sat on Brummel the same way he sat on me.

The marshal came over and removed a pair of steel handcuffs out of the back of his good book. He fastened them onto Brummel's wrists and hauled the man to his feet. The other two just held up their hands and surrendered. Denton hurried to embrace his

daughter. The marshal turned to Trouble and doffed his hat.

"Miss, I thank you kindly for the assistance in thwarting this dastardly attempt at train robbery. I wondered what divine intervention had prevented the rest of the gang from getting on board, then I recalled your... edifying discourse on the device your daddy was escorting on this train. My flock is taking care of the other porter at this moment, although some of them might never get over the wild ride they just had. They think your invention is the work of the devil, sir."

"It's all plain science, sir," Denton Kuhn said, looking mildly perturbed.

"I'd reckon it's a matter of perception, sir. The engineers are grateful for the distraction that enabled them to overcome the bandits that had joined them in the locomotive compartment and wired ahead for help. I assure you that as soon as the Denver sheriff's posse can round up the other robbers that they will see justice as well."

"Denver?" Trouble asked, her eyes bright. She clapped her hands with glee. "We're coming into Denver?"

"Well," the marshal said, laughter in his eyes. "I believe with your last blast of whatever that was that we have just passed through Denver at emulsifying speed, but sooner or later we're going to come to a stop. In fact," he said glancing over his shoulder at the passing landscape, "we're already about a mile north of the station. I don't think we're going to be able to stop for another ten miles at least."

"Well, that's all right!" Trouble said, reaching for the first of the fastenings holding her daddy's invention down to the floor. "If we wait until it stops, we'll turn the accelerator around. I can shoot it off again, and we'll back up again just exactly where we're supposed to go."

From the look on the marshal's face, he had the same picture in his head as I did of a hole that penetrated straight through the train all the way to the locomotive, and everyone's hair parted in the cars in between.

I came over and caught hold of her hands, and looked into those big blue eyes.

"I think we'll just do it the old-fashioned way, Trouble," I said. "I'm not sure anyone on this train is ready for any more of the modern method."

"Amen to that!" the marshal said.

# Old Bull

## By Ron Marz

H E appeared at the end of the street just after noon, sitting on an Appaloosa, ponying another behind. The horse walked up the street slowly, weary from a hard morning ride to reach Wichita.

A boy of eight or nine played in the street, trying to float a home-made boat in the spillover puddle next to a watering trough outside the hotel. He glanced up from his boat and watched the man on the horse ride past. He looked to the boy like one of the hard men who sometimes passed through town. His hat was pulled low, but the boy could see the creases in his face, his skin worn to leather by years of sun and wind. He was dusty from the trail. A rifle was slipped into the saddle roll on the back of his mare, the dull metal of the barrel poking out.

The rider glanced down at the boy as he went past, but said nothing. As the second horse passed, the boy noticed it was not without a rider. A body was slung over the horse's back, belly down, arms on one side, legs on the other. So, a bounty hunter.

The boy watched the rider continue down the street. He pulled his horse to a stop outside the sheriff's office, slid from the saddle, and wrapped the reins around a post. Then he turned his attention to the second horse, loosening the ropes securing the body to the saddle. Knots untied, he dumped the body in the dirt, where it landed on its back. Three bullet holes were visible in the chest, the blood on the corpse's shirt now dried and crusty, faded to the color of rust.

"That's Matthew Guilfoyle?" a voice asked from behind the rider.

The rider turned and looked at the sheriff, who had emerged from his office. "Used to be," the rider said.

The sheriff looked down at the body in the dirt. "I believe the poster indicated dead *or* alive. The latter option was not of interest to you?"

"It was not of interest to Mr. Guilfoyle. I gave him the option. He chose the other. Which, all things considered, was fine by me."

The two men shook hands. Sheriff Philip Braddock and Samuel Cobb were not friends, but there was mutual respect earned over years of acquaintance. Braddock endeavored to keep a peaceful town. Men like Cobb aided in that pursuit by bringing in gentlemen of ill repute, whether sitting a horse or stretched across one.

Cobb had been pursuing his particular vocation longer than Braddock has been sheriff. Longer, in fact, than Braddock had been in Kansas. Samuel Cobb had been bringing in bounties for the better

*Illustration by Bart Sears*

part of two decades, still plying his trade when most his age had retired, either from the good judgment of surviving a long career, or the poor judgment of choosing to confront the wrong man at the wrong time.

"What was he? Five hundred?" Cobb asked, nodding at the corpse sprawled in the dirt.

"Six," Braddock said. "I can have the money deposited into your account at the bank, if that suits you. Cash will take a few days to arrive, if that's your preference."

"Bank is fine," Cobb said.

"Finally starting that retirement fund?" Braddock said.

Cobb didn't reply. He didn't need to. They both knew Cobb wasn't the type to homestead and fritter away his remaining years sitting on a porch, nor a candidate to open a dry goods concern.

"Can sell Guilfoyle's horse at the livery. Seems a solid enough animal. Need to get mine fed and watered," Cobb said.

"You'll be staying in town?" Braddock said.

"For the night. Set out for Abilene in the morning, I expect. There's a thousand dollars on Ben Portnoy's head, and the Pinkertons haven't been able to catch a sniff of him. Thought I might have better luck," Cobb said.

"Long ride for an uncertain payday. Especially with Ben Portnoy's reputation for being less than agreeable," Braddock said.

Cobb shrugged, or at least what passed for a shrug with him. "Man's got to make a living," he said.

"There's a thousand-dollar bounty closer to home, if you're interested," Braddock said.

Cobb looked at him. He was interested. "Who is it?"

"Not so much of a who as a what. There's a thousand-dollar bounty on a buffalo," Braddock said.

Cobb tried on half a grin, which was more of a reaction than he'd usually allow himself. He unwrapped his horse's reins from the rail, intending to walk her to the livery before seeing himself to a hot meal and a room for the evening. Truth be told, he was looking forward to sleeping in a bed for a change, rather than on the ground. "Sheriff with a sense of humor," Cobb said. "Live long enough, you see everything."

Braddock did not relent. "I'm serious. There's a buffalo out there, part of the herd that's been moving to the north, and there's a thousand-dollar bounty for his head. Hand on the Bible, it's true."

Cobb couldn't help but stare. "Who the hell puts on a bounty on a buffalo?"

"Erasmus Sheridan, the rancher. That big spread west of here. He's the one who wants that buffalo's head on his wall, because it killed his oldest boy, Foster," Braddock said. "Foster and some of the ranch hands were out on a buffalo hunt a few weeks ago, looking to lay in meat for the winter. Story is, this big old bull turned on them, bowled over Foster's horse, then trampled Foster. The boy was dead before they ever got him home. So now Sheridan wants the beast mounted on his wall."

Cobb scoffed. "What's the herd, hundreds? Thousands? How's anyone supposed to find the one buffalo that killed his boy. He got a sign around his neck?"

"He might as well. The bull's got an arrow sticking out of his shoulder, so they say, red feathers on it. I expect that some Pawnee or Arapaho came to regret that shot," Braddock said.

Cobb shook his head, trying to convince himself there was in fact a thousand-dollar bounty on a two-thousand-pound animal. "So why hasn't anybody else taken him and cashed that check?"

Braddock shook his head. "More than a few have tried. Most never found the herd, the rest didn't manage to find the bull within the herd. But he's out there. Seems like the job calls for someone who's good at finding things."

Braddock inclined his head toward Cobb, and added, "Lot easier than trying to sneak up on Ben Portnoy before he manages to put a hole in your head. None of us getting any younger, Sam."

Cobb glanced away, looking down the street, or perhaps someplace more distant. Then he looked back at Braddock, heaved a sigh, and said, "Point me in the right direction."

THREE days later, Cobb found the herd. He'd ridden northwest, sleeping rough under the stars. More than once, he dreamed about the bed he'd slept in the night after arriving in town.

Toward the end of the third day, he crested a hill on his Appaloosa, and the herd stretched out in the broad valley below, like a great, black stain on the landscape. Once, the bison were so numerous that the plains shook with their passing. But now their time was almost past, once mighty herds hunted to mere shadows.

The herd Cobb beheld was a vestige of a bygone time, numbering well into the hundreds, perhaps as many as a thousand. They moved slowly, grazing as they went. Somewhere down there, supposedly, was a bull worth a thousand dollars. But how to find it? Walking into the middle of a herd like that was a surer way to the grave than bearding Ben Portnoy in whatever den he'd chosen.

Cobb eased his horse forward, walking down the hill, where the prairie wind ruffled the long grass on the slope. Needle in a haystack and he knew it. But Cobb was good at finding things.

He walked his mount closer to the herd, slow and steady, so as to not spook any. One animal bolting could start a stampede, with no telling what direction it would take. If that happened, neither Cobb nor his Appaloosa would be able to outrun it. Sharing Foster Sheridan's fate was not an appealing notion.

Cobb kept a distance, walking his horse parallel to the slow-moving herd, scanning the horde of animals in hopes of spying one with a red-feathered arrow embedded in his shoulder. Cobb reached the front edge of the herd, as the sun started to dip toward the horizon. Still no sign of the bull.

He turned his horse to the outside and started back in the other direction at a walk, once again looking across the herd for a glimpse of his bounty. Cobb listened to the grunts of males fussing at one another, the bleats of calves looking for mothers. He worked his way back, keeping his pace slow, scouring the herd with eyes that weren't quite as sharp as they used to be.

He eventually reached the rear of the herd, where the stragglers were struggling to keep up. Elderly, young, sick, the ones not able to match the herd's pace. A mother nosed her calf along, sending him forward at a trot. She quickened her pace to follow. As she moved out of the way, Cobb spied another bison, a large male, the hump on his back as tall as Cobb himself. An arrow with red feathers stuck out of his left shoulder.

The bull walked on. His gait was measured, perhaps a touch of arthritis slowing him. The animal shook his great head now and again to shoo the flies that swarmed.

Cobb remained still, watching the bull. He appeared to be keeping an eye on the stragglers, making sure none fell too far behind. He was old himself. But still formidable.

The setting sun had turned the sky blood red. Cobb could have taken the bull from the saddle, inching himself closer so that a well-placed rifle shot pierced the thick skull. But the herd was still on the move, and the report of a rifle could set it running in unpredictable directions. Better to wait until full night had fallen, and accomplish the task when most of the herd was sleeping, and less likely to spook.

Cobb kept his horse walking in parallel, never too far, never too close. On occasion, the bull would look in Cobb's direction, and decide the horse was no threat. The last streaks of red withered in the sky, and stars began to appear, first flecks against indigo, then diamonds against black velvet. The moon was little more than a crescent but bright.

When full night had fallen, the herd slowed and eventually stopped. Most of the great beasts settled to the ground, their comparatively stubby legs drawn up under the massive bulk of their bodies. The old bull remained on his feet, like a sentry posted on a perimeter. Cobb gave a slight tug on the reins and his mare pulled to a stop. They'd been a pair for years. Cobb hardly needed reins to tell her what to do. She knew already.

Cobb slid off her back quietly, his legs stiff from being in the saddle so long. He used to be able to ride all day, every day, and not feel a twinge. But that hadn't been true for the last few years. The bull wasn't the only one with a dose of arthritis. The horse would keep her place and wait, as she had countless times before.

Cobb pulled the Winchester out of his bed roll, checked to make sure it was loaded. It was. He planned to stay downwind from the bull, and get as close as he could. One shot to the side of the skull should put him down, and hopefully not spook the sleeping herd. Then Cobb could wait until the herd moved on in the morning, and harvest the head along with the arrow as proof.

Over his years of bounty hunting, Cobb had learned to move quietly, to not attract notice. That, more than anything else, had kept him alive this long. He'd taken more than his share of bounties without firing a shot, just by being a little smarter than his prey and having a plan. There were still a few bounty hunters his age, but no dumb bounty hunters his age. The vocation weeded out the incautious.

Cobb moved through the grass, much of it matted down or eaten away from the passing of the herd, working his way toward the bull. He crept closer, the only sounds an occasional snort or snuffle from deep in herd. The moonlight was enough to outline the bull's bulky shape. The wind shifted slightly, and Cobb shifted his path to the bull with it.

When he reached a distance of about fifteen feet, and a bit off to the side, Cobb went to a knee. He settled the rifle against his shoulder, and sighted down the barrel. The wind was still.

The bull turned toward him, and let out a low snort. A warning.

Directly in front of the bull was the worst place Cobb could be. His shot stood a fair chance of being deflected by the thick bone at the front of the

skull. And even if it wasn't, the bull could still trample him before the brain ever told the body he was dead.

The bull looked directly at Cobb with glassy black eyes. An old warrior, nearing his end, but not yet there. Cobb looked back, finger on the trigger, a hunter with at least a few more hunts left in him.

Neither moved. They studied one another, each surely capable of destroying the other. Cobb thought about the thousand dollars. He thought about the bull's life, all it had seen. He thought about his own life, all he'd done. In the moonlight, Cobb saw a reflection.

Two old bulls, with more trail behind them than ahead. But still, there was trail.

Cobb eased his finger off the trigger, never taking his eye off the bull. The bull remained motionless. Cobb stood up slowly, letting the rifle's barrel droop toward the ground. They regarded each other a moment more, some understanding passing between them, witnessed only by the firmament overhead. Then the bull huffed softly and turned away, walking deeper into the herd.

Cobb watched him until he was a shadow lost among the other shadows. The hunter retraced his steps to his mare, slipped the Winchester back into his bedroll, and mounted up. There was some scrub brush not far. He'd make a fire and bed down for another night of sleeping rough.

In the morning, he'd head back the way he came. There was still trail ahead of him.

# The Constantinople Affair

## By KARISSA LAUREL

MAGGIE Campbell stood outside executive producer John Mergenov's office door, her jaw hanging to the floor. *Did that really happen? Did Eddie really just shut the door in my face?*

She drew in a deep breath, smoothed her wavy blond hair, and threw back her shoulders as she wrenched the doorknob, telling herself it was an accident. In his excitement, Eddie must have assumed she'd walked into John's office ahead of him or something.

But the door handle refused to budge.

*Son of a bitch.*

Maggie raised a fist to pound on the heavy oak and demand entry, but she paused at the sound of a throat clearing behind her. At a desk in the executive-suite lobby sat Peg Reams, Metropolis Silver Screen's head receptionist, a middle-aged woman who had obviously taken her hair and make-up queues from her idol, Ginger Rogers. Peg caught Maggie's eye, offered a sympathetic wince, and shook her head.

Maggie wasn't going to let Peg's disapproval stop her from claiming her place at Eddie's side. She was co-screenwriter on this picture, by God. It was past time they treated her as such. But before she could knock, the front door across from Peg's desk swung open. A blast of hot Los Angeles air churned through the hallway, bringing with it a hint of lavender and moss.

Maggie froze again, her fist hovering millimeters from John Mergenov's door. Only one man that she knew of had the chutzpa to wear lavender cologne—*Pour Un Homme Caron*, to be precise.

"Oh, Mr. Montgomery, Miss Cortez," Peg purred. She patted her graying finger-waves and smiled. "We weren't expecting you."

"John in his office?" Tall, broad shouldered, slicked hair and dazzling smile, Lex Montgomery had been born not by ordinary human means. No, the Hollywood gods had fashioned him from the ideal leading-man mold. Even had the playboy reputation to go with his unearthly good looks. Beside him stood Lara Cortez, his number-one leading lady and a Hollywood idol in her own right.

Maggie dismissed Lara, preferring to focus instead on Lex, letting her gaze roam from the toes of his flawlessly buffed wingtips to the top of his elegantly coifed black hair.

*Illustration by Peter Krause*

As if feeling Maggie's eyes on him, Lex shifted, glancing at her standing outside John Mergenov's office. Even from several yards away, Lex's blue irises glinted as brightly as the Hope Diamond in a beam of sunlight. The man was too handsome for his own good. Even worse, he knew it and used it to his advantage, leaving a trail of broken hearts in his wake, *if* the gossip articles regularly published about him were true.

Lately the papers had been featuring Lex and Lara together, naming them Hollywood's most glamourous couple and speculating that Lara would be the woman to finally tame Lex's notorious libido.

"Mr. Mergenov's in a meeting right now." Peg gestured to a pair of plush club chairs next to her desk. "You're welcome to wait. It shouldn't take long."

Lex ignored Peg, his attention focused wholly on Maggie, who now felt like a marlin impaled on the hook of his piercing gaze. One corner of his luscious, wide mouth turned up, revealing a dimple. "Hey, doll…" His voice was warm bourbon. "Don't I know you?"

Maggie resisted the urge to snort. He *ought* to know her. She was co-writer of the screenplay for *The Constantinople Affair*, the same film in which Lex and Lara were currently starring. She was on the set with him every day. Not that he'd notice her tucked away in the shadows, hunched over her clipboard, furiously scribbling changes

to dialogue and set directions.

But she'd be damned if they didn't all remember her before they'd finished this movie. She'd be damned if hers wasn't the first name on the lips of every executive in Hollywood searching for the best screenwriter to pen their next box-office hit.

John Mergenov's door opened, and his balding head poked into the hallway. "Lex." He shot a grin at the movie star leaning against Peg's desk. "Thought I heard your voice. Join us, won't you? I'd like to get your thoughts."

Maggie folded her arms over her bosom. The producer's lascivious gaze lingered on the way her sweater set tightened and strained across her abundant curves. Maggie clenched her teeth again. "Mr. Mergenov, I also have a few thoughts—"

"Oh, good." Mergenov winked at her. "Glad you're here. Be a dear and bring us a couple of glasses and a bowl of ice from the kitchen. I've got a bottle of Glenlivet in here just begging to be opened."

Outrage stole Maggie's voice. She glared over Mergenov's shoulder, searching for the shock of unruly brown curls belonging to Eddie Fage, her supposed writing partner. Spotting him, she caught his eye and glared. His cheeks colored, and he looked away, pretending not to see her.

The air stirred behind her, and she caught another whiff of lavender. "'Scuse me, *doll*." Lex Montgomery's warmth burned against her as he slid by, slipping through the opening in the doorway that Mergenov provided for him. But not for Maggie. Apparently impervious to the daggers Maggie was staring into his backside, Lex greeted the other men in Mergenov's office—the director and another producer and Eddie. *The traitor.*

"Thanks, dear." Mergenov patted Maggie's shoulder, retreated into his office, and shut the door.

Maggie coughed. It was the only sound she could make. No words could properly convey her rage and indignation.

Lara Cortez's soft footsteps approached. Thoroughly mortified, Maggie refused to look at the other woman. There'd been a lot of that going around today. Why shouldn't Maggie follow the men's lead?

Lara patted Maggie's shoulder. "Peg will get their ice, honey. I think it's best that you go home. Kick off your heels and make a drink for yourself. Tomorrow will be better."

Tears of rage and shame mingled in Maggie's eyes. She blinked, refusing to let them fall. With her gaze pinned to the floor, she simply nodded, stepped around Lara, and strode down the hallway. She threw open the front door and marched into the dying Los Angeles daylight. The sun was setting on Hollywood, and possibly on her career as well.

Maggie strode across Metropolis Silver Screen's parking lot. She reached the sidewalk, but instead of stopping at her usual bench to wait for a streetcar, she kept walking, feet pounding the concrete as if trying to leave a mark, footprints as proof of her existence. She could go home as Lara had suggested, but nothing about wallowing alone in her misery appealed. The idea of having a drink sure did, though, and the Blue Bowler made the best dirty martinis in town.

MAGGIE had just ordered her second drink and was digging through her purse in search of a lighter when a small flame flared in her peripheral vision, close enough to warm her cheek. Startled, she flinched and fumbled the cigarette perched between her lips, catching it before it fell to the floor.

"Need a light?" Lex Montgomery, the smarmy bastard, winked and grinned, revealing that blasted dimple.

Too late, she caught a whiff of his distinctive cologne. The bar's miasma of cigar and cigarette smoke had masked his approach. Trying to appear nonchalant, Maggie puckered her lips around her cigarette, met Lex's blue gaze, and leaned close to the lighter. He flicked the ignitor again, and she inhaled until the tobacco caught flame.

She held the smoke in her mouth for a moment before exhaling into Lex's face. "Thanks... *doll.*"

He quietly coughed as she turned away from him and curled her fingers around her martini glass. *A little petty revenge is always good for the soul.* Before she could bring the drink to her lips, Lex slipped the glass from her fingers.

Her words of protest died when he tilted his head back and poured the drink down his throat—a long column of elegant muscle and bronzed skin. Martini drained, he swiped his wrist across his lips and set the empty glass beside her on the bar. "More of a vodka tonic sort myself, but Al always makes a dependable martini."

He raised a hand, catching Al's attention then pointed at Maggie's empty glass. "Another for the lady."

The bartender nodded. "And for yourself?"

"The usual."

Al shuffled away as Lex lowered himself onto stool beside Maggie.

She considered blowing another puff of smoke in his face, but at some point pettiness just became petulance, and that would give him the upper hand. *Who'm I kidding? I don't even have an upper finger in this situation.* "Is your being here merely a coincidence, Mr. Montgomery, or should I be concerned?"

His broad brow creased, black eyebrows drawing down. "Concerned? What would you have to be concerned about?"

Al returned and placed a martini in front of Maggie and a vodka tonic in front of Lex. She set her cigarette in a nearby ashtray and slid her drink farther from Lex's reach. "A lot of things that a big star like you wouldn't know about, Mr. Montgomery."

"Call me Lex, please." He frowned and studied his cocktail where it sat on the bar top.

Maggie glanced around the Blue Bowler's dim interior. Occasionally other patrons looked their way, but the bar had a reputation for attracting a wide spectrum from the Los Angeles population. Here, a secretary could rub elbows with a starlet without making a big deal out of it. In fact, those who did make big deals were invited to leave and not come back.

"Despite what people say, there's no silver spoon in my mouth. And it was more than luck that got me where I am now. I know more about worries than you might think, Miss Campbell."

Maggie arched an eyebrow. "I'm surprised you know my name. Could've sworn you thought it was *Doll*." She also could've sworn that, half an hour ago, he hadn't known her from Eve.

He set his finger gently under her chin, sending a tingle up her spine. "I'll call you whatever you like, if you'll promise to sit and have a few drinks with me."

"And what would Miss Cortez say about that?"

Grinning, he said, "I don't rightly give a damn what Miss Cortez would say about it."

His answer eased none of her concerns about why he was there. In fact, it only raised more questions. "All right, then what about the gossip columns?" Maybe no one would be so gauche as to approach Lex here in the Blue Bowler, but that didn't mean tongues wouldn't wag later.

"Don't give a damn about them, either."

Maggie hoped she was maintaining a cool exterior because, on the inside, her alarm bells were screaming. Men like Lex Montgomery didn't pay attention to little nobodies like her for no reason. "Then what *do* you give a damn about?"

"Would you believe I'm here because I think *The Constantinople Affair* has a brilliant script, that you're obviously the brains behind it, and that you got a raw deal today?" He shook his head, picked up his glass, and sipped enough to wet his throat. "I thought you could use a sympathetic ear."

"You thought you'd throw me a pity party?" Putting aside the complicated feelings his compliments aroused in her, she twisted her lips as if she'd sucked a lemon. "No thanks. And who told you I'd be here, anyway? I didn't even know I was going to be here until I decided I didn't want to go home."

"Alone?"

Maggie flinched. "What?"

"You didn't want to go home *alone*? Am I right?"

"It's none of your business."

His dimple flickered as if he knew he'd guessed correctly. And so what if he had? Did he think her living alone meant she was an easy target? "I'm not offering pity," he said. "I'm offering you a drink. And an ear."

Skeptical, she shook her head. "Still didn't tell me how you knew I'd be here."

"I've seen you here before."

"I thought you didn't recognize me when you saw me at the office."

He shrugged. "Yeah, well... I'm an actor. Pretty good one, they say."

She snorted and downed another gulp of gin and olive juice. He was better than good, which was why she'd been thrilled, ecstatic, *elated*, when Eddie, *the traitor*, had told her the studio had landed its biggest stars for their screenplay's leading role. *Their* screenplay, not Eddie's, though you'd never know it by the way he'd been acting.

If there was any chance of getting her foot through the door, getting Eddie and the others to take her seriously, having Lex Montgomery on her side couldn't hurt, right? She eyed him again, studying the square jaw, the nose that might have been too large on any other face but only gave his more character. The silk tie. The gold pins on his cuffs. She could do a lot worse. A *hell* of a lot worse.

"What's in it for you?" Maggie asked.

Montgomery's dimple flickered. He trailed a warm finger over her shoulder and down her arm. "Why, the enjoyment of your company, of course."

Maybe he was only using her, but maybe she could do the same in return. She raised a hand, signaling to Al. "Another round, bartender."

As they drank, they talked, and she confessed all manner of things she never would have under other conditions. She was in Hollywood completely alone, cut off from her familial support. Her father had wanted her to stay in Charlotte, marry one of his junior partners, and raise a new generation of Campbell babies to take over his law practice one day. Her mother had died from polio when Maggie was a child, so she'd had no maternal buffer to argue on behalf of her ambitions. If Hollywood didn't pan out, if she couldn't get her fair share of credit for *The Constantinople Affair* and leverage that into a studio contract for the screenplay she'd been working on in secret, without Eddie the Traitor's help, she'd have to go back to North Carolina, head hung in shame, and that was possibly more than she could bear.

Lex, as it turned out, had also lost his mother when he was a child. Perhaps Maggie had read that bit of information somewhere before, but while he kept his current life open for the media to meticulously document, his past was mostly a mystery. Even now he only gave her tidbits, enough to string her along, draw out her sympathy. A dead mother, a neglectful and borderline-abusive father, a childhood of poverty and instability.

*Damn*, Maggie thought. *I'm always a sucker for a vulnerable man*. She considered that his vulnerability was an act, a lie to weaken her defenses. Then she decided she didn't care.

She made an excuse to visit the ladies' room. On her way, she caught the bartender's attention and asked him to switch out the gin and vermouth in her glass for seltzer. She needed some sobriety if she was going to go through with the plan forming in the back of her mind, which simply came down to this: Win Lex's affections, and use that to ensure that her name appeared on the credits reel at the end of *The Constantinople Affair*.

Some tasks in life were tedious.

Attempting to seduce Lex Montgomery would not be one of them.

In the ladies' room, Maggie smoothed her hair and powdered her nose. She hoped the allure that had kept her social schedule full in North Carolina would be enough to entice a man like Lex Montgomery. She reapplied a glossy layer of carmine red lipstick. "The color of sexual appeal", the salesgirl at the City of Paris make-up counter had called it. *Well I guess I'm about to find out if she knew what she was talking about.*

Maggie avoided looking herself in the eyes. She wasn't quite sure she wanted to see what reflected in them. She might get cold feet. But whatever happened next, it would never be worse than admitting defeat to her father. She'd do whatever it took to prevent that scenario from happening.

"You want to get out of here?" she asked Lex once she'd returned to his side and they'd finished their drinks.

He paused, his gaze sharpening on her. Despite the cocktails, he showed no evidence of cognitive incapacity. She appraised his large frame, the bulk of graceful muscle playing under his button-down shirt. It would take a lot more than a couple of shots of vodka to inebriate a man his size. *Well good. I'd hate to feel like I'd taken advantage of him while he was in a debilitated state.*

But she worried his sobriety increased the chances of him rejecting her, too. Her qualms were unfounded, though. "My place or yours?" he asked, having obviously made up his mind about her.

She was *not* taking the golden boy of Hollywood back to her ramshackle, studio apartment. That would be an absolute deal breaker. With her luck, a roach would crawl across her bed at the most inopportune moment.

She winked at him playfully. "What do *you* think?"

He stood, tossed several bills on the counter, and offered her his arm.

She took it and followed him out the Blue Bowler's front door. They had just crossed the threshold when a blizzard of flashbulbs exploded in before her eyes. Voices shouted, asking for names, demanding details. "Who's the new dame, Lex? Where's Lara? Are you two an item?"

Under other circumstances, she might've been embarrassed, but if she wanted to use some of Lex's influence by proxy, then the press was one of the best ways to collected it.

Lex took Maggie's hand, tugged her across the parking lot, and guided her into the backseat of a bullet-gray Lincoln Zephyr. The door slammed behind her, and the car peeled away from the curb with such speed that she fell back, landing hard against Lex's broad chest. He caught her, wrapping his arms around her. "Whoa, there. I got you."

She blinked several times, trying to rid her vision of lingering spots of light. "It's very convenient that you found us this car, Lex."

"I didn't find it. I always keep a car waiting for me."

Gulping, she pushed against him, fingers splayed across the hard muscles of his torso. His arms relaxed, and she slipped out of his grasp, coming to rest on the plush leather seat beside him.

"I'm sorry about that," he said, and his regret sounded genuine. "I should've warned you about the press."

"No," she waved off his apology. "I should've known."

"Where to, Mr. Montgomery?" the driver asked, once they'd left behind the crowd.

"Home, Tony. Please, just take us home."

UPON their arrival, Maggie let Lex lead her into a small study on the second floor of his mansion in the Hollywood Hills. He poured her a drink and flipped a switch on his turntable. A record played, something unfamiliar but recognizably jazz. Maggie had never listened to much jazz, but the slow, winding song suited her mood.

Dim lamp light cast much of the room in shadows. Dark paneling covered the walls between rows of crowded bookshelves. Maggie reclined on a huge green velveteen sofa, trying her best to look casual and confident. But she was so far out of her league she might never find her way to the surface again. She could drown here, in embarrassment and shame, and that fear nearly set her on her feet, racing for Lex's front door and into the night.

Before she could act on her impulse, Lex sat down beside her, his heavy thigh pushing against her hip as he slid close. A comforting whiff of his lavender cologne calmed her enough to keep her in place. That and his blue eyes, which held her hazel ones and hypnotized her with their brilliance. "I wasn't lying," he said unprompted. "Or acting. I really do think *The Constantinople Affair* is brilliant. People give too much credit to directors and actors. Without a strong screenplay, we'd have nothing."

"I'm glad you think so." She sipped her drink. "I thought Eddie and I would kill each other before we finished it. I still might kill him before we're through."

Lex chuckled, deep and low. "He'd deserve it if you did, but I'd hate to see you locked up for murder." He reached out and raked his thumb over her bottom lip. "Prison wouldn't be kind to a beauty like yours."

Explosions of delight rippled across her scalp, and she wondered if her hair had lit on fire. He was clever to appeal to her intelligence first, calling her screenplay brilliant, but she was a vain creature if she were honest. Having a legend like Lex Montgomery remark on her beauty was something she couldn't easily brush aside.

Swallowing the last dregs of her trepidation, Maggie set her drink on a side table. She sat up and shrugged out of her cardigan, holding Lex's crystal blue gaze as she did. His breath caught. His pupils dilated.

*Such a reaction... And I'm still wearing my shell. What's he going to do when there's nothing left but skin and lace.* Flames lit in her cheeks at the thought of baring herself to Lex. She'd left home looking for more than a life as a dutiful wife. It might have been stable and secure, but it would have crushed her soul. This moment with Lex, however, was the stuff that lit hearts on fire and set spirits free.

She touched Lex's hand, stopping him as he reached for his tie. "Let me."

His Adam's apple bobbed. His exhalation quavered. For a man of his reputation, he certainly seemed... well... not nervous. But not quite so self-assured as she'd expected. She had as much of an effect on him as he did on her, it seemed. *How's that possible?*

She unknotted his tie, and before she could lose her momentum, she unfasted the button at his throat. He didn't stop her, so she unbuttoned the next, and the next. Bourbon forgotten, they drank in each other with their eyes, and once she had him stripped to his undershirt, his restraint collapsed. He gathered her close and pressed searing kisses to her throat. Her head fell back, giving him freer access as his fingers strayed under her top, stroking the camisole beneath. Lex's lips trailed the column of her neck and grazed her chin but paused before reaching her lips. Drunk on desire, she struggled to focus on the blue fire blazing in his eyes.

"Say yes, Maggie." Her name on his lips, in his low rough voice, was a spell of enchantment. She wanted him. By god she *ached* for him, and for more than merely his name and influence. For more than his body and his kisses. And that was a complication she hadn't anticipated.

"I thought I already had," she rasped, desire swelling in her throat.

"I want the words from you. Tell me what you want."

Her fingers clutched his biceps, like mounds of steel, and she blinked until her vision cleared. "Yes, Lex." She gave him the full intensity of her clear gaze. "I want this."

Before her last word had fully left her tongue, his mouth claimed her, hot, wet, and demanding. A moan escaped her throat, and his fingers burned a trail along her spine. His mouth was her sin, his tongue her confession.

She raised her arms and he slid cotton and silk over her head. He unfastened hooks and straps, undressing her until her bare skin glowed like pearl in the dim light.

He looked at her, his thumb stroking her breast, caressing the taut peak. "Stunning," he murmured.

"Am I?" Uncertainty loosened her tongue. "The world is full of gorgeous women, and you've seen more of them than I have."

Something sharp flashed in his eyes. "Need your ego stroked, too, doll?"

"Not at all." Absolutely she needed him to reassure her, but she knew better than to admit it. "But sometimes the ghosts of the past haunt you, whether you want them to or not."

"*You're* the only one here, right now." Tenderly, he caressed her cheek. "And you're the only one I want. Isn't that enough?"

For tonight, it was, but what about tomorrow? Tomorrows with Lex couldn't factor into her plans, though, so she shoved her doubts aside and tugged the hem of his undershirt. He relaxed, letting her pull the fabric over his head, ruffling that perfect dark hair so that it tumbled in thick waves over his brow.

His belt and trousers soon fell among the clothing heaped on the floor beside the sofa. He stretched alongside her and stroked her from hip to collar bone, again and again. His lips found her breast, and her back arched. He growled and his hard length pressed into her side. She trailed fingertips over its silken span until he shuddered. To have this much effect on him made her feel powerful, like a goddess. The Hera to his Hollywood Zeus.

"You pretended like you didn't know me," she murmured in his ear.

"Since the first day you walked on set, I've known who you were, Maggie Campbell."

"So why the game?"

"I needed to know you wanted me too."

"Is that really so important to you?"

Instead of answering, he gripped her knee, parted her thighs, and settled his hips between hers, pressing against her, teasing, taunting until she cried for him. "Lex, *please!*"

"There's no going back."

"I don't want to go back." She wasn't sure what his words meant, what he was implying or asking of her. All she knew is that she'd agree to anything in that moment if it would relieve the deep ache, the sharp and pulsing need.

"You want this? You want me?" He shifted his hips, pressing himself closer. She whimpered her affirmation. "The words, Maggie. *Please.*"

"I want this, Lex." His 'please' had been so suppliant, so raw. She would have died before telling him no. "I want *you.*"

He rocked into her. Her head fell back as she cried his name in satisfaction, the supreme pleasure of having him inside her. His rhythm was jazz music, not languid like the song he'd been playing for her earlier, but intense. Driving. Aggressive. She felt it in her heartbeat, in the rush of her blood, in the core of her utmost pleasure.

It was there, in her core, that the first wave of her bliss crested, a rising tidal wave. Each of his thrusts drove the mounting wave closer to her shore, and when it finally crashed over her, the torrential surge washed her whole world away, leaving her adrift among a field of starry constellations.

At some point in the night, he carried her to his bedroom, and between bouts of lovemaking, when they had paused for a late-night snack of cheese, crackers, and champagne, she told him of her current screenplay, the story that had been close to her heart since she first left home, the reason she worked up the nerve to come to Hollywood in the first place.

He'd listened until she ran out of words, and then he'd licked crumbs from her fingers and from her breasts and stomach. "Your dreams will come true, Maggie." He pressed a kiss to her cheek with gentle sweetness. "You're going to cast your spell over this town, the same way you have over me."

She wasn't the only one casting spells; in just a few passionate hours, Lex had cracked her tough façade, and he'd touched something inside her she'd allowed no one else to reach. Earlier, she'd told herself she was using him as much as he was using her, but this was fast becoming something weightier than anticipated. With farther reaching repercussions.

*What have I done*, she thought. *And what am I going to do now?*

But then Lex's lips were on hers

again, and her regrets and worries dropped beneath the surface, sinking deep into the darkest parts of her heart.

WHEN Maggie stepped off the streetcar at the stop closest to the Metropolitan Silver Screen Studio's gates, Peg was waiting for her. "Mr. Mergenov's in his office. He asked me to fetch you straight to him."

Trepidation chilled Maggie's blood, but she followed Peg across the studio lot and into Mergenov's office without an objection.

"Miss Campbell, please, have a seat." John Mergenov pointed at a chair across from his desk. "You must be exhausted after all your excitement last night."

Maggie narrowed her eyes, but she said nothing. She might not have attended law school like her brother but growing up in a family of attorneys had taught her a thing or two. She'd say nothing, offer no rope with which Mergenov could hang her, until she knew more about why he had wanted to speak with her.

Mergenov reached into his drawer, withdrew the morning paper, and tossed it to the edge of his desk. It landed wide open on the social page that clearly displayed a photograph of Maggie and Lex making their hasty exit from the Blue Bowler last night.

"Explain this," Mergenov demanded.

Maggie scanned the brief article that did not identify her by name but speculated about their association in less than respectable terms. The article also predicted the end of Lex's much lauded relationship with Lara Cortez. It could be a huge blow for the building publicity around *The Constantinople Affair* if the audience believed things between Lex and Lara had soured.

"Are you having an affair with Montgomery?" Mergenov asked in a demanding tone.

"That's a very personal question, Mr. Mergenov. I'm not sure how that's any of your business."

He bared his teeth and leaned toward her. He stabbed a finger at the photograph. "Everything involving Lex Montgomery is the studio's business. His is a carefully cultivated façade that has been maintained at great expense and even greater profit to this studio, and that won't be put in jeopardy by some two-bit tramp. So, when I ask you a question, Miss Campbell, I expect you to answer it, or else I expect you to take yourself off of this studio's property and never return."

Anger, hot and penetrating, flared in her chest. She used her fury to tamp down her feelings of guilt and self-loathing. If Mergenov was a devil, she was about to offer him her soul, and it made her sick. But not as sick as leaving in defeat. "This studio is Goliath, and I am but a small little David. But you'll remember how that story ended,

Mr. Mergenov. David defeated the giant with a stone and a sling shot. My stone and slingshot are my story, and I'll be more than happy to use it to bring down Metropolitan Silver Screen."

The livid stain in Mergenov's neck and cheeks and spread across his whole face and balding head. Rage quivered in his jowls. "What are you blathering about Miss Campbell? A stone and a sling-shot indeed."

"What I mean, since metaphors are obviously not your forte, is that there are any number of reporters who'd be quite willing to hear the more *scintillating* details of my encounter with Mr. Montgomery last night."

He scoffed. "You'd be risking your own reputation, Miss Campbell."

"I've got little of one to lose. Not nearly as much of one as you've built for Mr. Montgomery."

"You're a harlot."

"Takes one to know one." A petty rejoinder but so satisfying, especially when it made Mergenov scowl impossibly deeper.

"What are your terms?"

"A new contract, distributed among the studio executives, stating clearly that I get equal billing as co-screenwriter with Eddie Fage, my name on the credit reel with his, and full participation in all meetings involving script changes. No more locking me out or going behind my back."

"After this movie is released, I'll see to it you never work in this town again."

"If I don't get my name on this film, I'll never work in this town again anyway. I'll take the risk."

Mergenov held her gaze, his anger vivid enough for her to feel from a half-dozen feet away. But she didn't back down. "You'll regret this, Miss Campbell," he said, but he pointed at his office door. "Go get Peg. Tell her to grab her pen and notepad and get her rear in this office immediately."

Flush with the euphoria of her victory, Maggie leapt to her feet and strode toward the doorway. Only then did she realize Mergenov had not completely shut his office door, and in the hallway outside, as quiet and pale as a corpse, stood Lex Montgomery. The look of betrayal on his face told her he'd heard every word of her conversation with Mergenov, every threat, every manipulation. "Blackmail really isn't your color, doll," he said.

"Lex." His name came out on a breath of despair.

His blue eyes stared beyond her, refusing to meet her gaze. "Mergenov, whatever Miss Campbell says is true, and I'll corroborate any claim she makes. You better give her what she wants if you expect me to continue playing your games."

And with that, he spun on his heel and strode out of the office.

Maggie raced after him. "Lex! Wait, please let me explain."

It was too late, though. Nothing she could say would retrieve her words, rewind them like a film reel and put them back in her mouth.

She paused in the open studio lot, exposed under the burning Los Angeles sun like a slimy snail without a shell.

*It was nothing,* she tried to tell herself. Simply a night of meaningless, if passionate, distraction. It hadn't meant anything personal to either of them. But the look on Lex's face and the speed at which he hurried to get away from her contradicted her claims, revealing them for the lies they were. The tendril of guilt that had formed around her heart last night grew into a thick thorny vine. It squeezed until she shattered.

Hell *yes* it had been personal. No matter what she'd told herself, she'd known all along that she'd wanted him for more than his professional cache. Hell *yes* Lex had been asking for more than merely her body, and she had given it to him eagerly, with every good intention.

But the road to hell was paved with such things, as they say, and she was already well on her way to perdition.

THE next morning, as she stood before her worn and cracked bathroom mirror, she forced herself to look at her reflection and face the truth of who she was becoming. Dark circles ringed her eyes, evidence of her sleepless, guilt-filled night. A sickly pallor dulled her pale skin. Her blond hair hung in listless strands around her face. *Is success in this town worth the price of my loyalty? My honor? My credibility? Am I really willing to hurt the man I care about, to use him, to get what I want?*

As if the shame of yesterday's events hadn't been enough torture, the universe had further conspired against her by ensuring that a telegram for her father was waiting for her when she arrived at home.

*Dearest Margaret,*

*Come home. We shall devise a suitable a compromise to appease us both. Settling is what good lawyers do when engaging in battle is obviously not worth the risk of defeat.*

*Fondly,*

*Father.*

Her father was offering her an out, a compromise to save at least a morsel of her pride. What would conciliation involve, she wondered? What part of herself would she be willing to give up to? *Seems like you've already given away anything that would have been worth keeping.* Whatever her father expected of her, it would be a penitence she deserved to pay for what she had done here in the land of broken dreams.

As the morning wore on, Maggie paced her tiny apartment. Emotions warred inside her, shame and despair versus ambition and hunger. And there was something else, a softer feeling when she thought of her night with Lex, something she'd strangled before she'd had a chance to know if it might bloom.

She might have spent forever in that state of indecision if a semi-breathless Peg hadn't arrived on her doorstep after lunch. "Mr.

Mergenov wants you in his office. He says if you want that contract, you'll sign it now or you can, and I quote, 'cram it where the sun don't shine.'" Peg's nose wrinkled, demonstrating her distaste for the coarse language, but she was dutiful and stayed by Maggie's side during the streetcar commute across town.

"I think I've made a mistake, Peg," Maggie said as they stepped onto the sidewalk outside the studio lot.

"It's not my place to say," Peg said. "But I agree."

Maggie gave the secretary a curious look. "How much do you know?"

Peg smiled. "I know that Lex Montgomery has been at the Blue Bowler since they opened at noon. He's still there, alone."

"Lara's not keeping him company?"

"Lara Cortez wouldn't be caught dead in that place. She might be the most beautiful woman in California, but she's not real, and I think there's nothing that man craves more in the whole world than to finally have something real in his life." Peg lead the way into the studio office and gestured toward John Mergenov's office. "He's waiting for you."

Maggie paused outside Mergenov's door. It wasn't locked to her this time. It never would be again. At least not until *The Constantinople Affair* was done. But she was confident this film would be a major success and she'd be able to open any door she wanted, with or without John Mergenov's good word, so long as she was willing to scheme for it.

But she didn't want to spend the rest of her career scheming. She'd done it for only two days, and she was *exhausted*. She wanted something real, too, and she'd had it until she threw it away. Now she wanted it back, and she'd do something quite desperate to get it.

"Peg?" Maggie crossed to the secretary's desk. "Do me a favor?"

Peg grinned in a knowing way and pushed her glasses higher on her nose. "I'd be delighted."

IT hadn't taken Maggie long to pack and reach the train station. A single suitcase was enough to get her home—her father had already wired the money for a trans-continental ticket. She'd left everything else behind, and good riddance. She'd prefer to return home with as few memories of her time here as possible.

"All aboard!" The train conductor cried as the engine spewed a puff of smoke. On the platform around her, passengers rushed to embark. Rail porters assisted with luggage and herding the crowds inside. Maggie stepped forward, eyes glued to the train. There was too much chance she'd lose her resolve if she looked back.

A porter took her suitcase and gripped her elbow, steadying her as she stepped up and into the railcar. She showed her ticket, and he directed her to her cabin. Once he'd seen to her accommodations, she passed him a silver dollar tip. He tugged the brim of his cap and went in search of another passenger to assist.

As soon as her cabin door slammed, she slumped in her seat, buried her face in her hands and gave into her tears. Perhaps her loud sobbing explained why she didn't hear her compartment door open. But when a firm hand drew her fingers away from her face and offered her a clean handkerchief, she flinched, looked up, and gasped.

Lex Montgomery sat on the bench seat across from her, a manilla envelope clutched in his fingers. He opened it and shook out the contents. Shreds of white paper rained to the floor. "Peg delivered this to me in the Blue Bowler earlier this afternoon."

Maggie looked away, unable to meet that steely blue gaze.

"It's hard to tell," Lex continued, "but it appears to be the contract you negotiated with Hank. It won't do you much good in this condition." His dark eyebrows drew together as he attempted to put pieces of the torn contract together on the seat beside him like an impossible jigsaw puzzle. "I'm sure Hank has another copy in his office."

His charade had given her the time she needed to gather her composure. She blotted her tears and wiped her nose, but she held onto his handkerchief. It smelled of lavender, which she found comforting. "There is no other copy. I

tore up the original before it was signed." She cleared her throat. "Why are you here, Lex?"

He arched a black eyebrow. His dimple flickered. He reached into his suit jacket and retrieved a bundle of papers from his inner pocket. The papers were worn around the edges and stained. She recognized them immediately. "That's my screenplay. How'd you get it?"

"You left it in your apartment. The landlord was going to clean out your room, throw it away. Couldn't let that happen, could I?"

"You went to my apartment?"

"Seemed like the smart place to start looking for you."

She glanced away, focusing on the emptying platform outside her window. She shrugged. "It's no good to me anymore. He might as well throw it away."

Lex clicked his tongue. "Blackmail wasn't your color, and neither is self-pity."

"It's not self-pity. It's resignation to the truth."

"What truth?"

Keeping her head low, she risked a look at him through her lashes. If he was angry, he didn't show it. In fact, he only revealed that cool, perfectly poised exterior. Smooth hair, buffed shoes, tailored suit. He could have been marble, if not for the blue glint in his eyes. "This life wasn't made for me," she said. "Or me for it."

"I beg to disagree. *The Constantinople Affair* was brilliant, but this..." He waved her screenplay at her. "This is the stuff of Hollywood legend."

His compliment both thrilled and pained her. If he was exacting his revenge, she deserved it, and wouldn't object. "If you're here to punish me, I won't stop you."

"Punish?" His lips quirked into a wry grin. "I'm here to negotiate an investment. Leading man roles pay well enough, but they won't last forever. The *real* money is made in studio boardrooms." He tapped the screenplay. "I want to be in the boardroom for this one from day one."

She shrugged. "Then take it. It's yours."

"It's worthless without you to go with it."

A ray of hope burst through her, painful in its futility. There was no hope to be had here. Damn her heart for trying to tell her otherwise. "Lex, there are no words to make up for how I behaved. Any apology could only be offensive to you for being so utterly insufficient. But whether you mean the things you're saying or not, it doesn't matter. I'm going home. Take the screenplay or don't. It doesn't matter to me."

The flash in his eyes was the only warning he gave before he reached across the small cabin, grabbed her shoulders, and hauled her into his lap. "That's it? You surrender so easily? I saw the fight in you, Maggie. You were willing to callously betray me to get what you wanted. Where is that woman now?"

Maggie's throat and eyes were swimming again, but she clamped down on her tears. "That woman was atrocious, and I never want to see her again."

"But *I* do." Tenderly, he rubbed his thumb over her cheek. "I was falling in love with her, and I believed she felt the same about me. I thought I was a good judge of character. How could I have been so horribly wrong?"

"Maybe you're not the only good actor in Hollywood?"

He snorted. It turned into a chuckle. He stroked her cheek again and her lashes fluttered close. "Is going home what you really want, Maggie?"

"Of course not."

"Then what *do* you want?"

"I want to stay. I want to make it up to you. I want to make my movie. I want…"

Whatever she might have confessed next was interrupted by the train's sudden jerk. It shuddered again and her cabin swayed, slowly at first but quickly gaining speed as the train chugged way from the platform. Her eyes popped wide. "Lex! You have to get off."

He grinned. "I think it's too late for that, doll."

Still in his lap, she struggled to get away. He refused to release her, tightening his arms around her. "What are you doing?" she asked. "You can't just jump on a train and roll out of town on a whim."

"You did. Why can't I?"

"Because you're *Lex Montgomery.*

People will raise hell when they can't find you."

"Like I raised hell when I couldn't find you?" He arched an eyebrow. "Thankfully your landlord didn't take much convincing."

"You can't just... just..." She waved her hands in a gesture that encompassed their cabin and the Los Angeles landscape speeding past their window.

"Tell me to go, and I'll find a compartment of my own and never speak to you again."

She bit her lip. She *should* tell him to go. But the words wouldn't come.

"But I'd rather you tell me to stay."

She studied his eyes, looking for an answer, for anything that might explain how he could offer her such mercy. "I don't deserve second chance, Lex. I don't deserve *you*."

"I wouldn't be where I am today without them. Everyone deserves a second chance."

Hope flared again, this time less painfully. Could he truly be this forgiving? Before this moment she would have sworn that such grace couldn't exist in a place like Hollywood.

"Tell me you're sorry, Maggie." His voice was low and gravelly, and it stirred a familiar warmth within her.

"I'm sorry."

His chin dipped, bringing his lips closer to hers. "Tell me you won't betray me again."

"I'd die first." And she meant it, even if it was a bit more melodramatic than she'd normally allow in the dialogues she wrote.

"Tell me you love me." His smile was full of hope.

Her breath caught. Her heart stopped. His feelings for her were never in question—he'd treated her with more compassion than she'd ever deserved. She could explain it by accepting that he was one of the best men she'd ever met, which would be true, but there was more to it. He loved her, and she believed it. She'd torn up Mergenov's contract because she'd wanted to be a decent human being, but also because she'd realized she'd loved Lex too. Though, before now she hadn't been quite willing to admit it.

"I do love you, Lex." She pushed the words past the emotion swelling in her throat. "I'm sorry, and I love you."

Los Angeles was the city of dreams, blessed and cursed by hope and despair. It was the city of glamor and allure, make-up and masks, fantasy and facades. Here, fortunes were built on fabrications and pretense.

But this? This fragile new promise she was forming with Lex?

This was nothing but real.

His lips crushed against hers and his arms tightened until her ribs creaked, but she didn't object. She returned his passion, clinging to him as his touch restored her faith. "I love *you*, Maggie Campbell. Swear you'll stay with me."

"I swear," she said between his kisses. "I'll never leave you again."

# Hamburger Kiss

## By ROBERT GREENBERGER

*October 1998*

HER smile radiated, lighting up any classroom she entered. It was beamed at everyone she encountered but Ethan Calon was convinced no one felt about her smile the way he did. They'd met freshmen year, sharing one class and their passion for the school newspaper. She was the more gifted writer and quickly became assistant news editor while he was relegated to writing sports stories, and he hated sports, but refused to quit because he wanted to be near her.

She was slender, with a short bob of a haircut, a smattering of acne across her cheeks, but that smile more than made up for any of her plain features. He didn't pay much attention to her clothes, but she was always neat, favoring prints and pastels. She looked fine in whatever she wore, he decided, not really fussing much over fashion. Clothes were a necessity so went for the relatively solid color and plain styles, whatever his mom said was on sale.

Over time, they began to argue about what was important about covering for the paper since it came out haphazardly, a monthly scheduling turning into more of an every six-week affair, which drove their advisor, Austin McKean, crazy. The timeliness of the news stopped mattering so the debates went over what to cover and how to cover it. The sparring was good for them both, as he got to see how her mind worked,

When they argued, Ethan's glasses had a tendency to slip down his long nose, requiring constant adjustment so his mannerisms were that of a passionate teen in constant motion. His curly mop of brown hair vibrated with every gesticulation, his deepening voice rising to reflect his frustration.

"Bethany, how can you not see that our SA president is just doing it for the college app," he practically shouted. "He doesn't give one shit about running the school."

"But that's not news we can cover," Bethany Panzirer said in return.

When these two got into it, everyone else in the newsroom sat back and watched. Rarely had the juniors and seniors seen such passion from a pair of sophomores. It was also clear to everyone, including Bethany, how much Ethan was into her. How she felt was far less clear.

As the passions subsided, again, the room—a genuine newspaper office with desk and files, and large

*Illustration by Matt Haley*

screen for writing the stories to be designed—sprang back to life with everyone else griping about teachers and assignments. When conversation turned to an upcoming social event, Ethan looked up, directly across the space to Bethany, who was jotting something in her reporter's notepad, then back to his own work.

Later, as she was leaving for home, he called her name.

"Do you want to go to the movie with me?"

She hesitated, a small smile instead of her brilliant one, on her face. "Well, maybe, but it's got to be as friends. You understand, right?"

"Of course," he said without a moment's hesitation.

And so they went and sat beside one another, sharing popcorn and Coke but never holding hands or any real physical intimacy. At the end, as his father dropped Bethany off at her house, he walked her to the door, just as he had been taught, and while he hoped for a kiss, got a brief hug and she hurried inside.

*September 2002*

BETHANY spotted Ethan from across the rec room, looking a little scruffy around the edges compared to his high school look, but pretty much the same as when they graduated together two years earlier. She'd known they'd wound up at the same state school but lived in different parts of the campus. Since they shared no classes, his presence provided an odd touch of home. That said, she never saw him. But, here he was, in a denim shirt and jeans, in need of a shave. Idly she wondered why he was there, at her dorm's first mixer of the school year. *Duh,* she thought. He'd moved into the dorm. To be closer to her? Was he still *that* infatuated? She found his puppy dog affection for her during high school borderline obsessive. But it was also somewhat sweet.

Then she saw him slide his arm around a curvy Asian girl she didn't recognize. She leaned into him so clearly they were here together, an item. So much for *her* ego, she considered. He wasn't there for her, just a coincidence. Armed with that knowledge, she put on her smile and walked over to them.

"Hi Ethan!" she said brightly. It did warm her heart to see the instant recognition, his face shifting from surprise to that puppy look in an instant. He might have a girlfriend, but she'd bet he'd toss her if she said the right word. Not that she would. Their rivalry had been burnished over time into a friendship that got them through numerous AP classes and exams, finally working in tandem their senior year with her as Editor in Chief and he as Managing Editor, and genuinely finding equal footing with one another. They'd had dated others and were comfortable enough to discuss those relationships, seeking the other out to understand the mysteries of teen boys and girls.

"Bets," he said. No one at college called her that, for which she was thankful, but he was from home and could slide on that. He went to hug her, awkwardly disentangling himself from the girl.

"So, this is Linda. She moved in this year, and I couldn't be so far away so I made the move, too," he said. The women, practicing to be adults, shook hands. Bethany could easily read Linda's expression; she knew her boyfriend had or still has a thing for her, but she had the current claim and wasn't letting go. They made stiff conversation for a bit before others joined in and Bethany could relax, let her guard down a little. It genuinely made her feel good to see him happy with someone. She'd been single through most of freshmen year and was hoping to correct that this semester.

S HE'D barely unpacked after returning to the dorm after Thanksgiving break, a welcome week off from the crush of her pre-med classes, when there was a tentative knock on her door. Her roommate Cassie hadn't returned yet so she put down the folded sweater and answered it.

Ethan looked like someone had died. No tears, but the eyes were bloodshot. There were dark smudges under them, his face hung limply. He normally dressed

casually but here he seemed downright sloppy. He walked right in, just as he had so many times since they'd reunited two months earlier.

The friendship had resumed, pretty much right where it left off. He'd been studying poli sci while she vacillated between being a doctor or nurse, unsure if she had what it took to get through the medical boards. She'd thrown herself entirely into studies while he seemed to have time for his course work, Linda, and a role in student government. She envied him that while her bed remained occupied by just herself despite infatuations with a few fellow students and a TA. She'd always held back, never fully committing to a relationship. There was time for that later, she kept telling herself.

"What's wrong," she asked, seating herself beside him on the bed.

Ethan remain silent, shoulders slumped. "Is it your parents?"

A shake of his head. He'd at least gotten a haircut at home, somewhat taming the curls.

"Is it Linda?"

Silence then finally, a long, audible sigh that filled the room. "Yeah, she dumped me yesterday."

"Yesterday? Were you together?"

"No, it was a text. A long, emotional text saying she needed to be alone, concentrate on her studies, all that bullshit."

She waited him out, giving him time to collect himself and present the facts he wanted to share. They'd done this for one another so often, it was an old, familiar habit like making the bed or brushing your teeth.

"No one else?"

"I don't think so," he finally said. She doubted it too from the way she acted when they saw one another in the dorm lounge. Then again, she didn't understand where this breakup came from so something else was afoot. But, she wasn't going to get involved.

"Well, she's a bitch," Bethany said to cheer him up then gave him a warm hug.

They sat in companionable silence for a while. He had seemed to collect himself, which was reassuring. She'd seen Ethan fall apart before, but that was when his grandfather died the night before the AP English exam or when they had to put the dog, Chester, down. This was different, it was a girlfriend and although he'd had a few before, this one seemed to devastate him. They briefly discussed the awkward negotiations to happen when they encountered one another in the dorm halls or communal bathrooms, but that could all wait.

Finally, Ethan stood up and nodded in her direction, a silent thanks. He walked the short distance to the door, opened it, and said, without turning around, "I could wait for you...if you ever..." Then he left.

He'd said that before and she always took some comfort in knowing she'd grow old never needing to be alone. He was a rock for her, a touchstone of stability, a deep well of affection, maybe genuine love. But she had yet to feel anything but sisterly affection for him and doubted she ever would.

*November 2012*

HE loved grilling, always the first to signup for a shift at the church or school fairs. In his "World's Greatest Father" apron, he was flipping burgers, dogs, and sausages, exchanging banter with the other dads, who were grilling onions or toasting buns. This Fall Fair was raising money for a class trip and to help the homeless—who could say no to that? Looking up to gauge the line, he blinked once, twice.

The hair was longer and darker, the acne long gone, and her round face shone in the sunlight. There was an infant slung against her chest and she held hands with a little girl who had to be in the second grade. She was comfortably dressed and still damned attractive. He didn't catch her eye and resumed flipping burgers until she reached the table.

He'd moved back to his hometown right after college, getting his first job and marrying. It never occurred to him that Bethany, or many of their other classmates, would do the same thing. It just wasn't done these days. But there she was, back in town, in the same school district no less. Happenstance? Kismet? The stars aligning? He didn't care.

"Hiya Bets," he said.

She gazed at him, clearly taking in his fuller face, shorter hair, and recently acquired mustache. The brilliant smile, that peeled away the years, creased her face and he noticed the beginnings of crow's feet around the eyes, which he added to the all the things he loved about her.

"I can't believe it," she said. "Have you…"

"I moved into town right out of college," he said, filling in the gaps. "Liz and I bought a fixer-upper, which is not yet done of course. I have my son around here somewhere. Another one due in April."

"Wow, congratulations," she said, taking in the surprise, pleased with his news, which in turn pleased him. "This is Emily," she said, shrugging her body to indicate the sleeping infant. "And this is Isabelle, Izzy. Say hi to Mr. Calon." Instead, the little girl hid behind her legs and they both laughed.

"My boy, Peter, has an Izzy in Mrs. DeVoe's class."

"That's the one," she beamed.

"The world shrinks a bit more," he said. "So what'll it be? I'd love to catch up when I'm off shift."

"Well, Izzy's full, but I need a hamburger, stat."

He nodded and slid the freshest one off the grill and personally placed it on a bun, added tomato and lettuce with his plastic gloved hand, then arranged space for chips to be added at the cashier.

"How much will it be?"

"Three bucks, it's a fundraiser after all," he said, offering her the plate.

Before accepting, she rummaged through her pockets and the diaper bag slung over a shoulder. She came up with two crumpled dollar bills. Sheepishly, she gestured with them.

"Jeff, my husband, has all the cash. This is what's left after spin art and some games. Do you have a spare dollar? Or could you let me slide this once?"

"Hey, if it were my backyard, it'd be free, but they're counting every patty and every nickel. I can't…"

She adjusted Emily as she leaned over the table, her face growing close to his, perspiration quickly forming from the grill despite the fall air. "Ethan, come on, help me out. Do you have a buck? Tell you what, I'll sweeten the deal. I'll give you a kiss. I gotta eat or I'll pass out."

In all the years they'd known one another, they'd hugged, there'd been pecks on cheeks and foreheads, but a kiss kiss? They were married and *now* she offers the kiss he'd been dreaming of? Was she actually using his heart against him? He shook off the thought, cursed the timing, and nodded silently.

"I'll cover you," he said. And her face broke into *that* smile.

She grabbed the plate, tossed him the two bills which thankfully missed the grill, and strode off to pick up the bag of potato chips and ketchup. At the cashier's, she gestured his way and he nodded at Tommy, who nodded in acknowledgement. With a wave, she hurried off with the kids in tow; clearly the kiss was going to wait.

As he spread five fresh patties on the grill, Ethan reflected at how the world worked. He and Bethany were connected in ways that stated to feel mystical. School, college, and now as parents and neighbors. His heart panged with regret and memory as he sprinkled seasoning on the pink meat and listened to the sizzle.

By the time he got off shift, Liz, already showing under her windbreaker, and Peter were waiting for him. Their boy had wilted and needed to go home before a full-fledged meltdown. His wife never wanted a public display of bad behavior and cut more events and visits short to avoid any sense of embarrassment. As a result, he realized as he balled his apron up and slipped into his windbreaker, Bethany had vanished from sight, her promise broken.

That was one chit he was going to hang on to.

*March 2018*

"HE decided it was okay to read my diary," Bethany complained to her best friend Emnet.

"Without your permission," she asked, the incredulousness clear. Emnet and Bethany had met two years earlier thanks to their children being nearly identical in age, interests, and temperament. Where one went, the other could be counted on to also be on hand. They were active, involved mothers, always finding time to chat. She didn't allow herself many close friends, they were too hard to acquire, so she cherished each one like a fine wine.

"He can't be bothered to do his job, but has decided invading my privacy he has time for," she grumbled.

The two women were sitting on the unforgiving metal folding chairs as the PTA meeting was emptying out. Ideally, they'd both head to the nearby pub for white wine and a bitch session, but it was a school night and neither one had the energy for that anymore. She was starting to feel old when she was anything but that, just set in her routine.

"Is there anything in there he *shouldn't* read?"

Bethany nodded slowly, not meeting her friend's eyes. "Yeah. I don't want to fight in front of the kids so I pour it all into the book."

"Other men?" Emnet said, mostly teasing, but it stung. There hadn't been more than a passing flirtation with anyone in years. She'd been far from blind to those who would be happy to cheat with her, but she wasn't like that. No, she was committed to her marriage. Yet, she admitted to herself, as things with Jeff grew strained, she did indulge in what ifs. What would have happened had she reciprocated Ethan's interest in her at some point before she married? They had such a strong foundation of trust and honest between them. He'd turned out just fine, suppressing his puppy love and turning himself into a man, a husband, and a father she had to admire.

At night, when she sat with a glass of wine and her journal, she let her mind drift. Ethan had always been an abstraction to her, but he was a constant. He turned out to be the kind of man she imagined she'd marry. He remained handsome and seemed largely unchanged through the years. On more than one occasion, she did indulge in some thoughts which, in time, became fantasies. With every struggle with Jeff, Ethan was more and more of an ideal of what she wanted. On those occasions, she felt her heart beat just a little faster, but would never act on it.

She shook her head and said, "Not at all. His lack of ambition, his distrustful nature. His…"

"Hi," a voice sounded, drawing nearer. She looked up to see Ethan, his mustache beginning to show the first signs of gray. He was the one to attend these meetings, volunteer for the activities, not Liz, who never struck her as the social type. The two women never formed any real relationship and the one time the two couples had a dinner it was clear there wouldn't be a second. Jeff didn't like Ethan

and Bethany found Liz cold. Once more, the two had grown close. Now, she was playing with fire, knowing his passion for her remained smoldering in the background. But, they were married, and while she was truly angered by her husband, it wasn't permission to do anything that would jeopardize the family.

Still, his mere presence revved up her heart once more. The first time that had happened when they were near one another rather than the privacy of her mind.

"Hi Emnet," he said, nodding at her.

Emnet smiled back, rising to excuse herself, clearly aware if their deep bond and, if truth be told, also aware of his decades-long interest. "Well, I think this is something we need to discuss further. Play date?"

Bethany, pushing improper thoughts from her mind, also rose, already pulling out her cellphone to match calendars, a dance that could take some time. Ethan stood there patiently as the women waded through practices, appointments, and for Izzy, a math tutor. It was deemed miraculous that the women found a two hour block for the kids to play and the women to vent just a week away.

Emnet said her goodnights and left the pair to catchup. She felt it a good thing that she'd actually brushed her hair and did a little makeup before the meeting. Last time they met, she'd felt like a homeless person but then again, it was also after Emily had the flu, meaning neither had slept well in days. Still, she noticed and his appraising, and approving, look. He was developing the beginning of a paunch, well hidden by the loose button-down deep purple shirt.

"Bitching about Jeff again?"

Bethany nodded and grabbed her handbag, heading for the doors to the parking lot. "Again."

"Anything new?"

"He is perfectly content with his job, unwilling to ask for more money, unwilling to look for a better job. I had no idea he lacked this much ambition when we were engaged. He certainly pursued me with enough passion. I just wish he'd show some passion for his job." She hesitated, looking straight ahead. "Or the family." She wouldn't ever admit to him that he'd been looming in her fantasies. The timing was all wrong for so many reasons.

Ethan held the metal door for her, the snap of the November night air made her inwardly shiver. They paused on the sidewalk, uncertain if their cars were near one another. This had been a habit, the conversations each month after the PTA meetings. Izzy and Peter weren't in the same classes any more so their paths hadn't crossed as often as before. Still, they resumed their friendship, their confidences in one another right where things had been a lifetime before.

She knew, for example, that Ethan's wife had had a brief affair and they were in couples' counseling trying to heal. That was a year ago and she'd learned things remained brittle. She sensed his wife was staying around for the kids' sake, which was really doing no one any favors. Ethan deserved better. Hell, *she* deserved better. Jeff had proven not only without ambition but controlling, insisting he know where she was at every moment. He was no doubt at home, watching the clock, anticipating her return so they could walk the dog and go to sleep. If the meeting was running beyond 90 minutes, she was to notify him, so that was her internal alarm, keeping her chats with Ethan regular but frustratingly brief.

"Trouble?" he asked, wrapping the scarf around his neck, a bright plaid that clearly a child picked for him.

"The latest property tax increase is playing havoc with the bank account," she admitted. Over the years, nothing was off-limits. They'd discussed all the taboo topics: sex, religion, politics, and maybe the diciest of them all, money. "If he doesn't get a raise, we might need to start looking to move."

The alarm in his eyes told her everything she needed to know. His friendship, his concern, and his love remained steadfast. Still, she never held back before and she needed to float the idea that one day they might have to be apart once more.

"I don't want to. I love it here. I love the school and want the girls to graduate from their hometown. Uprooting them would be horrible. I *like* it here."

"Well, if it makes you feel any better, I would need to relocate to afford something on my own with room for the kids. Downwardly mobile, here I come."

"Is it definitely headed that way?"

"Damned if I know," he said. "There's no progress and I don't know if we'll get past this. It's weird, you having a distrustful husband although you've done nothing wrong and me willing to trust her again."

"Can you?"

"I want to. I can't imagine raising them on my own." He paused, took a deep breath, his exhalation formed a large white cloud between them. "Or being alone."

*April 2020*

**B**ETHANY and Emmet were chatting as the PTA meeting ended. Both were named co-chairs of the Spring Fling so had plenty of details to finalize, keeping them well after the meeting ended. In fact, they agreed to run out for a glass of wine to make the business more palatable.

Ethan looked up from his own beer as they came in. He was glad they were able to rely on one another for things like the fair. He was sitting with the few other dads

who actually attended the meeting, usually because they needed something for a class or their children. He had long since stopped caring about the actual agenda, since he just really wanted to have time to chat with Bethany.

Somehow, he wound up with enough equity in the house to manage to refinance the mortgage and stay in place, while his wife moved out six months earlier into a condo one town over. They communicated a lot more easily these days with a few miles between them and the kids were getting used to the shuttling back and forth. It was far from ideal, but he saw the toll the stress was beginning to take on them and pushed for the divorce. She folded fairly quickly since she was the one at fault.

But now he was a single dad, feeling like a failure at adulthood. The kids, the job, the life was feeling unsettled as the new reality was slow to feel real to him. Bethany, Emnet, and many of the other moms he'd gotten to know thanks to years of regular attendance were all sympathies and platitudes. Several even tried to fix him for blind dates but that was something he wasn't ready for. No, he needed to get right with the new routine and make sure the kids were better. He could worry about himself later.

He got a second beer as the other dads, David Chamberlain and Tom Longstaff, thinned out and he watched as the women had their second then third glasses of wine, energetically pushing through their joint To Do list. They had formed a good team and he knew she needed the friendship. Her husband, Jeff, had improved things for them, but only financially. She was still under his thumb and he hated the man for it. They'd barely interacted through the years and he found himself keeping his distance to ensure he wouldn't tell her husband what he thought.

Emnet got an alert on her phone, realized what time it was, and hastily shrugged into her overcoat and hugged her partner goodbye. Once she rushed out, he watched as Bethany orderly organized the papers and stuck them in a manila folder, then put on a peacoat and paid the waitress.

As she headed for the door, Ethan threw a five on the table and headed for the exit as well. He timed it so they would find one another on the sidewalk.

"Were you in there?" she said with genuine surprise.

"Yeah, me and the guys. The kids got themselves to bed so I had a night out."

"Good for you," she said.

"Let me walk you," he said and began pacing her as they headed for her maroon Forester. He held the door for her as she began saying something about Izzy. Quickly, he rounded the front of the vehicle and climbed into the passenger seat.

"She did what?"

"Mr. Piorkowksi found her kissing Mike McClellan after school."

"And?"

"Well, he thought it—how did he put it?—lacked decorum."

He chuckled at that. "Was she doing it wrong?"

"I don't think that's the point," Bethany said with a chuckle.

"So, what's going to happen?"

"I have to go talk to the dean," she said. "Not a conversation I really want to have."

"It's just kissing. They've found so much worse. Remember that viral video two years ago…"

"Sure do," she said with a wince.

They talked on about everything and nothing as they were wont to do. For a change, she wasn't on the clock as much and clearly the wine relaxed her. She seemed to be unwinding for the first time in ages, periodically looking out the window, letting their conversation help fog up the windshield.

"Speaking of kisses," he said and she turned, a look of alarm in her eyes.

"Yeah?" she said slowly with a hint of suspicion.

"You still owe me one."

She blinked. "For what?"

"When I loaned you a dollar for the hamburger."

"What hamburger…" she began but trailed off, the memory clearly being dredged back up. It had been years, he knew, but it was something he'd held on to while she tucked it away in the memory bin.

"You really going to make me pay up?"

"Sooner or later," he said, measuring the tone as to not appear eager, or worse, desperate. He looked at her but she didn't meet his eyes, lost in some thought. He understood; after all, it wasn't every day a man not her husband asked for a kiss.

She shifted in her seat, leaned over and kissed him.

Her lips were soft, the smell of wine still on her breath. It wasn't just a peck, it lingered for a few seconds. Of course he kissed back.

The pressure built and neither pulled apart.

He was lost in the kiss, finally achieving something he'd dreamt of for so long. They parted briefly and she looked at him, studying his eyes, considering. Making a decision. She leaned back in, a second kiss, and this one included her arm snaking around his neck.

Their tongues met this time, thrilling him.

He allowed his passion to show but was surprised to find she was displaying some passion of her own.

The fogged windshield kept them from being seen, giving them some protection. So, he continued to kiss her, waiting to see when she'd break off. She didn't and the minutes passed. He kept waiting for the spell to be broken by a cellphone alert, her sobering up, or something else to spoil the mood.

She'd told him when he was newly divorced that he might rush into a new relationship but warned him from it. "You need someone worth the risk of heartache and pain," she told him.

Ethan knew he was single. He knew she was unhappily married. She'd known heartache and pain. So had he.

He also knew he'd waited all this time and maybe, just maybe, they were finally about to get on the same page.

He wrapped both arms around her and kissed her again.

# *Casting Couch*

### *By* HEATHER E. HUTSELL

THERE it was—*Sizemore Studios*—larger than life in an arch across the lot entrance, and all lit up even though it was just before ten in the morning. He stood there looking at it, a smile half-cocked under his thin, black mustache, and hands akimbo. It was nicer than the sign to the lot at Shortfellows Productions, but it wasn't a flashy sign that had brought him here.

He passed through the gate and headed toward the main office building. There was plenty of tipping his hat to the ladies and tittering and whispering behind his back. People knew his face. The reactions were enough to float him above the packed-dirt roadways, if only in his head.

The office was bustling with the chatter of secretaries on telephones, writers commiserating over scripts, and various others coming and going. A good amount of that activity stopped when he walked in and removed his hat. He flashed smiles all around— they deserved that for giving him their undivided attention. He even winked at a few who recognized him and watched roses bloom on cheeks.

"Mister Ducats—"

He turned to see a lovely, little blonde with sparkling blue eyes and a nice pink dress. She had plucked up the receiver from her telephone the moment he walked in, likely to announce his arrival to the boss, and was now practically melting at his feet.

"Why, yes, miss?"

"Ms. Valentine will see you now."

"*Splendid.*"

He knew exactly who *Ms. Valentine* was. *Judith*. He'd never met her before, but someone like her didn't go long without someone like *him* knowing about her, or vice versa. Sure, *Judith* made her sound in charge—and she *was*, unusual as those things tended to be. But *Valentine? Valentine* was soft, warm, complacent. She'd probably give him anything he asked for, she just didn't know it yet. Why she'd never requested a meeting with him before now, he didn't know. Shortfellows had held him over well enough, kept him on the silver screen, made sure he had his public eating out of the palm of his hand. *But Sizemore*—better late than never.

Even though it was rumored that Shortfellows would catch up to raking in the same sort of dough Sizemore did, it had yet to happen. No one could really blame him for wanting to test the waters between studios to see who would pay top dollar for him. Maybe he could start a wage war in all this, making it better for everyone, all the way down the payroll. Just as long as, in the end, he was the one who ended up making bank.

The blonde doll went to a dark, austere-looking door and then opened it, quickly stepping aside so he could enter. From behind a heavy desk of cherry wood, a tall, voluptuous brunette in a scarlet suit stood up. Her eyes were so dark they were black, and there was an exciting, fierce look about her. She wasn't of the petite model brand like the secretary, but he couldn't argue that she was rather attractive in her own way.

"Mister Ducats—" She came around the desk to shake his hand.

"Misses Valentine. Pleasure to finally meet you."

"It's *Ms.*"

The Eastern European accent that carried her words reminded him of a flash-in-the-pan songbird named Naka Jovanovic, but still sent a delightful buzz through him as her hand remained in his.

"Is that so?"

"It is." She withdrew her hand before he could give it a squeeze and resumed her place behind the desk. "Please, sit."

He took a glance around and spied a black leather sofa. "Is that your *casting couch*?" he asked with a wink. She didn't respond, visibly unimpressed, so he took a seat on a matching armchair that squeaked under him in the suggestive way only leather could.

"So," he began. "This is a surprise—being invited here. Looking to do a little *star-napping*?"

"I beg your pardon?"

"Well, I'm sure you know—I've been acting for Shortfellows. And the invitation was from *you*, was it not?"

"Mister Ducats—stage name, is it? *Buck Ducats*?"

"Yes, ma'am. It didn't seem likely someone named *Charlie Diddle* was destined for the pictures—" He reined in the twang in his voice that only appeared anymore when mentioning his real name. "—So, I changed it."

"Mm." Her nod was curt and of disinterest. "Mister Ducats, I'd hardly consider you to be a star just yet—" The sting of her jab was unexpected, and Buck silently soothed it with a veil of smugness. *What did she know?* "But it has not gone unnoticed that your popularity has grown substantially over the past year—"

"So it would seem."

"I invited you directly because I think you have the potential to become the star you think you are. Clearly, you are here because you're interested in that prospect."

"Indubitably, ma'am."

"You're twenty-four, yes? You've done—" She looked at her notes. "*Two* films so far. I'm sure you've been led to believe that your face on the screen means big dollars for *any* studio that you're a part of."

"I do."

"Well, believe it or not, Mister Ducats, your face has nothing to do with it—it's your voice. That's where your value is and, look— I'm not going to mince words, Mister Ducats—whatever contract you may have with Shortfellows, I will buy it out. I want you to work for me. For Sizemore Studios."

The idea of making the switch— and so easily—was just as intriguing to him as the mysterious woman who offered to make it happen.

"You can do that?"

"Mister Ducats, would you even be here if you thought there'd be any complications for you?"

He would have come no matter what, just to see what it was all about, but Shortfellows was in the game for the money. Surely, they'd understand that he was, too.

"Well, no. But it just so happens that those two films I did for them were all I was scheduled to do, so you don't really need to bother them about it."

"Oh? Is that what was in your contract?"

"Oh, sure. Kind of a disappointment that was all, but I guess they didn't see what you do—things switching from silent pictures to talkies and all."

"So, you are interested then?"

The almost impatient prompt struck up visions of flashing camera bulbs and endless champagne in Buck's thoughts. She had invited him, in a world where a person's voice in film was starting

to equate to gold, and it was he her studio wanted. Never minding that something as naturally occurring as his voice was out of his control. Buck managed to refrain from huffing on his knuckles and then dusting them across his lapel.

When his pause was mistaken for indecision, she added, "You'll always have top billing with us, and be paid accordingly."

Buck was suddenly struck with elation over it all and this seemingly out-of-nowhere luck. "When should I start?"

"Tomorrow. And seeing as how I couldn't locate your agent—"

"Yeah, I don't have one."

"I see," she said after a pause. "Well, in any case, we have a new script that you can read for, though the part was practically written for you. Formalities—I'm sure you understand."

"Oh, of course."

"Good. Of course, if you work for me—and Sizemore—it will be exclusively. You will be under a new contract. We don't want you working for any other studios."

"Naturally," he accepted with a shrug and a schmoozy smile.

"Not even small, independent ones. I know how inconsequential they may seem. I promise you: it will be worth your time. You think you're a star now? You cannot imagine what you could become with us."

The idea of being banned from working with small, insignificant studios seemed odd. Sure, they paid less, but Buck knew of a few actors a step ahead of him who'd taken roles. They were mostly experimental, and that meant the possibility of something spectacular if things got stale with the bigger studios. Buck wasn't sure what the big deal was, but he shrugged again anyway.

"Whatever you say." In truth, and not that he needed to bother saying it, he just wanted the role and the money, and getting that contract signed would seal the deal on both. He wasn't worried about doing the part well—didn't Judith Valentine just say he'd become a star with Sizemore? No matter what her opinion, he already was one and he was sure she knew it. She probably just didn't want to inflate his ego. She used *Ms.* instead of *Miss*, after all, and it made her stand out. He could appreciate that—standing out and above the rest was what he lived for. He was *Buck Ducats*.

"Mister Ducats, I want to be sure you truly understand what it means should you be in breach of contract—there *are* consequences."

*That again?* Her warning prompted yet another of his nonchalant shrugs, a movie-worthy smirk, and bedroom eyes. Sure, she was laying it on thick, but if he got caught, so what? He was sure that Shortfellows Studio only fined its actors a hundred dollars for such an offense: how much worse could it be with Sizemore? It was probably peanuts compared to his future paychecks, and that was hardly something to be concerned about. Still, he could see she needed appeasing.

"Oh, I get it, ma'am. I get it."

Ms. Valentine pushed a folder and pen across her desk and Buck rose to sign the single sheet of paper inside.

"Don't you want to read it first?" she asked with a hint of surprise in her tone.

"No need. All contracts say the same thing and we're on the same page, *Ms.* Valentine." He wanted to liken the whole thing to taking candy from a baby, but he kept that to himself.

Buck left Sizemore after about an hour of touring the lot, ready for lunch and a celebratory drink. On his way out, he hooked one of the secretaries to take along with him. Not the dishy blonde, but a redhead in blue and with gams for days. She knew of a good place nearby. Buck didn't really care where they were going—it was on Sizemore's dime. From that point on, and as far as he was concerned, that meant *everything* was.

Lunch conversation with the redhead proved to be about as vapid as it ever was with any of them, never mind that Buck wasn't really listening to whatever she'd been saying, too preoccupied with visions of Judith Valentine. She was nothing like the rest of these dames. He wasn't even sure of his date's name. *Carol? Karen?* She knew his, and that was good enough. But *Judith Valentine?* How could anyone forget that?

The script reading for *Single Shot Swindle* went swimmingly the next morning, and as Buck went through his costume fitting, he scanned his lines in preparation for rehearsals that afternoon. The role was perfect: a young detective who was never foiled by a crime, who marveled everyone he crossed paths with, and who always got the good-looking dame in the end. Buck felt renewed, refreshed; he was flying high on life and nothing could bring him down. *This* was how he envisioned Hollywood to be. *This* was the life people dreamt of, and he was living it all.

There was only one little snag, and that was Shortfellows. They kept sending him letters—none of which he read past the greeting. He didn't need them anymore. They had been snoozing on coming up with a new picture, on transitioning to more talkies. They'd snoozed on *him*. Well, that was their dumb luck. He made a point to mention it to Ms. Valentine next time he saw her. Maybe she could get them to stop harassing him.

REHEARSALS went swell, but Buck noticed that Ms. Valentine was never around to watch them. An oversight on her part, he was sure. If she had been, he was sure she'd be changing her mind about his already being a star. Making his way through every eligible—and not so eligible—broad

on the lot went pretty well, too, especially when it came to getting them to keep quiet about their little trysts. Buck just told them all that he knew women could be petty and cruel toward each other, and he would feel terrible if jealousy were to result, should the rest find out that he was exclusive with anyone, so it was best that they just kept it between them. The line worked beautifully on every last gullible one. He saw them *all* at the various parties, but a wink here and there sufficed to keep them from approaching him, and unsuspecting of each other. These little escapades proved thrilling every time, even if the cozy nights out—or in—proved to run a little dull. Judith Valentine never failed to cross his mind and that spiced things up a bit. Whatever it was about her that made her so different, he knew he'd have to work his way up to her, and that could take a while.

Before Buck knew it, filming began, and in only a couple of months, his part in the production was coming to an end. Buck had enjoyed his time with Sizemore Studios all right. He'd enjoyed the paychecks substantially more. And even the women—at least the options were seemingly endless.

As ever, his mind went back to ponder Judith Valentine. She'd rarely been on set and when she had, she'd never given a hint as to her pleasure or disdain over his performance. He wondered if she was the kind to lurk in the shadows, unseen. A part of him thought she seemed it.

The day he collected his last check after *Single Shot Swindle* wrapped, he stopped in unannounced to see Ms. Valentine, momentarily inconvenienced when her secretary stopped Buck at the door.

"Mister Ducats, Ms. Valentine is very busy—"

"I'm sure she is." He flashed a smile at the young woman and the corners of her mouth started to lift, then fell again. Before she could protest again, he said, "I'll only be a moment." He didn't see her swoon, having already turned to open the office door, but he could clearly see it in his head.

Judith Valentine had her eyes on a document she had been perusing when Buck closed the door behind him.

"Well, hello there—" Why he'd thought he could speak to her in a wooing tone was beyond him, and her interjection was cold and steely.

"Mister Ducats, I'm *very* busy."

"Sure, I know. I just wanted to ask—" In his hesitation, through which he grinned to try and make it seem intentional, the woman finally looked up and gave a prompting gesture. "Well, I just didn't see you on set too much."

Understanding replaced her confusion. "Mister Ducats, my whereabouts during a shoot should be the least of your concerns. Anything else I can help you with?"

The dismissiveness in her tone stung a bit, but he still let the presence of the couch behind him cross his mind. The fact that he already had one feature in the bag with them didn't matter—he'd still get her on that couch. *Someday.*

"Mister Ducats?"

Buck felt her impatience in a twinge not altogether unpleasant in a rush right up the back of his neck.

"I was just wondering—now that the filming's done—what next?"

"What do you mean, *what next?*" She went back to whatever she'd been reading and was now making marks with a red pencil.

"When's the next production? When do I get started with rehearsals—?"

"You've got some time on your hands, Mister Ducats. Why don't you take it off?"

"Sounds marvelous, but—"

Her dark eyes lifted again, this time with a captivating spark. "Perhaps you would like to read your contract."

Something about her statement woke a sudden stubbornness in him. What could a contract possibly tell him that she couldn't just say directly?

"I just thought I'd be making a whole lotta movies, is all."

"You will be, Mister Ducats," she assured him, with no lack of irritation. "But not right at this moment. Don't worry: we'll call you when it's time. Now if you could—" She made a shooing gesture toward the door, and Buck had no choice but to leave.

He went without another word to her or anyone else and stepped just outside of the building, her words ringing in his head about taking *some time off*. If that was how things worked at Sizemore, then who was he to judge? She'd said more movies were coming, but in the meantime?

"*Don't mind then if I do*," Buck muttered and slipped on a pair of dark sunglasses, remembering only when he was too far to turn back for a second interruption, that he'd meant to bring up the unread letters from Shortfellows.

ONLY, Buck didn't take time off. He immediately went to speak with Jack Falltrapp, director and producer of the much smaller, independent Clandestine Pictures. Within two days, Buck was packed and headed for a few weeks in Catalina: on the set of *Dashville Splendor*. It wasn't his usual cup of tea, as far as movies he preferred to star in, but it was something kind of different—*artistic*—and he didn't mind the change of pace. For a fleeting instant, he thought how bad it would look for that billing to show up with his name on it, but these things didn't have the budget for a rushed premier. He would probably have another Sizemore feature wrapping before *Dashville Splendor* ever saw the light of day.

There was still the slightest niggling in the back of his mind while there—how Judith Valentine hadn't offered even one compliment on his performance. No *job well done*. She hadn't even mentioned him at the poor excuse for a wrap party, yet had lavished many thanks on the other talent. Maybe she didn't actually *know* what a real star was. With so many other swell things to focus on now—at the very least, a location that couldn't be beat—Buck managed to shrug off some of his annoyance toward Judith Valentine's ineptitude for praise. It didn't hurt that the vacationing women there just wouldn't stay away from him, and once he was gone, he didn't care if they found out about each other. He scarcely thought about the paycheck, which was a mere drop in the bucket compared to what Sizemore gave him. He had enough money from the picture he'd just finished with them to take care of him for the rest of the year—this chump change was a bonus—and it wasn't like *Dashville Splendor* was all that strenuous to act for. All Buck had to do was pretend to be a big spender at a tropical resort, who got into a bit of trouble with his bookie. It was a quick and easy shoot; a nice escape, and he was back to Hollywood in no time.

THE morning after his return home, Buck awoke to the loud, metallic slap of the mail slot flap. *Probably nothing important*—everyone knew that these days, important news came through the telephone. Still, and now unable to go back to sleep, he got up and had some coffee, some breakfast, and only remembered the arrival of mail when he passed by the front door and saw an envelope lying in the middle of the tiled floor. He felt that peculiar tingling sensation that came with every piece of adoring fan mail, and had yet to get old, but this time it shifted to surprise when he realized that it was from Sizemore Studios.

*Mister Ducats,*
*Report to Judith Valentine's*
*office at 10a.m.*

Buck checked his watch, seeing that it was half-past ten already. He scrambled to get dressed and presentable. What could she possibly be calling him in for, if not to tell him about the next production? He didn't want to miss that! And why didn't she just call him? For a moment, he wondered if it had to do with Shortfellows and his no longer working for them. Surely, Ms. Valentine had taken care of it like she'd said she would. It wasn't like they'd had anything in the works for him for a while now. Buck groaned. He hoped he wouldn't have to go to court over it.

Buck arrived at the studio lot at eleven. As usual, the place was buzzing and hopping with the activity of phones ringing, writers chattering, secretaries twittering,

but unlike his first visit there, or many of them after, no one stopped to even look at him. In fact, it seemed everyone did what they could to avoid it altogether. A few of them got up and, with hats and jackets in hand, left the building without even a nod his way.

Blondie—*Betty* or *Betsey* or somesuch—jumped up from her desk to rush to him. She looked too worried for something that surely could've waited until that moment. After all, and whether Judith Valentine was ready to acknowledge it yet or not, a show could not go on without its star.

"Mister Ducats—Ms. Valentine has been waiting for you—"

"Well, have her wait no more. I have arrived!"

His brilliant smile received only a twitch of one from her before she rushed to Ms. Valentine's office door. The little secretary hesitated and looked back at Buck who had finally caught up with her, before giving a timid knock. She opened the door at Ms. Valentine's command and Buck walked in. He might have noticed how the chatter behind him had stopped, or how the door practically slammed in the secretary's rush to get out of the way, had it not been for Judith Valentine's direct, icy stare. She had her hands folded and resting on her cleared off desk, as though she'd been sitting that way since ten o'clock.

"You're late."

Buck smiled and shrugged. "*Your*

*note* was late, so am I *really?*"

There was no sign of amusement on her part, and for an instant, Buck imagined a worm writhing on a hook, but even after his latest stint of tomcatting, there was something refreshing about seeing this woman again. He recognized that she tried to intimidate him, but it really was igniting.

"Sit down, Mister Ducats." Ms. Valentine remained like a statue, poised cold and tight behind her desk, watching as Buck raised a mischievous eyebrow at her. He thumbed over his shoulder toward the couch.

"There?"

"I don't care, Mister Ducats. Stand if you like. This won't take long."

The tone of her voice smeared his smile into a smirk. "To what do I owe the pleas—"

"Mister Ducats, you've been in breach of your contract."

"What are you talking about? I've been on *vacation!*" Buck laughed as though he'd just heard a real zinger, hoping to deflect the fact that she looked like a volcano near ready to erupt.

"Not only that, but you lied to me about your contract being finished with Shortfellows."

She was clearly riled, but she wasn't the first woman he'd had that effect on. It would be a cinch to smooth those ruffled feathers again—just like it always was with any other woman.

"*Judi*—"

"That's *Ms. Valentine.*"

"*Ms. Valentine,* about that— it really isn't that big of a deal. *Really.* I'm sure it's just some kind of misunderstanding with Shortfellows. And as far as Clandestine—you're not going to lose me to those jokers—they pay in peanuts." He was sure he gave her his most cherubic smile, but when she didn't ease up, he added, "Seriously: there was just such a gap between productions here, and, truth be told, I'm kind of addicted to the craft. I'm still *your* loyal star, but you can't expect me to just sit and wait around, and I'd never put you in a position of having to make that call. I just thought I'd pick up something quick with them. I'd *never* go work full time with them—they're *independent,* for Pete's sake."

"Mister Ducats, your reason for doing it makes absolutely no difference to me. You broke your contract with Shortfellows, and you've broken your contract with us, and you were warned that there would be consequences. You're dismissed."

She turned her attention to pulling some documents from a desk drawer, as though Buck were no longer there. The audacity struck him unlike any other insult he could imagine in the moment, leaving him with his indignation.

"Wait a minute—do you have *any* idea what you're doing? I'm *Buck Ducats.*"

Her smile—the first he'd ever

seen on the woman's face—was glorious and terrifying in its calm beauty and cut him off before her words could.

"*Yes*, you are. But *you should have read your contracts*. Goodbye, Mister Ducats."

"Are you *firing* me?"

Without responding to his weak, uttered realization, Ms. Valentine pressed a buzzer from somewhere beneath her desk, and the door flew open. Before Buck could do much more than turn, a flower sack was put over his head, and meaty hands had a hold of his arms.

"What do you think you're doing? *Wait!* Judi—*Ms. Valentine*—wait!"

The most he could assess was that two thugs had a hold of him now and they were in the process of dragging him out of the office. Hitting like a cold rush of water through his limbs, Buck realized how quiet the rest of the office had become. A telephone rang and he made a stunted attempt to struggle free.

"Hey—*hey!*"

But no one was there to answer him, and the telephone just rang and rang.

A HEAVY hand had come down on him, and the next thing he knew, Buck was waking up with a throbbing pain in his head. His wrists and ankles were bound. Prickly rope rubbed his skin raw where his socks and shirtsleeves should have been, and the ground

was hard and full of cracks that he could feel with the nudging of the toe of his shoe. The air around him had grown uncomfortably dry and hot, as though he'd been placed in a blazing furnace. His tongue felt like sandpaper against the roof of his mouth, and all he could see of the world was a white glow. His pulse began to race even before the flour sack was roughly removed from his head.

With the blinding, overhead sun in his eyes, it took a moment for Buck's eyes to adjust. In one moment, there was nothing. In the next, he could see the two thugs who had dragged him out of Ms. Valentine's office. They were big, faces scarred; one had a nose that had been broken one too many times. Buck scoffed and then smirked.

"Is this some kind of a joke?"

He finally took his eyes off of the two men to see that there was not another soul in sight. He wasn't sure how he felt about that. *Angry? Inconvenienced? Fine*, he'd been late and that had been unprofessional of him. He could admit to that. But that explained nothing.

"What, is this a test? It is, isn't it—just trying to get a rise out of me? Ms. Valentine says I'm canned, to get me all riled up, and then you all bring me out here to try and intimidate me? That's it, isn't it?" His impatience was rising. "What's the matter? Cat got your tongues? Why am I out here?"

By then, the thugs were smiling,

and did they ever look smug.

"Try to enjoy yourself, *Mister Ducats*. Best of luck to you," said one, and the truth of the situation finally hit Buck square in the melon.

"*Hey!* You can't just leave me out here! Someone's gonna come looking for me! Someone's gonna notice I'm gone!"

"Why would anyone notice? You're on *vacation*."

The thugs got a good laugh out of that and Buck attempted to kick at the ground, but since his feet were tied, he just landed on his backside and got a cloud of dust in his face.

"Sure—go back to Sizemore. Go get your pat on the back, *tough guys—*"

"*Sizemore*? Mister Ducats: we're with Shortfellows."

The sharp contrast of the chill in his veins against the desert heat turned his stomach.

"Should've read your contracts, Mac." They began walking back to the car, leaving Buck behind to squirm on the hot ground.

"*What?* Wait! I'll read it now! Come on—I'll read it now!"

But there was no negotiation to be had. He closed his eyes to try and recall any details of the few parts he'd played, to see if he might glean some helpful wisdom, but all he could hear were the two thugs as they got closer to the car.

"Say, Bernie—do you have a copy of that contract on you?"

Bernie gave his pockets a comical

pat. "Nope. Hey, you want to try that new place downtown?"

"*Would I*? I'm famished."

"You know what sounds good? A really big glass of iced tea."

"And a nice, cool slice of lemon meringue pie."

"That's *just* the thing for it."

Buck opened his eyes to the glaring sunlight and a fresh wave of panic, and hollered from behind them, "Tell her! Tell Ms. Valentine—we're supposed to make lottsa movies! I'm the star—*I'm Buck Ducats!*"

The men burst out in laughter as they opened the car doors, never looking back, and then drove away.

Buck scanned the area, frantic, the heat and hard pulse in his head making everything all spotty. Within a few feet of him, he saw movement on the ground: a sidewinder, stirred from Buck's commotion. Just beyond that, a few sharp-needled cacti. There was nothing else in sight but stretches of sandy-colored ground, waving from the heat, below a clear, blue sky. Overhead, a trio of buzzards quickly became a circling octet. There was nothing to do but panic and scream, and one last time, Buck did so up into the blazing sun: *"BUT I'M BUCK DUCATS!"* as though that had ever mattered.

# Tales of the Crimson Keep: Paper Wizard

## By Michael Jan Friedman

NO sooner had Joe seen the demon rise from the scarred, black hills into the iron sky than he reached into the pouch tied to his belt, took out his folded sheet of paper and a charcoal stick, and began writing.

He didn't have long. Less than a minute, he estimated, before the demon and its huge, beating wings covered the distance between them.

*Come on,* he thought, his hand pushing the charcoal stick from word to word. *You can do this.*

The wind howled, driving clouds of black grit across the blasted landscape. In the distance, lightning slit the sky like a knife. Under the weight of the ensuing thunder, the ground trembled beneath Joe's feet.

And all the while, the demon got closer.

Joe tried to hurry, but not so much that his handwriting became illegible. The last thing he wanted was to have to start his spell all over again.

He could hear the drumbeat of the demon's wings against the air, see the dust swirl in tight little twisters across the ground below them. The hairs on the back of Joe's neck prickled. *Come on...*

He'd memorized the spell before he got there. *Long* before. It wasn't hard—a great many spells started out the same way.

All he had to do was customize the thing so it pertained to the particular demon he was facing, and then—of course—write it. It was the writing part that was the problem.

*Quick as the wind,* he thought, cheering himself on. *Quick as—*

Suddenly, the demon was *there.*

It loomed above him, its eyes chips of red fire set into its skull, its black-veined wings blotting out the sky. As thunder droned in Joe's ears, his adversary alighted on the barren plain.

It wasn't the biggest demon Joe had ever laid eyes on, but it was big *enough.* It could snap him in half with a swipe of its talon.

*Let's go,* he thought, writing that much faster, for he no longer had the luxury of doing otherwise. *For the love of heaven, let's go...*

The demon tilted its long, reptilian head and regarded Joe with its smoldering red eyes. Then it asked, in the sort of deep, rasping voice one associated with a demon, "What are you doing?"

Joe wasn't finished. He needed *time.*

*Illustration by Mark Wheatley*

He'd always been a fast talker at heart. But fast-talking required some thinking, some strategy, and he didn't dare break his concentration. So he resorted to the only option open to him, which was also the last one the demon would expect: *Honesty.*

"I'll be with you," he said, "in just a moment."

The demon made a sound in its throat as if it were drowning in half-clotted blood. "You didn't answer my question, human. I asked what you were *doing.*"

"Sorry," said Joe, concentrating with all his might on his spell. "I don't mean to be rude..."

"Be rude all you like," said his adversary. "Be disgusting. I'm a demon. It's all the same to me."

"Thanks for understanding."

"I didn't say I *understood*," the demon rumbled. "I just said it wouldn't bother me if you were rude. Some demons might be bothered but I'm not one of them. What I *don't* like is to be kept waiting. That's a different story entirely."

Joe's fingers felt like they were on fire. "Again," he said, "my apologies."

"I'm on a schedule," said the demon. "A tight one, handed down to me by my superiors. It might not look like it to the likes of you, but it's so. Which is why I would appreciate a sense of urgency."

Joe could feel a drop of sweat tracing a path down the side of his face. He tried to ignore it, to keep working.

"And yet," said the demon, "you're still doing...whatever it is you're doing, aren't you? Exactly how long is this going to take?"

Joe sighed. "I wish I knew."

The demon scrunched up its hideous countenance. "You *wish* you knew? You must have at least an estimate."

Joe shook his head, his eyes still affixed to his paper, which he was gradually filling with the requisite words. "Sorry..."

"How is that possible?" The demon made a sound of exasperation. "How long did it take last time?"

Joe looked up apologetically. "Actually..."

The demon's eyes widened as the truth dawned on it. "Lords of Darkness...there *was* no last time. Is that how it is? This is your first attempt at weaving a spell?"

"Not at all," Joe assured the demon, returning his attention to his task. "I've done this many times. Just...you know, not under these circumstances..."

The demon's eyes slitted. "Meaning...?"

"Meaning in an encounter with a demon." Joe's hand was cramping—painfully—but he didn't dare stop. Not when he was so close. "I'm almost done," he said. "Shouldn't be long now."

The demon came closer and tilted its head to one side. "How do you expect to work magic when you're busy writing?"

"A good question," Joe replied.

"An *excellent* question. But as I said—"

"Wait a second...are you writing your *spell*?" The demon sounded horrified as it caught on. "Actually *writing* it?"

It wasn't the style of wizardry to which Joe had aspired as a youth. Not by a long shot. However, he hadn't much choice in the matter. "If you'll be patient just half a second longer..."

"This is none of my business, I'll grant you," said the demon, "but how do you expect to prevail over an adversary when you have to *write* your spell rather than *say* it?"

Joe had asked himself the same question. More than once, in fact. "Seems unwieldy, I know."

"Unwieldy? It's...absurd. The only reason I've let you go on so long is you're a novelty to me. Other demons won't be so easily entertained, I assure you."

Joe had no doubt. "I appreciate the advice."

"I don't offer it for your benefit alone. I'm thinking of the demons you'll encounter. If you take into account *their* needs as well as your own, everyone will be better off. Time is precious, after all. That's one thing we can all agree on."

Finally, Joe came to the end of the spell. "At last!" he exclaimed—and held his paper up before his adversary.

At which point...nothing happened.

Joe's heart sank. He'd worked so hard...

"At last *what*?" asked the demon.

"At last I banish you to whatever loathsome place you came from," Joe muttered.

The demon took a moment to examine itself. "I'm not banished."

"You're not," Joe conceded. "I can see that."

"You did something wrong."

*Obviously*, Joe thought.

The demon held out a claw-like appendage. "Let me see what you've got there."

Joe was understandably reluctant to hand his spell over to his adversary. "Um..."

"Come," said the demon. "If I'd wanted to destroy you, I've had ample opportunity, wouldn't you say?"

*Ample*, Joe conceded, *and more*. He handed over the spell.

The demon read it, using a long, curved talon to keep its place on the paper. Then it asked, "What's a *pissant*?"

Joe didn't recall writing such a word. "Where do you see that?"

The demon pointed to the word. "Right here. *Pissant*."

"No," said Joe, craning his neck. "It says *puissant*."

The demon read the word again, then shook its head. "I beg to differ. It clearly says *pissant*. And down here...where it says anniversary..."

"That's *adversary*."

"*You* may say it's adversary. But if you asked twenty scholars, I'd wager nineteen of them would say *anniversary*. And that's being generous."

Joe was about to object...except the demon was right, wasn't it? Joe's penmanship simply wasn't all that it might have been.

Nor was the demon the first to have remarked on it.

Back at the Academy, Joe's instructor, Norbert, had repeatedly pointed out Joe's inability to render letters in a recognizable and useful way. "Joe," he'd say, "your hand-writing is an abomination."

To which Joe had been forced to reply, "It is indeed."

To another wizard, it might not have been such a big deal. But to a wizard whose lot in life was to *write* his spells...

It was no small matter.

Determined to bolster Joe's prospects, Norbert had arranged for his student to receive remedial courses in handwriting. And Joe, for his part, had attended them religiously. They seemed to help a little too, especially at first. But in the end, his handwriting still left much to be desired.

"Practice," Norbert had told him. "That's what you need. Lots and lots of practice." And Joe had taken the advice to heart.

Every night, while his fellow aco-lytes were in bed, he stayed up to practice his penmanship. It was a good thing there were only twenty-six characters in the alphabet or he would never have slept at all.

Over time he refined his tech-nique, no question about it. *Yet clearly*, Joe thought as he stared into the demon's baleful eyes,

there on the Field of Twisted Iron, *it wasn't enough.*

"Pardon my saying so," said the demon, "but some humans are cut out for wizardry and some are not. I would say you're of the latter variety."

Joe wanted to argue with him. But how could he?

"From all I've heard," said the demon, returning Joe's paper to him, "there are *other* ways to make a living in your world. A great number of them. I suggest you pick one and pursue it, and forget about casting spells."

Then he turned his back on Joe, beat his wings, and ascended again into the iron sky. He didn't so much as cast a glance back over his shoulder to see if Joe was up to something.

Under different circumstances, it would have been a disrespectful gesture indeed—one that called for the most prodigious magical barrage Joe could manage. But he wasn't about to go after a demon that had so generously spared his life.

Besides, the most prodigious barrage he could manage wasn't going to happen in time to make a difference.

Joe heaved a sigh. *Perhaps the demon's right. Perhaps I'm just not cut out for this.*

But being a wizard was his life's goal, and had been for as long as he could remember. How could he give it up now, after he'd gone through the entire grueling course at the Academy?

Joe pulled back on the fingers of his writing hand, stretching the ligaments in their joints. They felt even more cramped than when he had labored over spells in his wizardry classes.

He had been lucky to find himself pitted against so reasonable a demon. He *knew* that. Nor would he find a monster so reasonable a second time, much less in the course of what he'd always hoped would be a lengthy career.

*If I expect to fight such adversaries effectively*, he thought, *I'm going to have to make some improvements.*

JOE wasn't a moron. Painfully aware of the limitations that came with spell writing, he had taken measures to streamline the process. At one point, he had considered writing his spells entirely in advance.

It was a clever idea. Unfortunately, it had drawbacks. One was that it meant carrying as many as fifty different spells, and going through them on the spot until he found the right one. That proved more time-consuming than writing the spells from scratch.

In an attempt to adapt, he'd organized the spells by category. In theory, a good idea as well. But in practice, he'd had trouble finding the category he was looking for. He found he could hide only so many pockets in his clothes, and only some of them could be close at hand.

*What about writing part of a spell and customizing it on the spot?* Not a chance, his instructors advised him, if he meant to get further than a sentence or two. His words had to be written in the right order. He couldn't leave a blank—say, to accommodate a particular condition or type of adversary—and just fill it in when necessary. Nor, for that matter, could he cross out a word and replace it with a different one.

Joe wished he had done better on his entrance exam and thereby earned himself a more promising course of wizardry. Water magic, for instance. Or fire magic. Or even the kind of magic that required spells uttered in rhymes. But he hadn't. He'd scored last in his class—*dead* last, he'd been notified—and there was no point in complaining about it.

Before he went to wizardry school, he could talk his way out of anything. *A real horse trader,* his grandfather on the Snyder side of the family used to say. And his grandfather would know, having been an *actual* horse trader for the better part of his life.

But horse-trading wasn't a skill they prized in wizard school. What they prized, it had soon become clear to Joe, were precisely the skills he lacked.

FORTUNATELY, Joe found himself the beneficiary of an idea.

Even before he quit the Field of Twisted Iron amid looks of disgust from the heavy-browed stalwarts commanding Man's armies...long before he left the threat of demon-kind behind, and returned to the safety of his own mortal world... he knew what he would do to improve his lot.

He would find the wizard known as Tom.

And he did. He found Tom on Tom's family's farm in the green hills north of Ulsper Town. Found him, unfortunately, in the season during which manure was spread liberally across the fields to encourage a bountiful crop. Manure so fresh and fragrant that Joe's eyes burned and filled with tears.

But then, an improvement in one's circumstances often required a measure of sacrifice.

On the surface, Tom was unremarkable in every way. He was of average height and average weight, with the most common shade of brown hair and the most common brown eyes. His face was the kind one might forget rather easily. And he spoke without any discernible accent, the first person Joe had ever met who could be said to do so.

Yet he was the sort of fellow who could do wonders for a magician of Joe's stripe, which was why Joe had decided to pay Tom a visit. "So you're on leave for a bit," Joe observed after he and Tom had exchanged pleasantries.

"I am," said Tom. "Not required back on the Field of Twisted Iron for an entire fortnight."

"That's good," said Joe. "Take your rest while you can get it, I say."

"Right," said Tom. "Under whom did you say you studied?"

Joe smiled. "Norbert."

"Ah, yes. I believe I met him one time. Had a wart on his nose, did he?"

"That was him, all right. A wart the size of my ear. So...is it true you were the fastest wizard in your class?"

Tom blushed. "I was. The fastest in *any* class, or so I was told."

"And how fast is that, precisely?"

"You mean, say, in feet per second?"

"That would do."

"In feet per second, I have no idea. That is, I've never measured myself that way."

"I see. Then how *have* you measured yourself?"

"That's the thing...I *haven't*."

Joe sighed. Tom, it seemed, was remarkable in at least one sense: He was rather dense. "Perhaps," he suggested, "you can just *show* me how fast you are."

"All right. How shall I do that?"

Joe pointed across the rolling fields of Tom's family's farm. "You see that chestnut tree? The one over there?"

"The one beside the road?" Tom asked.

"The same. Why don't you bring me a chestnut from that tree?"

"All right," said Tom. But he didn't move. He just stood there.

"Any time you're ready," said Joe.

"Actually," said Tom, "I'm done." He held out his hand and spread his fingers to show Joe the chestnut lying on his palm. "Would you like to see it again?"

"No," said Joe wonderingly. "That won't be necessary. I think we've established how fast you are. But there is something more I'd like to know. I've heard you can make others fast as well, just by placing your hand on their shoulder."

"That's so," said Tom. "Their shoulder or, for that matter, any other part of them."

"The shoulder will do," Joe said.

He was heartened. Tom was everything he had heard. With such a partner, he wouldn't have to worry anymore about how quickly he could write.

But first, he had to make Tom want to *be* that partner.

"So we'll work together," Joe said.

Tom's brow puckered. "Together, you say?"

"Indeed."

"I've always worked on my own."

"As have I," said Joe. "And I could continue to do—successfully, you understand—but that's not why I became a wizard in the first place. You know why I became a wizard?"

Tom frowned. "Because...?"

"Because I want to help people. And of all those I have encountered, whom do I wish to help the most?"

Tom's frown deepened. "The people..."

"The people with whom I share a passion for wizardry. *Exactly.* So I ask myself how I can help such people, and my answer is this: By giving them a chance to be more effective at their chosen profession than they have ever been before."

"And how—"

"How may I do this?" Joe was in full horse-trader mode. "By joining their power to mine, thereby creating a team the likes of which no demon can stand against."

"A team?"

"That's right."

"But...how would that work...?"

"Easy," said Joe. "Instead of one of us facing a demon, we would all three do so."

"Three?"

"Yes." And Joe described the third member of their team.

"She's agreed to this?" Tom asked.

"I've...um...yet to speak with her," he admitted.

"Then how—"

"Look," said Joe, "I've been able to convince *you* to join the team. How much harder can it be to convince *her*?"

Technically, Tom hadn't joined the team at all. At least not yet. And from what Joe knew of their prospective comrade, it might not be so easy to make her see things his way.

But Tom was the trusting sort. He shrugged. "All right."

Joe smiled. "Splendid."

A minute after they took leave of each other, Joe found it utterly impossible to remember Tom's face. But that didn't matter. It wasn't Tom's looks that would transform

Joe's wizardry into a force to be reckoned with on the battlefields of the Demon Wars.

RHEDIS, more properly known as Rhedis Alina Dickens, spent every morning sitting at the top of Tarrant Falls, which plunged more than a hundred feet from a forbidding granite crag into a frothing pool below, and eventually become the River Tarrant.

She did so without fail, or so Joe had been apprised by the gentlepeople in the local tavern.

Once he had learned that aspect of Rhedis's schedule, he made it his business to visit Tarrant Falls. Unfortunately, it wasn't easy to get to the top of them. The only path had been carved into the cliff face long ago, and was made slick by the unceasing spray. Nonetheless, Joe thought, if Rhedis could make the ascent, so he could he.

By the time he reached his destination, he was so wet his clothes were sticking to his skin, and his feet were squishing inside his shoes. However, he soon caught sight of Rhedis.

Joe had heard she was small, but she was even smaller than he'd been led to believe. As small as a ten year old, he reckoned. Her hair, on the other hand, was very long, and very black, and lustrous as a sable under the light of a full moon.

As for grace, she displayed no more of it in her bearing or her demeanor than the average woman. Perhaps less. But Joe didn't need the

grace she personified. He needed the grace she could bring to bear in a magical spell.

"I beg your pardon," he said as he approached Rhedis, greeting her over the roar of the water.

She turned to him in response, her eyes as wide and innocent as a doe's. But she didn't say anything.

*She's shy,* Joe thought.

It was all right. He'd met his share of shy people, and they'd proven no more impervious to his horse-trading skills than anyone else.

"My name is Joe," he said. He smiled his most charming smile. "We studied together at the Academy."

Rhedis's brow creased ever so slightly.

"My professor was Norbert? You must remember him. The fellow with the wart on his nose?"

The crease disappeared. *Progress,* Joe thought.

"Mind if I sit down?" he asked.

Rhedis just peered at him with her nut-brown eyes. *I'll take that as an invitation,* he thought.

Unfortunately, Rhedis had taken the only comfortable spot by the falls—a shaded patch of thick, green moss overlaying a portion of smooth, granite surface. Joe was forced to resort to a hard, mossless perch beside her.

He smiled his charming smile again. "Lovely place. I can see why you've grown fond of it."

Rhedis gazed at Joe a moment longer. Then she spoke, so clearly and distinctly that the thunder of the falls was no detriment to his hearing. And what she said was: "Get bent."

It took Joe a moment to absorb the words. After all, the remark was so out of keeping with Rhedis's diffidence.

*I misheard,* he thought. Sometimes words came out sounding like other words. It happened. Nor had he come all that way to fail in his mission thanks to a trick of his ears.

Joe was about to ask his companion to repeat what she'd said, if she didn't mind, when she leaned toward him and, with a curl of her lip, all but spat the word: *"Bent."*

Joe felt a hot spurt of anger, but he bit it back. He wasn't going to get anywhere if a little invective could stop him.

He took a deep breath and let it out. Then, softly and reasonably, he said, "Obviously, I've managed to offend you. I assure you, that wasn't my intent."

*"Bent!"* Rhedis screamed at him.

As a drowning man clings to a wooden plank, Joe clung to what remained of his resolve. "I'm certain," he said, putting one word in front of the other, "that it's been frustrating for you to apply what you learned at the Academy. Grace alone doesn't win the day against demons, no matter how lovely and mesmerizing your spellcasting may be."

Rhedis cast a withering glance at him, but at least she didn't say *bent* again. Joe took that as encouragement.

"What I'm offering you," he told Rhedis, "is the chance to *do* something with your ability. The chance to use it the way you always hoped to use it. *Effectively.*"

She was listening, it seemed to him. He kept going.

"I'm fine on my own, you understand. But personal accomplishment only goes so far. What good is my magical prowess if it can't improve the lots of others? *Your* lot, for instance?"

And he explained what he had in mind.

Rhedis nodded—always a good portent, if Joe's experience as a horse trader meant anything at all. Her gaze softened too.

"I spoke too soon," she said in a perfectly reasonable voice.

*I've got her,* Joe thought.

Then Rhedis's eyes flashed, and her mouth twisted, and Joe felt like he was in the embrace of a vicious, dark storm. "Don't just get bent," Rhedis told him, each word the crack of a whip. "Get torn to pieces so small and bloody no one will be able to recognize any of them as yours!"

Joe recoiled as if he had been struck with a giant fist. He had never witnessed such a venomous display. Not in his entire life.

Again, anger rose in him like bile. *Who the hell does she think she is?* Certainly, Rhedis contained a lot of nastiness for someone so diminutive.

He got up and brushed himself off. Then he took his leave of

Rhedis Alina Dickens.

*Well*, he thought as he descended from the crag overlooking the waterfall, *that could have gone better.*

IT was all right, Joe told himself. Tom's participation was the key. Rhedis's contribution would have made their lives easier, certainly, but they would get by without it.

A day later, Joe received new orders. He was to return to the Demon Wars and revisit the Field of Twisted Iron. His first mission, which had ended before it could get anywhere, had been simply to observe troop movements.

His second mission was the same. However, he was advised, this time he would do better to complete some actual observing.

Joe understood the lack of confidence in him evinced by the commanders of Man's armies. And were he on his own, it might be justified. But with Tom along, he had hopes of success.

"So what happened to her?" Tom asked as he and Joe left the tents of Man behind and started off across the blasted plain.

"Who?" Joe asked.

"The other wizard. Rhedis, her name was."

Joe pretended to study one of his barely-begun spell writings. "It turned out she wouldn't have been of use to us after all."

"But you said—"

"No need to worry," Joe interjected. He smiled at Tom. "We have all the wizardry we need right here."

That seemed to quell Tom's concerns.

AFTER what seemed like a long time, Joe spied movement on the horizon—that of dark figures made tiny by distance. "There," he said, pointing. "Demon troops."

"And we're to observe them," said Tom, appearing to fix the idea firmly in his mind.

"We are," Joe confirmed. "Nothing more, nothing less."

"And report back."

"That's correct. We needn't—"

Before Joe could finish his advisory, he heard the sound of leathery wings beating the air somewhere behind them—doing so in a far-off way, to be sure, but also unmistakably.

"Joe?" said Tom.

"I know," said Joe. "I hear it too."

He swore beneath his breath. *Could this not have waited until we did some observing? Even a little?*

The Field of Twisted Iron was a big place, after all. And demons didn't have the best eyesight. Yet for the second time, he had been spotted before he could do what he'd set out to do.

*It's all right*, he assured himself. *It'll be different this time. You've got Tom.*

Joe took a breath, opened his pouch, and extracted his paper and his charcoal. Then he turned around.

Sure enough, a demon was bearing down on them, its huge wings propelling it over the blighted ground. It was a particularly powerful and cruel-looking speci-men, one that bore no resemblance to the demon Joe had encountered the last time. A demon that looked utterly disinclined to show his adversaries the slightest hint of good sportsmanship.

"Now?" Tom asked.

"Yes," Joe said. "*Now.*"

Tom placed his hand on Joe's shoulder.

Suddenly, Joe's charcoal stick started to fly across the page. So quickly, in fact, that it was little more than a blur. Nor did his hand cramp up as it had in the past.

Tom's speed was every bit the difference-maker Joe had hoped it would be. He finished the spell in a matter of seconds.

There was but one problem: When Joe examined the spell, he found it completely and utterly unintelligible.

Tom was peering over Joe's shoulder, a look of concern on his face. "Are you all right?"

"I've been better," Joe said.

If Joe's handwriting had been a problem before, it was even more so now. Speeding up the process had put one problem to rest but it had rather energetically revived another one.

*I should have known this would happen,* Joe thought.

As a horse trader, he had prided himself on talking others into doing as he wished. This time he had done it to himself.

"It doesn't look so good," Tom observed.

"No," said Joe, "it doesn't."

*Grace,* he thought. It would have made a difference. *It still can,* he added silently.

But Rhedis had *dis*graced him. He wasn't going to get down on his knees and beg for her assistance.

The demon, meanwhile, was almost on top of them. Suddenly, rather than rake them with its talons, it pulled up, beat its wings to brake its progress, and landed on the barren plain.

And Joe had a feeling he knew why: The demon from his first encounter had spread the word. *He writes his spells, if you can believe such a thing! Actually* writes *them! With a charcoal stick!*

"You're the one," the demon looming over Joe and Tom rumbled, confirming Joe's suspicion.

Then, before Joe knew what was happening, the monster struck Tom with a sweep of its gigantic wing.

Joe had never seen a man fly—actually *fly*—through the air. But before Joe's eyes, Tom flew. He flew high and he flew far. But in the end, the worst part wasn't the flying.

It was the landing—and the *crack* that accompanied it.

Forgetting about the demon, Joe scrabbled across the barren ground. By the time he reached Tom, his pulse was pounding in his ears. *Let him be alive,* Joe prayed inwardly. *Please let him be alive...*

Tom's eyes were closed and he wasn't moving. Joe was afraid to touch him. What if Tom was all crushed inside? Moving him might finish him off.

Then again, *not* moving him might finish him off as well. And the demon might finish them *both* off before Joe decided one way or the other.

But it didn't. To Joe's overwhelming relief, the demon took to the air again, wheeled, and flew off, its immense wings carrying it swiftly across the Field of Twisted Iron—as if neither Joe nor Tom was worth its attention any longer.

A moment later, Joe saw why. The line of distant demon soldiers he had spotted had come up against another line—one of human soldiers, if the dark knot of conflict between them was any indication.

The winged monstrosity that had swatted Tom had flown off to back up the demons' ground forces—giving Joe a chance to look after his comrade. He put his mouth next to Tom's ear and said, "Tom...?"

Tom didn't respond. Was he even breathing?

Joe put his ear to Tom's chest. He could hear a heartbeat but it sounded faint.

*I've got to help him*, Joe thought.

But what could he do? He wasn't a doctor. He was just a—

*A wizard.*

There were lots of different kinds of magic—magic to fell demons, magic to move earth or air or water, magic to plant love or hate or courage in the heart.

And magic to heal the infirm.

Joe had never learned how to use his magic to help anyone—only to fight demons. With the Demon Wars raging, that was pretty much all he and his peers were asked to do.

But without his help, Tom would certainly perish.

*And it would be my fault. Mine.*

Joe knew the demon that had sent Tom flying might come back at any time. If Joe devoted all his attention to Tom rather than to escaping, Joe might end up dying as well.

It didn't matter. He couldn't abandon his companion. That in mind, he started writing.

It would take a strong spell to make Tom whole again, or anything close to it. Unfortunately, strong spells took longer than weaker ones, and Joe no longer had Tom's speed to draw on.

It didn't matter. One eye on the battle in the distance, Joe wrote as fast as he could, and hoped his spell was at least passably legible when he was done.

JUST as he had before, Joe found Rhedis seated on her patch of moss beside the waterfall that fed the River Tarrant.

Even when he came within a few yards of her, she barely spared him a glance. He waved. She didn't wave back. What she did was grimace, as if to say *You again?*

"I'm back," Joe said, "yes. But I'm not the same fellow who came to you last time with an offer of partnership."

Finally she turned to him, eyes narrowed. "You're not?"

"Not at all."

She looked him over, top to bottom. "In what way are you different?"

"I'm intent on telling the truth this time. And the truth is...I'm a failure as a wizard. A thorough and unmitigated failure. Though not for lack of trying. If trying were all it took, I'd be the champion wizard of all time. But I'm not."

Rhedis regarded him. Clearly, it wasn't what she had expected to hear.

"I'm not here to help you," Joe said, "as I professed earlier. I'm here because I need *you* to help *me*. You see, I took our colleague Tom to the Field of Twisted Iron in the hope that he would make me something I'm not. And I got him hurt. Killed, almost. Somehow I managed to pull him back together and get the both of us home, but it was close.

"I told Tom I'd had it—that I had no wish to risk his life again. Or mine, for that matter. However, he wouldn't let me off the hook. Innocent that he is, he wishes us to take on another mission.

"We've been lucky, all things considered. But we won't be lucky forever. We need a hand. *Your* hand.

"I won't blame you if you say no. Hells, no is certainly what *I* would say. But if there's even the slightest drop of pity in your heart, I'm hoping you'll make me the undeserving beneficiary of it."

Rhedis looked away. Joe hoped, as the moments passed, that she would look back, even a little. But she didn't. He waited for what seemed like a long time. The result was no better.

*All right, then*, he thought, accepting his fate. He had poured out his heart to the woman and failed to move her. *That's it.*

He turned to go. Slowly, in case Rhedis suddenly found it in her heart to pity him, or to reward him for his honesty, or perhaps both.

She did neither. In the end, Joe left empty-handed. But doing so didn't feel as bad as it had last time. At least he was leaving with a clean conscience.

THIS time, Joe and Tom weren't charged with observing troop movements. It was their job to convey a single message from one encampment of Men to another not so far away. Just that and nothing more.

After all, the commanders of Man's armies didn't give their most important assignments to wizards who had failed twice already. They reserved such assignments for mages who had proven themselves.

Still, it was a *mission*.

And it remained as much for several hours as Joe and Tom traversed the Field of Twisted Iron. Nor did they run into trouble of any sort. *None.*

Until, less than a mile from their destination, almost within spitting distance of the Black River, Joe heard the all-too-familiar sound of wings beating.

"Uh oh," said Tom.

*Uh oh indeed*, Joe thought.

He took a look back over his shoulder. This time, it wasn't just one demon in hot pursuit of them, but two. And though one was bigger than the other, even the smaller one—a speckled specimen with curved horns on his head—was no doubt capable of ripping them to shreds.

Without taking his eyes off them, Joe removed his writing implements from their pouch. "We can do this," he told Tom.

"Of course we can," said Tom, placing his hand on Joe's shoulder.

As Joe wrote—mindful not to write *too* fast, lest he turn out an unqualified mess—the demons dropped down in front of the two wizards, their eyes flashing with fiery intensity. Dust kicked up in front of them.

*Come on*, Joe thought, concentrating as he moved his charcoal across the page. He remembered the way the demon had sent Tom flying last time. *Come on...*

"Hang on," said the bigger demon. "I've heard of this one."

"Curse me," said the speckled demon. "It's the one who writes down his spells, isn't it?"

"I believe it is," said the bigger one. "What kind of wizard does that?"

"It must be an awful inconvenience."

"What do you suppose his friend does? Sing? Dance? Regale us with humorous stories?"

The two demons laughed. It wasn't a pleasant sound. In fact, it was less pleasant than the other sounds they made, and that was saying something.

Still, the longer they laughed, the longer Joe had to write out his spell. That was a good thing. But would it be good *enough*?

Joe wished he could be confident in the outcome. But well before he reached the end of his spell, he had reason to be otherwise. He could see some of the same problems as before had arisen, if not in quite the same number.

In time, perhaps he and Tom might find the right balance between speed and legibility. But, clearly, they weren't there yet.

*We're doomed*, Joe thought, seeing the demons had tired of taunting and were advancing on the wizards to do some damage. *Doomed.*

And Joe was the one who had recruited Tom in the first place. If they perished, it would be all his fault.

"Joe," Tom whispered.

"Not now," said Joe. "I'm writing."

Tom pointed.

Then Joe saw her. She looked so tiny making her way across the blasted landscape, even tinier than she'd looked sitting by the side of the waterfall.

*Rhedis...*

Unfortunately, Joe wasn't the only one who'd noticed her. The demons had caught sight of her too.

"She came," said Tom.

"Tom," Joe said, "we need to get to her before *they* do."

For once, Tom seemed to grasp the nuances of the situation. Putting his hand on Joe's shoulder, he said, *"Run!"*

Joe ran. But not as he'd ever run before. The land on either side of him became no more than a blur. And when it stopped blurring, Rhedis was standing there in front of him.

"Down!" Joe cried, and drove Rhedis to the ground.

A demon's scaly belly swept over them an instant later, so close that Joe could smell the enemy's hot, fetid breath.

Joe raised his head high enough to look into Rhedis's eyes. "I can't tell you—" he began.

"Shut up," said Rhedis, "and start a new spell."

"Right," Joe said, and did as he was told.

They had to duck another attack by one of the demons, of course. But thanks to Tom, the work went quickly. And not *just* quickly, because Rhedis had placed her hand on Joe's other shoulder

He was done in a heartbeat. And what he held in his hands wasn't anything like what he'd produced before. It was as if someone with handwriting much better than Joe's had sat down and taken their time and rendered the text of the spell as beautifully as they possibly could.

So beautifully that Joe wanted to take the parchment home, and frame it, and put it in a place of honor where the light that shone on it was never too thin or too harsh but always just right, as long as the sun was in the sky.

*That* beautifully.

It was a veritable masterpiece of spell-writing. But Joe hadn't made the thing to show it off. He'd had a purpose. And with that purpose firmly in mind, he turned to the demons and held up his spell.

"Here!" he cried, his voice echoing off the rocks of the blasted plain. "Take a look at *this*!"

The demons looked at him. Joe looked back at them. But nothing happened to the demons. Joe felt the blood leave his face.

*What now?* he thought.

He'd put it all together. Speed. Grace. *It should have worked.*

Then, suddenly...it *did*.

The demons looked as if invisible hands had grabbed them and begun to squeeze as hard as they could. The monsters writhed. They screamed. They cursed Joe and his mates with all manner of torment.

But they wouldn't get a chance to make good on their curses. Not when Joe's spell had so trapped them in its grasp.

"What now?" Tom asked.

*What now indeed?* Joe thought, unaccustomed to enjoying the upper hand on the Field of Twisted Iron.

Then he knew what he had to do. He had to let the demons go. That way they could spread the word: wherever Joe and his partners might be, demons were unwelcome.

So he released his adversaries—and watched them fly off into the iron sky with all the alacrity they could muster. It was exactly the sort of result Joe had hoped for when it first occurred to him to team with Tom and Rhedis.

Tom hugged Joe so hard that Joe thought his ribs would break. "We did it!"

Joe smiled at Rhedis and gasped, "We *all* did."

Just then, he saw Rhedis do something she had never done before—at least not in his presence. He saw her *smile*.

JOE had never before been called before the Council of Wizards.

He had glimpsed its members individually, of course, at some function or other during his time at the Academy. But never together, and never in their administrative capacity.

They were a formidable looking trio: Errisket of Sevenholm, Korrd of Kendisia Landing, and Milicron of Gordongasp.

"Have a seat," rumbled Milicron, whose gray beard was so long it ended in a pool in his lap.

"Yes, do," chortled Errisket, the only female on the Council. She extended a bony finger in the direction of the only unoccupied chair in the tower room, a rickety-looking wooden specimen set up to face the wizards.

"Thank you," said Joe. He sat down and regarded the wizards, who regarded him back.

For a time, no one spoke. Then Korrd—a thickset fellow with a snow-white walrus moustache—said in a voice punctuated with odd little gasps and grunts, "We understand you had some success recently. You and your compatriots."

"By the Black River," Errisket added.

"Is this true?" asked Milicron.

Joe nodded. "We did, in fact."

"Against not one demon," Korrd snuffled, "but two."

"That's so," said Joe.

Milicron nodded. "Impressive."

"I'm pleased you think so," said Joe.

"And your companions..." Korrd harrumphed. "An unlikely combination."

"That Rhedis," said Errisket. "Not an easy woman to deal with."

"Not easy at all," Milicron added.

"Oh, I don't know," Joe said, uncomfortable with the idea of discussing Rhedis's shortcomings when she wasn't there to defend herself.

"You disagree?" Korrd asked from under a pair of bushy eyebrows.

"She was a challenge at first," Joe noted, "but that had as much to do with *me* as with *her*. And once we understood each other, she couldn't have been a better comrade."

"Really," said Korrd. He exchanged glances with his peers. "And Tom? I've heard he isn't the brightest coal in the brazier."

Joe was starting to get annoyed. "What Tom lacks in one respect, he more than makes up in others. Much like me."

Korrd snorted. It was a distinctly disparaging snort, so disparaging that it made Joe forget where he was for a moment. Eyeing Korrd, he said, "Much like *you*, I imagine."

The words had barely left Joe's mouth before it occurred to him that he'd gone too far. Perhaps *much* too far. It was one thing to defend his teammate—his *friend*—and quite another to disrespect a member of the venerable Council of Wizards.

*Crap*, Joe thought, seeing Korrd's expression harden. *Crap, crap, crap...*

All he had worked for...all his teammates had worked for...had he squandered it with a single indiscretion?

He was certain of it—until Milicron began to make a sound in his beard. It took Joe a little while to realize that the sound wasn't an expression of discomfort but rather...a *laugh*.

A laugh that grew, and grew some more, until it became a full-throated roar. Red-faced, Milicron threw his head back and slapped his knee, and still he couldn't stop laughing.

"Sorry," he said, gasping for breath, "sorry, but I...I couldn't hold it in any longer..."

Then Korrd began to laugh too.

It was a hardy laugh, a thunderous laugh, worthy of a man as physically powerful-looking as he was. And a moment later, Errisket chortled a bit as well.

"Perhaps now," she said, "you understand the potential we saw in you."

Joe didn't know what she was talking about. "Potential? To write *spells...?*"

"Of *course* not," Korrd bellowed.

"But," said Joe, "writing spells was what I was trained to do."

Milicron dismissed the idea with a fillip of his hand. "It was *one* of the things you were trained to do. But not the thing we expected would be of the most help to us."

Joe shook his head. "Pardon my lack of clarity, but—"

Milicron held up a bony hand. "We have plenty of wizardly mechanics."

"Indeed," said Errisket.

"More than we know what to do with," Korrd added.

"They move rocks," said Errisket. "They bring rain. They cloud the mind."

"But good as they are," said Milicron, "they're not always successful in carrying out their missions. And why?"

Korrd leaned forward in his chair. "Because they work alone."

"It's as if they're trying to stand in a windstorm," said Milicron. "By themselves, they're no match for the wind. They get blown over. Roll around a lot, get sand in their eyes..."

"He's fond of analogies," said Errisket.

"In this particular analogy," said Korrd, slapping Milicron on the back, "a single wizard gets blown over by the wind. But two together just might stand their ground. And three—"

"May withstand a gale," said Errisket.

Milicron stopped her with a raised forefinger. "*Most* gales, you understand. Some are simply too—"

Korrd smiled at Joe. "You get the idea."

"Wizards do better when they work together," Errisket said, driving the point home.

"And yet they don't," said Milicron. "Or more to the point, *can't*. We have a theory..."

"Yes," said Errisket. "You see, the ability to wield magic is a rare talent. So is the ability to work with others. And the ability to do both? That's rarer still."

"Which," said Korrd, "is where *you* come in. Your wizardly talent, my boy, is coordinating the efforts of other wizards. And that you have done very well."

Joe shook his head. "Why... why didn't you *say* so in the first place? I—"

Errisket held a hand up. "Some things are best said, and some are best discovered on one's own."

Joe stared at her. At all three of them. "So my entrance exam...?"

"We lied," Milicron confessed. "Actually, you did rather well."

"And all those late nights..."

"Were necessary," said Korrd. "Not to teach you to write spells, but to teach you how much work a wizard must put in to learn his craft."

"Or," said Errisket, "*her* craft. Only then can you appreciate the value of another wizard's contribution. Or in your case, the contributions of *two* wizards."

"Not that your classmates were required to undergo the rigors you did," said Milicron. "Because, as we realized early on, you were different from your classmates."

"Special," said Korrd.

"Not unique, mind you," Milicron added. "I wouldn't say unique. We come across such as you every so often."

Korrd pointed at Joe. "But special nonetheless. And now that you've shown us you can lead a team, you'll have ample chance to do so."

"Of course," said Errisket, "you'll be in charge of a more strategically valuable assemblage of wizards. The kind who are impressively puissant on their own."

Joe nodded. "Of course."

Milicron shrugged. "It might take them some time to get accustomed to your leadership. But in the end, you'll whip them into shape."

Errisket smiled. "If you could whip Tom and Rhedis into shape, you can do so with anyone."

"No doubt," said Korrd.

*An assembly of wizards. The kind who are puissant on their own.* It would be a prestigious position indeed.

And yet...

"You don't look pleased," Errisket observed.

Milicron stroked his beard. "Why would you not be pleased?"

Joe told them.

"Ah," said Korrd. "*That's* why..."

WHEN Joe left the Council's chamber, he saw Tom and Rhedis waiting for him on the bench where he had left them.

"Are you all right?" Tom asked. "You were in there a long time."

"That was *your* fault," said Joe.

"Ours?" said Rhedis.

"That's right," said Joe.

"But we beat those demons," said Rhedis.

"Exactly. And now they want me to repeat that performance, albeit with better..."

Rhedis's eyes narrowed "Better *what*?"

"Better wizards," Joe said. After all, he wasn't going to lie to Rhedis ever again.

"What did you say?" Tom asked.

Joe shrugged. "I said *yes*. I'm not an *idiot*, am I?"

Tom looked like he was going to cry. "So...that's it?" He looked to Rhedis, then back to Joe. "We're not a team anymore?"

"Exactly," Rhedis spat.

Joe held his hands out to them. "Who said *that*?"

Rhedis made a face. "*You* did."

"I said I was going to repeat what we did with wizards better

than we are. *But with you as well.* I'm nothing without you two. You know that."

Tom frowned. "So...we're part of the team?"

"Not just part of it. The *core* of it. And we'll have the best wizards in the land around us." He named some of them.

"That's...impressive," said Tom.

"Not the same ones all the time," said Joe, "because I don't want us to become too predictable. But we'll be working with them all at one time or another."

"But will they listen to you?" Tom asked. "I mean, as powerful as they are..."

"They've already signed on," said Joe. "That's what the Council told me. They heard what we did and they couldn't wait to join us."

"Seriously?" said Rhedis.

"I've got a talent for bringing out the best in people." Joe poked a thumb over his shoulder. "That's what they told me in there. Are you going to argue with the likes of Korrd, Errisket, and Milicron?"

Tom paled. "Of course not."

"Then there you go. So what do you two think?"

"I'm in," said Tom.

Joe turned to Rhedis. "Get bent, I suppose?"

She smiled. "As painfully as possible."

Joe laughed. "I wouldn't have it any other way."

# Reliquary

BY DANIELLE ACKLEY-MCPHAIL

"Like a lily among thorns is my darling among the maidens."
—*Solomon 2:2*

**D**ELIVER us from evil... deliver us from evil... deliver...Oh, God!"

Do you know...despite having been raised by nuns...for the first time in my sixteen years, I meant that with all my heart. The church doors—massive portals of thick, carved mahogany that normally took three of us girls to prop open—groaned beneath an unseen assault. I grabbed Char's black-nailed, spiked-leather-gloved hand and ran for the sanctuary. In a twisted way, this felt reassuring. I was used to running off with my unlikely best friend and hiding from righteous wrath. Of course, that was generally after we'd actually *done* something to inspire said righteous wrath.

I could hear the echoes of times past as though they truly rang through the convent: *Maria Anna Martucci! Charlotte Evangeline Scalia! Show yourselves, you sinful children!* My throat closed tight, locking in a sob, while tears ran unchecked down my cheeks. I would never again hear Mother Superior's voice outside of my memories...or my nightmares.

Char and I would never stand before her awaiting assignment of our penance. Or duck our heads away from her exasperated gaze. My free hand tightened around the cloisonné pin she had pressed into my palm as she died. Other than her cross and the symbolic wedding band all nuns wore, the tiny lily was the only jewelry I had ever seen her wear. And she had given it to me.

The sob burst out, shredding my throat like asphalt does a bare knee.

Mother Superior had told me to find the others and get them out, but I had been too terrified by the time I found Char to look any further. I cried even harder with my shame, hesitating, though I knew it was too late to turn back.

"Hey, Mary Sunshine, save it and get us out of here!" Char tugged on my hand until my steps quickened once more. We had to reach the priests' hole hidden at the back of the nave before the bolt on the doors failed.

We approached the sanctuary, pushing through doors cousin to those behind us. Without a pause, we ran down the aisle, crossing ourselves with our free hands, though we dare not genuflect. Scrambling past the podium, we lunged at the bas-relief carved along the front of the altar, pushing and twisting at every lily we could, as Mother Superior instructed with her last breath. Suddenly, beneath my fingers, seemingly solid marble shifted.

"Char! Char!" I squealed, but she was already turning, her finger pointing toward the polished mahogany section separating from the paneling. As it swung away, there rose the rumbling groan of shifting marble as an inconceivably old mechanism dropped the massive block behind the paneling into the floor. Cobwebs wafted gently in the air current blowing through the gap. Char shivered beside me, and I drew a trembling breath. We looked at one another and took one step back away from the dark, dank hiding place. The sound of splintering wood behind us, however, uprooted any doubts we had. Char grabbed my forearm and yanked me onward. As one, we flung ourselves through the secret door just as hints of a rank, peaty smell drifted toward us from the back of the sanctuary.

Our weight pressed the marble down a fraction further, and as soon as we scrambled off it, the wood panel dropped, and the solid block rose once more, trapping us within the cloister walls. In the dark. In my heart, I lifted a silent, guilty prayer that the others had also gotten to safety.

I swear I could feel Mother Superior's spirit hanging above me in judgment as we half-stumbled, half-fell down the worn stone steps we had seen for just an instant. Without Char's hand gripping me tightly, I would have tumbled more than once. Both of us staggered as we reached the bottom. Part of me had expected never-ending stairs leading us... or at least me, down to damnation. Never mind that the passage was meant to save us. Guilt continued to gnaw at me.

For a long moment, we just stood there, gasping for breath, listening hard for sounds from above. I don't know about Char, but I heard nothing. Apparently, our pursuers were no match for a half-ton marble block.

Okay, so maybe it wasn't a half-ton, but fortunately for us, it might as well have been.

I yipped as a soft *click* ratcheted beside me, followed by a faint flicker of flame that fought to banish the darkness about as well as the Sisters had fought off those... *things,* succeeding only in staving it off a mere few inches. Enough that I could see Char roll her black-lined eyes at me but not much else. Even her close-cropped black hair disappeared into the darkness, though the flame did glitter faintly off the glossy onyx crosses studding her ears. She gripped one of those fancy lighters with the flip-top in her hand—the kind you don't have to hold down once you flick them.

"Do you think that will hold them?" I whispered.

"Of course," Char promptly answered, her gaze unwavering. I would have found that more reassuring if I didn't know she was a pro at lying without a blink.

Stumbling back as her arm darted past my shoulder, I pivoted to see what she was doing. There, in a cubby chiseled into the stone wall, lay a flashlight and a large lumpy knapsack. Char grabbed the hefty flashlight. As she clicked it on, she flipped the lid on her lighter closed and slid it into the pocket she'd sewn inside the waistband of her uniform skirt to keep the few precious things that mattered to her close.

The high-powered beam chased away the dark much better than the tiny naphtha flame. I gulped as Char started walking, revealing a close, dank corridor, the walls slick with condensation. Cobwebs draped from the ceiling. As the light receded, I would swear I heard a faint scratching, though I could not tell from where.

Gulping, I pinned Mother Superior's lily to my jumper, grabbed the knapsack, and hurried after the light.

THE cloister and orphanage grounds above us were vast— a relic from another era, centuries old. When we girls snuck into the unused portions to explore, we had to mark our path with chalk just to find our way back. I *really*

wished I had chalk about now. The tunnel went along forever, widening, but broken here and there by open niches or long, narrow patches of mortared stone stacked in the wall three-high—part of my mind supplied the word *loculi* from our study on the Roman catacombs, but the rest of my mind told it to shut up. I tried not to think of how many of those we passed. Other tunnels branched off, maze-like and disorienting. I did spy symbols chiseled into the stone beside each arch, but with no way to record them and no idea what they meant, I merely noted them and moved on.

Telling myself I was imagining the faint aroma of peat wafting behind us, I kept my eyes forward, locked to Char's back, turning when she turned and ducking when she ducked. Somehow, she never wavered. In my thoughts, I moved on from my recitation of the Lord's Prayer to the 23rd Psalms, desperate to drown out the scratching and shuffling I was certain I heard in our wake.

I would swear I felt a gentle touch upon my shoulder. Faint. There, then not quite gone. An air of peace settled over me, and I drew a slow, deep breath, able once more to follow my friend through the near darkness without hesitation.

The deeper we wended our way, the more my tension eased. After all, it wasn't as if the horrors hunting us would know how to open the secret passage, right? Anything I thought I heard or smelled had to be my well-exercised imagination.

I kept telling myself that.

Right up until the stones covering the walled-off *loculi* I was walking past tumbled to the ground.

I screamed as a desiccated hand snatched at my shoulder. I slammed the grasper with the heavy knapsack, both stunned and chuffed as the limb snapped off, falling to the ground, the fingers still scrabbling. *Revenants...* my mind finally made the connection I really could have done without.

"What the h..." Char pivoted and spun like a cowboy out of a spaghetti western.

I screamed again, interrupting her, and stomped hard on the brittle wrist grabbing for my ankle. Scurrying out of reach, I pushed Char back around, propelling her forward.

"Go! GoGoGo!" We ran the best we could, in the dark, through unfamiliar tunnels, the light bouncing wildly ahead of us. The sound of pursuing revenants grew fainter, but it seemed to come from both ahead and behind us, not to mention down every offshoot tunnel we passed. For the moment, we were clear, but I feared they were converging.

"This is ridiculous," Char murmured. She grabbed my arm and pulled me into an open niche. I slumped against the damp wall, gasping for breath. I swear I could

taste the rank odor of dust and decay on the air.

"Wha... whatever animated those corpses above is starting to affect the bodies down here."

"You think?!" Char asked in a surprised-not-surprised voice. "We don't have a lot of time here. What's in that bag slowing you down?"

Crouching, I unbuckled the flap and started to turn the bag out.

Char's hand darted out to stop me. "Better not. We might have to run."

I winced and nodded. I should have thought of that.

She nudged the bag in a silent reminder. I folded the flap over, waving her closer so I could see in better light. Char angled the beam, and we both looked at each other, confused. I reached into the knapsack and unfurled a thin tube about three-feet long, ending in a wand-style spray nozzle, like you would use for insecticide or something like that, only the other end attached to a plastic canister with "$H_2O$" stamped on it. Someone had taken a marker and drawn a cross above the writing.

"Seriously?" Char said softly, grinning down at me. "You have to be kidding me..."

I looked up at her, puzzled. "What?"

She gave me a look back and lifted one eyebrow.

I peered closer. Then my eyes widened, and I started to crack up.

"Shhh!"

I smothered my laughter, but tears still ran from my eyes.

It felt good to laugh, even if it wasn't appropriate. Getting myself under control, I took the flashlight from her and dove back into the bag. Snacks, batteries, first aid supplies, a bottle of sacramental wine (seriously?), and... jackpot! A map.

As I took out the map and tried to puzzle it out, Char pulled the bag toward her.

Leaving the nozzle and tube unfurled, she closed the flap on the bag and buckled it, snugging it down tight. I barely noticed as she swung it onto her back, both arms through the straps. She then knelt beside me and peered over my shoulder at the map. I pointed at a series of close vertical lines.

"I'm pretty sure this is where we came in." Then I pointed at a symbol that looked like a cluster of flowers. Maybe even lilies, if I squinted. "That looks like outside, so I'm guessing that's where we want to go to get out."

Char looked at me, expectantly. I stared back.

"Okay... and...?"

"And... what? Do you really think I have any clue where we are?"

Only...I scrambled to my feet, still clutching the map and the flashlight. I pushed past Char and hurried to the nearest arch. I admit I grinned like an idiot. I tried to point from the wall to the map with the hand holding the flashlight, and the beam went wild. Char grabbed my hand and held it still.

"Use your words," she quipped.

I turned the flashlight on the archway and then back to the map. "The marks...do you see them?" She returned my grin. Together, we searched the map for the tiny hash marks matching those chiseled into the stone beside the tunnel arch.

In the darkness down the tunnel, a scraping sound.

Mother Superior would not have approved of the curses either one of us swore. As we scrambled down the path we prayed would lead to safety, I tried to hand the flashlight back to Char. She waved it away, brandishing her spray wand and pushing me ahead of her.

WITH nothing more than a D-cell flashlight and about a quart of holy water, we battled the demons in the dark. They crawled out of the walls and even up through the floors, coming from every direction. I scrambled to read the map while dodging revenants, striking out with the flashlight like a club while Char spritzed her sprayer at the slightest sound. Under other circumstances, I would have felt well and truly blessed. Or maybe just wet and annoyed.

I tried to close my ears to the sizzling screech of the undead dying as Char's mist settled on their desiccated skin. Some scattered into dust, but the fresher corpses simply fell to the ground, tripping us up. As we stumbled over and around them, I hoped and prayed theirs was a *final* final rest. Even so, nightmare images plagued me as I fought... of the Sisters and the other girls from the orphanage facing this... *becoming* this...above.

Both Char and I bore wounds from our battle, scratches and bites we were unable to evade in the dark. I shuddered as they ached and burned but did my best not to think about them. I was too afraid to consider what consequences those injuries could lead to. Our journey seemed more and more like a trail of damnation, rather than salvation. I shook that thought off hard and continued in step with Char.

After what seemed like forever, we heard only our own panting breath.

In silence, we proceeded forward, the black surrounding our now-steady beam giving way to ever-lightening grey. A sharp click disturbed the silence as I turned off the flashlight to conserve the batteries. I handed it to Char, who slipped it into the knapsack.

For a moment, the tunnel widened into what appeared to be an antechamber containing—of all things—a battered red wheelbarrow and piles and piles of loose rocks similar to those that walled up the *loculi* we had passed on our

way here. I exchanged a look with Char, and we both shuddered. I doubted I would ever enjoy a haunted maze again. Not after fighting my way through the real thing. As we turned back to continue, a sudden flash of brilliant white light blinded me.

With a startled yelp, I whirled around, ready to head back the way we came.

And it was not there. As I blinked away the spots before my eyes, I beheld a solid stone wall with no passage in sight. A brief darting touch confirmed it as cool and rough and completely real. I turned and placed my back against it. My eyes widened at the sight of Char, bloodied chin raised and back straight, standing unmoved at the edge of a cavernous chamber transformed from moments before. Radiance glittered from the walls, and the ceiling rose three stories in the air, ending in one continuous crystalline dome. Refracted rainbows lit the chamber below. Such architecture matched nothing on the cloister grounds, to my knowledge.

I saw no sign of another way out to the surface.

At the center of the chamber sat an ornate shrine...a wide, creamy marble dais upon which stood a baptismal font and an ornately carved *cathedra*—a throne-like chair where the bishop or the priest celebrant sat. Luscious white lilies rising from vibrant green stalks filled the chamber, but for a narrow aisle leading to the shrine.

The air above the dais began to glow. I blinked, once, twice, three times in rapid succession, as the glow took on form, then color, and finally substance. When the light faded, I beheld a nun such as I had never seen before standing in front of the *cathedra*. If not for her familiar black veil, I would have thought her simply a holy warrior. In place of a wimple, she wore a chainmail coif. In place of a habit, she wore a white, long-sleeved version of a Crusaders' tunic, divided from the hips to below the knees, only marked with a familiar lily in place of the Teutonic cross. Simple leather greaves and sturdy boots peered out from beneath. In her right hand, she gripped a staff carved all over with lilies, and a rosary wrapped her left wrist.

The sight filled me with awe, in the truest sense. I slid down the wall, landing with a soft thud as my butt hit the ground.

"Our Father, who art in Heaven…" I murmured aloud without realizing it.

*'Charlotte Evangeline Scalia. I summon you forth.'* The words rang through the chamber, though the nun's lips did not move.

I scrambled to my feet as Char stepped forward, lowing the knapsack to her feet once she reached the dais. Guilt kept me from following.

*'Do you pronounce your faith upon your lobes, or do you mock those of true faith with your display?'*

Eyes wide, I turned my gaze to Char, my chest tightening, recalling the black onyx crosses studding her ears. What *did* they mean to her? I loved my friend. I believed her a good person, despite the rebellious face she showed the world, but even I did not know what faith she held in her heart.

"I believe in God, the Father, maker of heaven and earth, and in Jesus Christ his only Son…" I let out a shuddering breath as Char began to recite the Apostles'

Creed without once stumbling, not by rote, but in a voice ringing with true conviction. I mouthed the words silently in unison, fearful of drawing attention to myself, flinching and falling out of step as my lips formed the words "to judge the living and the dead."

I should have kept still.

*'Maria Anna Martucci. I summon you forth.'*

I was startled to find myself aligned shoulder to shoulder with my friend with no memory of crossing the chamber.

Without looking, Char took my hand and gave it a squeeze, stilling the tremors I hadn't realized rippled through me. I squeezed back. Slowly, I filled my lungs, and just as slowly let the air out again.

*'The charge of the Sisterhood has been passed on. Do you, by your own will, take up that charge?'*

*What the...?*

Even in my thoughts, I gulped back the rest of that response as tension drew me taut again. Charge?! I fingered Mother Superior's lily pin. I began to wonder, was this to be our final penance from her?

"Wh... what charge?" I stammered.

*'You are both called to the Order of the Lily.'*

Char snickered at that. I wanted to snatch my hand away and smack her, but part of me wouldn't dare.

"Listen, *Sister*," Char said with a smirk. "I don't know who you've been talking to, but I ain't

no saint..." If only Char knew... neither was I.

I could hardly believe it, but I would swear the nun smirked back.

*'Who is, as you mean it? Our Father calls many to service...all of us imperfect in His eyes, if not to His heart.'*

"No!" The word squeaked out of me, edged in panic even to my own ears. "I can't be a nun!"

This time there was no doubt. The nun outright laughed, her expression radiant and mirthful though she sobered quickly. *'All are instructed to guard against evil; only a chosen few are called to combat it.'*

I thought of what we'd just faced and quailed. "I'm not a fighter either." The words trembled over my lips as my chin tucked down, and my gaze darted, seeking a way out. Only Char's grip on me kept me in place.

*'Your wounds would deny your words. The Father does not call upon his warriors without also providing them the means to fight. If you have faith, can you not also trust? There are many ways of doing battle.'*

Char squeezed my hand once more at the nun's words. I fought a battle in my own heart. Ashamed of the doubt that even now crept over me, ashamed of the way I had abandoned the others to save myself. I straightened and drew a quavering breath, my heart begging for forgiveness I did not deserve. I would have expected the fragrance of the flowers to overwhelm me, but it added to my sense of calm acceptance.

"I am not worthy," I called out, taking a step back toward the antechamber.

Char turned to look at me, confused. I looked away in shame.

*'Who among us truly is, child?'* the spectral Sister interrupted before I could confess, her gaze knowing, but not judging.

I had no answer for her.

*'Do you accept the Blessing of the Lily?'*

It was but a thought. A moment of continued weakness. Fear taking over, as it had before. *What happens if I don't?* I wondered.

A barrage of images flooded my mind in that instant. Some heart-wrenching, some horrific. Some of them the fruit of my cowardice. All of them preventable. They mirrored the nightmare images that beset me as we traveled the maze. Only I was no mere observer this time. I felt the horror, the pain, the fear and despair, every emotion birthed of evil intent, with the knowledge I could have stood against it if only I had summoned the courage.

In my mind's eye, I saw Mother Superior as I had last seen her, the memory self-inflicted. She had not fallen to attack. She met her end in defense of the orphans and the Sisters in her care. Willingly, she stood between us and evil.

That is the charge she had placed

on my shoulders, and I had already failed her.

How could I continue to dishonor her memory by letting such evil reign? *Any* evil reign? I moaned and nearly crumpled to my knees, tears streaming down my face. "Enough! Enough..."

The images faded. The memory remained. Before Char could lift me, I straightened, squaring my shoulders.

"Why me?"

*'Your sister is your strength and courage, girl, but you are her wisdom and heart. Together, you forge a mighty weapon.'*

I let my gaze traverse the subterranean chamber taking in the unlikely field of white lilies. Straight and strong on their emerald stalks, bold and beautiful in their simplicity. Pure, but not perfect, not even these...

Yes. Yes, I could be a Lily. Chin lifted high, I stepped forward, and Char followed. Together we ascended the dais and knelt before the holy apparition, heads bowed, and hearts lifted.

*"O God, Who art the Creator and Preserver of all mankind, the Lover of spotless purity, the Giver of all grace and everlasting life, sanctify by Thy holy benediction these Lilies...'*

The blessing went on, but I confess, I didn't pay close attention. Being raised in a convent, I had heard it annually at the feast of St. Anthony and could probably recite it myself if I tried. The words did not matter. I marveled, however, at the intent. If we were literally called to protect against evil, what of the healing and granting of peace also cited?

'*One thing at a time, child…*' Somehow, it felt as if at this moment, she spoke only to me.

'*I, Lilja of the Order of the Lily, welcome my new sisters and accept your oath.*'

Her glow drew closer. I heard something dipping in water and remembered the font. I glanced sideways, watching as she made the mark of the cross on Char's bowed head. '*You shall be called Lys…in French, it means Lily, in Hebrew, it means 'God is my oath,' be you doubly blessed.*' As she moved toward me, I could not help but lift my gaze in awe and wonder, expecting at any moment to wake from this surreal dream. She gave me a gentle, understanding smile and gestured with her left hand that I should bow once more. With a start, I noticed she was missing her fourth finger, but now was not the time to ask or wonder. I lowered my gaze and received her benediction.

'*You shall be called Shousnan… in Armenian, it means Lily, be you equally blessed.*'

Not only did I feel my physical wounds heal at her touch, but also the spiritual ones.

I waited as her words trailed off for whatever came next.

And still, I waited.

Char…*Lys*…whatever…she cleared her throat expectantly, to no effect.

And we waited some more.

It wasn't long. A few moments that felt like forever. Neither of us had ever mastered patience. I did not lift my head, but I peered up through my lashes in a manner long-perfected during twice-daily times of prayer and once-daily— except for twice on Sundays— times of worship. Lys must have done the same. We gasped together, and our heads came up as one. The glowing, translucent figure was gone. Before us, with two carved staffs now leaning against its back, stood the previously empty cathedra.

Two objects sat upon the cushioned seat: what appeared to be a jewel-encrusted vial—a little longer than finger-length—suspended from a chain and a hand-stitched, leather-bound book, both older than anything I had ever seen before. I did not look too closely at what I recognized as a reliquary… a blessed object containing a piece of a saint's remains. I shuddered at the macabre relic and turned my gaze to the book. Now that…that fascinated me. The cover bore no words, but the now-familiar symbol of the lily had been burned into the leather. I wondered what wisdom it held as I remembered what Lilja had said about God providing us the means to fight.

By instinct or divine inspiration, we each reached for a different object. Lys slipped the reliquary into her secret pocket, rather than around her neck. Me? I clutched the book to my chest. Interestingly, only after that, did we reach for our staffs.

"Now what?" my sister murmured. "How do we get out?"

I started to shrug, only to jump with an undignified squeak as Lilja spoke directly into my...or, I assume...*our* heads.

*This is a crypt, my sisters. None are expected to leave, but by the way they came, or the way they are bound.* There was no doubt by that last she meant the afterlife.

By the grace of God, not now, not today.

Lys retrieved the knapsack. Handing me the flashlight, she then refilled the sprayer from the baptismal font. Armed, if not armored, we squared our shoulders once more and turned back to the catacombs.

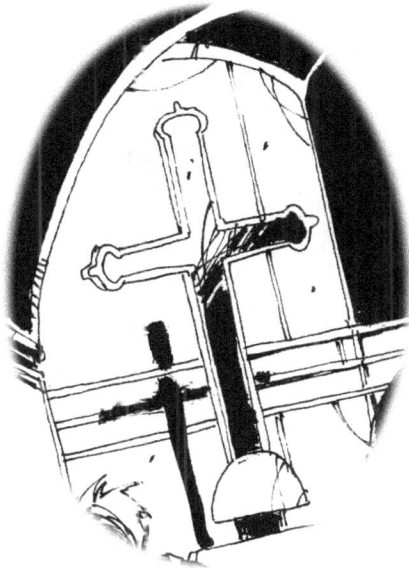

# They'll Never Let You In

## BY MARY FAN

You've probably met Grace Chang. She's the sleek-suited lady on the subway clutching the pole with her right hand and scrolling through her work emails with her left. She's the one in fashionable athleisure behind you at farmer's market. You probably took one glance at her in Pilates class and saw her entire life story in her impeccable form.

But if you, like so many others, were appalled by what she did, you must have asked yourself: If you knew her so well, how could she have shocked you so?

THE gold-colored pin, with its finely etched medieval shield, glinted under the restaurant's garish florescent lights. Grace glanced away. Matt hated it when she mentioned that thing. He liked to pretend it didn't exist, even as he flaunted it.

His chestnut eyes turned to her, and he smiled—perfect white teeth against perfect white skin. "What were you looking at, babe?"

"That print on the wall." Grace quickly gestured at the fading, cheaply framed image of a Chinese village.

Julia, sitting across from Grace between two of their other friends, gave her a joking pout. "C'mon, stop knocking this place! I know it's not as fancy as the restaurants you usually go to, but the food's good, okay? Probably the only authentic dishes this side of town."

"I didn't say anything!" Grace exclaimed.

Julia narrowed her dark, upwardly swept eyes. "You were going to." She pushed back her long blue bangs, which formed a ragged curtain over her gold-complexioned forehead. "You all still trust me to order for the table?"

Beside her, Viano nodded enthusiastically. "Heck yeah, we do! And since I'm the guest of honor, I get to decide."

Matt laughed. "Fair enough! Hey, before we do that, let's have a toast!" He raised his minuscule glass, which was filled with a powerful sorghum liquor. "Welcome back, Viano!"

Julia raised her own drink along with everyone else. "And don't you dare stay away so long ever again! *Ganbei!*" With that, they all emptied their glasses.

All except Grace, who'd given up alcohol as part of her latest cleanse.

"I can't believe it's been three

*Illustration by Dan Schkade*

years since we graduated." Julia shook her head then waved over the waiter and began ordering in Mandarin.

As the only other person at the table who knew what she was saying, Grace clenched her fingers nervously and tried not to look at her boyfriend. Julia's choices were all very traditional—and probably very unfamiliar to everyone else. What if Matt hated everything and thought less of Grace's own tastes?

That gold-colored pin flashed as he turned to chat with Kennedy, another friend from their old dorm, and Grace once again looked away.

This time, she caught Amara's piercing brown glare. From her knitted black eyebrows to her tight burgundy lips, which complemented her warm brown complexion, everything about her expression radiated anger.

"What's wrong?" Grace asked.

Amara arched her brows. "Are you kidding me? After what you pulled, you have the nerve to ask?"

"I don't know what you're talking about."

"Oh, so you're playing the clueless nice girl now. Classic."

"Amara—"

"You made me look like an idiot at work today in front of all those executives! You threw me under the bus to cover up your own damn mistake. You know, when I found out we'd been hired to the same team, I was so excited because I thought I'd have a friend at the office. Guess I was wrong."

The table went silent. Grace lifted her chin. "Look, I'm sorry you were offended, but I just told them what really happened. If you'd followed up with that prospect like you were supposed to, we wouldn't have lost the account."

"It was *your* account!" Amara gave her an incredulous look. "I was doing you a favor by helping out!"

Viano held up both hands in a placating gesture. "I'm sure it was a misunderstanding. Hey, let's not ruin this reunion by talking about work."

Grace gave smooth smile. "Of course. Sorry, Viano."

Amara pointed an accusing finger at Grace. "I'll back down for now because this is Viano's big welcome-back dinner, but we're not done. Why don't we circle back on Monday," she added sarcastically.

Grace started to retort, but Matt put a hand on her arm. "Relax. Whatever happened, I'm sure there's no need to get emotional."

"I'm sorry." Grace sighed. "I just wanted to land that account so badly. It's been three years, and they still won't promote me, even though I have the best numbers of all the business development specialists. I've also worked so hard to network with Brad Wexler—the regional director—and he was in that meeting. I didn't want to look bad… especially since he's a member of the League."

Viano leaned closer. "What's the League?"

Matt laughed. "It's an urban legend."

Grace caught the glitter of the gold-colored pin again, and a strange, deep-seated fire burned in her chest.

*Of course he would say that.* The voice, bitter yet brittle, whispered through Grace's head. She blinked and ignored it, as she'd done so many times before.

"The League is real." Amara leaned forward and gave Grace a pointed look. "Listen, I get why you did what you did. I don't blame you for wanting in with the League or trying to impress a member. But you shouldn't have trashed me to get what you want."

"You're right." Grace sighed, hoping she sounded sufficiently remorseful to satisfy Amara, who was known for holding grudges.

Viano threw up a hand. "Is anyone going to tell me what the League is?"

"It's a club for elitists." Julia wrinkled her nose. "Like those secret societies they have at Yale or whatever. They say all the most powerful people are in it—CEOs, politicians, A-list celebs. Everyone knows it's real, but no one can prove it." She turned to Grace. "I don't get why you're so obsessed with it."

Grace shrugged. "I just see it as an opportunity—"

"They'll never let you in." Julia's expression grew serious. "You can do everything right, but you'll never be one of them… and I think, deep down, you know that."

Grace didn't answer. Of course Julia wouldn't understand. Julia was the starving-artist type—who always begged Grace to feed her while looking down her nose at the career Grace had chosen. The very career that allowed Grace to back Julia's crowdfunding campaigns and buy her mediocre creations.

Kennedy shook her head of dirty blond hair. "Why are we even talking about the League—which probably doesn't exist—when there are real issues to discuss? Like how factory farming is destroying the world?"

"For real." Alessandor, a tall young woman in a yellow shirt, snorted. "We're not going to have an ozone in a few years. What does it matter if a bunch of rich people have a secret club?"

Grace wanted to say that joining the League could be her only way to move up in the corporate world, but the last thing she wanted was to cause a scene.

"Calm down, babe." Matt curled his fingers around hers. "You're the smartest person at that company. I'm sure you'll get to where you want to go, with or without some mythical League."

Grace smiled. "Thank you."

Viano pointed at the pin on Matt's collar. "Been meaning to ask: What's with that thing?"

Matt shrugged. "Old family heirloom. My grandfather made me promise to wear it before he passed."

The identical pin Brad Wexler

wore on his lapel had come with a similar story, but Grace chose not to point that out.

THE woman in the mirror looked nothing like the girl Grace had once been. That girl could never have imagined wearing a blue sheath dress worthy of Ivanka Trump with a pair of classy heels and artsy—but not too artsy—earrings. That girl had loved to keep her hair long and wild, not neatly clipped by her chin. And that girl had hated garden parties.

The doorbell rang. Grace crossed her apartment, which her friends had compared to a hotel room with its sparse furniture and generic paintings of landscapes, and opened the door.

Matt stood on the other side, that gold-colored pin gleaming against his casual gray suit. "Ready, babe?"

"Yes, let me just grab my purse."

He cocked his head. "Are you sure you want to wear that necklace?"

Grace touched her jade pendant—the one with a carved dragon that her grandmother in Nanjing had given her. It was probably the only thing she still shared with that girl from the past. "What's wrong with it?"

"Nothing—I love it, actually. Something about it just seems off... maybe because of the color?" He held up his hands. "Just thought I'd point it out since I know how much of a perfectionist you are."

*This isn't about jewelry.* The voice floated against her thoughts, and the sensation of heat flared through her core. *You know what it's really about.*

Ignoring it, Grace glanced down at the pendant. Its pale green *did* clash with the rich blue of her dress. "Thanks. I'll change it."

She rushed back to her bedroom, took off the pendant, and replaced it with a string of pearls.

THOUGH Grace had been to the Dawsons' grandiose suburban property several times since she and Matt had started dating, its stern stone facade and elegant fountains never failed to awe her. The moment the two of them stepped into the marble-floored foyer, a rake-thin woman with the same chestnut-brown eyes as Matt swept forward with outstretched arms, the red soles of her pale pink pumps flashing.

"Matthew, honey! So good to have you home!" She embraced her son then turned to Grace. "And how lovely to see you again, dear!"

Grace smiled. "Lovely to see you, too, Mrs. Dawson."

"You know, I finally watched that new American adaption of *The Monkey King.* What a beautiful film—so much culture! And such a unique take on the story. That director—I'm sorry, I can't remember the name—saw something in the legend that no one else had before. It's breathtaking—the pinnacle of international filmmaking."

Grace nodded. "Yes, I watched

it with Matt when it came out. We loved it."

*He did. You didn't.* A dry laugh accompanied the voice this time. *Didn't you say something about how it felt like a stereotypical imitation of what Chinese filmmakers had been doing for years?*

She hadn't, but she'd wanted to.

"Did I hear you talking about that *Monkey King* movie?" A white-haired man in an impeccably tailored suit approached with a glass of scotch in one hand. "My wife and I loved it!"

Grace's gaze fixed on his lapel pin.

Same gold color. Same medieval shield.

Same perfect white-toothed smile as Matt—because this was his uncle, James Dawson, CFO of an international bank and half the reason Grace had agreed to attend this function.

James glanced at her. "I'm James Dawson, by the way." He held out his hand.

"Grace Chang." She took it and tried not to wince as he crushed her fingers.

"You and Matt have been seeing each other for quite a while now, haven't you?" He clapped his hand on his nephew's shoulder. "Why didn't you introduce us earlier, Matty? She's a delight!"

Grace blushed. "Thank you."

*You haven't even said anything other than your name.* The voice slithered through her head, accompanied by an unsettling rumble in her gut. *The only thing he could find delightful about you is how you look.*

That didn't matter. All that mattered was that he liked her.

"I'll bring her by more often." Matt grinned at Grace. "Assuming my family hasn't scared you off yet."

She laughed. "Of course not."

Matt's mother placed one delicate white hand on her chin. "Grace, didn't you mention once that you studied Taoism?"

"How wonderful!" James exclaimed before Grace had a chance to say no, and that Matt's mother must have had her mixed up with someone else. "I've been trying to incorporate more Eastern philosophy into our corporate culture. Some of the other executives only want the newest and latest, but I believe taking a more patient approach, one drawn from ancient wisdom, will behoove us in the long run. Don't you agree?"

Grace nodded. "'Be not afraid of growing slowly. Be afraid only of standing still.'"

"Exactly!" James gave her an appraising look. "You must have learned that from your parents. They're from China, right?"

"Yes." Though she'd actually learned the quote from a dorm poster.

He pointed at her, pulsing his hand slightly. "There's something special about you—I can tell. I'd be very interested to see how your career develops. Add me on LinkedIn when you get the chance.

I'll make sure my assistant accepts the connection request."

"Y-yes, of course!" It took all of Grace's self-control not to jump with excitement. James Dawson— CFO James Dawson, world-famous James Dawson—was interested in her career. Perhaps she had a chance after all.

THE words "Your Exclusive Invitation" had lost all meaning for Grace thanks to retailers and e-marketers, but this time, it was different. In the age of emails, envelopes made of expensive paper and cards with gold embossing felt especially luxurious.

And the fact that the embossing depicted the same medieval shield engraved on those gold-colored pins made the invitation more valuable than diamonds.

Ostensibly, the event was hosted by James Dawson's company. An evening of networking and industry education, it said.

But Grace knew what it truly meant.

And she didn't hesitate to RSVP with a "yes."

THE driver pulled over on the side of a dark road in the middle of the woods. "This is it."

Grace looked out the window but saw nothing. "Are you sure?"

The driver shrugged. "This is where the GPS took me. Gotta say, I don't get a lot of rides specifying coordinates instead of an address."

"There must be some mistake."

Grace grabbed the invitation from her purse to double check.

A LinkedIn notification popped up on her phone—a new message from James Dawson:

*You're in the right place. We require discretion. Once the driver leaves, the gates will open.*

She stuffed the paper back into her purse. "Never mind—this is right. Thank you."

She stepped out, and the driver sped off.

Not a single ray of light penetrated the shadows. Darkness thickened around her, and stillness settled like a shroud. Her pulse quickened, and she grabbed her phone again, aiming to turn on the flashlight.

The device didn't react when she pressed the unlock button. No matter what she did, the screen remained lifeless.

White lights, powerful and blinding, burst through the blackness. She whirled to see a pair of intricate wrought-iron gates at the end of a wide pathway through the forest. Staring, she stepped into the light of the pathway's gracefully molded lamps. Behind the gates lay an enormous stone building with giant windows and ivy-covered walls.

The gates opened, and a golf cart appeared, heading toward her. Grace exhaled.

"Grace!" A familiar high-pitched voice rang through the dark.

It wasn't until the golf cart had stopped before her that she recognized the waving woman as Alessandor. Her brown hair, colored pink at the tips, bounced by her round, cream-toned chin. Instead of the casual jeans-and-tank-top outfit she'd worn to the restaurant, a tie-dyed sequin-covered qipao now adorned her figure. The design struck Grace as bizarre.

"Like it?" Alessandor gestured at the dress. "Kennedy designed it—genius, right? Sorry about the intrigue by the way. We've got a lot of celebrities here, and we don't want the paparazzi finding out."

Grace stared at her. "You've been in the League this whole time?"

"Don't be silly." Alessandor winked. "There is no League."

As Grace climbed into the golf cart, a sudden clap startled her.

Alessandor wiped her hand against the side of the vehicle. "Gross! Stupid bug. I should have just let it go, but old instincts die hard."

"Great reflexes."

"Thanks!" Alessandor steered the golf cart toward the building. "My parents made me study martial arts when I was a kid. I didn't want to. It seemed like a stereotypical thing for someone like me to do, and my classmates made fun of me enough for not fitting in. Meanwhile, my teachers always wanted me to talk about my 'culture,' and my parents would do anything to accommodate Americans, so they agreed whenever teachers made me demonstrate my skills in front of everyone. It was so embarrassing,

and I used to resent my parents for that, but now, I'm glad they kept me connected to my family's roots, and martial arts have helped me embrace my heritage."

Alessandor's chipper voice seemed incongruous with the deeply personal story she'd just told—and to Grace, who barely knew her.

"That's wonderful," Grace said. "Where did your parents emigrate from?"

"Oh, my family's been here since the *Mayflower*." Alessandor laughed as the golf cart passed through the gates. "I'm so white, I embarrass snow."

"But..." Grace stopped herself. Perhaps she'd misunderstood what "accommodate Americans" had meant.

*You didn't... you know whose story that truly was...* The voice seemed louder this time.

*It was mine!*

Grace jumped. "What was that?"

"What?" Alessandor gave her a puzzled look.

That second voice—it was stronger, harsher than the subconscious rumblings she'd grown accustomed to. Had she imagined it? "Never mind."

Alessandor parked the golf cart by the side of the building, and the two of them headed up a wide stone staircase. The elegantly carved wooden door at the top opened as they drew closer.

Grace's breath caught. This was it—she was finally going to meet the League.

*Don't enter.*

Grace took another step.

*Turn away.*

She ignored both voices... and the echoes of others behind them. If she was having some kind of breakdown, she'd worry about it after she'd impressed the League and—hopefully—taken her first steps toward gaining membership.

*They'll never let you in.*

She stepped over the threshold.

Dim yellow candlelight threw jagged shadows upon the dark, tapestried walls. Twisting iron chandeliers dangled from the high stone ceiling. People ate and drank and laughed beneath them, some swaying to disembodied music so garbled beneath the mishmash of conversations, it was impossible to pinpoint a melody beyond "something jazzy."

Grace's eyes wandered past the tuxedoed caterers and their plates of Asian-fusion hors d'oeuvres, across the glittering guests in their fashionable suits and evening gowns, and over the sculptures of Zodiac animals that looked as if they'd been stolen from an archeological site near Beijing. Except there was something off about them, though she wasn't enough of an artist or historian to pinpoint what. Her gaze settled on one of the tapestries, which depicted what appeared to be the Forbidden Palace rendered in a modern style with a red sunburst design across the front. It looked uncomfortably like the old Japanese flag—the

one flown during World War II. A disturbed feeling snaked through her, but she reminded herself that she wasn't knowledgeable enough in such things to have an opinion. And this was the League—she wasn't about to make a fuss over something so trivial here.

She followed Alessandor deeper into the foyer, looking this way and that, though for what, she wasn't sure.

*You're searching for anyone else who isn't white.* Swirling voices repeated the words in her mind, surrounded by distant yet distinct echoes.

*You won't find them here.*

*You're alone.*

Grace pressed her hand against her head, wishing she could silence them.

"Well, *ni hao*, Grace."

Grace turned to find James Dawson behind her. "Hello, Mr. Dawson."

"Please, call me James." He grinned broadly. "Welcome."

Matt approached, the pin whose presence he so often denied now proudly glinting on his lapel as he gestured at it. "Hey, babe, sorry I couldn't tell you before." He planted a kiss on her cheek. "I've wanted to so many times, but I took an oath."

*He's lying... You know he's lying...*

"I understand." As usual, Grace smiled.

"I swear, it wasn't up to me. They had to make sure you were worthy."

"Of course."

"Are you mad at me?" He lowered his chin with something of a pout.

"Why would I be?"

"I knew you would get it." He wrapped his arm around her. "Honor is as important here as it is to your culture."

Once again, she smiled.

Once again, she ignored that deep, burning sensation quaking in her core.

"Oh, Grace!" Alessandor's brown eyes lit up. "I've been meaning to tell you about my next book idea. Ever since I won the Pulitzer, I've been stuck on what my next novel should be about. I mean, how do you follow the work that got you called 'the voice of American youth' by every major publication? But then it hit me: a modern-day retelling of the myth of the Weaver Girl and the Cow Herd. It's such a beautiful legend, yet no one's really adapted it yet. Doesn't that sound great?"

Grace shrugged. "I'm unfamiliar with the myth."

"Oh, you mean your mother didn't tell it to you when you were a kid?"

Grace shook her head. "I grew up on Cinderella and the Little Mermaid like everyone else..."

She trailed off as Alessandor abruptly walked away.

"My nephew tells me you play." James gestured at the grand piano at the edge of the foyer.

"She does more than play—she won medals and such at school." Matt placed a hand on her arm.

"Hey, babe, want to show them?"

She did not, but she nodded. "Sure."

"Wonderful!" James clapped his hands together in delight. "Stop the music—we have a virtuoso among us!"

The room went silent, and the jazzy background music vanished. He gestured at the instrument.

*Don't...* Whispers, indistinct yet harsh, filled her consciousness. Though they had no words, they all carried the same sensation. *Don't...*

But she couldn't let anyone see the nervous sweat trickling down her neck. She couldn't let anyone sense her tightening breaths.

She sat at the piano with her chin lifted and placed her hands delicately over the keys.

The first song she played was the one she felt most comfortable with, the one she'd composed herself. A simple, pretty melody she hoped would calm her. And it worked.

Until the song ended, and she realized no one was watching or listening—not even Matt, who was engaged in conversation with Alessandor... and Kennedy, who was also, apparently, a member.

She needed their attention—she was supposed to impress them. The League would never offer her membership if she seemed mediocre or forgettable.

So she played another song, one that had won her "medals and such in school." A classic yet complicated piece from the Western canon.

Polite, spattered applause ensued.

That wasn't enough.

*Don't...* The voices burrowed deeper into her head. *Turn away...*

She took in the Zodiac statues, the corrupted image of the Forbidden Palace, the occasional qipaos, hanboks, and kimonos adorning the guests, and she knew what she needed to do.

"This next piece is a folk song my grandmother used to sing when we'd visit her in China. I hope you enjoy it."

She'd never tried adapting this piece for the piano before, and the improvised accompaniment was crude at best.

Yet she'd never heard such thunderous applause before in her life.

"Perfect! Simply perfect!" James walked up to her. "Friends, family, meet Grace Chang!"

Roars of approval.

Yet she could barely hear them over the voices, whose words remained garbled and yet whose sensation was clearer than ever: *You shouldn't have done that.*

*You should have left.*

*They'll never let you in.*

She should have been ecstatic. She should have laughed and carried on and worked the room. The League was impressed with her—she only needed to keep it up. Yet she could barely keep up her calm facade with the voices infiltrating her mind and the burning sensation embedding itself in her core.

"Thank you." Grace stood. "Excuse me, I need the ladies room."

What she really needed was a quiet place to collect herself. Just a few moments, she told herself. A chance to breathe and get over her nerves. Then, she could return and dazzle the League with her charm. They *would* let her in... They had to...

Her feet carried her forward as if on autopilot; she had no idea where they were taking her. The voices seemed to be leading, though she wasn't sure how. It was as if they'd hooked onto her sense of navigation and yanked her forward.

Mixed-up hallways full of mixed-up decor... Steep staircases leading downward... All blending together... Twisting... Turning...

*You wouldn't listen when we tried to warn you. Now, you have to see.*

A metal door stood before her.

*Open it.*

She didn't know where she was or how she'd gotten there.

*Open it!*

Her hand shot up of its own volition and seized the door handle.

The heavy door swung open.

A wide room stood before her, so large, she couldn't see the wall at the other end. Countless vertical slabs stood before her, stretching into the distance.

And bound to each, with wide yet blank eyes, was a person. Breathing, blinking—alive. Though otherwise motionless.

Dressed in hospital gowns and pressed against the slabs—which resembled upright hospital beds—they stood bound by cuffs with tubes protruding from their limbs and necks. They couldn't have spoken if they'd wanted to with the breathing tubes down their throats.

Rows upon rows upon rows... so, so many... and every single one she could see looked East Asian—like her.

Grace screamed.

A pair of hands grabbed her shoulders.

She spun in a panic, tears spilling from her eyes.

"Babe! It's me!" Matt looked down at her and shook his head. "What were you doing, wandering off like that? How did you find your way down here?"

"The voices..." Grace gripped his arms. "What is this, Matt? What's happening?"

"Oh, this?" Gesturing at the room, he laughed. "It's no big deal."

"What? Of course it is! Why—" She broke off as several others appeared behind him, white faces emerging from the shadows, illuminated by the harsh lights from the room behind her.

Among them stood James Dawson, the CFO of a global bank. Alessandor Earnest, the Pulizer Prize winner at 25. Kennedy Thomson, the friend from college who'd become a one-to-watch fashion designer. Brad Wexler and several other executives from work... Politicians she recognized from the news and celebrities she'd seen in various shows...

"Why did you come here?" Matt's expression turned cold.

"The voices..." Terrified, Grace backed away.

"There are no voices."

"I heard—"

"Why did you come tonight? Why did you accept the invitation?"

"I wanted to be one of you." She froze as she realized she was surrounded. "I wanted... I wanted to be part of the League..."

"You should know better by now." A cruel smirk curled his lip. "There is no League."

Hands reached out to her—countless pale, grasping hands. Cruel, yet calm. Powerful, yet desperate.

BLACKNESS fractured by flickering candlelight engulfed Grace's sight. All she felt was the hard surface pressed against her back and the cold restraints anchoring her body. No muscle would obey when she tried yanking.

Bit by bit, the faces reappeared, reflective and blank. Some, she recognized. Some, she didn't. Yet it made no difference—they might as well have been one amorphous entity. A multi-tentacled monster.

Strange chanting filled her ears, and an icy, burrowing pain stabbed her heart. Yet she didn't react—she couldn't even scream.

At first, she couldn't understand anything that was being said. Then, she caught a few Mandarin words among them, though they sounded as if they'd been strung together at random.

*The words don't matter.* The voices floated through her head.

*They don't care what they're saying... only how pretty the syllables sound...*

*Yet their curse works nonetheless...*

*Thanks to the brutality of their ancestors...*

*They need no knowledge for their power to take hold...*

Once, she would have ignored those voices in hopes that they would go away. Now, she clung to them, since they were the only ones speaking to her at all. *Who are you?*

*We are the remnants...*

*We are the parts they didn't want...*

*And you're about to join us...*

"MY parents made me start taking piano lessons when I was five. I would have started at three, but my fingers were too small. I hated it for years. But my mother would force me to practice for hours a day, yelling at me and forbidding me from doing anything else until perfection was achieved. Sometimes, I'd try to have some fun by playing the Chinese folk songs my grandmother sang to me, but my mother only wanted me to play famous songs by European masters. It was stifling."

A young red-haired woman Grace had never seen before sat down at a grand piano—the only dark item in a room otherwise filled with white. White walls, white lights, white faces.

The woman, dressed in a blood-red gown that sharply contrasted her pale complexion, placed her fingers delicately on the piano keys and looked up at the people crowded around her... the others from the event. Matt and his uncle. Alessandor and Kennedy. The executives from work and myriad people of fame.

"I composed this song in college." The young woman inhaled sharply. "It relaxes me... When I play it, I finally feel like a musician, and not a clone."

The song flowing from the piano was a simple, pretty melody.

It was Grace's melody; the same one she'd played that evening.

And that story—it was hers too.

When the woman finished playing, the others applauded enthusiastically.

"A genius deconstruction of Eastern and Western influences!" exclaimed one woman, who Grace recognized as an acclaimed journalist.

She wanted to scream, but all she could do was blink.

The woman at the piano stood and bowed, then walked off.

A young man in a sharp black suit with slick blond hair walked up to the piano and lifted its lid. Instead of strings, an assortment of pens and paper lay before him.

"I've just come up with the showstopper for my next collection." He picked up a pen and arced it across a piece of paper, quickly sketching out a long ball gown. Tigers and lotuses adorned it, reminiscent of the various prints that had once decorated Grace's childhood home.

The dress was one she'd doodled in high school, back when she'd fantasized about designing her own prom dress.

The young man held up the finished drawing to roars of approval.

"A cross-cultural delight that fuses the best of both worlds!" The woman who said that was one of those fashion editors so famous, even people who weren't into fashion knew her name.

The young man curled up his drawing and retreated.

The next one to step up to the piano was Matt. He, too, reached for a piece of paper, except his utensil of choice was a brush.

"I used to hate studying calligraphy." He dipped the brush in ink and began writing. "I thought it was boring. Something for old people. But my father forbade me from watching TV until I'd finished practicing. I used to think he was a tyrant, but now, I understand that he only wanted me to hold on to my heritage. I wish I'd paid more attention... I'm afraid this is the best I can do now."

He held up the finished calligraphy. It spelled out Grace's Chinese name in her handwriting.

Cheers and applause followed.

"Isn't my nephew a most sophisticated and cultured young man?" James Dawson grinned. "He will do well in his new international role at the company."

"It's gorgeous, Matt!" Kennedy approached, clapping. A jade pendant bounced against her rich blue top.

It was identical to the one Grace's grandmother had once given her.

The famous fashion editor turned to Kennedy. "Such a lovely choice of accessory, dear. A bold yet elegant color pairing."

All Grace could do was breathe and blink as League members claimed pieces of her one by one— to ecstatic exclamations and adoring applause.

Yet the burning sensation in her gut was stronger than ever. Instead of trying to douse it, she let it rage. It was all she had left of herself.

"Who should we invite as our next guest?" James turned to Matt. "Your friend Julia, perhaps?"

Matt shook his head. "Julia doesn't have enough of what we're looking for."

The crowd retreated from the room, closing the thick metal door behind them.

Leaving Grace alone in the terrifying whiteness.

*Welcome.* The voice sounded louder and more distinct than it ever had before.

If she could have moved, Grace would have jumped. *You again.*

*Yes, us again.*

*Who are you?*

*We told you. We are the remnants.*

*What do you mean?*

*You already saw us.*

An image filled Grace's mind— the room she'd stumbled upon.

Rows of motionless yet conscious people bound to upright slabs with breathing tubes down their throats. Except this time, there was one more.

She took in the vision of her own body, now a husk of a person. Yet she still *felt* herself, didn't she? At least her mind was still her own…

She tried to recall what the melody she'd composed in college sounded like. She couldn't.

She tried to remember what that fanciful prom dress she'd designed in high school had looked like. She couldn't.

She tried to envision herself practicing calligraphy under her father's stern instruction. Even that was gone.

*We tried to warn you.* The voice now sounded like legions. *They took everything they wanted from you, and this is what they leave behind.*

*That's what you meant by 'remnants.' You're the… ghosts… of their previous victims.*

*Not ghosts. If we were ghosts, we'd be dead. But if we died, they'd lose what they'd taken from us.*

*They want our creations, our memories… our souls…* The burning within Grace felt stronger than a firestorm. *You led me here. Why?*

*You didn't run when we told you to. They would have forced you to join us no matter what. But now that you're listening… you can free us all.*

*How?*

*You know how.*

The firestorm spread through every inch of her that remained,

until it was no longer a sensation. It was all she was. *Why me?*

*We needed one more. You are not a chosen one. If you'd been a single person earlier, you'd be speaking with us now instead of listening.*

*I don't understand.*

*Yes, you do.*

Flames tore through Grace, yet she couldn't define exactly what the heat meant. It was powerful, all-consuming. It was more than anger, more than rage. More than passion, more than desperation. *Yes, I do.*

*Let us in.*

METAL screeched. Plastic clattered. Liquids splashed.

Grace's ankle was the first piece of her body that was freed. Her bare foot clunked heavily against the ground. Tearing her other ankle and her wrists from the rest of the restraints should have been painful. Ripping the breathing tube from her throat should have been excruciating. Yet she felt nothing but the heat as she moved.

For these movements weren't hers alone—they belonged to the voices. They *were* her. She'd become them.

*They've taken too much from us.*

*They'll take no more.*

*Let's destroy them.*

Her feet carried her forward toward the closed door. She didn't slow as it drew closer. Neither did she start at the impact when her face slammed into it. Instead, the door fell, and she continued forward as if no obstacle had stood in her way.

Flames burst through her fingers. Not just the heated sensations before—real, roaring fire that incinerated everything they touched. Her own body was not impervious to their effects—the very hands that held the flames bore angry red burns. Though she saw them, she didn't feel them.

*We're already gone.*

*We can't get back what was taken from us.*

*Let's destroy them.*

No more would fall to the League. Not here, at least.

She moved up the stairs, spreading her flames. No—not her flames. The collective fire of so many who'd already been lost, so many whose names no one would know.

Cries of alarm sounded ahead. She strode forward, unmoved. Many ran for the doors, but the flames reached them first. Yellow fire crawled up the walls, the windows, the decor with a will of their own. They swallowed the image of the Forbidden Palace, incinerated the Zodiac statues. They consumed the faces that had watched so mercilessly, yet now screamed so desperately. Brad Wexler, flailing as the flesh melted from his face. Alessandor Earnest, writhing as the heat fused her sequined dress to her skin. Kennedy Thomson, throwing her arms up in vain as a burning beam crashed down on her.

Grace caught Matt's eyes. Tears of terror streamed down his face.

*Cry, asshole, cry.*

*All of you, cry.*

*Cry with the pain you've inflicted upon so many.*

Panning her gaze across the sea of white faces, she laughed. "If there is no League, why do you scream when we burn it down?"

*Recovered security footage showed Grace Chang laying waste to all around her. By the time emergency responders arrived, only the burned-out walls of what was once a magnificent stone building remained. Tearful memorials were held for those who'd been inside, all speaking of what angels the dead had once been, none speaking of the terror they'd inflicted.*

*The police concluded that Grace must have perished in the disaster, but others aren't so sure. They say she escaped and resumed her life with a new identity but the same face.*

*She's been spotted on the subway, the sleek-suited lady clutching the pole with her right hand and scrolling through her work emails with her left. She's been seen at the farmer's market, the one in fashionable athleisure. Some glimpsed her in Pilates class, yet saw none of her life story in her impeccable form.*

*So, where is Grace Chang now? Like I said, you've probably met her.*

# Hell Dogs
# of Eldorado Canyon

## By Jonathan Maberry

-1-

"**Y**OU pretty much just killed that fellow," said Buck Merker. "You know that, right?"

The rancher, Joshua Fowler, turned to look at the man who'd just spoken.

"What's that, Buck?" he asked.

Buck took a long pull of his beer, wiped foam from his mustache, and nodded in the direction of the open saloon door. Outside a medium-sized man was untying his horse from the post. The fellow was an oddity. Half redhaired second-generation Scotsman and half Comanche. And looking like equal parts of each. Flame-red ponytails, blue eyes, but swarthy skin and shelf-like cheekbones. The clothes were no different than most drovers wore, but the earrings—pieces of shell dangling from silver wire—were part of the Comanche culture. The expression the man wore was Comanche, too—bitter and disappointed.

"Wasn't eavesdropping, Joshua," said Buck, "but I overheard you selling him on the idea of treasure up in those hills. He came to point like a bird dog and there he goes, riding off."

"Nothing wrong with hiring someone to do some looking around," said Fowler.

"I didn't hear you tell him what happened to the last four people you sent up there. Or the others who heard about the treasure and decided to give it a go. What's it now? Eighteen total in three years?"

Fowler, a squatty man with furry sideburns and plump little lips like a girl, just shrugged. "I didn't tell him any lies."

"Sure, okay," conceded Buck, "but you sure goldurn didn't tell him all the truth."

Fowler rapped the bar and pointed at his glass. Only after it was full of whiskey again and he'd taken a sip, did he reply.

"Guess you don't know who that man is," he said.

Buck sniffed. "Another half-breed looking for work without knowing what he was signing on for, I suspect."

"Two things," said Fowler. "Unless you want your meat and veg sliced off while you sleep I wouldn't let him hear you call him a 'breed.'"

"It's what he is."

"But he doesn't like the word, so

maybe hold your tongue around him." Fowler smiled thinly. "That fellow there is a sight touchy about that. Tends to take offense."

"Okay, sure, whatever," said Buck. "What's the *other* thing?"

"His name," said Fowler. "Though I'll bet a shiny half dollar that you've heard of him. And once I tell you I'll bet the other half of that dollar that you'll be a little more careful of what you say around him, should he actually come back here."

Buck looked interested. "His name? And what would that be?"

"That there, son," said Fowler, pointed to the man who had just swung into the saddle, "is Red MacGill."

Buck, who was a small-time farmer and part-time scout, went pale.

"*That's* Red MacGill?" he gasped.

"In the actual flesh."

Buck got up and walked over to the door, then went outside to watch MacGill ride away. Fowler, amused, joined him.

"You still think I just sent a man to his death?" asked the rancher.

Buck shook his head. "Lord a'mercy," he breathed, "but I pity anyone who gets in his way. Anyone living...or dead."

-2-

RED MacGill had heard a little of that conversation while he was untying Nightmare. He'd heard some variation of that in a hundred towns.

Who is that man?

That's Red MacGill.

Or...*that's the one they called the 'sorter'*.

Sorter.

That was one of the few words someone had hung on him that Red didn't mind. A sorter of problems. A sorter-out. Someone who could get to the bottom of things.

As adjectives went, it wasn't bad. And it was accurate enough. His business was that of a 'sorter of problems'. Not figuring out who stole a horse or cut a fence or robbed a train. He felt himself drawn to less simple problems. What his mother's people called 'old troubles'. Things that haunted the land before the white men came; but which were stirred up and confused because of the clash of old medicine and new influences. Troubles that came from the ghosts, gods and demons of Europe invading the lands and causing problems with the spirits who already lived in the plains and mountains, in the valleys and caves.

Like the one he'd just been hired to sort out here in near the town of Nelson, Nevada. Up in Eldorado Canyon. Away from farms and families; deep in country pockmarked by gold mines. On lands where ancient cities were carved into the living rock walls—but long since abandoned. Lands where Paiutes and Mojave lived—or, where they tried to live when the white men left them alone. And

where those people died when settlers, ranchers, or the government
decided that stripping gold and
silver from the ground mattered
more than the less enforceable
rights of whomever was pitching a
tipi or constructing a lodge.

There was trouble there. In and
around the mines, and near the
winding blue snake that was the
Colorado River. Maybe it was his
kind of trouble, and maybe it was
claim-jumpers, bandits, or other
white men playing the manifest
destiny game.

Red rather hoped it was a real
ghost causing the mischief. There
would be some justice there—
depending on whose ghost it was.

But he didn't hold much hope
of that. He'd sorted a lot of haunt-
ings over the years, and had found
very few ghosts. Or even hints of
haunts. Mostly it was people being
afraid of the dark and refusing to
admit it, and instead blaming spirits from the larger world.

That didn't matter all that much
to Red. The money they paid him
to figure it out spent the same in
either case.

He aimed Nightmare in the
right direction and settled into the
saddle for the ride. The morning
sun was playing games behind the
clouds and there was the smell
of wildflowers, horse dung, and
cooking smoke on the breeze.
Rather nice; but he wanted to
smell the desert outside of town.
Where the air was cleaner and it
didn't smell like the invaders who

called this their country.

He rode into the big open lands,
heading for haunted mountains.

-3-

THE job seemed simple enough—
but they always did at the out-
set.

"Need you to go out to Eldorado Canyon and see about those
dogs," was how Mr. Fowler had
put it.

"Dogs…?" Red had smiled.

"Dogs," agreed Fowler.

"No, that was a leading question," said Red. "The 'what the
heck do you mean by dogs' was
implied."

Fowler frowned at that. "You
making fun of me?"

"Having fun," corrected Red.
"Not the same thing."

It took the rancher a moment to
sort through that, but in the end
he nodded. He sipped his whiskey,
nodded again, and said, "Not sure
what you know about the mining
rush out here."

"Lots of folks came out here in
a hurry and filed claims," said Red
with a shrug. "Some made it rich.
Some lost their shirts. And a lot of
red men got kicked off their land."

Fowler looked down into the
golden depths of his glass. "Yeah,
I guess that about says it."

"I'm not here to judge," said
Red, lying because there was no
benefit into picking a cultural fight
with this man. "What about all
that has you shook up? I thought
most of the mines were played out

or never hit a lode at all."

"Most are shut down," said Fowler. "A few are still working. Since things have slowed down, the owners of the last working mines had formed a coalition. Sharing the costs, and chipping in for security that oversees the whole area."

"Okay," said Red, who'd heard about that kind of arrangement elsewhere. "But how exactly do dogs figure in? Someone been killing guard dogs? Maybe leaving out poisoned meat?"

That was a common trick used by the slyer and more vicious claim-jumpers. Using poison was a safe method. Killing dogs using something quite like a bow and arrows did the trick, too, providing the archer can stay upwind of the dog, and if they had the right skill level. It also allowed the blame to be shifted to local natives rather than white rivals. Some even went as far as to fabricate tribal markings and fletching techniques on the arrows. When there was a potential fortune to be had, it was often worth going that extra mile.

But Fowler shook his head. "No. If it was only that, those of us in the coalition would just hire more men to work sentry. And, by the way, we actually did that, but not for the reason you think."

"Okay," said Red.

"The problem is the dogs have turned on our people up there."

"Turned...?"

"Yes sir. Started a couple months ago," said Fowler, leaning closer and lowering his voice. "When some of the mines played out the owners just up and left. Too expensive to sell off their equipment—most of which was leased or bought on credit. So some just up and left everything, and in some cases even leaving their dogs."

Red nodded, having heard about that sort of thing, too. The miners would keep the guard dogs chained up outside or loose inside as a way of making it look like someone was planning on coming back. By the time it became apparent they'd skipped out on employee wages and store debt, the owners were long gone. And the dogs? They generally starved to death or went feral. When he asked Fowler about this, the man shook his head.

"There were a few dogs left behind and died out there, sure, but they aren't the ones I'm talking about," said Fowler. "I'm talking about the coalition's dogs, the ones we had up there. Well-fed and well taken care of. So it's *our* dogs that have started wandering off at night. No traces. Just up and gone. First a couple, but and since it started all ten of them have vanished." Fowler paused and sipped, needing the courage that came out of strong spirits. "Then they started coming back at night, you see."

"Came back?"

"In the dead of night, yes sir," said Fowler. "They been attacking some of the guards and even went after our foreman, who was asleep in his cabin near the mine."

"How bad were these attacks?"

Fowler's eyes went hard. "Bad as bad can get. Tore those poor sons of bitches to pieces—God rest their souls. Eight good men dead, and one man missing. Dutch Gunderson. Big ol' boy, too. Must have taken the whole pack to drag him off. Guess we'll find his bones somewhere out in the canyons. With all those rocks there's a million places where those dogs could have dragged him. And we had all that rain, so there's no trail worth following."

"Dogs did that?"

"Dogs," agreed Fowler. "Damn near ate the foreman down to his bones, too. It was a sight to makes a man want to go to church and pray like he means it. Pray for his soul."

"Not wolves?" asked Red. "Or maybe mountain lions? Hell, even a bear's more likely to do mischief like that. Makes more sense than guard dogs turning on folks."

That's when Fowler had given him a smile that was part smug and part scared.

"If this made sense, Mr. Mac-Gill," he said, "we wouldn't be drinking this much whiskey this early on a Sunday, now would we?"

-4-

AS he made his way toward the mining settlement, Red went over the details.

The first attack was just shy of two months ago. Three men were killed on two consecutive nights, though only two bodies were actually found. The first man to die, Curly James, was technically only presumed dead. He'd been riding around the perimeter of the largest mine, a loop that covered quite a few miles. A couple of miners staggering back to their bunks after a night of beer and cards heard the screams. A man's voice and also the terrified shriek of a horse. They alerted the rest of the guards and a group went out looking for Curly. They found his horse first—it was slain by claws and teeth and was barely able to stagger. Later, when the bites were examined it was determined that, without a doubt, they were made by dog teeth. Maybe by several dogs, since one hound could never take down half a ton of horse.

The searchers followed the horse's blood trail and it led them to a clearing where everything—ground, trees, rocks—was splashed with fresh blood. They found Curly's clothes, longjohns and all, torn and soaked with gore. They found his gunbelt, the leather slashed open but the pistol still in the holster, as if the poor bastard never had a chance to draw his sidearm. And that was all they found. No trace of Curly was ever found, and the mining coalition had made sure the search was thorough.

And as for Dutch Gunderson, they never even found bloody clothes. He was simply gone. Left all of his belongings behind, including personal items he would have taken with him if all he wanted to do was leave a failing mine and skip out on any debts he might have with the company store.

It wasn't until later that awful night that the rest of the miners realized that all of the camp's dogs were gone. The footprints they left were so confusing that it was impossible to tell where they'd run off to.

The next night there was another attack, and this time a pair of guards walking the perimeter were attacked. Both men were killed, their throats torn away by fangs. Doc Wheeler came out from town and pronounced that it was definitely dog bites that did for those men. And it was an opinion that held because a few weeks later three more men died. In those cases, it was one man per night.

In two cases, there were shots fired, but no dead dogs found anywhere. Nor were packs of dogs spotted. And that was very odd. From what Fowler told him, more than a dozen large mixed-breed dogs had gone missing, and that was a very large pack. Hard to believe they hadn't been spotted at all and yet loitered in the vicinity to make a series of careful attacks.

The oddities in the case were many, and if it hadn't been for them, Red would have passed on the job. He had a fair stash in a couple of banks—one in Dodge City and another in Abilene—so he was drawn more by the genuine mystery. Not that he said as much to Fowler, because even on a curiosity job, Red still liked to get paid a good wage. He wanted the word spread as well as about what he did to earn his coin.

Something shook him out of his reverie and Red looked up abruptly. It took a moment to find what had triggered his awareness, but then he saw it. Or, rather, them. Off to his left, maybe a mile to the west there were three buzzards circling slowly on warm up-currents.

"Whoa, Nightmare," he told the horse, and it obediently stopped, swishing a tail to chase away flies. Red stood up in the stirrups and squinted into the still air. The sun was edging toward the west and he reckoned that he had about three hours of good daylight left. Red let the sounds of the horse's breathing and the creak of saddle leather fade out of his awareness as he studied those birds.

On any ordinary day vultures in canyon country would mean little. This was a hard landscape, and out here death was common. Animals dying natural deaths were less common than being hunted and killed. That painted the land with red and put the scent of red—fresh or spoiled—into the dry air. He sniffed, but if there was anything to smell it was either faded or too far away.

Until it wasn't...

A rogue breeze came wandering through the rocks and it brought with it the faint, sweet, sickly smell of death. Red nudged Nightmare and they turned from the road that led to the mine and heading in the direction of those buzzards.

Red was a tracker and knew the difference between the smells of old death and new. This stink had a bit of both, as if there were more than one dead thing out there.

-5-

DEATH waited to be found. Nightmare began making nervous grunts before they rounded the last turn, and Red made sure his pistol was loose in the holster. He similarly adjusted the handles of several knives and the stock of his rifle. He was no quick-draw gunslinger like the ones he read in dime novels, but he generally hit what he aimed at. He had a cool head and tended not to panic or react out of alarm. And he'd seen every kind of death there was to see out in the natural world. From the leavings of animal kills to mass buffalo slaughters by bastards like Buffalo Bill to what was left of villages after cavalry came through to 'settle the redskins down'—as the phrase was often noted in newspapers.

But when he rounded the turn he stopped and stared in shock.

The lonely trail through the ageless rocks seemed to vanish in a heartbeat and he sat on his horse on the killing floor of an abattoir.

It was a scene from hell. Or from the kind of opium dream that turns dark and bares your neck to demons.

The missing dogs were there. All ten of them. Though not all of any of the hounds. Red had to count skulls and spines to tally it up. There were patches of torn fur and splintered ribs, cracked hip bones and scores of cracked teeth. What little flesh remained was spoiled and crawling with maggots and flies.

But that was not the worst of it. Not by a long mile.

There were other bones, other leavings. Horses and goats, most of a cow, and smaller animals, too. Raccoons, gophers, lizards, and birds. All dead. All torn to pieces.

Red swung from the saddle, drawing his pistol as he did so. The barrel was covered with a filigree made of runes and symbols from a score of faiths, and the sandalwood handle was inlaid with silver that had been blessed by the great Comanche chief and medicine man Isa-tai. Even the bullets in each chamber were cut with special runes and bits of prayer. All of that was part of his method, his rhythm and system; and most of the time it gave him both comfort and protection.

Now, though...

This slaughter was horrific and as he stood there, Red could feel all of the heat leak out of the day.

If all of the miners' dogs were dead, then what had killed them?

More to the point, what had killed those men?

What had killed and eaten them?

Red moved cautiously from one ruined corpse to another. He read the orientation of bones, looking for the patterns of killing and feeding typical of cougars and bears. Many of the bones were bitten or gnawed, the bigger ones cracked open and the marrow sucked out.

The bite marks were strange. All of the bites seem to have been made by the same animal, but how could a single animal—even a bear—do this much damage. Strong as bears are, a pack of dogs would have torn it to pieces, or at very least driven it off. Besides, the shape of the tooth marks didn't fit any kind of bear Red ever saw. And the bites were definitely not those of a big cat. That left other dogs, coyotes, and wolves, but even there Red had his doubts.

The radius of the bites were simply too big, even for a timber wolf. Maybe a great Dane could have a bite that wide, but they weren't the kind of dog to do this kind of thing. And, again, if one dog was hunting these hills and canyons, the other dogs would have killed it by now. Fowler said that the mining camp guard dogs were all big—with mixes of French Berger Picard, English and Irish setters, German Pointer, bull mastiffs, and bull terriers.

The floor of that clearing was hard rock that did not take a print, and the rain Fowler mentioned probably washed right through here. Spoiled any hope of picking up a clear trail. Even so, it had to be something that big to do this kind of damage, which meant there would be prints somewhere.

Red looked up at the sky, debating whether to search now or come back at first light. The downside to waiting was that the biggest rocks in this part of the canyon were to the east of where he stood, which meant that morning light would create dense shadows. That might mean he'd need to wait until close to noon before he could hope to pick up a trail.

That wouldn't do. It wasted too much time, and it risked another night of attacks in the dark.

"Damn," he murmured, knowing that the decision was already made for him.

He sheathed his knife, and then checked his pistol to make sure it was loaded. Then he began walking around the kill site in an outward expanding spiral. Lizards scampered away to find cover under rocks. The buzzards still circled above, and crows gossiped in the trees. Flies buzzed around and the sun baked the rocks to the point where Red had to put on a pair of old gloves to keep his fingers from being scorched.

He found tracks here and there, but they were inconclusive and confusing. There were prints from a number of animals, incl:-ding many dogs and coyotes, but -here were also human prints. Boots and bare feet, though why on earth anyone would take their shoes off out here was beyond him. No moccasins, which was a bit of a relief. Last thing he wanted to find was proof that this was some kind of revenge thing against the white miners. Not that Red disagreed in principle, but every year there were more and more whites out here. Black men, too, who'd come west to escape the Civil War, or who were freed slaves looking for a better life as a miner or drover. Retaliation by these invaders was swift and often spilled over into the lives of red men and women who had nothing whatsoever to do with mischief of this kind.

But his relief at that was short-lived because he could not make sense of the evidence he found. Red MacGill was a superb tracker and hunter, but he felt like a blind novice.

The sun slid further toward the edge of the world and he realized that he'd spent too much time looking. Even if he left right away it was unlikely he'd reach the Eldorado Mines before sunset. It was a day past the full moon, so there would be light to ride by.

Right now the early twilight allowed the slanting rays of the sun to hit the ground at angles that cast small shadows in ways that helped him find less obvious

tracks. There was one set of tracks that was particularly puzzling to him. It was clearly made by whatever animal did all this killing, because those tracks circled and returned to the killing floor from a dozen different directions. The problem is that the tracks were weirdly distorted. They overlaid and sometimes obscured the bare footprints and some of the booted prints, and the confusion made it hard to find all four animal prints. He mostly found hind paw prints and few corresponding front paw marks.

He squatted by one clear set of prints, measuring them with his own palm.

"That's a big damn dog," he said aloud. "Real big and—"

Which is when Nightmare screamed.

-6-

RED whipped around and rose to a fighting crouch, the knife clutched in a tight fist.

A man stood fifteen feet behind him.

A man who Red had not heard approach.

A man who pointed the big black mouth of a shotgun directly at him.

Red froze.

"Who...," began the man, but he faltered and had to try it again. "Wh-who are you?" There was a tremolo in his voice.

Red straightened slowly, lowering the knife and holding his

other hand out, palm toward the stranger.

"I'm working for the mining company," he said, keeping his voice calm.

Doubt clouded the man's eyes. His gaze darted to the big horse, to the bones and gruesome debris on the hard ground, and then back to Red.

"I work for the coalition," the man said slowly. He was medium height—perhaps two or three inches shorter than Red—and dressed in baggy clothes. His shirt was four sizes too big and the cuffs of his blue jeans were rolled up. The belt was cinched tight around the baggy waist, causing the fabric to be rippled like drapes. He wore no hat; however his face was pale and unburned by the scorching sun. He had a cap of curly brown hair and gray eyes that were filled with suspicion. The man raised the gun barrel from Red's chest and pointed it at his face. "I've worked for them for three years and I don't know you at all."

"I'm new," said Red quickly. "Mr. Fowler hired me just this morning. I'm heading up to the mine now."

The gray eyes narrowed. "This clearing isn't on the way to the mine."

"It's not far from the trail," said Red. "I saw buzzards and came over to see what was what."

"Why? What's it to you? And since when does Old Man Fowler hire injuns?"

Red let that pass. "I'm a scout," he said. "A tracker. Fowler hired me to look for the dogs that have been killing the men at the mine."

"Is that so?"

"It is. So...since we're working for the same man, mind telling me your name?"

The man studied him, the shotgun barrel unwavering. Then, after nearly half a silent minute, the gun sagged down until it pointed at the floor.

"Maciej Gunderson," he said. "People call me Dutch."

Red nodded. "Dutch, eh? People think you're dead. They think the dogs dragged you off."

Dutch said nothing, but merely shook his head.

"You went missing though..." prompted Red.

"No," said Dutch. "I went hunting."

"Hunting?"

"For whoever killed my friends."

"For the dogs, you mean?" asked Red.

Dutch used an uptick of his chin to indicate the bones all around the clearing. "What do you think?"

Without looking around, Red said, "I guess it wasn't dogs after all."

"It wasn't dogs," agreed Dutch.

"Not these dogs, anyway." Red explained about the bite marks. "Either we have the biggest coyote known to man, some new breed of wolf, or a mixed-breed dog that has a bite that a grizzly would be proud of."

Dutch's eyes flicked again to the carcasses. "How do you know that?"

"As I said, I'm a tracker."

Red walked slowly over to his horse and made a show of checking and adjusting the saddle buckles.

"Mr. Fowler will be pretty happy to know that you're okay," he said.

Dutch said nothing.

"Though I do have to ask... why'd you stay out here all this time?"

"I told you," said Dutch, watching everything Red did with those pale gray eyes. "I've been out here hunting."

"Sure," said Red amiably, "but as I understand it, you didn't leave a note or anything. Didn't take any of your gear..."

"I left a note," said Dutch. "I told one of the guys there, too."

"Fowler didn't say anything about that."

The shadows were growing long, as if every rock and tree was leaking black oil in expanding puddles. Red glanced at the horizon and saw that the sun was above to topple over the canyon wall. Soon the whole area would be plunged into darkness. He looked over his other shoulder and saw that the moon was already above the horizon and beginning its climb. Red kept his face bland as he tightened a girth that didn't need tightening. It was the one closest to the Winchester in the leather scabbard.

He turned back to Dutch, hoisting a faint friendly smile onto his mouth.

"Maybe we should both head back to the mine. I could use some rest and I think we can both use some grub. You look half starved."

"Me?"

"Sure," said Red, his fingers brushing the side of the rifle stock, "you must be hungry. You came up here with no supplies and you've been gone two weeks. Your clothes have gotten all baggy."

Dutch absently touched the puckered waistband of the jeans. His fingers idly traced the pot-metal belt buckle. However, his eyes weren't fixed on Red. They looked past him.

Past... and up.

Red nearly turned to follow the man's line of sight, but he knew what Dutch was looking at. And it made his blood turn to ice.

He said, "Why are you wearing Dutch Gunderson's clothes?"

The man said nothing. However a smile was beginning to crawl onto his lips. It was a small, sly, secretive smile. An ugly smile.

"Or should I guess?" asked Red.

Without looking at him, the man said, "Sure. Go ahead. Let's see how clever you are."

"You don't have even a trace of an accent," said Red. "Not Dutch or anything."

The man said nothing.

"Fowler told me that Dutch was a big fellow."

"Yes." The smile was growing.

"A real big fellow, and you're shorter than I am."

"Big enough," said the man.

Red's fingers rested on the stock of his rifle.

"And there's you with all that curly hair." He leaned on the word 'curly'.

The smile grew and grew.

"They found your clothes all torn apart," said Red. "Torn and bloody."

"Did they now?" The man's voice seemed different. Thicker and deeper.

Red felt a fat bead of icy sweat trickle down his spine. "Why don't you come back to the mine with me, Curly?"

Curly James—for it was clearly the mine foreman—smiled even more at the mention of his name. "Oh, I'll head that way tonight," he said.

They looked at each other. The distance between them was less than twenty feet. Despite the conversation they were having out loud, Red knew that they were both keenly aware of a separate and altogether more important conversation unfolding on a different level. In look and the attitudes of their bodies, in Curly's smile and Red's hand on his rifle stock. So much was being said, and it terrified Red.

It took a lot for him to ask the question that burned in his mind.

He looked around at the bones and spoiled meat and then raised his eyes to meet Curly's. The man's eyes were no longer pale gray. The iris was ringed by a yellow that glowed like molten gold, and the gray itself has become stained with a pale green that was at once sickly and vibrant. In the center of the black pupil there were sparks of red, as if the man's hungers were ignited fires inside him.

"Why?" asked Red.

That smiling mouth grew wider still. It stretched the corners of Curly's mouth so far the skin at the corner tore and thin lines of blood ran down over his chin.

"Why?" he echoed. "Why not?"

"You worked with those men," said Red. "You knew them. They were your friends. What did they do to deserve what happened to them?"

Curly did not answer. His tongue—now strangely long—lapped out to lap up the blood. Nightmare whinnied and shifted; his big eyes rolled in fear. Red had to hold onto the edge of the saddle and the stock of the rifle to keep the horse from bolting.

"At least tell me how this happened to you," pleaded Red. "Were you attacked by someone? Is this a family curse? Was a curse put on you?"

Curly shook his head slowly, the smile never wavering. His eyes burned with green and gold and red.

"You wouldn't understand," he said.

"Try me," said Red. "You might be surprised at how much I understand."

As he spoke he could hear the quaver in his voice. The sun was little more than a flickering spark on the western horizon. In the east the world was already dressing for night, and the moon was rising behind the skeletal arms of pinyon trees.

Curly took a step forward, making Red flinch backward and half draw the rifle from its scabbard. The man saw that and laughed.

"People tell tales," said the foreman. "They make it a romance. A curse on some innocent soul. An evil spell that awakens the beast within."

As he spoke his voice changed even more. Not only becoming deeper and rougher, but the accent changed from a drover's drawl to something else. German, thought Red, or something close. And there was a heavier sense of gravity to his diction.

"But this is no curse," said Curly. "I am no one's victim. I've never been anyone's victim. That's not how this works. It's passed from father to son, from mother to daughter, along the road of years. This is has been who we are going back three and a half thousand years. My ancestors have hunting your kind since the Hittites swept across the Eastern Mediterranean. We hunting through the rise of Rome and glutted ourselves as it fell. You think it was only swords and spears that toppled the empire? What is a battlefield but a dining hall for my kind? What are any of you but cattle?"

"But why here? Why this place?"

demanded Red. "Why this mine and these people?"

Curly James looked genuinely confused. "Why? Why not? Those miners…so hardy, so fit. So much meat on the bone." He plucked at his stolen clothing. "So much to enjoy."

Now, though, the clothes were less baggy. It was as if Curly were swelling inside those garments. His chest was already broader, and the shirt sleeves were now stretched tight over biceps that, moments before, were half the size.

He looked down at the shotgun he still held and laughed as he let it drop from fingers grown curiously long. Red saw that the man's nails had grown, too. Each was dark, almost black, and they curled over the pads as they tapered toward wicked points.

"You murdered all those men," said Red as he very slowly, very gingerly began to slide the rifle free.

"I hunted them," said Curly, and his voice was no longer even remotely human. "You can only murder your own kind." His taloned fingers fumbled a bit as he unbuttoned the shirt and let it fall. His torso was still man-shaped, but the muscles were swollen and stood out with rigid tension. Black hair that was as curly as that on his head seemed to grow before Red's eyes.

"You're st-still human," said Red, tripping over the words. "There are only three days of the full moon. Those are the days you kill. I figured that out from the dates Fowler gave me. May 12th and 13th, the full moon and the day after. April 13, 14, 15—all three days. And tonight is the last of this month's cycle. Tomorrow you won't be a...a..."

"Oh, have the courage to say the word," sneered Curly as he kicked off his shoes and unbuckled his jeans. He stepped out of the trousers with legs that were strangely deformed. And his feet were the most transformed, with the heel thinning and rising so that Curly's weight was shifted onto the balls of his feet. Toenails grown long and strong, clawed at the ground. And now Red knew why he had not found tracks of a four-legged predator. This creature stood upright like a man, even though his humanity was fading before Red's eyes.

Red pulled the rifle free and swung the barrel around toward the creature.

"Werewolf," whispered Red.

"Yesssss," said Curly, letting the word hiss out. "And I'm soooooo hungry."

Red raised the rifle, tucking the stock into his shoulder.

"I can't let you kill anyone else," he said.

Curly threw back his head and laughed. It was the worst sound Red had ever heard. It was as if thunder broke inside the man's chest and boomed out through a mouth that had stretched too wide. It smashed through the clearing and into the trees. The sound was so loud, so intensely wrong that creosote bushes burst into flame and the crows in the trees pitched forward dead, their hearts exploding in their chests. Blood welled in Red's nose and ears and he staggered backward, the rifle falling from his hands as he screamed. But his own scream was lost beneath the weight of the werewolf's laugh, and blood sprayed from his mouth. Red's knees buckled as the monster's laugh became a howl that tore the twilight apart.

Above them, the moon broke free from the cage of tree branches and soared into the darkening sky. It was a day past full, but it was massive—swollen and unclean. It leered down on the drama playing out between man and monster.

Red dropped to his knees as the last of the façade of humanity fell away and Curly James became fully who he was. His true self—freed of the disguise of humanity he was forced to wear—was this thing. This beast.

The werewolf towered over him, limbs twisted with hard muscles, skin covered now in a gleaming black pelt. The growls that rose from his throat were filled with hate and hunger and red joy.

Red MacGill looked up at the monster and saw his doom. Blood choked him and ran freely from his nostrils. His head rang from the assault of that evil laughter.

His rifle lay in the dirt and he fumbled for his pistol, but even as he drew it the werewolf lashed out and slapped it away. The gun, with all of its sacred bullets, went spinning off into the brush.

Then the creature seized him by the shirtfront and jerked him to his feet. Then further still, lifting him until the toes of his shoes were barely touching the ground. The monster pulled him close and exhaled a fetid breath that smelled of brimstone and rancid meat. This was death's champion and Red's heart was fit to burst as a tidal surge of horror swept through him.

But even as the werewolf's massive jaws gaped wide for that killing bite, Red's hand moved—more of its own accord rather than any conscious action. His trembling fingers touched the handle of his knife, scrabbling and clawing at it. The blade rasped as it cleared the leather and Red almost—almost—dropped it.

Those wicked fangs shone in the moonlight and a growl of bottomless, aching hunger filled the air as the monster bent forward to bite. It did not even try to stop him from using that knife. What, after all, was steel to a creature like this?

Red screamed.

He screamed as the teeth clamped around his shoulder.

He screamed as his blood exploded from the savage wound.

He screamed as he thrust the blade into the werewolf's iron-hard stomach.

He screamed as he wrenched the knife sideways, ripping through muscle and skin and intestines. Steam erupted from the monstrous flesh as the knife's carved runes passed through inhuman tissue.

The werewolf screamed, too.

In hunger. In pain.

They both shrieked as they fell.

-7-

RED had no idea how long he lay there.

Hours.

Forever.

He woke when Nightmare came and licked his face.

Red opened his eyes and stared up at the horse. Nightmare's eyes were huge and white showed all around the iris. His mouth was flecked with white foam and ripples of awful tension rippled through the big animal's heavy frame.

Above the horse, Red could see the wicked moon riding across the sky. Much higher now, nearly overhead.

It took such great effort for Red to move because of the weight that lay across him, pressing him against the rocks.

It was Curly Janes.

Not the beast. Only the man. What was left of the man. His body looked flattened, the muscles slack from the massive loss of blood. It pooled around Red's body, black as oil, stinking of copper and wrongness.

And Red knew that his own blood was mixed in with Curly's. His shoulder hurt as if white hot coals were searing their way into his skin. He could feel each separate puncture. When he moved his arm there was a grating sound as bones ground against each other.

It took Red a long time to worm his way out, pushing and shoving the corpse off of him. He had to do it one handed because his left collarbone was broken, and possibly his shoulder blade. The bite had been devastating.

He grabbed onto Nightmare's stirrup to pull himself to his knees, and then used the saddle to climb to his feet. It took forever and each movement ignited fresh agony. But he got up. Then he leaned wearily against the horse, head resting on the animal's neck.

The moon was so bright above him.

So bright.

Red tried not to look at it because he was afraid that it would be looking back. Afraid that it would be staring at him and into him. He did not want to see recognition in that pale and bloated face above him in the night sky. He did not want to see a knowing smirk on that distant rock.

"Please," he said, gasping it out. "Please."

When he was strong enough, Red staggered over to Curly's body. He gripped the handle of his knife and with a cry of mingled horror and pain, tore it free. Moonlight etched each rune, each sigil carved into the steel.

"Please..." he begged as he pressed the sacred blade against the terrible wound in his shoulder. Hoping, praying that all he felt was cold steel. Begging the night, the darkness, his ancestors, and any gods who might be listening for there to be no steam rising from his own flesh.

"Please," he said, and he said it over and over again. "Please."

Above him, the moon leered at him.

# About Our Contributors

AWARD-WINNING author, editor, and publisher DANIELLE ACKLEY-MCPHAIL has worked both sides of the publishing industry for longer than she cares to admit. In 2014 she joined forces with husband Mike McPhail and friend Greg Schauer to form her own publishing house, eSpec Books (www.especbooks.com). Her published works include six novels, *Yesterday's Dreams, Tomorrow's Memories, Today's Promise, The Halfling's Court, The Redcaps' Queen,* and *Baba Ali and the Clockwork Djinn,* written with Day Al-Mohamed. She is also the author of the solo collections *Eternal Wanderings, A Legacy of Stars, Consigned to the Sea, Flash in the Can, Transcendence, Between Darkness and Light,* and the non-fiction writers' guides *The Literary Handyman* and *LH: Build-A-Book Workshop.* She is the senior editor of the *Bad-Ass Faeries* anthology series, *Gaslight & Grimm, Side of Good/Side of Evil, After Punk,* and *Footprints in the Stars.* Her short stories are included in numerous other anthologies and collections. In addition, she crafts and sells original costume horns under the moniker The Hornie Lady Custom Costume Horns, and homemade flavor-infused candied ginger under the brand of Ginger KICK! at literary conventions, on commission, and wholesale. Danielle lives in New Jersey with husband and fellow writer, Mike McPhail and one extremely spoiled cat. To learn more about her work, visit www.sidhenadaire.com or www.especbooks.

JUNE BRIGMAN has enjoyed a long and varied career as a cartoonist, drawing such comic book titles as *Alpha Flight, Supergirl,* and *Star Wars.* She is the co-creator (with Louise Simonson) of the *Power Pack* series from Marvel Comics. She is also the co-creator (with Stuart Moore) of the *Captain Ginger* series from Ahoy Comics. Assisted by her husband, inker/colorist Roy Richardson, she illustrated the *Brenda Starr* comic strip for fifteen years, and has drawn many educational comics, as well as doing illustrations for *Horse & Rider* magazine. June and Roy have recently taken over the artistic reins of the long-running *Mary Worth* comic strip. June has a BFA in Sequential Art from Empire State University, and an MFA in

Illustration from the Savannah College of Art and Design. She is currently an adjunct professor of Sequential Art at Kennesaw State University. When not at the drawing board, June is in the saddle riding Isabelle, her beautiful gray mare.

MICHAEL A. BURSTEIN has earned ten Hugo nominations and four Nebula nominations for his short fiction, which is collected in the volume *I Remember the Future*. Burstein lives with his family in the town of Brookline, Massachusetts, where he is an elected Town Meeting Member and Library Trustee. He has two degrees in Physics, once worked at Los Alamos Labs, and has appeared in not one, but two Woody Allen movies.

KERRY CALLEN has been an writer/artist for *MAD magazine*, creator of the indy comic *Halo and Sprocket*, and a longtime Art Director for Hallmark Cards. His current comic work can be found in various places around the internet.

GARY CARBON is a Chicago-based artist, who grew on up on a steady diet of comic books, TV, and movies. This inspired him to follow his interest in art and focus on trying to bring fictional and mythological characters to life. His art focused on these characters in several formats—comic books, graphic novel illustrations, and photography. Gary work includes working with multiple publishers for the pulp character the Spider as well as small publishers and characters such as Athena Voltaire and Erin Storm, a character he co-created with Rob Jones. Gary works both traditionally in pencil, pen and ink, pastel, charcoal, gauche and oil paint as well as digitally. To see more of his work, visit garycarbonart.com

RUSS COLCHAMIRO is the author of the rollicking sci-fi adventure, *Crossline*, the zany sci-fi/fantasy backpacking series *Finders Keepers*, *Genius de Milo*, and *Astropalooza*, editor of the sci-fi-themed mystery anthology *Love, Murder & Mayhem*, and co-author and co-editor of *Murder in Montague Falls*, a noir-inspired collection of novellas. His latest novel is the sci-fi mystery *Crackle and Fire*, featuring his intergalactic private eye Angela Hardwicke. Russ has also written short fiction for more than a dozen sci-fi and fantasy anthologies, and hosts the *Russ's Rockin' Rollercoaster* podcast, interviewing a who's who of sci-fi, fantasy, and mystery authors. He lives in New Jersey with his wife and two children. For more on Russ's fiction, visit www.russcolchamiro.com, follow him on Twitter and Instagram @AuthorDudeRuss, 'like' his Facebook author page www.facebook.com/RussColchamiro-Author, and watch his podcast on

YouTube at https://www.youtube.com/channel/UCUb7MDUN-QxyVRBDOTVEqOaw

**M**IKE COLLINS has been working in comics, books and TV for over 25 years, producing graphics for publishers including Marvel, DC and Warners Comics in the USA, Rebellion, Panini and Eaglemoss in the UK. For TV, he contributed art to the *I'm In A Rock'n'Roll Band* and *Boy Band* series, also Planet Dinosaur; for *Doctor Who Confidential* and *Totally Doctor Who*. He has also been involved in set design for S4C. He is a storyboard artist for animation, including *Horrid Henry*, *Hana's Helpline*, *Cym Teg* and *Igam Ogam*, and produced illustrations for *The Daily Telegraph*, *Western Mail* and *The Daily Star*. He wrote and illustrated *Matthew Daemon* for *Weekly World News*. He has also worked extensively for Future Publications on a variety of titles, principally *SFX Magazine*. In advertising, Mike has worked on campaigns for Colmans and Coca-Cola. He has worked extensively in using comics as a way of promoting learning, in workshops and in publications, for various initiatives and educational plans, most prominently with Read A Million Words in Wales.

**G**REG COX is the *New York Times* bestselling author of numerous novels and short stories, including the official movie novelizations of *War for the Planet of the Apes, Godzilla, Man of Steel, The Dark Knight Rises, Ghost Rider, Daredevil, Death Defying Acts*, and the first three *Underworld* movies, as well as books and stories based on such popular series as *Alias, Buffy the Vampire Slayer, CSI: Crime Scene Investigation, Farscape, The 4400, Leverage, The Librarians, Riese: Kingdom Falling, Roswell, Star Trek, Terminator, Warehouse 13, The X-Files*, and *Xena: Warrior Princess*. In addition, he is a Consulting Editor for Tor Books. He has received six Scribe Awards, including one for Life Achievement, from the International Association of Media Tie-In Writers. He lives in Lancaster, PA. You can visit him online at: www.gregcox-author.com

**P**AIGE DANIELS grew up reading and watching as much science fiction and fantasy as humanly possible. When it was time for college it was clear that she watched one too many episodes of *Star Trek*, because she chose Physics as her major with the intent of being an Astrophysicist. After graduating from Northern Kentucky University, she went on to earn her Electrical Engineering degree at the University of Kentucky. She is the author of the dystopic near-future science fiction trilogy, Non-Compliance and a space opera series, The Singularity

Wars. She has also co-edited the Brave New Girls anthology with Mary Fan. Despite being surrounded by a bunch of Hoosiers, she has lived happily in Indiana for the past twenty-one years. When she isn't working her 9-5 job or writing she manages a hobby farm with her delightful husband and two kids and coaches an afterschool robotics team. You can cyber-stalk her at www.nerdypaige.com or http://www.goodreads.com/PaigeDaniels Or www.facebook/paigedanielsauthor.com or www.twitter.com/TClosser.

BEFORE he created the seminal superhero Doc Savage in 1932, Missouri writer LESTER DENT (1904-1959) mastered most of the pulp-fiction genres popular at the dawn of the Great Depression. Breaking into the field with a string of aviation-centered adventure stories, Dent quickly branched out into other sub-genres, penning Westerns inspired by his upbringing in Wyoming and Oklahoma, acclaimed hardboiled detective mysteries, and briefly, several so-called "air-war" tales set during World War I. "The Man Cut in Half" was written circa 1932, and shows the strong influence of Dent's favorite writer, Dashiell Hammett.

MARY Fan is a sci-fi/fantasy writer hailing from Jersey City, NJ. She is the author of the Jane Colt sci-fi series, (Red Adept Publishing), the Starswept YA sci-fi series, (Snowy Wings Publishing), the Flynn Nightsider YA dark fantasy series (Crazy 8 Press), and *Stronger Than a Bronze Dragon*, a YA steampunk fantasy (Page Street Publishing). She is also the editor of *Bad Ass Moms*, an anthology from Crazy 8 Press. In addition, Mary is the co-editor (along with fellow sci-fi author Paige Daniels) of the Brave New Girls young adult sci-fi anthologies, which feature tales about girls in STEM. Revenues from sales are donated to the Society of Women Engineers scholarship fund. Her short fiction has appeared in numerous anthologies, including *Pangaea III: Redemption, Keep Faith, Thrilling Adventure Yarns, Magic at Midnight, They Keep Killing Glenn, Tales of the Crimson Keep: Newly Renovated Edition, Mine! A Celebration of Liberty and Freedom for All Benefitting Planned Parenthood*, and *Love, Murder & Mayhem*. When she's not writing, Mary can usually be found shadow boxing, singing opera to her cat, or falling off a flying trapeze.

KELLI FITZPATRICK is a science fiction and fantasy author, English educator, and community activist based in Michigan. Her *Star Trek* story "The Sunwalkers" won the Strange New Worlds 2016 contest, and her essays on pop culture media appear online at StarTrek.com and

Women at Warp, and in print from Sequart and ATB Publishing. She is a contributing writer for the *Star Trek Adventures* role-playing game from Modiphius. She is a strong advocate of the arts, public education, and gender rights and representation. Kelli can be found at KelliFitzpatrick.com and on Twitter @KelliFitzWrites

MICHAEL JAN FRIEDMAN is the author of 78 books of fiction and non-fiction. Eleven of his titles, including the autobiography *Hollywood Hulk Hogan* and *Ghost Hunting* (written with Sci-Fi's *Ghost Hunters*), have appeared on *The New York Times'* primary bestseller list. He is currently working on yet another short-story collection of sci fi, fantasy, and superhero tales. A cofounder of Crazy 8 Press, he is seen as our spiritual guru. Mike continues to advise readers that no matter how many Friedmans they know, he's probably not related to any of them.

ROBERT GREENBERGER, unofficial mayor of the speculative fiction and comic book communities, has written *Star Trek* novels and short fiction in addition to short works of science fiction and fantasy. His adult fiction includes the award-winning novelization of *Hellboy II: The Golden Army*, *The Essential Batman Encyclopedia*, *Iron Man: Femme Fatales*, and *Captain*

*America: The Never-Ending Battle*. A cofounder of Crazy 8 Press, he continues to produce short works. He spends his days as a high school English teacher in Maryland, where he makes his home with this wife Deb. For more, see www.bobgreenberger.com.

DAERICK GROSS has been around for a while...I'm old. However, I am a wide-ranging craftsman with adaptable styles and mediums and adapting to this new 'digital-thingy'. I am most known for my use of fluid lines, body-language and color. Over the decades, I have created illustrations for newspapers and magazines; movies, television and videos; RPG games; advertising; and... comic books. And, I have a snarky sense of humor that comes with the package.

MOST recently the creator of "The Unsung" and "CommsCon" campaigns for Microsoft, MATT HALEY has been illustrating Marvel and DC Comics for years, as well as for TV shows like *Gotham*, movies like *Wonder Woman* and for famed designer Jean-Paul Gaultier. A longtime collaborator with comics legend Stan Lee, Matt helped create the cult TV series *Stan Lee's Who Wants To Be A Superhero* and the film *Comic-Con Episode IV: A Fan's Hope*. Matt is the director of the viral hit *Blackstar Warrior* and just completed his latest TV project *Cyberfist*. For more, see http://www.matthaley.com

GLENN HAUMAN, alternately known as "Da Big Guy", "G to the H", and "Party Of The First Part", made the mistake of asking his friends during a Cards Against Humanity game, "What's missing from my biographical blurb?" The responses included "Spectacular abs", "A low standard of living", "The secret formula for ultimate female satisfaction", "Pretty Pretty Princess Dress-Up Board Game", and "Some god-damn peace and quiet". You can find out more at http://www.glennhauman.com, @glennhauman, or at his day job at ComicMix.com.

HEATHER E. HUTSELL began writing stories at age eleven. Her first—a murder mystery—won her an award through the Young Authors program, as did two more detective mysteries in as many years. She published her first novella, *Awakening Alice*—a sequel to Lewis Carroll's *Alice in Wonderland*—in the collaborative work *Ghost on the Highway* in 2006. She went on to self-publish an illustrated version of *Awakening Alice* along with its sequel, *A Ticket for Patience*, in 2007. Heather has since written and self-published eleven novels, two novellas, and four short story collections, with her newest book being the second volume of humorous and macabre short stories involving dolls, marionettes and automata. Her works include romantic horror, absurdist fiction, dystopian tales, fairytales gone awry, dark comedy, and steampunk mystery series, The Case Files. She has a story contribution in Crazy 8 Press's anthology, *Bad Ass Moms*. Heather has also written for two historical documentary series: *The Indian Wars: A Change of Worlds* and *Emancipation Road*.

KARL KESEL loves his job far more than he has any right to. He has written, inked, and occasionally penciled: *Superman, Superboy, Harley Quinn, Spider-Man, Suicide Squad, Fantastic Four, Captain America* and many others—although he has an inexplicable fondness for obscure characters no one else remembers. His current obsessions are his creator-owned comics with Tom Grummett—the Jack-Kirby-does-the-*X-Files*-esque *Section Zero* on Kickstarter now at sectionzero1959.com—and David Hahn—the grin-and-gritty *Impossible Jones* (coming soon)! He lives in Portland, Oregon with his wonderful wife Myrna, their joyful son Isaac, and cute-as-a-bug daughter Eliza. He really can't complain about much.

PETER KRAUSE is a graduate of the University of Minnesota, with a B.A. in both journalism and studio arts. For ten years, he was a full-time artist for DC Comics, New York. Peter drew Captain Marvel, Superman and other DC super-heroes. He was the artist for the series *Star Trek: The Next Generation, Metropolis: Special Crimes Unit, and The Power of Shazam!* Peter was also a guest artist on the series *Adventure of Superman, Superboy, Birds of Prey* and "Secret Files. Since the mid-1990s, Peter has worked with a number of advertising agencies and production houses in North America. His work includes storyboards, print concepts, ad layouts, billboard designs, interior retail concepts and depictions of promotional events. The drawings are done with markers and Photoshop. Peter lives in Minneapolis, Minnesota with his wife Lisa. They have three sons—Timothy, David and Nicholas.

**P**AUL KUPPERBERG is the author of more than two dozen books and over 1,000 comic book stories, ranging from Superman to Scooby Doo and Batman to Bart Simpson. He wrote the critically acclaimed *Life With Archie: The Married Life* series for Archie Comics, which featured the controversial and bestselling "Death of Archie" story line, and is executive editor and writer for Charlton Neo Comics. You can follow Paul at PaulKupperberg.com and on Facebook or Twitter.

**K**ARISSA LAUREL is a science fiction, fantasy, and romance author living in central North Carolina with her son, her husband, the occasional in-law, and a very hairy husky named Bonnie. Her favorite things are superheroes, *Star Wars,* Southern cuisine, and Hindi cinema. Karissa serves as an assistant editor at *Cast of Wonders,* a young adult speculative fiction podcast—part of the Escape Artists family. Most recently, she is the author of *Touch of Smoke,* a paranormal romance novel available from Red Adept Publishing. She's also the author of *The Norse Chronicles,* an urban fantasy series, and *The Stormbourne Chronicles,* a young adult, epic steampunkish fantasy series. Her short stories have appeared in various anthologies including *Bad Ass Moms, Thrilling Adventure Yarns, Volume 1, Wicked South: Secrets and Lies, Magic at Midnight, Love Murder and Mayhem,* and *Brave New Girls; Stories of Girls who Science and Scheme.* Her short fiction has also appeared at *Daily Science Fiction, Luna Station Quarterly,* and *Cast of Wonders.*

**W**ILLIAM Leisner is happy to return to the ranks of Crazy 8 authors, having previously contributed to all three volumes of the *ReDeus* series. He is the author of numerous *Star Trek* stories, including the novels *The Shocks of Adversity, Losing the Peace* and *A Less Perfect Union.* His original fiction includes the ebook *A Dimension of Death*, which sees Rod Serling team up with Gene Roddenberry to solve a murder on the set of *The Twilight Zone*, and has recently appeared in the anthologies *Second Round: A Return to the Ur-Bar* and *My Battery is Low and It Is Getting Dark*, from Zombies Need Brains, LLC. He is co-developer (with Scott Pearson) of *Tales of the Weird World War*, an alternate history/horror/sci-fi series set to debut in late 2020. A native of Rochester, New York, he currently lives in Minneapolis.

JONATHAN MABERRY is a *New York Times* bestselling author, 5-time Bram Stoker Award-winner, and comic book writer. His vampire apocalypse book series, *V-WARS*, was a Netflix original series. He writes in multiple genres including suspense, thriller, horror, science fiction, fantasy, and action; for adults, teens and middle grade. He is the editor many anthologies including *The X-Files, Aliens: Bug Hunt, Don't Turn Out the Lights, Nights of the Living Dead*, and others. His comics include *Black Panther: DoomWar, Captain America, Pandemica, Highway to Hell, The Punisher* and *Bad Blood*. He is a board member of the Horror Writers Association and the president of the International Association of Media Tie-in Writers. Visit him online at www.jonathanmaberry.com

DAVID MACK is the award-winning and *The New York Times* bestselling author of more than thirty-six novels of science fiction, fantasy, and adventure. His writing credits span several media, including television (for episodes of *Star Trek: Deep Space Nine*), short fiction, and comic books. Mack currently works as a consultant for two *Star Trek* television series, *Lower Decks* and *Prodigy*. He lives in New York City.

RON MARZ has been writing comics for three decades, starting his career with a lengthy run on *Silver Surfer* for Marvel. Since then, he has worked for virtually every major publisher and compiled a long list of credits, including stints on *Thor* for Marvel, *Green Lantern* and *Superboy* for DC, *Star Wars* for Dark Horse, and the historic *Marvel vs. DC* crossover. Among Marz's more recent work is his acclaimed run on *Witchblade* for Top Cow/Image, the *Skylanders* series for IDW, *Turok* and *John Carter: Warlord of Mars* for Dynamite, and *Fathom* for Aspen. In 2020, he cowrote DC's popular Endless Winter crossover event. He is the Editor-in-Chief and Lead Writer for the revived Ominous Press, penning *Dread Gods, Demi-God, Beasts of the Black Hand*, and *Harken's Raiders*. Marz's creator-owned series include the all-ages tale *Dragon Prince* at Top Cow; the historical adventure *Samurai: Heaven and Earth* at Dark Horse; and the vampire tale *Shinku* at Image. Marz has also written video games, including multiple Skylanders titles, *Marvel Ultimate Alliance 2, Spider-Man 2,* and more. His website is www.ronmarz.com, and his Twitter is @ronmarz.

LUKE McDONNELL is an artist and designer who broke into comic books in 1980. His many assignments include a lengthy run on Iron Man prior to joining DC Comics where he worked on *Justice League of America.* He gained fame with his two-plus year run on *Suicide Squad* and also drew *The Phantom.* After leaving monthly comics, he went to work for Craig Yoe's design studio.

STUART MOORE's novels include *X-Men: The Dark Phoenix Saga* (Titan Books); three volumes of the bestselling middle-grade series *The Zodiac Legacy* (Disney Press), created and cowritten by Stan Lee; and *Thanos: Death Sentence* (Marvel). Recent comics work includes the original series *Captain Ginger* and *Bronze Age Boogie* (both AHOY Comics) and *EGOs* (Image), as well as *Batman: Nightwalker* (DC Ink), and *Deadpool the Duck* (Marvel). Stuart has also been an award-winning comics editor, and consults on a freelance basis for AHOY Comics, where he holds the mysterious title of "Ops."

WILL MURRAY is the author of more than 70 novels, including some 20 posthumous Doc Savage collaborations with Lester Dent, and 40 books in the long-running Destroyer series. Other Murray novels star the Executioner, Pat Savage and the Mars Attacks characters. His year 2000 book, *Nick Fury, Agent of S.H.I.E.L.D.: Empyre,* foreshadowed the 9/11 terrorist attacks. Murray has penned several milestone crossover novels. He pitted Doc Savage against King Kong in *Skull Island,* and followed up with *King Kong Vs. Tarzan.* His 2015 Doc Savage novel, *The Sinister Shadow,* revived the famous radio and pulp mystery man. Murray reunited them for *Empire of Doom.* His first Spider novel, *The Doom Legion,* revives that famous crime buster, as well as James Christopher, AKA Operator 5, and the renowned G-8. *Fury in Steel* finds The Spider being hunted by the FBI's Suicide Squad. *Tarzan, Conquerer of Mars* is another historic crossover. For anthologies, Murray has written such iconic characters as Superman, Batman, Wonder Woman, Spider-Man, Ant-Man, The Hulk, The Avenger, The Green Hornet, The Grey Seal, John Silence, Honey West, Sherlock Holmes, Cthulhu, Dr. Herbert West, The Secret 6, Zorro, and Lee Falk's immortal Ghost Who Walks, The Phantom. Ten of Murray's Sherlock Holmes short stories have been collected in *The Wild Adventures of Sherlock Holmes. The Wild Adventures of Cthulhu* is forthcoming. For Marvel Comics, Murray created the Unbeatable Squirrel Girl.

JODY LYNN NYE lists her main career activity as "spoiling cats." She lives northwest of Atlanta with three feline overlords, Athena, Minx, and Marmalade, and her husband, author and packager Bill Fawcett. She has written over fifty books, most of them with a humorous bent, and over 170 short stories. Jody has been fortunate enough to have collaborated with some of the greats in the field of science fiction and fantasy. She wrote several books with Anne McCaffrey or set in Anne's many worlds, including *The Death of Sleep, The Ship Who Won, Crisis on Doona* (a *New York Times* and *USA Today* bestseller), and *The Dragonlover's Guide to Pern.* She wrote eight books with Robert Asprin and has since his death continued two of his series, the *Myth-Adventures* and *Dragons.* She edited a humorous anthology about mothers, *Don't Forget Your Spacesuit, Dear!,* Her latest books are *Rhythm of the Imperium* (Baen Books), *Moon Tracks* (with Travis S. Taylor, Baen Books) and *Myth-Fits* (Ace). She is one of the judges for the Writers of the Future fiction contest, the largest speculative fiction contest in the world. Jody also teaches the intensive two-day writers' workshop at DragonCon.

You can find her online on Facebook, Twitter, and her website, www.jodylynnnye.com.

SCOTT PEARSON is a full-time freelance writer and editor. He has published across a number of genres, such as lit fic, humor, mystery, urban fantasy, horror, and science fiction, including three *Star Trek* stories and two *Trek* novellas. He's the canon editor of the *Star Trek Adventures* role-playing game and the cowriter of the IMAX space documentaries *Space Next* and *Touch the Stars.* He is the co-developer, along with William Leisner, of *Tales of the Weird World War,* an alternate history/ horror/sci-fi series which debuted earlier this year. Scott lives in personable St. Paul, Minnesota, with his wife, Sandra, and their cat, Ripley. He and his daughter, Ella, cohost the podcast *Generations Geek* at generationsgeek.com. Visit Scott online at scott-pearson.com and also follow him on Twitter @smichaelpearson.

RON RANDALL's work has appeared in all the major comics publishers in the United States, including Marvel Comics, DC Comics, Image, Dark Horse and IDW on properties as varied as *FutureQuest, Spider-Man, Supergirl, Predator* and *Star Wars.* His own on-going science fiction series *Trekker* is his signature project.

AARON ROSENBERG is the author of the best-selling DuckBob SF comedy series, the Relicant Chronicles epic fantasy series, the *Dread Remora* space-opera series, and—with David Niall Wilson—the O.C.L.T. occult thriller series. Aaron's tie-in work contains novels for *Star Trek*, *Warhammer*, *World of WarCraft*, *Stargate: Atlantis*, *Shadowrun*, *Eureka*, *Mutants & Masterminds*, and more. He has written children's books (including the original series STEM Squad and Pete and Penny's Pizza Puzzles, the award-winning *Bandslam: The Junior Novel*, and the #1 best-selling *42: The Jackie Robinson Story*), educational books on a variety of topics, and over seventy roleplaying games (such as the original games *Asylum*, *Spookshow*, and *Chosen*, work for White Wolf, Wizards of the Coast, Fantasy Flight, Pinnacle, and many others, and both the Origins Award-winning *Gamemastering Secrets* and the Gold ENnie-winning *Lure of the Lich Lord*). He is the co-creator of the *ReDeus* series, and a founding member of Crazy 8 Press. Aaron lives in New York with his family. You can follow him online at gryphonrose.com, on Facebook at facebook.com/gryphonrose, and on Twitter @gryphonrose.

DAN SCHKADE is a cartoonist from Austin, Texas. He's best known for the Eisner and Ringo-Nominated Webtoon *Lavender Jack*, as well as *Will Eisner's The Spirit Returns*, *San Hannibal*, and other words published by Dark Horse Comics, Dynamite Entertainment, IDW Publishing, and others. He lives in the American Midwest with his girlfriend and cat.

AFTER attending the Joe Kubert School of Cartooning and Graphic Arts, BART SEARS burst into comics in 1986. His muscular work could be found in the pages of *Secaturs*, *G.I. Joe*, and *C.O.P.S.*, before gaining fame as the illustrator of *Invasion!* and *Justice League Europe*. He has worked for Valiant, CrossGen, and Marvel in addition to co-founding Ominous Press, where he serves as Chief Creative Officer.

DANIELE SERRA is an Italian illustrator and comic book artist. His main influences and inspirations arrive from weird and horror fiction written by H. P. Lovecraft and William H. Hodgson, Ridley Scott movies, Japanese horror films and Clive Barker's works. His love for horror culture started before his painting career, making him quickly develop his signature style: high contrast paintings with bright, as well as strong dark colors, curved strokes and shadows, and a particular attention to his character's gaze and expression.

DAYTON Ward & Kevin Dilmore are not the same person, no matter what is written on Men's Room walls. Instead, DAYTON WARD is a *New York Times* bestselling author or co-author of nearly 40 novels and novellas, often working with his best friend, Kevin Dilmore. His short fiction has appeared in more than 25 anthologies and he's written for publications such as *NCO Journal, Kansas City Voices, Famous Monsters of Filmland, Star Trek Magazine* and *Star Trek Communicator* as well as the websites Tor.com, StarTrek.com, and Syfy.com. Before making the jump to full-time writing, Dayton was a software developer, discovering the private sector after serving for eleven years in the U.S. Marine Corps. Though he lives in Kansas City with his wife and two daughters, Dayton is a Florida native and still maintains a torrid long-distance romance with his beloved Tampa Bay Buccaneers. Find him on the web at http://www.daytonward.com.

KEVIN DILMORE has contributed to publications including the Village Voice, *Amazing Stories, Famous Monsters of Filmland, Hallmark* and *Star Trek Communicator* magazines. He has teamed with author and best pal Dayton Ward for 20 years on novels, shorter fiction and other writings chiefly within the Star Trek universe, including *Purgatory's*

*Key*, the final novel in the *Star Trek: Legacies* trilogy, published by Pocket Books in September 2016. Kevin works as a senior writer for Hallmark Cards in Kansas City, Mo.

JEFF WEIGEL is an illustrator and author who lives in Belleville, Illinois. Since 2017 he has been the artist for the Sunday newspaper adventures of the classic comic strip *The Phantom*. He has written and illustrated multiple children's books and graphic novels, including *Quantum Mechanics*, published by Lion Forge, and *Dragon Girl: The Secret Valley*, published by Andrews McMeel. He was a regular contributor to Image Comics' anthology title *Big Bang Comics* for more than fifteen years.

MARK WHEATLEY, Overstreet Hall of Fame inductee, has been awarded the Eisner, Inkpot, Mucker, Gem, Speakeasy and nominations for the Harvey and the Ignatz. His work has appeared in *Spectrum*, the Library of Congress, The Norman Rockwell Museum, and other museums. He has designed for Lady Gaga, The Black Eyed Peas, ABC's *Beauty and the Beast*, and Square Roots, as well as *Super Clyde, The Millers*, and *2 Broke Girls* on CBS. His most recent print projects include *Doctor Cthulittle, Tarzan and the Dark Heart of Time, Swords Against the Moon Men, The Philip*

*Jose Farmer Centennial Collection, Mine!* and *Wild Stars*. Past creations include *Breathtaker, Return of The Human, Ez Street, Lone Justice, Mars, Black Hood, Prince Nightmare, Hammer of The Gods, Blood of The Innocent, Frankenstein Mobster,* and *Skultar* as well as *Tarzan, Baron Munchausen, Jonny Quest, Dr. Strange, The Flash, Captain Action, Argus, The Spider, Stargate Atlantis, Torchwood* and *Doctor Who.*

R ICHARD C. WHITE is a science fiction/fantasy/fantasy noir/action-adventure/non-fiction author. His latest release is a fantasy noir collection: *Chasing Danger: The Case Files of Theron Chase.* Other recent works are *Harbinger of Darkness, For a Few Gold Pieces More,* the short story "Dangerous Memories" appearing in *The New Adventures of Rocky Jordan,* and *Terra Incognito,* a non-fiction book on world building. He's appeared in various anthologies, such as *Monsters, Robots,* and *Space* for the Origins Game Fair, as well as *Liberty Girl: Fight for Freedom, All for One: Tales of the Musketeers,* and *Charles Boeckman Presents: Johnny Nickle.* He's also written the novella, *The Dark Leopard.* As a media tie-in writer, he's written for the Star Trek, Doctor Who, Battletech and The Incredible Hulk franchises. His novel, *Gauntlet Dark Legacy: Paths of Evil,* was a best-selling tie-in for his publisher. His latest tie-in

works are *One Night in Freeport* and *Storm Wreck* for Nisaba Press (Green Ronin Gaming). Richard is a member of the Science Fiction and Fantasy Writers of America and the International Association of Media Tie-in Writers. Additionally, Richard serves on the SFWA Writer Beware committee.

S HERRI COOK WOOSLEY earned a M.A. in English Language and Literature from University of Maryland, where she taught Academic Writing and Introduction to World Mythology. She's a member of SFWA. Her short fiction has been published in *Pantheon Magazine, Abyss & Apex Magazine,* and *Flash Fiction Magazine* while her debut novel, *Walking Through Fire,* was long-listed for both the Booknest Debut Novel award and Baltimore's Best 2019 and 2020 in the novel category.

# *Special Thanks*

THE following people backed our Kickstarter campaign at the appropriate levels and are hereby thanked for their generous support.

Russell J Handelman
Ray Riethmeier
Stephen Ballentine
Mary Anne Espenshade
Judith Waidlich
David Palmer
Ryan Permison
Debra Hussey
Jim Shan
Adam E. Falk
Tim Tucker
Matthew Wang
CapnDon
Trisha Baker

IN MEMORIAM

DAVE GALANTER

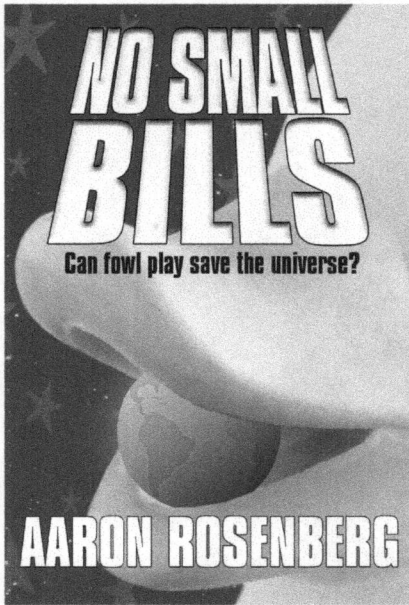

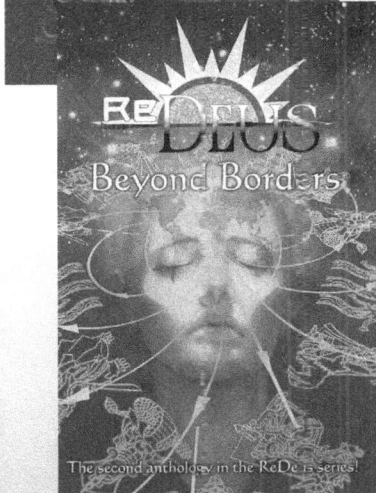

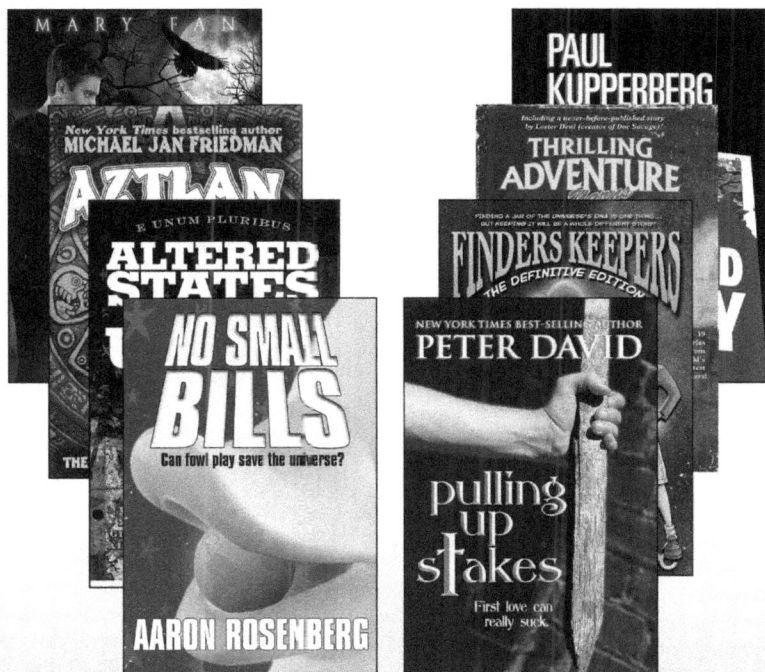

CPSIA information can be obtained
at www.ICGtesting.com
Printed in the USA
JSHW041929230321
12840JS00002B/5

9 781732 040649